ORPHEUS RISING

ORPHEUS RISING

BATEMAN

headline

First published in 2008 by
HEADLINE PUBLISHING GROUP

1

Cataloguing in Publication Data is available from the British Library

ISBN 9 780 7553 3468 1 (Hardback)
ISBN 9 780 7553 3469 8 (Trade paperback)

Typeset in Meridien by Palimpsest Book Production Limited,
Grangemouth, Stirlingshire

Printed and bound in Great Britain by
Mackays of Chatham plc, Chatham, Kent

Headline's policy is to use papers that are natural, renewable
and recyclable products and made from wood grown
in sustainable forests. The logging and manufacturing
processes are expected to conform to the environmental
regulations of the country of origin.

HEADLINE PUBLISHING GROUP
An Hachette Livre UK Company
338 Euston Road
London NW1 3BH

www.headline.co.uk

For Andrea and Matthew

Forward

You have to understand this. I die in the end.

Michael Ryan's murder – and I believe that is what it was – was a shock to everyone, but especially to me. After all, I discovered him and, to some extent, have my career to thank him for. He was also my friend.

My relationship with Michael Ryan began at S*****, although I did not actually meet him until after I'd left. I was paying my way through college with a part-time job there. It really amounted to nothing more than idling away a few hours leafing through the thousands of dusty manuscripts that made up their slush-pile. I was not expected to find anything remotely publishable.

Love & Rockets was probably the fifteenth manuscript I picked up that afternoon, and I almost put it right down again, because the title was so unoriginal and the pages were somewhat battered; it had clearly done the rounds of other publishers, and the author hadn't had the sense to send in a nice clean script each time it was rejected. The fact is, my inclination was to sign off on a rejection note without going any further than the title page, but I was sitting with the script on my lap, and in reaching for my coffee it slipped off. It was only in trying to gather up the pages

1

that I discovered that the author had failed to number them. I have, as my first ex-wife will attest, an inherent sense of neatness, and nothing would do but for me to attempt to put Michael Ryan's manuscript back into numerical order, and that is how I came to start reading what would become *Space Coast*.

I have never been one for making grand claims for it, but if you look at the back cover today you will see quotes from the critics such as 'simple but profound', 'a gritty love story that will stay with you for ever', 'an intimate portrait of America' and perhaps my favourite, 'a God-damn American classic'. When I took it upstairs in S*****, tears in my eyes and drained, having read it in one session, my boss (the most junior editor at the company), nodded patiently while I raved about it, then indicated for me to place the manuscript in his in-tray. 'I'm backed up to Wyoming,' he warned me.

Six weeks later, he said, 'Not for me.'

I took it to four different editors at the same company, and they all said, 'Not for me,' or thereabouts.

My time at S***** was almost up, I had exams to study for, but I couldn't get the book out of my head. I knew it was a winner. And, quite frankly, I no longer wanted to continue as a Classics scholar. It just seemed *pointless*. I had not previously considered publishing as a career – it was simply a summer job that was less demanding than working tables in a restaurant, though the tips weren't as good. But the sheer thrill of discovering *Space Coast* changed everything. On my final day at S***** I picked up my cheque and walked out with the manuscript under my coat. The next morning, I flew down to Orlando, rented a car, drove to Brevard, and told Michael Ryan that I was going to get his book published if it was the last thing I did.

He was very excited by my news, right up to the point where he discovered I was an unemployed college dropout who'd stolen his manuscript. Then he wanted to throw me down and jump on my head. It was Claire who calmed him down, who convinced him to give me a chance. She was beautiful. A Florida tan, short blonde hair, funny, charming, very much in love. She told him

I was the first person who'd shown any interest at all in his book, and even if I was a thief, and looked about twelve years old, maybe it was a sign, and he should give me a chance. They were living in a rickety old wooden house which had once enjoyed stunning sea views but was now overshadowed by a huge apartment block. She was working in the local bank, allowing him to write at home, but there clearly wasn't much money around.

So he agreed. Once his temper cooled he was good company. Claire made dinner while we sat on the porch and pretended to look at the sea. I convinced him to change the title from *Love & Rockets* to *Space Coast* by arguing that it sounded more upmarket, more literary. I've never met an author since who hasn't also fallen for that one. Mostly it was just to cover my tracks in the unlikely event that S***** later claimed some kind of ownership. I would be his agent. I promised to take it to every publisher in New York. Failing that, London. Then on to Paris and Frankfurt. And failing all of the above, whatever the capital of Estonia was. It would, I swore, be published *somewhere*.

I phoned Michael every week and tried not to sound too dejected, but there isn't much of a positive spin you can give to complete and utter rejection. As time went on, it was mostly Claire I spoke to. Michael was losing heart. He was thinking about going back to journalism. I urged him, through her, not to. At the same time, it was clear that I myself was going to have to get a job. New York is not cheap, and the savings I had been living on were fast running out.

Then, out of the blue, the Maitland Press, a small publishing house with links to the University of Maryland, e-mailed and invited me to their small, cramped office for a meeting. I had barely shaken hands with their senior editor – and owner – John Maitland before I launched into my spiel. It was the first sliver of interest I'd had in the book, so I was determined to give it everything. I talked up a storm. I paced, I gesticulated, I hammered my fist into my palm to emphasise a point. *Space Coast* was the future of American fiction. Michael Ryan was a Mark Twain for the twenty-first century. If he rejected Michael

Ryan, he was rejecting The Beatles. John Maitland looked exasperated throughout.

When I was finished, and slightly out of breath, he clasped his hands before him and said quite gently, 'I have no idea what you're talking about.'

A number of rather confusing exchanges followed, but it gradually emerged that I had never sent *Space Coast* to the Maitland Press, and that John had contacted me as a favour to a former professor of mine who had heard I was out of work and had rung him to ask if he could help. The Maitland Press specialised in academic works. It hadn't published fiction in twenty years. Was I interested in a job? They couldn't pay much.

Much is relative.

John had been left in the lurch by an editor who had probably wilted under the workload and failed to earn the aforementioned 'much'.

I didn't hesitate. 'I will edit your history books, if you will publish *Space Coast* and give me ten per cent of the profits.'

He blinked at me and said, '*What* profits?'

John Maitland read *Space Coast* overnight. He called next day to say he quite liked it, and when could I start work. An hour later I phoned Michael, but expected to get Claire. When he answered, I just launched straight into it. I didn't tell him I'd taken a job at Maitland, I just said I'd received an offer from a small publishing house. There was a $2,000 advance on the table, take it or leave it. I didn't tell him I'd traded my health insurance for it. I was just fantastically elated. As far as I was concerned, it was the deal of the century. My faith in *Space Coast* was finally vindicated. When I finished ranting, there was only silence from the other end.

'Michael?'

He said: 'Claire is dead.'

I don't know whether it qualifies as fate or karma or irony. It meant everything to him, getting a book deal, and suddenly it meant nothing. He went through the motions, of course, as *Space Coast* ground its way casually towards publication. It's safe to say that it was not the Maitland Press's top priority. Only two thousand copies would be printed, and the budget for advertising and promotion would not have been adequate for a nine-year-old girl to alert the neighbourhood to her missing cat. There is a pearl of publishing wisdom to the effect that if a book is good enough, it will be discovered. And it is probably true. But it helps to have big bucks behind it. *Space Coast* did not even have small bucks.

I did not include in the publicity materials the fact that the author's wife, who bore an uncanny resemblance to Cathy, *Space Coast's* heroine, had been killed during a botched robbery at the First National Bank in Brevard. But I let it be known. The jacket photo showed a handsome young man with a brooding demeanour and sad, sad eyes which suggested the tragedy of his wife's violent end. The fact that I knew that it was a vacation snap taken long before the bank robbery, and that his apparent suffering was nothing more than a raging hangover, was neither here nor there.

In the end, it *was* word of mouth that really did it. First small bookstores, then local newspapers picked up on it. Orders began to come in from out of state, and then from *every* state. It began to sell. And sell. It got to the point where the Maitland Press simply could not cope with the demand, and licensed *Space Coast* to its current publisher. I went with it. Sales went through the roof. Nobody could quite say why: it was a love story, but there was also murder and a family secret, redemption and a little sex. There are a hundred thousand books with those ingredients. But there was something else as well: it was so simply written, so quietly funny. The romance felt real, but it was also the way romance should be, but rarely was. It made people feel good. They also knew what had happened to the author's wife. The question of exactly how much this contributed to the sales is unknowable, incalculable. Certainly it drove much of what was written about it, and about its author. If Michael knew or cared, it is impossible to say. He did not conduct any interviews, he did not read to an adoring audience or burst into tears on *Oprah*. He simply disappeared. No – perhaps *disappeared* is too strong. He *withdrew*. He was certainly aware of how well his book was selling, that it had passed the mark from where it could be described as merely a best-seller and was now a bona fide phenomenon. Once it arrived on the *New York Times* bestseller lists it stayed there for an astonishing 175 weeks. It dropped out for three months, then pre-production of the movie version was announced and it went straight back in, rising to number one as the film was released (to generally poor reviews).

In the ten years following *Space Coast*'s publication it earned Michael Ryan $110 million. This money remains in his bank account to this day, largely untouched. The book you are holding is his Last Will and Testament.

I was in the Sad Café, that week's restaurant *de jour*, trying to woo another hotshot young author to our imprint and not making a very good job of it, when Bernie phoned from the office to say it had just been on the news that Michael Ryan, the reclusive author of *Space Coast*, was dead. It struck me like a thunderbolt, and yet . . . I had been half-expecting it. The surprise, of course, was the manner of his passing: not the suicide of a lost romantic, but shot to death at a rundown motel on Brevard Beach.

I immediately led the young writer to a bar next door, and asked the barman to switch through the news channels. Michael Ryan was everywhere, but it all boiled down to this: *A spokesman for Brevard County Sheriff's Department said that police attended the motel in response to a call reporting an armed man acting in a suspicious manner. When challenged, Mr Ryan ran towards police officers while brandishing what appeared to be a gun. He was shot five times, and died instantly. Police have not yet commented on reports that the gun was in fact a cell phone. They did confirm, however, that drug paraphernalia was found in Mr Ryan's motel room.*

'Did you know him?' the young author asked. 'The movie sucked.'

When his fame was at its height I only heard from Michael perhaps three times a year, and then only in late-night phone calls. If there was crucial but mundane book business that absolutely required his signature, he would give me the address of some remote hotel where the documents could be sent: Idaho, Oklahoma, North Dakota. Paris. Moscow. Manchester, England. If for any reason their delivery was delayed, then they would be returned because he had already moved on. As the buzz around his novel finally began to fade, when it began to inch from the front of the store to the rear, when the movie had played one too many times on cable, Michael's calls gradually became more frequent, a little more upbeat. He even talked about getting an apartment in Manhattan, putting down roots again. One morning he called me at work and said, 'Let's do lunch.'

'Seriously, Michael? When?'

'Today. *Now*. I'm outside.'

In my mind's eye I had expected to be confronted by a haunted, hollow-eyed wreck, but Michael looked fit and tanned. He shook my hand warmly and asked after my first and second wives. He had not heard about the third. We ate in Pizza Hut. His choice. He was chatty and witty and we laughed. Was his sunny demeanour forced? I did not think so then, but in retrospect – well, retrospection is a wonderful thing, and rarely accurate. My memory of our meeting is that the talk flowed both ways, but when I was later quizzed by my colleagues about it I could recall very little of real substance. Of course, the letter I gave to him did not seem important then. I have wondered since whether, if I had chosen *not* to hand it over, he might still be alive today – but I think not. It may have been the catalyst for his decision to go, but I believe he was being drawn there anyway. He had fought his demons for a decade, all the time knowing that he could really only confront them by returning to Brevard. I was just the messenger. The piano player, if you will.

About a month after his death I was spending a long weekend at my place in the Hamptons when a woman knocked on our front door and introduced herself as Lena Olson. She was – is – pretty, petite, with dirty-blonde hair. She said she'd come to see me about Michael Ryan. You must understand that his death and the manner of it had reawakened interest in *Space Coast* and my office was very quickly deluged with inquiries from potential biographers, newspaper journalists, movie-of-the-week producers, longlost relatives and lunatics. Getting away for the weekend was a pleasant relief. I presumed this Lena Olson was just another coffin chaser, albeit somewhat more tenacious than most.

'I'm sorry,' I said, 'if you could just contact my office on Monday, I'm sure . . .'

'I was his doctor. I've been trying your office for days – I keep getting put through to a machine.'

'Yes,' I said, 'it's to keep the nuts at bay.'

She gave me a long, steady look. 'I'm not a nut.'

'Can you prove that? I mean, can you prove that you were his doctor?'

'Actually, I don't think I can. I didn't bring . . .'

She sighed, then gave me a warm smile. She was not obviously deranged and I was slightly bored with my weekend, so instead of closing the door I stepped outside onto the porch and indicated for her to sit opposite me in one of our fine wicker chairs. She was carrying a computer bag, which she set down carefully beside her.

'If you were his doctor,' I said, 'you could tell me where his birthmark was. It was quite distinctive.'

'If I was his doctor,' she replied, 'I wouldn't divulge that information.'

I smiled indulgently. 'If he was alive, that would be perfectly understandable. However . . .'

Lena Olson clasped her hands in her lap. 'Michael had no birthmarks.'

'I'm afraid he did.' I began to rise from my chair. 'The inside of his thigh. We swam together several times. Now if you don't mind, I'm expecting my wife—'

'That wasn't a birthmark, Mr Naiffy. It was a scar. He had an accident with a Bowie knife when he was a child.'

'Well,' I said, lowering myself back down, 'I suppose it's a possibility.' I nodded thoughtfully at her. 'Were you his doctor for very long?' It was a trap, of course. Michael had lived such a peripatetic lifestyle in recent years that I very much doubted that he actually had a doctor he could call his own.

'For four days.'

'That's not very long at all.'

'No, it wasn't. But it was long enough to fall in love with him.'

I blinked at her for fully half a minute while she smiled shyly back. Her cheeks had reddened significantly. Finally I ventured: 'I don't quite know what to say to that. Ahm. So. What . . . what can I do for you?'

Lena reached down to the computer bag and unzipped one of its side compartments. She withdrew a single sheet of paper, then studied it for a moment before holding it out to me. 'This is a copy of an e-mail Michael sent to you. If you look at the top corner, you will see the date and time it was sent at – and if you've read the newspaper reports, you will appreciate that he sent it just a few minutes before he was shot dead.'

'I don't understand. I didn't receive—'

'No. It was obviously a very stressful time – he misspelled your e-mail address, put an extra letter on your first name, so it was returned by the server. You know, *address not recognised*. I found it on his laptop after . . . well.'

I nodded, then glanced down at the e-mail. The top corner indeed showed that my e-mail address was erroneous, but that it had nevertheless been sent at 8.03 p.m. on the evening of his murder. The message is reproduced below for the first time, exactly as I read it that day:

Subj: Death

Date: 05/03/2006 20.03 GMT Standard Time

From: *ryanm@aol.com*

To: *Robertt.naiffy@clarion.com*

Bob. You have to understand this. I die in the end.

9

They're outside. In a few moments I will lift my cell phone and hold it in my fist so that they can't quite see what it is. Then I will open the door and run out. They will think it's a gun and, according to their training, shoot me dead. It will be so quick I probably won't feel anything. But even if I do, I think when they come up to me, when they turn me over, there'll be a smile on my face.

I can barely breathe. The adrenaline

Bob I trst . . . need you to make sure I'm not remembered as some slobbering psycho. I mean, this is suicide . . . but not as we know it. I've taken my time – put it down . . . this is real, it has to be real. If I'm glty of nything its being in lve.

Theyre comin

Pray fgrme

MR

I have to say that reading it, and knowing that my friend was shot to death approximately three minutes later, it sent a chill through me, then and now. Before I could really gather my thoughts, Lena said: 'There was an attachment with the e-mail. It's also on the laptop.' She patted the side of the bag. 'I haven't read it.'

'Why not?'

'Because it was addressed to you. I knew he was writing it. He spent the last week holed up in that motel. I don't think he slept. He was just desperate to get it down. I went there every day, but I just couldn't talk him out of it . . .'

'Out of what? What do you mean?'

'Look – it would be better if you read it yourself. That's what he wanted. If you could read it now, that would be even better. I brought it to you because it was right to do so. But there are things I need to know as well. I would very much like to read it as soon as you finish. It took me longer than I thought to track you down, and I really have to fly home tomorrow.'

Lena slid the computer bag across the wooden floor until it rested against the leg of my chair. Then she stood up. She held out her hand and I shook it. She didn't let go.

'He said you were his friend,' she said. 'Yet you weren't at his funeral.'

'No,' I said.

'As I understand it, his book made you millions and millions of dollars. I think he would have expected you to be there.'

My position on funerals, on death, is perhaps unusual, but not unique. I'm not shy about it either. 'Doctor Olson – it's quite simple. I believe that once you're dead, you're dead. I've been to one funeral in my life – my mother's. There was an open casket. Ever since, whenever I think of her, I think of her as a corpse. I don't wish to think of anyone like that ever again. So I don't do funerals. I remember them as they were. I will remember Michael Ryan as I knew him.'

She gave me an odd look, which I took then as one of disapproval, but you will understand it better when you read what follows.

It is Michael Ryan's particular curse and destiny to have his only two works implacably intertwined with death. In the case of *Space Coast* it was his wife's. In *Orpheus Rising*, it is his own demise which hangs over it.

Read it and weep.

Robert Naiffy, Publisher
New York 2007

MAYOR'S OFFICE
Brevard Town Hall
City of Brevard Beach, Florida

3 March 2007

Dear Mr Ryan

We are sending this to you via your publisher, as we have been unable to ascertain a home address.

As you are no doubt aware, this year will be the tenth anniversary of the tragic events at the First National Bank in Brevard. We have been talking for some time about marking this dark day in our history, and have decided to build a memorial garden at Brevard Avenue. It will be ready by 25 June, when we plan to hold an official opening, a memorial service and also host an official dinner at the Town Hall. We very much hope that you can attend, together with the relatives and friends of the other victims.

I did not know Mrs Ryan, as I only moved to this area five years ago, but I am told she was a good, upright citizen and a credit to Brevard. I am also very much aware of how much benefit in terms of tourism, jobs, etc. your novel Space Coast bestowed on this area, so it would be a pleasure to welcome you back.

If you would care to contact this office, my secretary will happily assist with travel arrangements.

Sincerely,

Thomas Heise

Thomas Heise
Mayor

1

Bob, the only way I can do this is kind of scatter-gun. You know I always felt a book was like a sculpture: you start with your big block of material and chip away everything that doesn't look like a sculpture, but I haven't time for that approach now. You're getting the whole block, and I know I can rely on you to edit out whatever is surplus to requirements.[1] I just need to put it down as it comes to me, because I'm desperate to go. I will get to the letter and what happened shortly, but first you should know about how I met her and fell in love. Obviously some of it ended up in *Space Coast*, but that had been put through the fiction blender. I can't remember ever talking to you about how it actually happened, and I simply don't know if she told you. You two got on pretty well, and I suppose a lot of the times you called I didn't want to talk because you couldn't sell my book. I seem to remember you had a lot of long conversations with her. Anyway. When I arrived in Brevard I wasn't particularly looking for love. I was looking for *sex*. Show me a twenty-four-year-old single man who isn't.

I had spent the previous eighteen months working as a reporter on the *Addison County Independent* in Middlebury Falls, Vermont. It was a weekly paper, and paid me by the word, in cash, because

---

[1] I haven't removed any material at all – just rearranged the order where I felt it helped the narrative. *RN*

I'd travelled over from Ireland and didn't have the right papers for them to employ me properly. I didn't go there directly. Like a million other Irish illegals I'd started out on New York's building sites, but I should have known better. I'd never done as much as fifteen minutes of manual labour at home, and within five minutes of starting I knew that I'd no aptitude for it. I was hopeless, and the warm welcome I received to the city's building trade through several loose family connections soon grew cool.

I had harboured romantic visions of building a kind of hard labour camaraderie, of putting on some muscle and getting a good tan, but the guys were immediately wary of me, plus I arrived in winter and almost froze to death. I also came by a nickname: Dropper. I dropped near everything there was to drop, and if it wasn't for pure luck and the proper builder's innate sense of something coming his way, I might have claimed a couple of lives. So I soon started to hear the guys talking about a job in this bar, or that bar, but I was too cold to take the hint.

Eventually the foreman took me aside and told me bluntly that he'd arranged a job for me in an Irish bar in Brooklyn and that I should take it because the men had had a meeting and decided that if I didn't take it, the only way they could ensure their future safety would be to drop something on *me*.

So I took it, and then spent six months cultivating an alcohol problem.

It didn't seem like one at first because, like I say, I was young and there were plenty of young ladies who seemed to find freckles quite novel, but it meant a lot of partying, which inevitably led to a lot of hangovers. Eventually I was on my final warning. I thought because I got on well with the boss – I got invited to Sunday dinner with his family, we both had an interest in the soccer from home – that he wouldn't fire me, but he did. This was in April. He sat me down in the bar and said, 'Michael, you've been drunk since October,' and he wasn't wrong. 'You're not indestructible,' he said, which was news to me. 'You need to wise up and you need to decide what you want to do with your life. And if you take my advice, it won't have anything to do with building sites or bars.'

14

I nodded along with this, mostly because I was still drunk from the night before, but at least a small part of me knew he was right. I started to get up, mumbling my thanks anyway and could he pay me to the end of the week, but he pushed me back down and said, 'Listen, Michael, it's none of my business, but I got a few things to say, right?' From reading this, you probably think he was this old guy, wise in the ways of the world, looking out for the snotty-nosed kid, but it wasn't like that. He was maybe five years older than me. He was just grown up. 'I notice you always have your nose in a book,' he said. 'When you work, there's a paperback in your back pocket. When you get real drunk, you go into a corner and start reading. One time you left your journal on the bar.' He raised an eyebrow.

'Sorry,' I said quickly, starting to colour up. 'I didn't mean . . .' I'd been writing about my life in the bar, and my descriptions of the boss hadn't been exactly flattering.

'It's all right, Michael. I thought it was real funny. I can't hardly write a birthday card, but you've got a cute way with words.' I shrugged. It was just a diary, really. I had always kept one. 'That's what you should be doing,' he concluded. 'Writing stuff.'

I laughed. 'Yeah, I wish. Jimmy, it's not that simple. Writers are . . . well, they know things, the meaning of life; they understand poetry and Shakespeare. I don't.'

'Michael, I didn't know how to pull a pint of Guinness till I went to bar school, you hear what I'm saying?'

'It's not the same.'

'It's not? You don't think you got the smarts?'

'I know I don't . . . got the smarts.'

We both smiled. He was from Waterford, originally.

He said, 'Last night, you nearly got into a fight,' and I thought he was changing the subject.

'Yes, I did. I'm sorry. I know Ambrose is a friend of yours, but he's been in here four nights a week ever since I started, and he just never shuts up. He has a dumb opinion for every occasion, and last night I just lost it. I don't mind an argument, Jimmy, but there's reasoned discussion, and then there's Ambrose.'

'So you threw a pint of Guinness over him.'

'Yes, I did. I'm sorry. It was a dreadful waste of a pint of Guinness.'

'Well, I heard most of it, and he *was* being a pain in the ass. And when you say he's a friend – he's a customer, that's all. But you gotta be nice to the customers. You know what his job is?'

'Vice President of being an asshole, somewhere.'

'He's New York bureau chief for the *Washington Post*.'

'You're *shittin'* me.'

'Nope. He won a Pulitzer Prize a few years back. He's written three books. One says *New York Times bestseller* on the front, though I never did see it there.'

'But he's so . . .'

'Dumb. I know. Michael, this is my point. I see people you think would be real smart, but set them down at the bar, put a drink in front of them, they're just as dumb as you and me. Believe me, Michael, I've met brain surgeons who ain't no brain surgeons.'

I sat nodding for a bit, then shrugged again. 'So what's your point?'

'Point is, we both agree he's dumb and yet he has this big job and he's written all these books. So, I figure, if he can write books, why can't you? Very least you could be as crappy as he is.'

I suppose this approach was pretty simplistic, but it was exactly what I needed. I'd always had these dreams of being a writer, but I'd buried them way down, figuring I didn't have the smarts, but what Jimmy said really changed things for me. Maybe I was never going to win the Nobel Prize for Literature, but I knew I could at least be as bad as Ambrose Jeffers. I picked up his books from a Borders that night and could hardly get past the first page of any of them. In the past I would have just figured I was too stupid to understand what he was writing about – but I'd met the man and now I knew it wasn't me: *he* was the stupid one, and despite what the rave reviews on the back said, I knew his books were stupid as well. It gave me this bizarre kind of confidence in my own abilities.

Bob, you know that unless you're stark raving mad, or a complete genius, that you can't just sit down and write a great novel. Like Jimmy said, before you could run a bar, you needed to know how to pull a pint. However, I hadn't the patience, the money, the papers or indeed the inclination for college. I wanted to be writing *now*. So journalism was the obvious solution. I could learn to write *and* get paid for it. But I was hardly going to walk straight into the *Times*. I had to start small. I spent a day in Borders looking up the names of small newspapers within a couple of hundred miles' radius, then with the help of the neighbourhood copy shop, wrote to about thirty of them, explaining that I was an Irish student looking for vacation work. The *Addison County Independent* was the only one to reply, saying they had a sudden vacancy, they couldn't pay much and when could I start.

I told Jimmy. He said, 'Go for it.'

'All right,' I said.

'And when you make a million bucks off your first novel, come back here and I'll buy you a pint.'

The *Independent* was incredible. Middlebury was a nice, quiet, picturesque college town where not much happened, which meant the newspaper had a ton of space to fill every week. So outside of my daily reporting tasks I was given almost complete freedom to write whatever I wanted. Eventually, I produced columns, reviews, features, interviews – and then, as my confidence grew, some poetry, then short stories and finally a kind of a serial, which was really a local soap opera. I don't make any great claims for it now, and to be truthful it didn't make a huge impact, but it did attract kind of a cult following. What the *Independent* really did was give me the time, the space and the opportunity to essentially teach myself how to write. I was only supposed to be there for two weeks, filling in while one of their reporters took a career break.[1] When he failed to return

---

[1] He went off to climb Everest. He made the summit, but lost five fingers to frostbite on the descent. On the plus side, he discovered God, but kept His location to himself. Both his lack of fingers and his sudden religious conversion brought him to the decision that he was no longer compatible with journalism. I think he became a prison guard.

they decided to keep me on, but continued to pay me according to how much I wrote – but I was writing all day and half the night, caught up in a glorious fever. If I'd kept it up I probably would have bankrupted them. They soon realised it would be cheaper to put me on salary, though it was still in cash so I could be kept off their books.

My decision to leave wasn't entirely voluntary. I was getting itchy feet, and the news stories I was covering were becoming repetitive. I was still enjoying the writing freedom the paper gave me, but I was also enjoying simultaneous affairs with two women. One worked at the paper, the other worked in a downtown bar called the Ice House. That they didn't know about each other in such a small town was something of a minor miracle, but eventually, *inevitably*, the shit hit the fan and I had to get out of town fast – not because I was afraid of confrontation, but because my workplace paramour took it upon herself to inform the authorities that I was an illegal immigrant. I could have stayed and fought it – but I didn't want to get the paper into any trouble after they'd been so good to me – and the truth is, I was ready to go. Although I had worked exhaustively as a journalist, I had never really felt like one. I wanted to write a novel. I had wanted to write one my whole life. I had saved some money, I had a battered Oldsmobile which was dependable rather than sexy, and I now had the conviction that I really could be just as bad as Ambrose Jeffers. Even, perhaps, a tiny bit better.

For the ten years after what happened in Brevard happened, I looked upon my moonlight flit from Middlebury as both the best and worst decision I ever made. Best because it led me to Claire, worst because if I'd never left, Claire would undoubtedly still be alive. A world with Claire in it is an infinitely better place than one without.

For one reason or another, not so long ago I found myself drunk in Brooklyn and spotted Jimmy's bar, and it came back to me, what he'd said about him buying me a pint. I thought I'd go in and surprise him, and we could talk about older, happier times. Except the staff didn't have a clue who Jimmy was. The bar had changed hands at least three times in the years I'd been gone. But you know who *was* sitting at the bar?

Yup.

Ambrose.

I should have gone up and shaken his hand and thanked him for indirectly inspiring me to become a writer. But like I say, I was drunk and he was still talking crap. I asked him if he knew anything about Jimmy and he said he didn't keep track of barkeeps.

So I said, 'Maybe you can keep track of this . . .' and poured a pint of Guinness over him.

They threw me out, of course. Literally. I landed on the sidewalk. Someone gave me a kick with such enthusiasm that the exertion of it caused his chest to whistle. But I hardly felt it. I was too busy laughing.

2

First day I arrived in Brevard, a writer called Paul de Luca had his feet bitten off by a shark. I remember it for three reasons: one, it's pretty damn memorable; two, I remember thinking afterwards that if it had been his hands instead of his feet, it would have been a better story, and three, it was the first time I saw Claire. After the initial shock of seeing the man without his feet, I remember thinking, God, she's pretty. If half the women here are half as pretty as she is, I'll drop anchor. I had been driving for fourteen days, moving kind of carelessly south, looking for somewhere that felt right, and suddenly Brevard, with its marvellous beaches, stunning climate, author with the missing feet and the surfer girl with blood on her bikini, seemed like the place to be.

Best decision I ever made.

No regrets.

Honest.

Paul de Luca was a local who'd written a couple of crime novels, both of them featuring a private detective called Mark de Luca, who specialised in environmental cases. When he wasn't saving the Everglades, this tall blond detective spent every spare moment surfing off Brevard Beach. In real life Paul de Luca supported his writing career working in an adult video store north of Brevard – and spent every spare moment surfing. He too was tall, blond and buff. Women were fascinated by him not only because he was handsome and intelligent, but because he had this air of mystery about him. Why, when there were clearly so many other avenues open to him, did he choose to work in a seedy video store? Later he would say he was just doing research for his novels, but nobody was ever quite convinced, particularly when, after his accident, he used his insurance pay-out to actually buy the video store. Then he extended it – putting in a small theatre for visiting strippers and 25¢ peep-booths for those who found stripping either too intimate or not intimate enough.

I learned all this later from Claire. She knew everything about everybody, and delighted in telling me during those first long delicious days on the beach. She never told it in a nasty, duplicitous way. She was just describing the natural history of a place, how every single thing in it was connected in some way to every other single thing, and the way she told it, her brow furrowed and her eyes tight, then suddenly throwing her head back and roaring with laughter, it was just magical.

I can see her now.

I can hear her. Laughing about mean old Judge Wheeler who used to terrify them as kids, and how after he retired they used to sneak up to his house in the middle of the night and ring the bell and run away, then hide and watch as he prowled his garden with a shotgun; and how in the end he gassed himself – story was, he found out a man he sent to the chair was innocent, and he couldn't live with himself. And how one of her friends had said, 'I couldn't live with him either,' and at the time it was just the funniest thing she'd ever heard. And even funnier – the Judge's house got knocked down and the adult video store went up in its place, so old Judge Wheeler would be spinning in his grave.

Of course, she wasn't laughing first time I saw her: she was screaming.

I'd not been in Brevard for more than five minutes. I'd just bought an ice cream on the pier, and was leaning on the rail, looking out. There was a tattered banner stuck in the sand advertising a Ron Jon Surf Shop Surfing Competition for the following day, and there were a few surfers out getting some practice in. The wind was whipping the sand up, keeping most of the tourists

22

off the beach, so when she struggled out of the waves, dragging Paul de Luca behind her, nobody noticed; when she collapsed beside him nobody saw; and when she hauled herself up again and came screaming up the beach for help, nobody heard but me, licking my cone and hardly paying any attention because, well, this was America, land of the free and crazy. It was only when she got close and I saw the plain terror in her eyes and the blood on her bikini that I realised how serious it was. I vaulted over the rail, down onto the sand where she'd sunk to her knees, fighting for breath and whispering, 'Shark . . . *shark* . . .'

Hell of a way to meet someone.

We stood together as the paramedics fought to stabilise Paul de Luca. He was moaning, his eyes rolling back in his head. They wouldn't let him look at his feet – or where his feet used to be. Then they gave him a shot that knocked him out, and loaded him into the back of the ambulance. One of the paramedics turned to Claire and asked if she wanted to go to the hospital with him, but she shook her head and said she had to get back to work, which I took to mean that she wasn't in any way related to him, that she wasn't his wife or lover, that they weren't dating, that she just happened to be in the vicinity when the shark attacked. You see, she was beautiful. You may consider it reprehensible of me to be thinking in this way when a man was fighting for his life right in front of us, but I couldn't help it. Even – or especially – at that age I had a kind of moral detachment when it came to my love life, but this was beyond even that. Something just went *ding* in my head when I saw her, and you can't fight the *ding*.

Besides, there was nothing further we could do to help Paul de Luca: we had fashioned tourniquets out of a torn beach towel and two metal spikes used to secure a volleyball net which hadn't quite stopped the bleeding, but it had slowed it. We had saved his life. They told us that. I felt pretty good about myself, and even better about Claire. By this stage I'd also borrowed a second towel from a display outside the beach shop at the foot of the pier and draped it around her shoulders, which were caked in sand, although not so much that I didn't notice that the skin beneath was smooth and tanned and very lightly freckled. She was shivering. As I smoothed the towel down, she leaned against me for a moment and I felt the soft curve of her breast press into my arm. She smiled a thank you. Her eyes were watering.

Then Sheriff Newton arrived, along with the Mayor and a TV news crew out of Orlando which had been diverted from covering a house fire in nearby Indian River Beach. There were also about 200 people standing around watching and comparing notes. A bronzed reporter informed Central Florida that there hadn't been a shark attack at Brevard Beach for forty years. The Mayor said he hoped it would be another forty before it happened again. He was ordering the beach closed for the day, but had every expectation that it would open in time for the Ron Jon Surfing Competition the following day. I suspected the entries would be down. As the ambulance wailed away, I said to Claire, 'Are you okay?'

She nodded vaguely.

I said, 'You're in shock, let me get you a coffee.'

But before she could respond, the TV news crew pounced again. I was available, but for some unaccountable reason they chose the beautiful girl in the bloodstained zebra bikini over the freckle-faced Irishman with a bad case of sunburn.

I went and got the coffee anyway. When I came back, she was gone. I wasn't particularly disappointed because I had enjoyed her beauty without expectation. There were a dozen similar towns along this Atlantic coast, but something had clearly drawn me to this one. I had parked my car, bought an ice cream, experienced the aftermath of a shark attack, been sprayed with blood, saved a man's life and draped a towel around the fine shoulders of a beautiful woman. If all that didn't amount to a sign that this was the place to stop and wait for the muse to strike – well, what would?

As I booked into the Comfort Inn, three blocks away, I kept my bloodstained T-shirt on. It was my own personal red badge of courage.

3

Bob, I kind of lied to you when I said I was thinking about moving back to the city. Truth is, I'd already been there six months. I have an apartment a few blocks from where you live. One morning, I was three places behind you in a Starbucks queue. You said, 'Excuse me,' as you went by. There was even eye-contact, and I was all set to pump your hand and marvel at the coincidence, but then you were gone. I suppose I looked a bit different, and when you haven't seen someone in that long, and consider there to be no possibility that you might, then even if he's standing right there in front of you, you just don't take it in. It was no bad thing, really. I was back, but I wasn't quite ready.

Ten years is a long time.

I won't bore you with the details of every place I stayed, or we'd be here all night. Some places it was just a few days. Others it was months. I was in South Dakota for a year. Before you picture me riding the range, I worked in a library. Book punching, if you like. I did Europe, the Far East. Even went home to Ireland for a while, which was a mistake. A hard lesson to learn: you can't go back, because it's never the same. That's why, when I got back to my apartment and opened the letter from the Mayor of Brevard, I immediately crumpled it up and threw it in the trash. I only had fond memories of my childhood in Ireland, yet returning was such a painful experience. How much worse would returning to Brevard be? It was the cause of the nightmares I had spent the last decade trying to escape. Do you know, it was seven years before I got a proper night's sleep? When you lose someone to illness it is bad enough. When you lose them through a violent act it is so much worse. When it is a violent act that could and should have been prevented, you not only lose them, you carry this huge open wound festering with anger and bitterness around with you. Nobody but you can see it, yet every day someone pokes at it with a stick because everything, *everything* reminds you of what happened. Once, I was walking close to the Kremlin when I saw a blouse which was just like one Claire used to wear, and I burst into tears. Why would I *ever* want to return to Brevard?

And yet.

It niggled me.

The letter stayed in the trash – but I didn't take the trash out.

Eventually I showed it to my shrink. It was badly creased and there was a dried smear of chicken fried rice on the back.

He said, 'Why not?'

I said, 'Why so?'

He took another drink. We were sitting in Jimmy's. His name was Ambrose Jeffers. He wasn't half as bad as I remembered. You grow up a lot in ten years. You realise that other people are entitled to an opinion, and just because you don't agree with it, it doesn't make them a dumb-ass – or at least, not a complete dumb-ass. A couple of nights after I threw the Guinness over him I went back and apologised. He accepted it gracefully and swore that he hadn't been the one who kicked me while I was sprawled on the sidewalk. He was fifty-eight years old, was on to his third wife, but had added another Pulitzer to his collection. We'd been meeting up a couple of nights a week ever since.

'Because it's the right thing to do.'

'Right? How? It'll just stir up some shitty memories.'

'From what you tell me, Michael, they've been stirred up for ten years. This might settle them down. All they're saying is, "Look, a terrible thing happened here, we want to pay our

respects to the victims, we want to remember them, we don't
want people to forget".'

'Who's ever going to forget?'

'People do forget. They move on, they move away, new people
come in.'

'Well then, why dredge it all up again?'

'To remind people, to educate them, to say, "This happened
once, let's not let it happen again". Or maybe it's an election
year. Whatever the reason, I think you should go. But it's your
call.'

'Yes, it is.'

I bought him another drink. He watched sports and I brooded.
After a while he said, 'If you haven't been back in ten years,
then you haven't been to her grave in ten years.'

I shook my head.

'Why not?'

I shrugged.

'Michael, am I your psychiatrist or am I not?'

'You're not.'

'I'm just surprised you've never visited her.'

'Ambrose – it's not like fucking *visiting*. She wouldn't be putting
the coffee on.'

'You know what I mean. Who looks after the grave – her
family?'

'She doesn't . . . City Hall does it, I'm sure.'

'As long as you're sure. As long as it isn't all overgrown and
vandalised.'

'Don't. Look, I've avoided publicity for ten years, what do I
want with walking right back into it? It'll just start the whole
thing up again.'

'It's not about you, Michael. It's about *them*, the ones that
died.'

'The ones that died are dead and gone.'

Ambrose drummed his fingers on the bar for half a minute.
'Okay. Michael – say you meet someone at a party and they ask
you what you do for a living, what do you say?'

'I don't go to parties.'

27

'Michael – please.'

'Okay. All right. "I don't know. I do – this and that".'

'Let me put it another way. You get hit by a truck and you go to heaven and Saint Peter is standing at the pearly gates and he's looking in his ledger and he asks, "Michael Ryan, what was your profession down there on earth?" What would you say?'

'Writer, if you insist.'

'Not me, him. And he would look up in his book and say, "You didn't publish much. I can only find one book, although it did sell amazingly well and the reviews were excellent". And you would say . . . ?'

'"I only had one book in me".'

'And he would say, "Nonsense! Did you ever hear of a hat-maker who only made one hat? God gave you this talent and you failed to make full and proper—"'

'Is there any relevance to this, Ambrose?'

'A writer writes. Is it the case that you continue to write, but don't publish?'

'No. I don't write.'

'You don't want to write?'

'I *can't* write.'

'Since the day and hour this terrible thing happened to your wife?'

'More or less. Yes.'

'But the desire to write: is it still there?'

'I don't know. I really don't.'

'Do you want my honest, professional opinion?'

'As a psychiatrist? Because I have to tell you, you're not a psychiatrist. You're just a reporter who drinks too much.'

'Excuse me. I'm a multi-Pulitzer Prize-winning reporter who drinks too much.'

'Either way, your advice is about as valuable as *Dear Abby*'s, and twice as expensive.'

'Young man, I could drink *Dear Abby* under the table. However. Here's what I think, cards on the table, no bullshit and don't interrupt. Michael – you are a phenomenally successful writer, if over-praised. You should be writing again. I think you should go back to your publisher and say you're going to accept this invitation, you're going back to Brevard, you're going to write about it and he's going to publish it.'

'Ambrose, I'm not—'

'He'll say, "That's fantastic, Michael, of course I'll publish it – but what kind of a book are we talking about?" And you'll say, "My life changed for ever the day my wife was killed. I was so mad and angry that I blew out of town before I had a chance to face it head on, and I've been running away from what happened ever since. I want to go back and talk to the people who were there that day; I want to talk to the people I've blamed for what happened before and after the robbery; I want to talk to the relatives of the other people who died; I want to learn who their sons or daughters or parents were and what they were like. I want to talk to the wives or parents of the bank robbers, I want to know why they did what they did. I want to understand. I want to visit my wife's grave and say goodbye to her because I've never managed it yet, and even though I still love her I have to let her go, and move on, otherwise it's going to kill me as well".'

'Jesus Christ, Ambrose.'

4

I only learned her name was Claire from the Channel 12 news. Claire Roth. She'd been surfing right beside Paul de Luca when he suddenly went down screaming. She hadn't seen anything of the shark. Not even a fin. Nor, I thought, had she heard the theme from *Jaws*, but it didn't stop the station playing it. The interviewer described her as 'the heroine who works as an unassuming clerk in the First National Bank in Brevard'. That evening, I strolled around Brevard and found myself outside the bank. It was located halfway up Main Street and seemed to be extraordinarily large for a small-town bank. Then, in walking the length of it, I realised it must have been extended at some point to make it stretch as far as the end of the block to facilitate an automated drive-thru. There were four separate lanes, three of them in use. I had a sudden urge to switch banks.

Bob, I've never been big on research – even when I was a reporter. You can look up Brevard on the net and know that these days it has a population of around sixteen thousand, and it wasn't much smaller when I first arrived. You will discover that it was founded by fishermen in the 1860s as Indian River City, but quickly had to change its name because US Postal Authorities claimed it was too long to use on a postmark. The extension of the Jacksonville, St Augustine and Indian River Railway Company line to Brevard proved a catalyst for growth around the turn of the twentieth century, but it wasn't really until the 1960s that it took off as a tourist resort. This was partly because it is right next door to Cape Canaveral. The space race may now have slowed, but satellites are sent up nearly every month and they're still a big draw. They are spectacular.

Claire and I had a satellite.

The city is strung out along four miles of the Indian River and there's all the usual water activities, if you're into that (ha!). Downtown is made up of narrow tree-lined streets. There are dozens of antique stores and art galleries. It describes itself as 'historic Brevard' and makes like it's a centre of the arts and culture, but really it is, and was, quite rundown. You don't notice it so much in the blistering sun, but in the cool of the evening you'll see it's a little decayed, a little threadbare. A lot of the antique shops are just junk shops. It's no bad thing – and hardly unique in Florida. The important thing was that after the exhilaration of my arrival, I very quickly felt relaxed in Brevard. I could do my work there. I knew it.

Naturally, I also quickly found a bar. It was called McDaid's Char Bar and Grill. It was right on Main Street. There were tables outside, and I sat there for a while, already making notes in a yellow legal pad, just first thoughts really. A waitress called Jo-Anne, both arms heavily tattooed, detected Ireland in my accent and asked me whereabouts I was from. I told her Dublin and she said she had a friend there who ran a tattoo shop and did I know it. I showed her my arms and told her that people with freckles were already tattooed and she kind of smiled at that. I should have left it, but when she came back with my next drink I explained that some people thought that freckles were actually secret maps of the universe, and after that a different waitress served me. I should have returned to the Comfort Inn then, but instead the siren call of rock'n'roll drew me inside – a six-piece band on a small stage, blasting out 1960s' hits. If it's loud enough, and you're drunk enough, most bands can sound pretty good.

Jo-Anne, having finished her shift, sat down at the bar beside me at the end of their first set and asked me if it was true about the freckles. I said I had no idea – I'd read it in a book somewhere. She asked me my name and if I was on vacation and had I heard about the shark attack, and I said I had been there. I told her about the spraying blood and the makeshift tourniquets and she said she'd heard all about it and I said, 'It was on the news,' and she said, 'No, I was working, but I actually know the girl that saved his life, Claire – she's in the restaurant right now,' and she pointed further down the bar.

'Is she?'

She could tell by the way my eyes lit up that she'd already lost me, and I could certainly tell from the way her own smile faded and her eyes lost a little of their lustre that it wasn't the first time she'd talked herself out of what might have been a fun night (although it wasn't going to happen, not with the tattoos, one of them of a tiger and another of a Harley, neither of them very good). I craned my neck, but the restaurant was around the curve of the bar. I said, 'I should go and say hello.'

'She's with Tommy. I wouldn't tell Tommy about the freckles being like a map of the universe.' Jo-Anne got up off her stool and moved along the bar. Someone asked her to get a drink and she snapped that she wasn't working.

I lifted my drink, about to go. Then I sneezed and spilled half of it. In truth I'd started to feel a bit fuzzy. I had a brief thought about going back to the hotel and getting my head down. I've never been one for small talk, and although it comes easier when I'm drunk, I didn't want to sound drunk or say something stupid, so instead of going home I thought for a bit about what to say, and how, and then I ran through how it might go a couple of times, and how she might possibly respond, and what not believing in secret freckle maps of the universe might say about her boyfriend's character, if he was her boyfriend. Then I thought it might be better to say nothing at all, to leave it until I was sober. That was the coward in me coming out, and also the realist.

'Hey.'

I turned. 'Hey.'

There she was.

'I was just on my way to the . . .' she nodded towards the rest rooms. Her hair was down. Virtually no make-up. 'I thought it was you.'

'It's me,' I said.

She was wearing a lacy white top and black shorts to above the knees. She smiled widely. 'I never got to say . . . the camera crew just whisked me . . . did you see me on the news?'

I gave her a quick rendition of the *Jaws* theme.

She laughed suddenly and splendidly, then clamped a hand to her mouth. 'That was awful! How could they do that! Poor Paul. Will you join us for a drink? Tommy would love to meet you. But I have to pee.'

She hurried away and I had three minutes of just standing there thinking how nice she was. She was warm and friendly; her eyes were tactile but her hands weren't, which I like in a stranger. When she returned, she led me to the small restaurant which consisted of half a dozen tables laid out in two columns. She pulled out a chair for me and said, 'Sit down. Tommy, this is . . . oh my God, I don't even know your . . .'

'Michael. Michael Ryan.'

'Tommy, this is him – the guy on the beach. You were such a hero.'

I laughed. 'No. God, no. You did all the work.' I extended my hand.

Tommy took it and squeezed it hard enough to crack. His face was weatherbeaten and his hair straggled. He wore a black T-shirt raggedly cut at the shoulders to show off his muscles and tats. 'She's been talking about you all night,' he said. I smiled somewhat awkwardly. Tommy playfully punched her shoulder then smiled at me. 'Paul's a good friend of mine. Son of a bitch lost both feet – imagine that. Owes his life to you – and my girl here, though he don't know it yet. Not entirely sure he knows about the feet either. Wouldn't like to be the one to tell him. When I was in the Marines, guy in my section, he lost both arms. Hell of a thing. Son of a bitch lucky to be alive. Both of them. Get you a drink, Michael?'

'No – really, I'm fine. Bit of a summer cold.' I sniffed up. 'Early night.'

'You on vacation, Michael?' he asked.

'No. I just moved here. Today, in fact.'

Tommy nodded. 'Hell of a thing to lose your feet,' he repeated.

'Where are you from?' Claire asked.

'New York. Dublin, originally. I'm a writer. I've come here to write a book.'

'Really? Why here?'

'No particular reason.'

'What sort of a book?'

'A novel.'

'A novel! What's it about?'

'I don't know yet. But I think it will start with a man getting his feet bitten off by a shark.'

Bob, looking back now, I can see why this might have annoyed Tommy. It reads as cheesy now as it probably sounded then.

Claire clapped her hands. 'Tommy! I'm going to be in a novel!'

Tommy laughed, but it sounded forced. 'If I go to a bookshop, I'll find your other books?'

'No, this is my first.'

'And you haven't started it yet?'

I shook my head.

'You know,' he said, his voice suddenly gruff and low, 'I didn't call myself a Marine until after I killed my first man in combat.'

He gave me a kind of a bug-eyed look. I was aware of the point he was making, and the barely concealed hostility that came with it, but also, I was drunk. 'Man,' I said, 'that's awesome. You were in Vietnam?'

Claire snorted.

'The Gulf, man. How fucking old do you think I am?'

'Tommy, he's only joking.' She put her hand on his and squeezed.

I sneezed again.

Claire said, 'Bless you.'

'Thank you.'

We smiled at each other. Tommy smiled at neither of us.

I took another sip of my beer, then stood up and said, 'Listen – no offence, I'm beat, I'm coming down with something and

I'm half-drunk. I need to lie down. It's good to meet you both.' I nodded at Tommy. 'And I'd guess about forty-five.'

Tommy's brow furrowed. 'About forty-five?'

'You look maybe forty-five. But good, too. Listen, nice to meet you and your daughter, and maybe see you around.'

I took care to keep my face straight, then turned away. As I crossed the restaurant he hissed, 'Son of a bitch,' and I heard the scrape of chair legs on the wooden floor, then Claire trying to calm him down, her voice serious but with a hint of barely suppressed laughter.

I started back towards the Comfort Inn, pleased with myself for about five seconds – that is, until I started thinking that I hadn't actually achieved anything apart from making myself an enemy who was used to killing *his* enemies. Despite my conviction that the pen is mightier than the sword, I found myself ducking into shop doorways every time a car approached. Eventually I managed to convince myself that I was being foolish and paranoid. Besides, the chances were that he was having a much better time in bed with the girl of my dreams.

5

You won't be aware of this, but Ambrose got me as far as the lobby of your publishing house in his efforts to make me pitch you his idea for me to write a book about my return to Brevard. But then I balked and we returned to Jimmy's and he sulked for a while. Then he had what he likes to think of as a brainwave.

'I've got it, you bog-Irish cretin – I'll go with you to Florida!'

'No, Ambrose.'

'Why not?'

'Because it would be a nightmare. I would murder you.'

'Nonsense! It'll be fun.'

'Fun!'

'It'll be like a spiritual quest. A quest for the wayward soul of Michael Ryan.'

'No, Ambrose.'

'I'll be like your muse, your moral compass. Don Quixote and Sancho Panza!'

'No, Ambrose.'

'And if you don't write it, I will.'

'Now we're getting to it.'

'No, what I mean is – the threat of me writing it, and getting it totally wrong, at least in your eyes – is exactly what you need hanging over you to make *you* write it. Michael, listen to me. I'm not blowing hot air up your ass here, but you are far and away a much better writer than I am . . .'

'Granted.'

'. . . and you know it's a fantastic idea for a book . . .'

'Yes, it is.'

'. . . but you know you're never going to do it of your own accord; you need someone there to help you along, to encourage you, to support you, to bounce ideas off. And even if you disagree with every single article I've ever written, you'll have to agree I am good at getting stories and talking to people – which you, frankly, are not. I won't just be along for the ride, I'll contribute.'

'No, Ambrose.'

'Come on, Michael. I've got *months* of vacation time, and I'm not freakin' wed to Jimmy's, I can get drunk anywhere. What are you scared of?'

'*Everything*. You, especially. Ambrose, when we went to see Bob Naiffy today, it's the first time I've ever been with you outside of this bar. And you nearly got into a fist-fight with the cab driver.'

'He didn't know where the fuck he was going.'

I sighed. 'Ambrose, listen to me. I don't even know if I'm going back to Brevard. The whole memorial thing bothers me. Then there's the publicity – I've spent a decade avoiding it, but the moment I step off the plane it becomes less about what happened back then and more about me. What are all the other relatives going to think of that?'

'Who gives a shit?'

I laughed. He had, however, hit the nail on the head. I *was* scared to go back. Scared about how I might react, scared of what I might find out, scared of breaking down, the way I had before. Oh yes. It wasn't all just wandering aimlessly and looking grim during those years on the road, Bob. I was in hospital. For a while I didn't know who I was or what I was about. It was a long hard road back to Jimmy's and a loud-mouthed, overweight hack trying to persuade me to return to the scene of the crime.

'I got it all figured out,' said Ambrose. 'I do the driving, you do the navigating and think your deep thoughts.'

'I still know Brevard pretty well, so there won't exactly be a lot of navigating.'

'No, I mean driving from here to there. New York to Brevard, Florida, shouldn't take us more than—'

'Ambrose, not that I'm going, but there are big things with wings that can get us there the same day and out the same night.'

'That's not the point. You have to recreate your original journey. Michael, we drive right down the eastern seaboard, just the way you did the first time. These things, it's as much about the journey as about the arrival.'

'That's bullshit, Ambrose.'

'Well, maybe it is, but you never know. It'll be fun.'

'Jesus Christ, Ambrose! It's not about fun!'

'Why not!?'

He kept at it. He would not let me off the hook. I had the choice of not meeting him in Jimmy's, but I kept turning up, and he kept planning. One night he brought me an internet print-out of the cars that were available from Avis.

I said, 'I'm not going, Ambrose.'

'Sure you are.'

The next night he showed me a map and got me to point out the towns I'd stopped at on my way to Brevard originally, and where possible to name the hotels, motels and restaurants I'd used.

I made a lot of them up.

Twenty-four hours later, he said, 'Do you know, every one of those towns has a Comfort Inn. We could get a good rate if we block book.'

'It's not about the rate,' I said.

'I understand completely,' said Ambrose. 'We're seeking to replicate the original journey, and you didn't stay in a Comfort Inn until you arrived in Brevard. But for the towns where you can't remember where you stayed or I can't find the hotels, we could use Comfort Inns and still get a hit on the rate.'

'It's not about the rate, Ambrose.'

'I understand completely. You have money. I didn't want to take advantage.'

'Ambrose, it's about the fact that I'm not going.'

'Sure you are. Where did you stay in Myrtle Beach, South Carolina?'

On 10 June, fifteen days before the opening in Brevard of the memorial garden and its attendant events, Ambrose breezed into Jimmy's, sat down beside me, ordered a drink then gave me the thumbs-up. 'All done,' he said. 'The car's booked, the hotels are secured and I e-mailed the Mayor's office to let them know you're coming – but relax, I made it perfectly clear you didn't want any personal publicity, you just wanted to blend in with all the other folks, and I didn't even mention you were writing a book about it all.'

I stared at him.

'*What*?' he asked.

'You're such a fucking asshole, Ambrose.' Then I walked out.

Bob, there are all sorts of psycho-babble you (and I mean *you*!) could come up with to explain my reluctance to return to Brevard. The simple fact is that I did not want to do it. (My reasons for being reluctant to travel with Ambrose should be perfectly obvious). And *yet* . . .

When I was nine years old, my father took me to the local swimming pool at Blanchardstown, outside Dublin. There was a diving pool there with one low board (although it seemed high) and one high board (which was really, *really* high). I had no interest whatsoever in jumping off either of them, but then a boy a year younger than me went flying off the top one and I got it into my head that I had to do the same. I climbed the steps, with my dad shouting encouragement from below, but I got to the foot of the board and I just couldn't step out. I tried and I tried but I couldn't force myself – at which point I burst into tears and then had to walk past all the other kids queuing up to jump. They weren't laughing at me. They didn't look away, embarrassed. They probably didn't even notice. My dad was very good about it. He said I was too young, maybe in a couple of years, nothing to be ashamed of. No one said I had to do it. I went

40

home and had a miserable week, and then on the Saturday we went back to the pool and I walked straight up there and jumped off. I hated every second of it, but I did it because I had to.

Ambrose, who had never been to my apartment, and who, to the best of my knowledge and by my determined effort, didn't know where it was, appeared at my front door a few hours later. I don't know how he got past security downstairs, because he was steaming drunk, but he made it, a shambling figure in a too-tight mac with a box of Kentucky Fried Chicken squashed into one pocket. He almost fell inside when I opened up. He steadied himself, then pointed a chubby finger at me and exploded: '*I'm* an asshole?!'

'Ambrose . . .'

'You're the one had his wife killed on him and ran away! You're the one blames himself for what happened and won't face it! You're the one who pussied out of visiting his own wife's grave! You're the one petrified of writing anything 'cause you think you've lost it! You're the one with millions of dollars in the bank!'

'Ambrose . . .'

'Shut the fuck up! You could write a grocery list and it would sell! I've won two Pulitzers and my book sales are still in double figures! My boss says my stories are shit and I've been in New York too long and they're going to move me somewhere else and I know as sure as hell that my wife and kids won't go with me! I need to get away! I need to rejuvenate! I need to sort my friggin' head out! I've drunk too much! But *I'm* the asshole? *You're* the fucking asshole!'

He was breathing hard, and sweat was lashing down his brow; his mouth was curled up into a snarl and he rolled back and forth on the balls of his feet as if ready to attack.

'Ambrose,' I said quietly. 'I've decided to go back to Brevard. I want you to come with me.'

It took several moments to sink in, then he nodded once. 'All right,' he said, 'I'll go home and pack.'

Then he turned and staggered back down the corridor.

6

Where does lust stop and love begin? How thin is the line that separates unrequited love from stalking? I think *crush* is the most accurate word, letter for letter, in the entire dictionary. It does exactly what it says.

After a few false starts I found a cheap and cheerful efficiency apartment that was more than adequate for my needs. It was triangularly equidistant from the beach, the Publix supermarket and McDaid's Char Bar and Grill. The first two are self-explanatory, but the bar, *this* bar, was important because it was where my muse hung out. Or, to be perfectly honest, my *anti*-muse. She *became* my muse, certainly, but back then I think she actually stopped me from writing for the simple reason that she inhabited my every waking thought. Every writer is a great *excuser*. He will find a thousand excuses *not* to write. My plan, you see, was to write the great American novel. Nothing like setting the bar high. Within a few hours I reined in my ambition to attempt the great Irish novel. By the end of the first week I had resigned myself to writing possibly the third best novel ever to come out of Blanchardstown. The simple fact was that although I had arrived in Brevard with a case full of plots and twists and characters, I had dreamed of being a novelist for so long that now that I had the opportunity, I was like an orphanage kid let loose in a Toys'R'Us – overwhelmed by possibilities to the point where I couldn't make a decision about anything. Thus

I was ideally placed to propel Claire Roth into position as my primary excuse for hardly writing a damn word.

She didn't know she was my anti-muse. She hardly knew I existed. We had had one exciting, adrenaline-fused encounter on the beach, and then an awkward, somewhat drunken exchange. I did not know her at all, I hardly knew if she was bright or dim, left or right, funny or raging, but I knew *something* and it was enough to stop me in my tracks. Until it was settled, one way or another, I couldn't start my novel.

I knew McDaid's Char Bar was her local because Jo-Anne told me as much, but for the next four nights Claire failed to appear. However, Tommy was there. He worked the sound desk for the band. I noted that he wore a wedding band and tried desperately to recall if Claire did. He spoke to me a couple of times when he came up to the bar for a drink. First time he said, 'Hey, Chapters, how's it goin'?' The second time, two nights later, he said, 'Hey, Chapters, how's it goin'?' From this I understood that he – or *they* – had a nickname for me. Perhaps they giggled about it in bed. I nodded and smiled but otherwise did not try to engage him in conversation.

Jo-Anne said, 'You're not the first, you know.'

'Not the first what?'

'Guy to hang around waiting for Claire to show.'

'I'm not waiting for Claire to show.'

'One night I counted three in a row, one, two, three, just right along here, just here to look at her.'

'I'm not here to—'

'What*ever*.' She moved away to serve someone. When she came back she said, 'It's not exactly her fault. She just attracts people. I don't mean because she's beautiful, though she is, there's just something about her that makes you smile and want to be with her. Some people are blessed with that.'

I weighed that up for a few moments. Then asked, with studied nonchalance, 'Not that I'm interested, but these guys, do they ever . . .'

'End up with her? No, course not. She's with Tommy, ever since they were kids. No, they just hang around for a while, she's nice and friendly and that's enough for some of them. Occasionally one asks what she's doing with a loser like Tommy, saying, "I have a yacht" and all that shit, but she just smiles and tells them she really likes them and all, but she's with Tommy.'

'I see. Then what?'

'Oh, I usually feel sorry for them and jump their bones.'

'That's uhm, very accommodating of you.'

'Relax, Michael, I'm not going to jump you.'

'Okay.'

'I would be interested, but I had my clit pierced yesterday and I think it's gone septic.'

I nodded, and raised my drink.

You will be wondering by now why, if I was so desperate to see her again, I didn't just walk into her bank or hang around outside until she came out for lunch or finished work. The fact is, I did. I went into the bank on my first morning in Brevard, then walked straight back out when I couldn't see her. I did see a security guard and perhaps a dozen staff, but no sign of Claire Roth. After that, if I just happened to be passing by around lunchtime – every day, that is – I would walk very slowly, backwards and forwards, hoping to bump into her. At the end of my first week in Brevard, and still not having seen her again or written a single useful word, I finally resorted to phoning the bank and asking for her, only to be told that she was on vacation. When I was asked who was calling, I hung up.

Although my muse was on vacation, I found a temporary solution to my writing malaise in suddenly recalling what I had flippantly said to her in the restaurant: that my novel would start with a surfer getting his feet bitten off by a shark. Why not? It might serve as an extraordinary introduction to my story.

As a writer, you have no weekend. Quite often you have no week *start*. You have no days off. Even if you can't write a word, there is no respite, because what you should be doing, but cannot, hangs over you like a giant bird, pecking. No escape. You feel guilty all the time. I know that now, and have had ten years of it. Then, I only knew it as a horrible feeling. I had to get started. Even if what I wrote was garbage, I had to physically start writing. The act of it would surely get the juices flowing.

So, on a steamy Sunday morning, by way of research to inspire this new beginning, I drove three miles out of town to make an unannounced visit to Paul de Luca in his private room at Merritt Island General Hospital. When I arrived I explained who I was to the nurse in charge and she said she'd check with Mr de Luca. I asked how he was and she said that he was 'a little bit down'. A few moments later, she ushered me in. She smiled valiantly and said, 'Paul, this is Michael Ryan. He was on the beach with you when it happened.'

Paul, propped up, with an IV connected, glared at me. 'What do you want – a fucking reward?' he snapped.

The nurse, who had moved across to fluff up his pillows, glanced nervously towards me. 'Now, Paul, when you said you'd see him, I didn't expect you to abuse—'

'What the fuck do you *want*?' he demanded.

'I just thought I'd come and see how you are.'

'How the fuck do you *think* I am?'

'Paul!' the nurse scolded.

'And if there's anything I can do for you.'

'Yeah, right! Like take me out for a walk! I'm starting to get itchy feet in here!'

'Perhaps some other time,' said the nurse. She crossed towards me, and I turned for the door.

'Wait,' said Paul, his anger suddenly deflating. 'Wait.'

I turned.

'You were there?'

I nodded.

'With Claire?'

I nodded again.

'Why hasn't she been to see me?'

'I don't know.'

He sighed. 'She saved my life, but she hasn't been to see me. I think maybe she's afraid of hospitals. If you see her, will you tell her it's all right to come? It's horrible, but I'm coping. They're going to fit me with titanium feet. A man with titanium feet climbed Everest not so long ago, so there's hope for me yet. Will you tell her to come?'

'I can ask her.'

'Good. Okay. Good. Look, I'm sorry. It's just . . .' He had been looking directly at me, or the nurse, but definitely not at his bed or the outline of his legs, which just kind of tapered off under the blankets where his feet should have been. Now he tilted his head back and stared at the ceiling. 'I need some *fucking* pain relief.'

'Paul, we've discussed this.' The nurse turned to me. 'If you want to leave . . .'

'No,' muttered Paul. 'Look – just sit down.'

I glanced at the nurse for some kind of direction, but she just gave an exasperated shrug and hurried to the door. 'I'll ask the doctor about increasing your meds, Paul,' she said.

As she left I lowered myself onto a plastic chair set against the back wall. I forced myself not to look at his legs. 'So . . .' I began.

'I'm not talking about the shark. Every asshole been through those doors wants to know about the shark. I didn't see nothin', I didn't hear nothin' – all I know is I woke up in here with all these tubes sticking out of me, footloose and fancy free.'

'Okay,' I said. 'So what would you like to talk about?'

He looked at me for several long moments, then gave a slight shake of his head and turned his attention to the window. I think we both knew what we really wanted to talk about. It was just a matter of who started first.

'So, what makes you think she's scared of hospitals?' I asked.

7

This is a list of cities where we argued:

Asbury Park
Wilmington
Newport News
Portsmouth
Newport News (we had to return because Ambrose left his wallet behind there)
Elizabeth City
Edenton
Plymouth
New Bern
Beaufort
Wilmington
Wilmington
Wilmington (left his wallet, then remembered he'd forgotten his laptop)
Myrtle Beach
Charleston
Savannah
Brunswick
Fernandina
Jacksonville

Jacksonville (wallet again – he had a thing about leaving it under his mattress instead of in the safe)
St Augustine
New Smyrna Beach
and finally, memorably, Titusville.

You see, Bob, in a buddy movie, what really makes it work is if, actually, they aren't buddies at all, but they *become* buddies by the end of their journey. They are physical opposites. One is handsome, the other not. One is tidy, the other messy. One laid-back, the other quick to anger. One is a pessimist, one an optimist. They will fight and sulk and learn and make up and grow, all in the space of ninety minutes. I was on the road with Ambrose Jeffers for twelve *days*. It was a mad director's cut of a road movie; except when the credits rolled we were anything but friends, and had learned nothing but mutual mistrust.

He drove; I navigated. There wasn't a lot to it. Just keep going south until we reach Brevard.

We were bar mates. We had no shared history or interests, and it was clear to me that he wasn't driving thousands of miles with me out of friendship. He was after a story. I would, in his words, pussy out of writing it, and then he would swoop. He didn't really care if I found salvation or enlightenment at the end of our journey. So the question is, why did I allow him to travel with me? Why did I go along with his absurd idea to recreate my original journey? Why did I not get him to sign all sorts of paperwork which might one day prevent him from exploiting our 'friendship'?

I suppose, better the devil you know. Because, sad as it may seem, after a decade on the road I didn't have anyone else. I needed the support, the encouragement, even someone to blame. To his credit, he didn't exactly pepper me with questions, nor did he try to analyse me or get me to relive the events of ten years ago. It was much more subtle than that. Sometimes I found myself telling him things I'd kept bottled up for ever. We had joked in the bar about him being my psychiatrist, but we'd never really gotten deep down into it. But on the road, long-suppressed

50

details began to leak out. Then I would suddenly realise what I was doing and abruptly shut up, and there's nothing worse than that for a listener, just when you're getting to the nitty gritty. So he would get annoyed, and I would get defensive, and then we would go at it. At night, he got very drunk. And often, during the day. Don't get me wrong, I can drink with the best of them. Ambrose just happened to be amongst the worst of them. In Jimmy's he was interesting, argumentative and self-righteous, but funny with it. On the road, it wasn't quite so funny.

Titusville is a stone's throw from Brevard. We arrived there just as darkness fell, and although we had pre-booked a hotel, I was for continuing on. I wanted to arrive in Brevard under the cover of darkness, although I can't adequately explain why. Ambrose, however, was adamant that we arrive fresh in the morning – and besides, I'd stayed in Titusville on my original trip, and he thought it important to stick to that schedule. So, fatigued from the driving, and the continual bickering that went with it, I allowed Ambrose to steer us towards the Luna Sea Motel.

Really.

It was one of the most boring, functional motels I've ever stayed in, and I've stayed in thousands, so maybe they just didn't get the joke. We ended up in a nearby Outback restaurant, two good steaks, fries too salty. Ambrose was on his third pitcher of beer, with me yawning and Coked out. He wasn't in good form. Something had clearly been festering, and I supposed it was because I'd been withholding information. But it wasn't.

'Do you know something?' he asked.

'What?'

'I didn't like *Space Coast.*'

'That's good to know.'

'It annoyed me very much that the obnoxious little shit I used to argue with in Jimmy's wrote something that sold millions.'

'That's understandable.'

'And a little bit of me was quite happy that you had a miserable life afterward.'

I eyed him curiously. 'That's quite mean, Ambrose.'

'Yes, it is. There is an old quote, and I can't remember who it's by, that says, "every time a friend succeeds, a little piece of me dies".'

'Good quote.'

'And you weren't even a friend.' He burped loudly. 'Better in than out,' he said. 'My point is, while I was planning this for you, I reread *Space Coast*. It's very good, Michael.'

'Thank you.'

'But from what you've told me over the past few months about Claire and everything that happened, it raises a lot of questions.'

'What sort of questions, Ambrose?' I didn't much care for the way his mouth was twisting inwards and his eyes suddenly seemed quite predatory.

'About her contribution to the book.'

'I'm not sure what you mean.'

'That you couldn't have written it without her.'

'I've always said that.'

'I mean that you really, *really* couldn't have written it without her.'

'Are you suggesting she *wrote* the book?'

'I've heard it whispered. But no, Michael, I'm not suggesting she wrote the book. I'm suggesting she *is* the book.'

'And what the fuck is that supposed to mean?'

'What do *you* think it means?'

I glared at him. 'You are such an asshole.'

He was drunk. I should have known better than to either allow him to steer the conversation in this direction or to rise to it.

'An asshole,' Ambrose grinned, 'is a useful thing.'

'Shit comes out of an asshole, Ambrose,' I said. It wasn't exactly a Wildean exchange. I retired to the rest room before he could respond, threw water on my face, then dried it and stared at my reflection. I was thirty-five years old, but looked older. Felt ancient.

There was a little blackboard hanging on the wall with a saucer filled with sticks of chalk on a stand below it and a printed invitation to leave a comment. I picked up the chalk, then stared at the board. Claire was my *muse*. She wasn't my ghost writer. I took a deep breath. *Relax, he's just trying to provoke a quote out of you. It had to come sooner or later.* I shook my head and laughed. I wrote: *Michael Ryan was here*, put the chalk down and turned for the door. Ambrose was just coming in. We passed each other without speaking. I'm not entirely sure he recognised me.

When he returned, Ambrose put two damp hands on the table and asked breezily if I was nervous about tomorrow. He had either forgotten what had made me jump up from the table, or he had chosen to.

'Kind of,' I said.

'It could be a dreadful anti-climax, you know. Anything that has a Mayor involved generally is.'

'I *hope* it is, Ambrose.'

'Don't say that, Michael. We're here for a reason. We have to go looking for our, *your* story. People aren't going to volunteer information, not about something like this. We're going to have to squeeze it out of them.'

I shook my head. 'That's not why I'm here.'

Ambrose snorted, and it probably would have all kicked off again if the waiter hadn't arrived. Then it kicked off in a different direction. We'd finished our dinner, turned down a dessert. I guessed he was there with the bill. Ambrose immediately said, 'Another pitcher, my good man.'

'Did you write this, sir?'

I hadn't registered that he was holding the blackboard from the toilets by his side. He brought it forward so that it was facing us, then tilted it first towards me, then Ambrose.

It said: FUCK THE POPE.

Green chalk.

My mouth dropped open slightly. 'Absolutely not,' I said.

'No *way*,' said Ambrose. 'Who would do . . .' Then his brow furrowed slightly as he looked down at my hands – and the green chalk dust on them. The waiter noticed at about the same time.

'May I remind you that this is a family restaurant, sir?'

'I swear to . . .' I began weakly, lifting my balled napkin and wiping my fingers, 'I didn't . . .'

'If you would settle your bill now, sir, it would be very much appreciated.'

He turned away. Ambrose had his fist in his mouth.

I punched him outside. He punched me back. I punched him again and he fell over. When I went to see if he was okay he kicked my feet out from under me and I went down hard. As I lay on the ground, winded, he kicked me, and the exertion of it caused a chesty whistle to issue, just as it had six months before.

8

I do believe in fate, and I'll tell you why.

Families fall out for all sorts of reasons, and mine was no exception. Quite often the reason for the fall-out becomes obscure with the passage of time, but once torn asunder, fences often are not repaired, sometimes for generations. My family was like this. I had an uncle in Dublin I never knew. He was my father's younger brother. As my parents both died relatively young I had the occasional urge to track him down but never did anything about it. One day, when I was collecting a prescription from my local pharmacy, the girl behind the counter reappeared with the medicine in a paper bag, and as there were half a dozen people waiting, called out my surname. Two of us stepped forward to claim it – the other Ryan turned out to be my uncle. What are the chances of that happening in a city the size of Dublin? But that isn't all. I certainly didn't bear a grudge over whatever had gone before, so we made the usual promises to keep in touch. Almost immediately, however, I lost his number and, truth be told, and out of sheer laziness, never made much of an effort to track him down again. Three years later I was in our local supermarket. As I was about to pay for my groceries I reached into my pocket for the ten-euro note I had placed there a few minutes before, only to find it missing. I left the shopping basket at the till and retraced my steps around the store. Failing to find it, I returned to the till, only to find another man standing there:

he had just lost a *five*-euro note, but in looking for it had found my own, larger note. Instead of making off with it, he took it up to the girl behind the counter and was just explaining his situation. At this point she gestured at me and said that the ten-euro was probably mine; he turned to me, and it was my uncle. What are the chances of that happening? *Twice.* I think we were supposed to meet, to renew family ties, and this time we did, and really became quite close. It was fate.

So, I like to think that what happened with Claire was fate as well. Obviously Brevard is much smaller than Dublin, so the chances of us meeting again were much greater, but I still think *someone* was moving in a mysterious way to make it happen just the way it did.

My visit to the equally smitten Paul de Luca had given me some idea of how to open my novel, but hadn't sufficiently inspired me to get started. So robbed by love or lust or plain lack of talent of my *raison d'etre*, I decided to get the engines fired up by getting myself into shape. I've never been much of a one for going to the gym, but I was a decent runner when I was younger, and so I took to early-morning jogging along one or other of the Brevard beaches. Floridians are early to rise, and the beaches can become surprisingly crowded along the waterline where it's easiest to run. Preferring solitude at that time of the morning, and wishing to avoid collisions along the narrow sand-strips with the numerous labouring seniors, I quickly moved from using the closest beach to town to pounding one that was much further out. It wasn't as long and it was somewhat rockier, but I thought it was by far the most beautiful of them. On the third day of my second week in Brevard I arrived at Suntree Beach at a little after seven a.m., parked and made my way down to the edge of the water. The sun was just coming over the horizon, giving the water a marvellous red hue. At the point where I started running there was a dead fish lying in the sand. As I moved along I saw another, and another, and then realised there were dozens of them. I was thinking, That's unusual, but I kept moving, just stepping back up onto the more powdery sand to avoid them. Yet as I ran on, I saw that it wasn't some small isolated occurrence, but that the waterline along the full length of the beach was littered with dead fish.

Then I started coughing.

I had asthma for a few years when I was a kid, and it was just like that. I couldn't catch my breath. It wasn't a stench from the fish, as they were still quite fresh, it was something altogether more acrid. I actually staggered back across the sand and sank to my knees, thinking, Jesus Christ, I'm going to die on this deserted beach because some deadly chemical has washed ashore. I'm a writer, Bob, so I tend to exaggerate; in retrospect it really wasn't that bad. I was just confused, mildly panicked – and then utterly surprised, as a voice beside me said: 'They call it Red Tide.'

It was Claire. In a white bikini. I started coughing again.

'If you just move back up the beach a little, you'll be fine.'

I got to my feet, then stumbled. Claire took hold of my arm and led me back towards the car park.

'Red *what*?' I gasped.

'Tide. It happens a couple of times every year. It's like a build-up of algae in the water. It kills the fish and it makes you cough like that. But you'll be fine, unless you've bronchitis or emphysema or something. Then I'd have to give you the kiss of life.'

Despite the fact that I was blushing (I could feel it but the sunburn, which had still not graduated to a tan, helped to hide it), I said, 'Actually I suffer from both.'

She laughed and looked at her feet. Maybe she was embarrassed as well. 'It's been happening for centuries. It turns the water kind of reddish for a while, but it's nothing to worry about. We just don't, you know, put it on the tourist brochures.'

I smiled. She was beautiful.

'I come here for a swim most mornings,' she said.

'God – not this morning. And are you not scared, after the shark?'

'No, not at all. What are the chances of it happening twice?'

I could have told her all about my uncle, and lightning striking twice, but I just kept smiling.

'We keep bumping into each other,' I said.

'You mean, *I* keep bumping into *you*. You're going to think I'm some mad stalker or something.'

'I don't think you're mad,' I said.[1]

She smiled kindly, then looked towards the sea. 'It'll be gone in a few days, but no swim for me today. Are you going to finish your run?'

I shrugged. 'I've just had a brush with death; I think I need caffeine. I don't suppose you'd care to join me?'

'Okay,' she said.

We adjourned to a Starbucks. There's *always* a Starbucks. She made me follow her car so it wouldn't look like she was still stalking me, then surprised me by driving away from Brevard and into Titusville. She'd pulled a short dress over her bikini. Once inside she spent three minutes making her mind up what sort of coffee to have, then ordered it black. We shared a bagel. She said she was on a diet, and I snorted.

'I was going to look you up anyway,' I said.

'Really?'

'I went to see Paul de Luca.'

'Poor Paul – how is he?'

I had already decided that honesty was the best policy. I looked at her for a long moment, then said: 'Well, it's kind of strange. He's lost his feet, yet it seemed to me he was more upset that you hadn't been to see him.'

'Oh, Paul – he's so sweet. He's probably all doped up.'

'Yeah – I suppose. But he was really quite annoyed. Do you know him well?'

'I know him from the bar; he's an old friend of Tommy's. He would speak to him more than he would speak to me. You wouldn't think it, but he's quite shy, really.'

'Well, I told him I'd tell you, if I saw you. I might go back and visit him. Will I tell him you'll drop by?'

---

[1] Three months later she fessed up – she'd spotted me sitting at a traffic-light and *followed* me to the beach. Not quite as fateful, but the fact of her seeing me at the red light at all still qualifies as fate.

Claire looked down at her coffee. 'No, I . . .' She sucked on her bottom lip for a moment. 'I have this . . . thing about hospitals. They give me the creeps. People die there. They go in, and they don't come out.'

'You could argue that people get born there, and that if they're ill, they are nursed back to health.'

'I know it's stupid. They just scare me. I *should* go and see him. I *will* go and see him. He must feel dreadful. To lose your feet, I can't imagine.'

'He was talking about getting titanium replacements. Apparently someone with titanium feet recently climbed Everest.'

Claire nodded along with that. Then her eyes flitted up. 'Wouldn't they rust?'

'I imagine they've thought of—' Then I realised she was joking. 'Oh. Right. I see. Very good. How's that old fella you were with in the bar?'

'That was *so* funny.' She put her hand to her mouth. 'I mean I shouldn't, but Tommy's so uptight about his age, it was all I could do to stop him going after you.'

'Bring him on,' I said. '*Very* slowly.'

She began to stir her coffee. 'He's very protective of me,' she said quietly.

'I can understand why.'

Our eyes met, and held.

'He must love you a lot,' I said.

They held for another few moments, then she looked back to her coffee. 'Tommy says that anyone who believes freckles represent a secret map of the universe deserves to be beaten to death with a tyre iron.'

9

There is something very odd about standing in a cemetery, talking to a patch of grass and a rectangle of carved granite. It is embarrassing to address yourself to a bunch of hidden bones. Even the knowledge that they belong to the great love of your life, that they once propelled her around your house and home, that they allowed her to surf and make love, does not detract from the abstract grotesqueness of it. I do not recall now quite what I said, but I know it was a labour, a duty that lay heavy on me. In the ten years since her death I had spoken to Claire every day, without fail, and without response. To be finally standing in the Brevard Town Cemetery, six feet removed from her physical remains, did not have the huge, paralysing impact I had dreaded; it merely rendered me virtually speechless. I had said all the big, important things to her in my head so many times that all that was left there on my first morning back in Brevard, with the sun burning the back of my neck, was small talk.

Small talk!

Even with so little to say, I still glanced around to make sure nobody was watching, or, indeed, that Ambrose had not sneaked up and was surreptitiously taking notes. It was too early to check into our Comfort Inn, so I'd left him nursing his hangover and kicking his heels in an IHOP – an International House of Pancakes, in case you didn't know, Bob. Yummy. He had been all apologies that morning about kicking me while I was down and had sworn never to drink again. While I had forgiven him, I wasn't in the mood to have him witness what might have turned out to be a devastating experience.

I spent a maximum of ten minutes by Claire's grave. It had been tended with the same efficiency as all of the others thereabouts. The stark words carved into the black granite gave no indication of the manner of her death. Only the dates reflected the appalling brevity of her life. When she was murdered and I was taken to the morgue, and saw her lying there, Dick Schulze, who had married us, made the mistake of saying to me that Claire looked quite peaceful. I threw him up against a wall and would have punched him out if I hadn't been dragged off. There is *nothing* peaceful about violent death. And there was nothing peaceful, spiritual or sacred about that graveyard. I was standing in a junkyard for old bones.

As I walked back towards my car, following the course of a path that twisted between the gravestones of generations of Brevardians, I had to step off it onto the grass to pass by a young woman standing in my way. She was crouching to examine the floral tributes surrounding a freshly dug grave. The top soil had not yet been dried out by the sun and the gravestone was not yet in place.

I said, 'Excuse me,' as I passed. She smiled and gave a slight nod, but I had only gone a few yards further when she called after me.

'Mr Ryan?'

I stopped. My immediate thought was: It's started, the recognition, the first of the *'Didn't you write?'* conversations. It wasn't just that I had an over-inflated sense of my own importance – I was merely aware that in Brevard I was a very large fish in a very small pond. Even in the IHOP, Ambrose had picked up a tourist guide that proudly claimed Brevard to be the home town of the surfer Kelly Slater, the rapper Carrot Top and the author of *Space Coast*, Michael Ryan. There was a photograph of me, a clipped version of the ten-year-old picture which still adorns the paperback version of the novel.

She came towards me and extended her hand. 'Mr Ryan – it's

Lena. Lena Olson.' My brow must have furrowed. 'From next door – Dr Olson's daughter.'

She had short, dirty-blonde hair and sad green eyes. There was a tiny, long-healed scar just below her hairline. It came to me suddenly. 'Lena – the girl on the swing!'

She smiled. 'I think you were better at writing books than making swings.'

Claire and I had only been married a few weeks when I attempted to build a swing in our yard. The plan was for our children to enjoy it. As it happened, Lena was home from college for the summer and happened to be sunbathing in her back garden when I finished putting the swing together and she volunteered to go first. It wasn't a good idea.

'You could have sued,' I said.

'I still haven't ruled it out.'

'Lena – my God! Look at you, all grown up.'

'Mr *Ryan*.'

'Michael – please.'

'Michael.' She grinned awkwardly. 'It feels funny, saying Michael. Dad always called you Mr Ryan.'

'I think he was being kind. I'm only seven or eight years older than you, Lena. Anyway, how is the old . . .' And then I stopped, and my eyes flitted to the flowers on the grave behind her. 'Forgive me, Lena. He's . . . ?'

'Last week.'

'I'm sorry. He was very good to us. And then, to me, after . . . Did he suffer?'

'No. It was very sudden.' She glanced back at the grave. 'I've been coming every day, but I think my patients are starting to lose patience, if you'll excuse the pun.' She held up an apologetic hand. 'Mr . . . Michael, are you walking down?'

There was just about room for us to walk side by side on the twisting path. Our hands touched once and she immediately said, 'Excuse me.'

'So you're a doctor now?' I asked.

'It's in the genes. Dad had a toy stethoscope in my hands

before I could manage a knife and fork – although there was a brief period when I was about fourteen when I rebelled and decided to become a veterinarian. It soon fizzled out.'

'Lena, do you remember what happened when the swing collapsed under you, and you cracked your head?'

'Of course I do. You ran about in a panic. When you realised Dad was out on call, you wanted to call 911.'

'*You* calmed *me* down, then you stitched yourself up.'

'It was only two stitches.'

'Lena, you *stitched yourself up*. Without so much as a Tylenol.'

'Tylenol is for wimps.'

'That's exactly what you said! I thought you were very brave. I was absolutely petrified about your dad coming home and blaming me – quite rightly, I might add – but all he did was examine the wound, nod and say—'

'"She's as tough as old boots"! I was furious! I wanted him to admire my technique. I'd dreams then of being a surgeon, not some old country doctor. Now look at me.'

'You look . . .' But I stopped. 'I'm only back for a few days. There's a memorial service . . .'

'I know. Ten years – it's hard to believe. Nobody was sure if you would come.'

'Well, it's kind of against my better judgement.'

'Really?'

'I'm just not really into – you know, making a big thing of it – but I was persuaded that it would do me good. And I suppose it's nice to be invited, but to tell you the truth I don't have a lot of time for these do-gooders who've nothing better to do with their time. These things are mostly designed to make the organisers look good rather than . . .' I cleared my throat. 'Obviously, you are one of the organisers.'

She laughed suddenly and unexpectedly. 'Yes, I am.'

'I'm sorry, I really didn't mean to be rude.'

'It's fine. Honestly. A lot of them *are* like that.'

'All the same, I shouldn't have said that.'

'Forget it. Tell you what, if you want to make it up to me, you can buy me a drink at the dinner. But I warn you, after this,' she pointed at her scar, 'and *this*,' meaning my thoughtless comment, 'it's definitely three strikes and you're out. And you wouldn't want to get on the wrong side of someone who's *still* as tough as old boots.'

I couldn't help but smile. 'Then it's a deal.'

Our vehicles were side by side. Lena, looking a little embarrassed at the formality of it, nevertheless extended her hand. We shook, but as I turned to open the door she suddenly said, 'You were such a happy couple.' I nodded. 'I used to watch you playing around together and wish that some day I'd be that happy.' She leaned against her car and looked back up the hill. 'I've been staying at Dad's this past week. Whenever I'm there I always take a walk next door, around the garden. Sometimes I peer through the shutters – it's just so sad to see all your stuff still there.' She stopped as she suddenly registered the surprised look on my face. 'Michael? I'm sorry, I didn't mean to bring up the past.'

'No – no, it's not that.' I actually felt a little weak at the knees. 'I didn't realise . . . I mean, after it happened, I was in such a state . . . I asked my friend to sell the house for me, to get rid of the contents. I just wanted nothing more to do with it. You . . . you're sure it's still all there?'

'Michael, it's exactly as it was. There's a property management company comes by and looks after the garden once a month, but apart from that, the house has been shuttered ever since.'

'I just never in a million years thought . . .' I shook my head.

'Michael, my dad keeps – he *kept* – a key to your house in his study in case there was any storm damage and the company couldn't get out for a while. If you want, we could go and take a look now.'

My eyes were unfocused and my heart was hammering, but I'd no choice, really. No choice at all.

Bob, what the hell were you thinking of?[1]

---

[1] I thought his decision to sell up a trifle rash, given the circumstances. It was a beautiful house, and I believed in time he would reconsider, or at least want to have Claire's personal effects. I signed up the property company and charged it to my employers, but it was only ever meant to be a temporary arrangement. To be frank, I then forgot about it, and was quite shocked to learn that they've been paid for the past decade to look after the house – including quite a substantial payment for a new roof following a hurricane – RN.

10

Claire phoned while I was in the shower getting ready. I had finally persuaded her to go and see Paul de Luca. He wasn't responding well to treatment and the doctors couldn't quite figure out why, but I, being a self-proclaimed expert in matters of the heart, had a pretty good idea. I was to meet her there and hold her hand, metaphorically speaking, while she tried to conquer her fear of hospitals. Her message said her car had broken down, and was there any chance of me taking her? Could I call her back?

Well, my heart leapt and sank simultaneously. Of *course* I would take her. I would take her anywhere, be it a piggy-back across a crowded room or a camel ride across the Sahara, with me in the camel suit. But calling her back – what if Tommy answered the phone? What would I say? Or, more importantly, what would *he* say? Or threaten? As I dried myself off, I tried to work it through logically. Claire was looking for a lift from *me* – which meant that (a) Tommy was already away to work and she didn't want to bother him; (b) Tommy had refused to help; (c) Tommy was happy to help, but she preferred to go with me; (d) Tommy had forbidden her to go, but she was going anyway; (e) Tommy had discovered how often we were meeting and was using her to lure me to the house in order to stab me 167 times.

The truth was that Claire and I were meeting up at Suntree

Beach every morning. It was never planned; there were no surreptitious phone calls, I just turned up at the same time and so did she. That second morning, with the Red Tide already dissipated, I arrived and changed into my swimming gear. She appeared a few minutes later, all set to go jogging. We laughed, without any need to explain why, and then we compromised on doing both. As we ran or splashed, we talked and talked – about Brevard, movies, books, ambitions, dreams. We laughed a lot. She was funny and sharp and her eyes were just so alive. She had worked in the bank for three years and was bored by it, but had no clear idea of what she really wanted to do. She didn't particularly want to travel or see the world. She loved Brevard. Her family had been there for generations but as an only child she was now 'the last of the Mohicans'. Her mother was dead from cancer but her father was still around. He was the editor of the local newspaper, the *Brevard Herald*. I told her about my stint as a journalist and she suggested approaching her father about getting some part-time work and I said, 'No, no, no, no, no, no and no. I'm writing my novel.'

'Can't you do both?'

'No, no, no, no, no, no, no and no. Absolutely no.'

For three weeks, every morning, including weekends, we met up like this. Tommy was mentioned, of course – the occasional 'Tommy says this' or 'Tommy did this', but what we ignored was any allusion to their relationship, their history, their future. I did not want to know if they had a sex life or how often they did it or how fantastic it was, but I thought about it. I did not ask if they were planning children, though I obsessed about it. She did not complain about him, she did not criticise, she did not give me details of arguments and fights. I was not a sunburned shoulder to cry on. We were becoming friends, and as much as I loved it, I hated it.

Claire asked if I had a girl, and I said no. She asked me if I was waiting to meet the right one and I said I was happy to meet *any* one. She volunteered to set me up with Jo-Anne from the bar, and I told her about Jo-Anne's piercing. Claire scrunched her face up in horror and then asked, 'Wouldn't it rust?' and I was halfway to answering before I realised she'd suckered me in again.

So, to the phone call.

I took a deep breath and dialled. My plan was to cut the line if Tommy answered. I'm not ashamed of being a coward. I was clinging by what amounted to advanced osteoporosis of the fingertips to the notion that the pen was still mightier than the sword.

'Oh – thank God,' I said, almost without realising it, when Claire answered.

She laughed. 'Why are you thanking God?'

'I . . . well, you know.'

'No, I don't know.'

'Claire.'

'Michael.'

'You know what I'm talking about.'

'I haven't a clue.'

'Tommy, Claire, Tommy.'

'What about him?'

'Claire.'

'I'm serious, what about him?'

Okay. Cards on the table. Bull, horns, all that shit. She was teasing me, but I'd had enough. It had been building up for weeks. 'Claire, I don't know if Tommy knows about us going running every morning, and I'm sure you can argue that it's all perfectly innocent, but if I start calling to your house and taking you places, even if it's only this one time, then if I was your husband, and I found out, I'd be extremely angry and jealous, and rightfully so. I really like you, Claire. I think you're lovely and amazing, but you're with Tommy, and I don't like sneaking around. It's not fair to me, to him, even to you. So that's why I said "Thank God", because I don't want Tommy in my face, at least until I know where you stand. Do you understand what I'm saying?'

I could hear her shallow breath. After a little she said, 'Michael?' very quietly.

'What?'

'I only asked you for a ride to the hospital.'

I sat on the edge of the bed and pushed thumb and forefinger into the corners of my eyes.

'Michael?'

'Look, I'm sorry, okay? I didn't mean . . . If I got the wrong impression, I . . . Look . . .'

'Michael.'

'*What?*'

'I'm not married to Tommy.'

'Okay, so you're not married, but—'

'He doesn't live here.'

'Oh.'

'And I've never even kissed him.'

This information was *staggering*.

'But you – you – you said . . . and everyone . . .'

'Everyone was wrong.'

'Claire, if you're bullshitting me . . .'

'Maybe I am. Come and pick me up, Michael. *If* you dare.' She giggled, then cut the line.

You see, Bob, you read about twisted women luring men to their doom. Claire had not previously shown any indication of being even slightly twisty, but she might easily have been hiding it, or been adhering to her meds, and now she had decided to strike, or skip a couple of pills. Remember, a *femme fatale* is pretty useless if everyone knows she's a *femme fatale*, so she has to show a little more guile than that. I *thought* I knew her, but that knowledge was largely derived from idle chat while jogging. Just because I knew that her favourite movie was *Annie Hall* and that she found Tom Petty oddly attractive, it didn't mean she wasn't crackers. You can like *Annie Hall and* be insane, although I'm not so sure about Tom Petty. Or it could mean that she and Tommy were both in it together. That they had hatched this plot in order to rob me of my fortune, which at that moment in time consisted of around fifteen hundred dollars and several notebooks which might one day inspire a bestselling novel, or probably not.

But there was nothing else for it. If she was telling the truth, I was in heaven. If she was teasing me, then hell it was. I sped to what was known locally as the Blue House. It looks pretty much as I described it in *Space Coast* (although, obviously, a different colour!) save for it being slightly smaller and perhaps a little better kept. There was kind of a brittle feel to it, you know the way painted wood goes in the sun? The creaking of the steps as I mounted them was loud enough to eliminate the possibility of me sneaking back down them again if I had a renewed crisis of confidence.

I knocked on the door.

Claire, wearing a white T-shirt and bikini bottoms, opened it. She did not smile. She folded her arms. 'Have you been behaving impeccably towards me because you're afraid of Tommy?' she asked bluntly.

'I've been behaving impeccably towards you because that's what I do.'

'*Are* you afraid of Tommy?'

'Absolutely. He has killed men in combat. And possibly women.'

'But you're still here.'

'Yes, I am.'

'You're either very foolish or very much in love.'

'Yes, I am.'

She smiled. 'Permission to kiss me is granted then.'

I stared at her.

'That's an order,' she whispered.

Again, the kissing scene in *Space Coast* is more or less exactly as it was, although, obviously, this was better because it was real. I'm not a good enough writer to ever do justice to a first kiss.

You might suppose from this that I was so captivated by our kiss that a Boeing 747 could have landed in the front yard and I wouldn't have noticed, but actually the very opposite was true. I heard *everything*. You call it heightened reality. Nature's wonder, a distant TV soap, the crunch of a stick shift a block away, and

71

then, so much closer, the creak of wood. My eyes flitted open. I saw a pair of feet appear at the bottom of the stairs in the hallway behind Claire and heard the not so subtle click of a shotgun being cocked.

11

Funny, of all the things that could have set me off crying, it was the fridge magnets that did it. From the very second Lena had invited me to tour the Blue House I had been on the verge of losing it, but it had not come as the door opened to swirling dust motes, nor as I mounted the stairs to our bedroom (it seemed inevitable that this would be the first room I chose to visit) and entered what was our home within our home. We spent so much time there. Not just because of the obvious, although there was plenty of that. It was a huge room, stretching from the front to the back of the house, with crumbling balconies at both ends so that in our many idle moments we could catch the sun almost whenever we chose. Although the house had not been touched in ten years, it had been tidied by hands other than our own immediately before it was closed up, so that the bedroom was not as I remembered it – a mess of papers, discarded clothes, damp towels, jumbles of Claire's underwear and toppled columns of books. It was neat. It was what it was: a room that has been put to order after the death of its occupant. Most of the rest of the house was like that. Lena was kind enough to remain downstairs while I entered the bedroom, only calling up to ask if I was okay when I had been silent for a while.

'Fine,' I said, but obviously not loud enough, as a few moments later she appeared in the doorway and repeated her question, her voice soft, almost hesitant. I nodded. The room was stuffy, so I tried to open the balcony doors, but the key was missing.

'Dad probably had it somewhere,' said Lena.

'Doesn't matter.' I shook my head. 'It's like a hotel room.' I knelt and ran my hand over the bedside table. 'There was a permanent circle of water here, condensation from the glass of Pepsi she would have sitting here twenty-four seven. And here, there were always little flecks of ash; she didn't think I knew she had sneaky cigarettes when I went out.' My fingers traced up the stem of the small lamp. 'She would pretend that the lamp wasn't working and I'd have to reach across her to try it myself, and then she would kiss me and we would lose concentration and for months I never got to find out if it was working or not, or if it was her fiendish plan to seduce me.' I pushed the button. No light. I sighed. I glanced up at Lena. She was looking quite embarrassed. 'Sorry,' I said. 'Too much information.'

She gave a half embarassed shrug and tried the lamp herself. 'It's just the bulb,' she said.

We went back downstairs. The rooms again were neat but dusty. There were plenty of cobwebs, but not big horror film ones. A ten-year-old TV guide. Lena lifted it and smiled at the long-faded star on the cover. 'I *loved* him,' she gushed. Then she shook her head. 'I saw him on one of those infomercials last week, pushing haemorrhoid cream. Don't love him so much now.' She smiled, then led me down the short corridor towards the room I had used as a study. She hesitated before opening it. 'Mom and Dad did most of the tidying, but they asked me to do this room.' She turned the handle and pushed the door open, then stood to one side for me to see.

It was *exactly* as I remembered it. Papers were strewn every-where. Two broken printers lay on their side in one corner. Books about Brevard and the Space Coast and the Apollo missions and fish and fauna lay scattered across the floor. My laptop screen was open and covered in a coating of grey dust. There was a half-full ashtray peeking out from under a yellowed copy of *USA Today*, evidence that I too had enjoyed a sneaky cigarette.

'You didn't touch anything. Teenage rebellion, was it?'

Lena shook her head and looked at her shoes for a moment. 'Well, I'm a big girl now, so I suppose I can say it. I had this terrible crush on you.'

'Me?'

'It was a long time ago. I thought you were very sexy.'

'Me?'

'And you were a writer, and teenage girls love dark and moody writers.'

'Was I dark and moody?'

'I have no idea, we hardly exchanged two words, but I imagined you were. Teenage girls can imagine quite a lot.'

I nodded along with this for several moments. Then: 'But you weren't teenaged, you were off at medical school.'

'Yes. Well. I was a late developer.' She moved into the room then and placed her hands on the back of the leather swivel chair. It had once had a small hole in one of the arms which, over the course of several months, I had picked into a huge chasm, exposing the yellow stuffing within. 'It took several days to get the house in order, but I would come in here and lock the door. I'd sit in your chair and . . .' she sat in the chair and opened the second drawer down in my old desk, then smiled as she withdrew a thick wedge of paper and set it on the desk before her '. . . read this.' She patted the top sheet. It said *Love & Rockets, A Novel, By Michael J. Ryan.*

I laughed. 'Michael J. Ryan. I thought the J would make me sound more sophisticated.' (As I recall, Bob, your reaction was, 'J for Jackass'.)

'It just sent shivers down my spine. I knew it would be huge. I didn't know you at all, I *imagined* you, but there was so much of Claire in it.'

'Living next door, you must have known her pretty well.'

'I'm an only child, but I always dreamed about Claire being my big sister. She was so pretty and popular, and whenever I did talk to her she was lovely, but I really didn't know her that well. She was always going out. There were always boys hanging around. At least, until Tommy roared up on that bike of his.' I wasn't aware of it, but she must have noticed a change in my demeanour. 'I'm sorry,' she said quickly. 'I didn't mean to mention Tommy.'

'It's okay.'

She turned slightly in the chair. 'He was evil, wasn't he?'

'I don't know,' I replied, as honestly as I could – *then*. 'I think maybe he was just in love.'

Lena shook her head. 'Funny kind of love.'

A few minutes later, Lena found me in tears in the kitchen. I'd wandered off while she tried various keys to get the back door open, and when she came back my head was pressed against the refrigerator and tears were rolling down my cheeks.

She put a hand on my arm and said, 'Oh Christ, I shouldn't have mentioned him.'

I turned. She wanted to hug me. And I wanted her to. But we'd only just met, and there was an awkward stand-off. Then I moved towards her, but veered off, rubbing my sleeve across my face and mumbling apologies. I turned back to the fridge and ran my hand gently over and around the nearly two dozen fridge magnets stuck to its front.

'It's not Tommy,' I said, 'it's these damn stupid magnets. We . . . well, we . . .'

'The author of *Space Coast* collected fridge magnets?'

I laughed. 'No, of course not – that would be sad. It was more a case of, well, accumulating them over a very short space of time.' I peeled one off the door and showed it to her. 'We were in one of those crappy antique shops downtown and Claire showed me this and said, "Every home should have a fridge magnet of Donald Duck". And I looked at the price and said, "Not for fifteen bucks it shouldn't". I remember she looked kind of disappointed, but money was tight, so she understood. A few weeks later I made a big thing of taking her out for dinner, hinting that I'd something for her, and I think she got it into her head that it was an engagement ring – which was exactly what I'd hoped she'd do. I even got this little jewellery box . . . So we went out and she could hardly eat she was so nervous, and then at the end I slipped this box across the table and she'd tears in her eyes – and then she opened it and saw Donald Duck . . .'

'That's so cruel!'

'I know that now. I thought I was being clever. I thought it right up to the point where she threw it at me and stormed off.'

'I don't blame her.'

'A couple of weeks later she started being sick in the mornings. She'd lock herself away and be evasive when she came out. But I guessed what was happening. I sat her down on the bed and said, "Claire, are you pregnant?" She burst into tears. She said, "I don't know, I've just done the test but I wasn't brave enough to look at the result. It's in the top drawer in the bathroom cabinet. Will you look for me, Michael, please?" She was so scared. And so was I. It's a big thing, when you're only in your twenties, to think you might be a dad. I remember taking this deep breath, the biggest moment of my life, then pulling the drawer open. And what do you think? A Minnie Mouse fridge magnet. And Claire, from the bedroom, shouting, "Sucker!"'

'That's even worse!'

'Don't get mad, get even. Funny thing is, the Donald Duck – I'd stolen it – and Claire had gone back and stolen the Minnie Mouse, and neither of us knew it. It wasn't like we were habitual shoplifters, it was just overpriced tat and we resented paying fifteen bucks for it. But always after that, wherever we were, and we spotted a fridge magnet, it became like a dare thing to slip it into our pockets. Junk stores, wedding showers, christenings, every opportunity, one of these babies ended up back here. If I ever wanted to write a romantic novel, I could tell the entire history of the relationship through these fridge magnets. It would be quite a hook.'

'You did write a romantic novel,' said Lena.

'No,' I said, 'I wrote a tragedy.'

Lena shook her head. 'She didn't die in the novel, Michael.'

And I shook mine. 'I know that. But it is my particular curse that most people believe she did.'

Then the tears were rolling again, and this time I did get a hug.

When I returned to the Comfort Inn, Mayor Thomas Heise was waiting to greet me. He had with him twelve councillors, the head of the organising committee, the organising committee (*sans* a doubtlessly shamefaced Dr Lena Olson), and a brass band. There was a banner that read *The Space Coast welcomes the author of 'Space Coast'*. The brass band played 'Happy Days Are Here Again'.

12

When you see two gun barrels pointing at you, you tend not to focus on who's holding them. You focus on those two dark holes, your quick route to eternity. Claire, despite the fact that our tongues were intertwined, was instantly aware of the sudden frigidity that swept across me and turned quickly. It was only when she let me go, that my eyes settled on the man holding the gun and I realised with the tiniest smidgen of relief that it wasn't Tommy but an older man. Nevertheless, *anyone* aiming a gun at your heart is still a huge cause for concern.

Immediately, Claire yelled, 'Daddy, will you stop that!' But it was not yelled with genuine anger or terror. She was laughing.

'Daddy' jabbed the gun in my direction. 'What are your intentions? What are your prospects? Have you ever been in prison?'

'Daddy!'

Mr Joe Roth, sixty-seven, silver-haired and heavily built, owner and editor of the *Brevard Herald*, finally lowered his shotgun. 'Daughter of mine,' he said, 'a father has the right to ask.'

Claire shook her head and smiled apologetically. 'He does this every time. It wasn't funny the first time and it isn't funny now.'

'Gotta sort the men from the boys somehow,' said her father. 'Remember that boy who ran a mile? All I could do to stop myself shooting him in the ass.'

'Dad, he was fourteen.'

'Fourteen and spineless. You, sir,' and he nodded at me, 'stood your ground. I'm Joe.'

He extended his hand and I shook it. 'Mr Roth,' I said.

'I said, Joe. Unless you're working for me. *Are* you working for me?'

'No, sir.'

'It's Joe.'

'Joe. Is that thing loaded?'

'You bet your ass.'

Claire tutted. 'All right, tough guy, tell him what happened the day Tommy came by.'

'Son of a bitch.'

'Shall we say Tommy disarmed you, Daddy? Is that diplomatic enough?'

'Son of a bitch jumped me when I wasn't ready.'

'Threw you down in the yard and would've cut your throat if I hadn't hollered.'

'Son of a bitch is the only son of a bitch I know caught Gulf War syndrome before he went to the damn Gulf.' Joe shook his head, then nodded at me. 'Come on in, Michael.' He turned back into the house. 'Claire tells me you used to be a journalist. Could do with some help . . .'

As I began to follow, I gave Claire a look and she raised her hands helplessly.

'We have to talk,' I said quietly.

'We have to kiss,' she replied.

Joe Roth argued strongly in favour of my working for his paper. He said the long hours and miserly pay were more than adequately compensated for by the satisfaction of serving your local community. Uhuh. I told him I needed to concentrate on my novel, and he said to come see him if I changed my mind, or was starving. He said every journalist thought they had a book in them. I said usually it was the telephone directory. He laughed. I think it was a laugh of approval. I didn't get the impression that he would like anyone his daughter liked. I got the impression he had been down a long and rocky road with

Claire's choice of male companion, probably starting about the age of seven. He was gruff on the outside, quite gruff on the inside, but also funny and opinionated, and the love for his daughter shone through. Maybe my love for his daughter shone through as well. I thought the ultimate seal of approval for our relationship was that he went off to work and left us alone together.

I am a writer, Bob. Worldwide, writers are pale, shadowy figures who bare their souls on paper, who mangle the juice out of their emotions to satisfy the demands of a chapter. They are not exactly sociopaths, but have certainly taken several classes in it. Unless they're Hemingway or Shakespeare (and I have my doubts about Shakespeare), they are not generally babe magnets. Or, to put it another way, I couldn't believe my luck. Alone, in the house, with Claire – beautiful, kissable, lovely Claire. Therefore, understandably, I immediately moved in for the kill.

Claire put her hand in front of her mouth. I kissed it anyway.

'No,' she said. 'Not here.'

I tried to kiss her forehead. 'Here?'

'No, stupid. Let's go for a walk.'

Walking was the last thing on my mind. When you are that age, the phrase *but you have the rest of your lives together* does not even enter the equation. If, lying in bed that morning, I had struck a bargain with the devil allowing me to kiss her in exchange for my soul, I would have happily fulfilled my contractual obligations. But in the Blue House, ourselves alone, and not having struck that deal, the kiss was no longer some impossible fantasy, and I wanted more. I wanted to move our fledgling relationship to the next level of intimacy.

Or, as it's commonly known, second base.

She was having none of it. Within a matter of moments she had me outside and was locking the door behind her. Then she slipped her hand in mine and pulled it slightly, the way you might do with the reins on a horse to make it change direction, so that I was facing her and she kissed me again. Then we walked down the steps and out into the yard and she kissed me again. It didn't seem to make much sense to me that while the kisses were getting increasingly passionate, at the same time we were moving away from the place where second base, or, Allah be praised, even third might be achievable without running the risk of getting arrested.

Claire led me out of the yard and across the street. There was a path leading between the twin apartment blocks and a sign that said NO BEACH ACCESS. We ignored this and continued on to the thin strip of sand dotted with sunbeds which constituted the beach.

'It used to be the best beach in town,' Claire said, 'but then they built the apartments and something happened and most of it washed away. Paul should get his detective to investigate. I'm sure bribes were paid. We used to have this fantastic view.'

At that moment in time I didn't give a damn about bribes or sand erosion. I pulled Claire to me. We kissed.

She sat on a sunbed and patted the one beside her. 'Sit,' she said. I sat. 'I'm sorry,' she said. 'I feel funny about doing stuff in the house.'

'That's okay,' I said, although my face probably said it wasn't. 'I just—'

'I know.'

The sea was dead calm.

'Are we sitting on someone's sunbeds?' I asked.

'We are. And we don't care.'

'What will we do if they come along?'

'We will fight them. They are mostly retired tailors from Brooklyn. We will probably win.'

'And what if Tommy comes along?'

She turned slightly. She put out her hand. I took it. 'I have to tell you about Tommy,' she said softly, 'and I have to warn you.'

The first time I met Tommy, I had my doubts. He was so gung ho. In the same way that we suspect someone who protests too much, I had guessed that he probably hadn't seen that much combat, if any, and that if he was a Marine at all, he was a Marine typist. But no, actually, according to Claire, he *was* a god-damn American hero, and had the medals to prove it. Was his behaviour a direct result of his combat experience? Was he traumatised by the death of his comrades, poisoned by a cock-tail of chemicals – or were his brains scrambled by a cluster bomb? No one I ever spoke to detected any change in Tommy before the war or after. He was a Marine, he didn't take no shit, and nobody messed with his woman.

Except, she wasn't his woman.

'Right up to fourteen, no one took much notice of me. I was quiet, kind of spotty – your typical dorky kid, right? Then it seemed like overnight . . .'

'I *am* a swan.'

'. . . guys started to hit on me and it was confusing. Some of them wouldn't take no for an answer and I was too young to look after myself and too old to go running back to Dad all the time, and so I kind of fell in with Tommy and his gang and they looked after me. He was always getting into trouble, but he never laid a finger on me. Everyone presumed we were together, but we weren't, ever. Swear to God.'

'Why not?'

'Because he's not for me.'

'And he's okay with that?'

Claire shook her head. 'I thought he was. I thought we were just friends. We *are* just friends. We haven't fallen out. I still see him. It's just . . . Look, he always said he loved me, and he would wait for me to come round, but I didn't, and I think he went off to the Marines to impress me and he came back the big hero, all clean-cut and everyone slapping him on the back, and he asked me to marry him and he was really stunned when I said no. And after that he started to change. Before, when I went out with a boy, Tommy would just shrug, or sulk for a while, but when he came back and I met someone, well, they'd pretty quickly stop calling me or they'd show up with their nose busted or say they had a sudden urge to move to Idaho or somewhere.'

'And did you confront him?'

'Of course I did, and he would deny it, but I knew.'

'If he can't have you, no one else can either.' Claire nodded. 'Yet you still hang around with him.'

'I just feel . . . responsible, you know? It's like borrowing a book from the library. It's your favourite book and you want to keep it but it's not yours and you have to give it back.'

'Unless you beat up the librarian.'

'I'm not saying it's right. I'm saying I kind of understand why he does it. I don't mean because I'm so wonderful, but if there was someone I was absolutely dying about, I'd want to be with them all the time, and not have anyone else get in the way. But I've been trying to put a little distance between us. That's why I took the vacation time and stayed home out of his way.'

'And why we go running on distant beaches and drink coffee in outlandish places.'

'I was just trying to protect you.'

'But now we've come out of the closet, so to speak.'

'No, we've kissed and we're holding hands on a beach over-looked only by blind tailors. The question is, after what I've told you, do you still want to kiss or do you want to move to Idaho?'

13

It gave me a small measure of relief to learn from Ambrose that the *Brevard Herald*, the newspaper owned by Claire's father, had long since been sold to the Gannet Group and now operated out of a sleek new office behind Main Street under an entirely new management team. I didn't want to meet any old faces. Although Claire and I weren't together for a terrifically long period, and I never did work in the place fulltime, when *Space Coast* didn't immediately find a buyer I did take a few shifts on the news desk. Really it was just helping Joe out of a vacation hole and I also hoped it might serve to get my own creative juices flowing.

We went to the *Herald* because Ambrose wanted to see how the bank robbery had been reported, and because I wanted to escape from the Comfort Inn. The brass band continued to play in the parking lot out front. It seemed to know only uplifting tunes. The organising committee was drinking coffee in the lobby. There was a table set up for people attending the memorial service to pick up their welcome packs and ID pins even though it was still two days until the festivities got under way. After posing for some photos with the Mayor, and signing several copies of my novel, I made an excuse to go to my room, collect Ambrose, then we escaped out the back way.

At different periods for the rest of that day we caught ourselves whistling 'Happy Days Are Here Again'.

The *Brevard Herald* of old had inevitably reflected the personality of its owner and editor. Every week Joe wrote an op-ed piece called *The Voice of Reason*, which was more like *The Voice of a Crotchety Old Man*. It wasn't quite conservatism with a capital K, but it wasn't far off. I think he would have made a fine Indian chief. Not the scalp-hunting warrior type, more like Sitting Bull, the wise old man sitting in his tepee shaking his head at progress. In his writing, Joe had an economy of words one associates with movie Injuns: not always grammatically correct, but short and to the point. Joe was against Big Agriculture, Big Arms Sales, Big Army, Big Corporate Takeovers, Big Judgements in Law Suits, Big Labor, Big Medicine, Big Real Estate Development. He believed small was beautiful. Just like the circulation of his newspaper.

The new *Brevard Herald* was full-colour, professional, and lacked even a whisker of personality. The editor, Adam Harrington, gave us a tour of the office and talked excitedly of demographics and sales targets, and tried to persuade me to give an interview, but I put him off. He showed us into a storage room where copies of the pre-Gannet *Herald* were kept in bound copies going back forty years.

I asked Adam if he had met Joe, but he said he'd only been in town for three years. 'They move us around a lot. Sad, though, to lose your daughter like that,' he said. 'He sold out to us soon after – then he had a stroke, didn't he? How is he these days?'

'I don't know,' I said bluntly. I had, somehow, heard about the stroke (perhaps from you, Bob?) and back then it was just something I really didn't need to know anything more about. I was in a bad enough place. So I kept moving and didn't follow it up.

'You don't keep in touch?'

I shook my head. 'I thought he was dead.'

'We thought about giving him a call, since we're obviously doing some articles on the robbery and the memorial garden, but then we heard he wasn't too well. He's in one of those gated communities along the coast a bit.'

I nodded. Ambrose *computed*.

I was back on speaking terms with him by this stage. We did not discuss the fact that he had kicked me when I was down

– *twice* – nor that one of his eyes was mostly closed over from my expert punch.

Adam asked a few more questions. He seemed to think Ambrose was my minder. Perhaps he was. When he didn't get much out of me he gave Ambrose a try. Ambrose responded by giving him a business card. Adam studied it.

'The *Washington Post*?'

'The very one.'

'The Ambrose Jeffers who won a Pulitzer?'

'Two,' said Ambrose.

Adam flicked the card between his fingers. 'Don't you think,' he said gravely, as if attempting to raise his game in the presence of a higher form of life, 'that the Pulitzer has been greatly devalued by recent press scandals?'

'No,' said Ambrose, then turned quickly and opened the bound newspaper file for the correct year. I looked at my toes. Adam took it as a none too subtle signal to leave us alone.

You see, Bob, it would have been different with a daily newspaper. There you might expect a big front-page report on the day of the robbery, perhaps a follow-up the next day, and then some smaller reports, until by the time a week was up it was consigned to the archive. Local weekly papers, depending on the date of a big news story, usually have the luxury of time and space. The *Herald* publishes on a Thursday. The robbery happened on a Friday. By the time the next edition came around, the entire paper was devoted to the tragedy at the First National. Even in the poor light of the storage room Ambrose was able to observe that I 'went grey' when he turned to their account of the robbery.

It was dealt with in excruciating detail, which was all the more excruciating for the knowledge that the man who must have written most of it was the father of one of the victims. Claire was given no more or less space than any of the others. Her obituary was no less charming and heart-wrenching than those alongside. Just as my own words are forever associated with her murder, so every single person reading that newspaper must have known what it took for Joe Roth to produce it, for him to recount the exact nature and impact of the gunshot wounds that robbed him of his daughter and me of my wife.

After twenty minutes I couldn't handle any more. I left Ambrose to it. Adam looked up as I passed through the open-plan editorial office and I held up my cell phone as if I had to take an urgent, private call, and went outside. I gulped in fresh air. I started walking. I wasn't thinking about where I was going. Or maybe I was. Within three blocks I was opposite McDaid's Char Bar and Grill. I just stood, kind of looking at it, remembering. The same row of metal tables was set up outside and a middle-aged, overweight woman in a blowsy skirt was taking a customer's order. As she turned away she glanced across at me, moved on a few steps, then stopped again and looked back.

'Son of a bitch,' she said.

I smiled. 'Jo-Anne.' I crossed the road.

'Son of a bitch,' she said again.

'How are you, Jo-Anne?'

'Jesus Christ, it's like seeing a fucking ghost.' She came right up to me and before I could stop her she'd enveloped me in her thickly tattooed arms and crushed me against her voluminous chest. 'You never came back, Michael. You never came back.'

'I'm back now,' I said.

Jo-Anne had bought the bar five years ago. 'It was a good price. Once word got out that two members of our resident band were involved in that damn robbery, business just fell away. They thought we were all involved, like it was some sort of Mob hangout. I'll tell ya, the only murdering done in here was to some classy songs.' She looked at me, then gave a short nod acknowledging that it might be a crass thing to say, but she wasn't about to apologise for it. 'So how the hell are you?'

'I'm fine.'

'You're back for all this . . . crap.'

'Seems like it.'

'They came round wanting me to sponsor one of the events,

then someone must have realised and the offer was quietly with-drawn. It had fuck all to do with me, Michael.'

'I know that, Jo-Anne. So – did you ever get married and settle down?'

'What do you think?'

'Probably not.'

'Married twice, divorced twice.'

'I'm sorry.'

'I'm not. How do you think I could afford this place?'

'Well, that's good.'

'And I'm still waiting for Mr Right. Who knows – one day he'll cross that road, and sit down right there, just like you did.'

I asked for the menu.

I had just finished eating when Ambrose arrived. He slumped into the chair opposite and shook his head. 'Whatever way you look at it,' he said, 'it's a real mind fuck.'

'Yes, it is.'

He drummed his fingers on the table. He turned the menu over in his hand. He checked his cell phone for messages. Then he snapped, 'Who do you have to screw around here to get a drink?'

'Me,' said Jo-Anne, from behind him.

14

Brevard, for all its qualities, wasn't exactly coming down with things to do, especially when I wasn't with Claire. Her vacation time was up, she had a job to do, which theoretically left my days free for writing. The Ron Jon Surf Competition had been and gone without any fatalities and as the summer season drifted towards its close the tourists began to melt away. Many of the beach-front stores and attractions closed up until the arrival of the snowbirds around Thanksgiving. Bored with my own company, I found myself drifting into McDaid's Char Bar and Grill in the early afternoon two or three days a week. In retrospect, I should have known better.

Jo-Anne was good, friendly company, and not half as scary as she looked. Her reputation as a man-eater seemed to be greatly exaggerated, and possibly entirely of her own creation. It was a defence mechanism masquerading as an attack mechanism. I would sit outside with my notebook and sip a beer or two. The idea for what would become *Space Coast* was beginning to take shape, fuelled jointly by Claire's own enthusiasm for smalltown life and my own fascination with the carnal desires that can shape a man's life. Bob, you probably haven't made the connection before between Claire's 'friend' Tommy and Taylor in the novel, but there are very strong parallels. I was (and am) convinced that nearly everything in this world, from accountancy to woodwork, has something to do with sex and love, that

91

there is barely a moment in any person's life when they are not obsessed or consumed by hidden passions, and that everything that happens in this world has something to do with the fact that most of them remain unrequited. Genuine love between two people is extremely rare. I was so lucky to have Claire. For most people the object of their affections loves someone else, and that someone else loves someone else again. It means that 99 per cent of mankind settles for second best, and that is what causes so much turmoil. How awful was it for Tommy to have found the one person he could love, only to have her reject him? He had devoted himself to her for years, living in hope, when really, from day one, he was on a hiding to nothing. You don't grow into love, it hits *wham* from the first instant, and anything else is wishful thinking. That's what I believe, anyway. Often I am wrong.

Taylor in *Space Coast* started off as a smalltown rebel who couldn't convince the girl of his dreams to go out with him; he then went off to the war, won a fistful of medals and came back convinced he'd done enough to win her hand, only to find that she had been killed in an automobile accident. Except war has never interested me, and it was all very melodramatic. Her death actually weakened my story.

After I'd been in Brevard about a month, I arrived at Suntree for one of my early-morning runs (Claire had long since stopped joining me on these – having bagged her man, so to speak, she confessed that she hated running with a passion) and was astonished to find the beach already crowded with people, all staring intently out to sea. I immediately presumed that Paul de Luca's shark had struck again and a *Jaws* frenzy was about to kick off. Many of them had chairs and blankets and breakfast all prepared, and my next thought was that I'd stumbled upon some aquatic version of *The Wicker Man*. Before I could even ask anyone *why*, there was an almighty roar, like a thousand tanks starting up at once, and I saw this incredible juddering brightness to the east as a satellite was launched from Cape Canaveral. It was two or three miles away, but the power and majesty of it was quite unlike anything I'd ever seen before. Since then, I've been to a

World Cup Final and sat in the Coliseum and camped at the foot of Everest, and never have I been as impressed as I was then (or later, as you will see).

It only lasted a minute. Soon the finger of white heat had faded away, leaving only a wispy smoke trail across the vast expanse of blue sky, and the people were packing up their belongings. I said to no one in particular, 'That was fantastic.' An old man nodded beside me. 'You should see it at night – amazing!'

I started my run, and before I'd gone more than a few hundred metres I realised that I'd cracked my story problem. Taylor didn't need to be a Gulf War veteran. That had been done a thousand times. He would be an astronaut! He had been on the space shuttle, walked in space, walked with *God*, if you will – but still couldn't convince this one woman to love him. How much of a pisser would that be?

To be clear though, Tommy *is not* Taylor. In the wake of *Space Coast*'s publication I know that you received thousands of letters from women (and a few men!) confessing heartbroken sympathy for Taylor. I think there are very few of them who would have had similar feelings for Tommy. Taylor at his heart was good; Tommy as it turned out, was bad. I had thought him merely boorish on our first few meetings, and while I was aware of Claire's warning about his habit of scaring off her boyfriends, I hadn't really taken it on board. Besides, we were still being quite careful about being seen together in public. We weren't hiding, exactly. We just weren't rubbing his face in it. Claire wanted it that way.

Paul de Luca loved his titanium feet. That is, he would have preferred his real feet, but as substitutes go they weren't bad. He moved with considerable speed, although his gait was occasionally quite robotic. Sometimes when he walked he looked as if he was crossing a ploughed field, stepping over invisible furrows.

Over the course of those first months in Brevard I had been to see Paul perhaps half a dozen times – the first few times in the hospital, then later at his place of work in the XXX Video Store. We seemed to be becoming friends. I've never been quite sure why – we were opposites in so many ways. It wasn't just that I felt sorry for him. For some strange reason I also felt quite responsible for what had happened – if we had gotten to him sooner on the beach, if either of us had been a surgeon special-ising in feet – but mostly because I felt his heartache at not having Claire. I was very definitely the instrument of that pain. And of course, he was a published writer and I was not, and that was attractive. I read his detective novels and was positive to his face but quite snobbishly critical in private. But I had sincere admiration for anyone who could actually write a novel and get it published. I reread the novels recently, by the way, and they're actually quite good. His agent was the first I approached with *Space Coast*. He told me to cut it in half, add more sex and get rid of the intellectual shit. I didn't.

Paul appeared quite brash on the outside, and needed to be, working where he did, but once you got talking to him he came across as quite sensitive and thoughtful, and funny. It felt some-what strange to be having a conversation with him while other men urgently masturbated in curtained-off cubicles; I couldn't see them, of course – you just heard the occasional groan. Sometimes Paul would break off mid-conversation to scream down the hallway for his customers to put more quarters into the machines, then return to our chat as if nothing had happened.

The police appeared to believe that the XXX was a magnet for local lowlifes, but they didn't give him too much hassle. Once in a while a squad car would roll across the car park and out again. Paul hinted broadly that he paid them to look the other way. I didn't believe or disbelieve, it was none of my business. Claire teased me about going out there. I invited her to join me. She refused. She still hadn't seen Paul since his encounter with the shark, though they had spoken on the phone. Her allowing me to go out to the XXX was at least partly to do with her own guilt. He always asked about her, and always encouraged me to talk about her. I had the feeling he was nurturing his side of the friendship because of my connection to Claire. He loved her.

So did I.

*   *   *

One afternoon I was actually thinking about the Tommy/Taylor thing, sitting at my regular sidewalk table, when Tommy himself sat down opposite me.

'Hey, Chapters,' he said. 'How's it going?' He was wearing a white T-shirt that bulged in all the places mine didn't.

'It's going just fine,' I said.

'You written that bestseller yet?'

'Getting there,' I replied. I could see Jo-Anne eyeing us curiously from inside. When I lifted my beer for a sip I cracked the glass off my teeth. A little spilled onto my T-shirt. I wasn't frightened *at all*. I was just unsettled.

'Ain't seen Claire around, this while,' he said.

'Haven't seen her here at all,' I replied honestly. 'Get you a beer?'

'No, thanks. Not staying. You hear about the band?' He nodded back into the bar to where several members of Hey Rock'n'Roll, the six-piece covers band with a permanent residency in McDaid's could be seen dismantling their equipment. I shook my head. 'They got a contract with Carnival Cruises, six weeks, six cruises, east and west Caribbean; it works out, could be permanent.'

'Good for them,' I said.

'Even better, they need a roadie. So I quit being a mechanic, ship out Sunday.'

'That's fantastic,' I said, again honestly.

'Yes, sir, yes it is.' Tommy nodded.

I nodded.

'Six weeks,' he said again.

'Six weeks.'

'When I get back, I expect you'll be gone.'

'Well, I'm not sure what—'

'Let me put it another way. You *will* be gone.'

It sat in the humid air between us for a while. Jo-Anne arrived to clear the table immediately behind him. I was aware of her making eyes at me, but I kept my gaze steady on Tommy.

'You think I don't know about you and Claire?'

It was a statement in the form of a question. I just looked at him.

'You think there's a damn thing goes on in this town I *don't* know about?'

'Tommy . . .'

'You just shut your god-damn fucking mouth.'

I nodded slowly, then eased back in my chair. If he was going to do anything, I didn't think he'd attempt it in broad daylight in the middle of Main Street. It would be more like a Special Ops midnight surprise.

'You think I haven't been down this road before?' He leaned forward, resting his arms on the table and gripping the side of it with his hands. 'See, she has these infatuations, time to time, never go anywhere, she always comes back to me. That's the kind of relationship we have. Open. She knows it. I know it. Only poor jerks like you get caught in the middle, don't know it. Now I'm thinking maybe she likes you a little better this time, 'cos you're a smart kid; maybe you will write a book, but then maybe you're just selling better quality bullshit. But she'll get tired of you just the same. I know it. So I'm letting you off light. I'm saying have your fun, spin your little stories, but I come home in six weeks and you're still here, I'm not going to be happy. Do you understand me?'

'I hear what you're saying, Tommy.'

'And what the fuck does that mean?'

'It means I love her.'

Tommy laughed. 'You god-damn jerk-off, *everyone* loves her – isn't that the whole fucking point?'

He stood up.

'Six weeks,' he said, then stepped back into the bar.

15

'Truman Capote made his name with *In Cold Blood*. Norman Mailer sealed his comeback with *The Executioner's Song*. And remember *The Onion Field*? If you give true crime a literary gloss, there's a fortune to be made.'

Ambrose was on his third drink. He had a notebook on the table. It was already half-filled.

'Ambrose, I have a fortune.'

He nodded for several moments. Then: 'I wasn't necessarily thinking of you.'

'Why does this not surprise me?'

'Michael, are you going to write this book?'

'I don't know.'

He nodded some more. Then: 'Well, it's your decision.' He flipped open the notebook. 'These four guys, you knew them all?'

I knew them all. But I just looked at him.

'Tommy Ford, worked in a car shop. Ty Whitelaw and Lawrence Shaw were musicians. DeMarcus Hall was bank security, the inside man. Whitelaw and Shaw were shot dead in the bank, but the other two escaped and were cornered at DeMarcus Hall's mother's house outside town and killed there. None of them had any criminal history to speak of. Now what do you think would make four pretty ordinary guys, steady jobs, just up and rob a bank?'

'Wild guess, Ambrose – do you think maybe it was the money?' A headache had arrived.

'I'm talking motivation, Michael. They killed six innocent people.'

'Ambrose.'

He flipped another page. 'Matthew Nesbitt, a nineteen-year-old student, about to negotiate a loan for a car – except his girlfriend said it was really for an electric guitar. Michelle Del' Appa, a fifty-five-year-old nurse, been putting thirty dollars into her account once a week for twenty-five years, due to retire in three weeks.'

It was like being prodded with an ice pick.

'Three bank employees. Claire . . .'

'Ambrose!'

'. . . Roth, obviously, then—'

'Ambrose!'

'What?'

'Shut the fuck up.'

His eyes met mine. He gave a slight nod. He closed the notebook. He looked at his drink. He sang quietly: 'How many roads must a man walk down . . .'

I stood up.

'Michael, where are you going?'

'I don't know.'

'Sit down then. I thought the idea was to face these things head on.'

'No, Ambrose. That was your idea.'

'There's a story to be told here, you can't just run away from it. I swear to God, if you don't do it, it'll haunt you to the grave.'

'No, Ambrose. I think it'll haunt *you*. I'll call you later.' I turned on my heel.

'That's it,' Ambrose called after me. 'Walk away!'

As I passed the entrance to the bar, Jo-Anne was coming out with a tray of drinks. 'Is everything okay?' she asked.

I looked back. Ambrose was studying the menu. 'Everything's fine, Jo-Anne.'

'Good. I think he's quite sweet.' She smiled warmly in his direction. 'He tried to hit on me when you were at the john. What's a Pulitzer anyway?'

'Ask him,' I said, 'if you have an hour to kill.'

What had been annoying me, of course, wasn't Ambrose dredging up the past – that went with the territory – it was the knowledge that Joe Roth was still alive. I was pleased obviously, but also shocked. Joe was a big, proud man who had entrusted me with the safekeeping of his daughter, and it still somehow felt as if I had betrayed him. Even if it wasn't strictly true, at that precise moment it felt as if I had fled the scene of the crime only to avoid facing him. Later I'd heard about the stroke and callously written him off. What if whatever money he made from the sale of the paper had been quickly eaten up by medical bills and he had spent the last decade in penury? What on earth would Claire think of me, with all the money in the world, enjoying an eternal vacation while her father suffered?

Bob, I don't mind admitting that my initial reaction was to just ignore the fact that Joe was still alive. But Ambrose, as annoying as he is, got to me. I *had* been walking away from things for ten years. The fact that I was in Brevard at all showed that I wanted to change that. This was no time for backsliding. I had to find out how Joe was.

While it would have been easy enough to track him down through the newspaper, I preferred a slightly less direct approach (read into this what you will). I knew old man Olson had been Joe's doctor a decade ago, and it seemed reasonable to assume that if his daughter had inherited the practice she had also inherited his patients. If not, she would very probably know where he was and how he was. It was a small town. Besides, I wanted to know why she hadn't even mentioned my father-in-law.

I phoned her at home and got her machine. I then tried her surgery, and was told she was unavailable, but I could leave a message. She called back less than five minutes later.

'Michael, hi, how did—'

'You didn't tell me Joe Roth was still alive.' It came out a little sharper than I intended. It was the headache.

'You didn't ask.'

'We were standing in his house, Lena. All this time I presumed he was dead.'

'Michael, I had to make a judgement call. You were in quite a fragile state and—'

'I'm not fragile,' I cut in. 'I'm sorry if I got emotional over seeing my wife's clothes, and her handwriting, and our fucking fridge magnets.'

I cut the line. I walked on. A few seconds later she rang back.

'Sorry,' I said.

'Usually when they call it a gated community it's about keeping the bad guys out. This one's about keeping the residents in. Down at the police station they call this Alzheimer's Alley.'

We had already been waved through by a sleepy-looking security guard and were now parked in a pretty courtyard surrounded on three sides by bungalows with lanai in front and a communal swimming pool which glistened with criss-cross patterns in the late-afternoon sun. There was a high fence around the pool and a padlock on the gate.

'It's not exactly user-friendly,' I observed.

'It's a necessity. But they still manage to climb the fence.'

'Wouldn't it be better just to drain the pool, then?'

'Nope. They'd still try and jump in, and then they'd end up breaking their necks. At least if there's water there's a fifty-fifty chance of getting to them before they drown.'

'Are you serious?'

She smiled. 'Not entirely. Are you sure you're up to this?'

I nodded.

Lena wasn't Joe's doctor, in fact, but attended other patients here and regularly called in to check on him. She had already cleared my visit with his own MD and been updated as to Joe's condition. There had been a succession of strokes, each one a kickback after he'd been making good progress. He was like a fighter who didn't know when to stay down, or couldn't afford to.

As we waited to be buzzed into the reception area, Lena put a hand on my arm. 'Don't expect too much,' she said softly.

An hour before, I hadn't been expecting *anything*. Lena left her hand where it was until a nurse arrived and escorted us across the pristine reception and down a corridor towards Joe's room. Although it looked like the facility was made up of individual bungalows, it was merely a piece of architectural trickery. They were all interconnected.

'Maybe I should have brought something,' I said.

Lena and the nurse maintained a diplomatic silence.

This isn't Joe.

'His eyes open occasionally,' the nurse said. 'Perhaps he'll move a finger. But there's no communication. He's fed via these tubes, all his vitals are monitored, and he has manipulative physiotherapy five days a week.'

'Is there anything else he needs – or more of what he has? Whatever it takes.'

'There's nothing else, Michael,' said Lena. 'Everything is covered.'

'Perhaps you'd like to sit with him for a while?' asked the nurse.

I didn't, actually. But it was the thing to do. Lena gave me a smile which mixed sympathy and encouragement and said she'd wait in the car. The nurse closed the door behind her and left me with my catatonic father-in-law lying enveloped in the greenish hue of a life artificially sustained.

I stood at the foot of the bed.

'Hey, Joe,' I said.

I used to say, 'Hey, Joe,' all the time to him. One day Claire started to tell him about Hendrix. He cut her off by snapping, 'Degenerate!'

There was a TV high in the corner behind me, switched on but with the sound off. Baseball. His bedside locker was clear on top. Because I am a curious fellow, I opened the drawer below and peered in. There was shaving gear and a toothbrush sitting beside a zipped-up leather washbag. Underneath there was a badly creased paperback copy of *Space Coast*. I took it out. It fell open naturally to the title page. Beneath my name there was scrawled, in Joe's handwriting:

Welcome home, you son of a bitch.

16

Space Coast was written during the six months Tommy Ford was gone from Brevard. Hey Rock'n'Roll had their contract with Carnival extended several times and he stayed with them. According to some of Claire's acquaintances, he was having a whale of a time. I couldn't have cared less. All I knew was that from the day and hour of his departure it was as if someone had lifted a weight from our shoulders. I imagine it's like when a gay man comes out after twenty years in the shadows, or when Bambi emerges – hesitant steps at first because the world seems like such a dangerous place, and then your confidence rapidly grows until you're strutting about the place thinking, Life is great! Why didn't I do this ages ago?

As a journalist I was never very good at research; as a novelist, probably worse. But I didn't really need it. It was fiction. I made it up. When I really *had* to find something out, it didn't seem like such a chore. There were plenty of people living in the area who had come out to work at Cape Canaveral during the heyday of the Apollo programme, and several of them were regulars at our favourite bar. Talking to them was a delight. I also got to know Mary Haagen, who had been the librarian in Brevard for thirty years. She maintained a collection of newspapers and letters and official documents dating back to before the First World War – a treasure trove of information which I eagerly plundered.

However, it was Claire who was my greatest resource; she

knew everything there was to know about the town and the beaches and the hinterland. Every house I pointed at she could tell me when it was built, who built it, who had lived and died there. Much of her knowledge came through Joe, of course, and growing up around the newspaper, but it was presented fresh and new: history, Claire flavoured. She had a take on things which was cynical without being depressing; she could keep a straight face when we met boring people and yet her eyes would hit mine and I would dissolve into laughter and they'd look at me like I was mad – and so would she. She took me to Brevard Community Theatre and whispered of its bawdy origins during *Death of a Salesman* with such enthusiasm that I was almost thrown out for laughing so hard. She took me surfing (me!) and I came back with my feet intact and a new appreciation both for the beasts of the sea and for her skimpiest bikini yet. We lay in the sand, we browsed the junk stores, we gazed and loved and planned. We walked hand-in-hand. She couldn't put a salad together to save her life.

One day when I was writing, she lifted up one of my empty notebooks and began to sketch me.

I said, 'I didn't know you could draw.'

'You still don't.' She slanted the notebook away from me.

I kept working. Or, after a while, pretending to. I kept looking up at her. She was concentrating so intently.

Ninety minutes later, she handed me my likeness.

Or, my unlikeness. My dislikeness.

Claire looked at me, eyes big, soft lips open just a fraction. 'Well?'

'Do you want marks out of ten?'

'Would you mark da Vinci out of ten? Would you give Picasso an A plus? Just tell me what you god-damn think.'

'What do *you* think? Are *you* happy with—'

'Michael!'

I cleared my throat. I set down my own notebook. I had decided when I first met Claire that honesty would be the best policy in all things. It was quite an easy policy to adhere to, but occasionally there were little moments like this which proved an unexpected challenge. If she'd been reading what I was writing I would have preferred her to avoid the truth. At that point I needed encouragement, not criticism (actually I made a point of not letting her see my work in progress – partly out of shyness, partly out of fear) and I could have treated her to the same well-meaning dishonesty. After all, it was only a sketch. But I was setting the bar high for this relationship. Three failures and I might be out. So I wasn't about to waste one.

'You don't like it,' she said.

'I don't like it.'

'You really don't like it?'

'I really don't like it.'

'What about the eyes?'

'I don't like the eyes.'

'Is the nose not quite accurate?'

'No.'

'What about the chin? It's a strong chin.'

'It is a strong chin. Unfortunately, it's not mine.'

She gave me a hard look. 'Is it not perhaps the case, Michael Ryan, that you just don't like yourself . . .'

'I love myself.'

'. . . and therefore you will never appreciate a likeness?'

'It's considerably short of a likeness.'

She sucked on her lower lip.

'Claire, I'm sorry. I know nothing about art, and it may be that an expert might say it's perfect. All I know is that if I tried to pass through immigration looking like this, I would be arrested. If this is truly what you think I look like, I am either committing suicide, or murder.'

Claire slowly uncoiled from her position on the L-shaped sofa that dominated the apartment, then crossed the short angle to kneel before me. She took my head in her hands and kissed me.

'What was that for?' I asked.

'For passing Art 101.'

'I don't follow.'

'Every boyfriend who successfully avoids Tommy also has to

105

sit a practical exam in art appreciation. I deliberately compose the most god-awful picture I'm capable of, then sit back and watch them squirm. You're the first one who hasn't lied to me. I approve of you.'

I nodded. I turned to my work again. She set her chin on her elbow, and her elbow on the cushion and gazed lovingly at me. Without looking up I said, 'How do you know *I'm* not lying?'

She thought about that for a moment. 'I see. Like a double bluff. You realised it was a test. You actually quite like the picture, but think I'll respect you more if you're critical of it. Either that or you think it will inspire me to get better. Or, you don't think there's room for two artists in one family.'

I made another note. I corrected a hasty spelling. Again, without looking up, I said: 'Are we a family?'

'No. No, we're not. We'd have to be married to be a family. And we hardly know each other. That would be foolish.'

'To the extreme,' I agreed.

She lay on the ground and looked up at me. 'Which brings us back to your reasons for lying. Or *possibly* lying.'

'It's a triple bluff,' I ventured. 'Or is it?'

Her eyes narrowed. 'You think you're very smart, don't you, Michael Ryan?'

'I have my moments.'

'And I'm just a dumb country girl.'

'Are you from the country?'

We were both quiet for a while. Then she poked my knee gently. 'I'm never really going to know, am I? The question is, even if you despise it, and it makes you want to commit suicide and murder, will you put up with it if I stick it on your fridge, because you love me?'

'Yes,' I said.

'Okay.' She stood up and took my notebook into the kitchen. I heard a page being torn from it. When she returned a few moments later she said, 'I'm going now.'

This was a surprise. I had presumed that it was all leading up to sex.

'You said you could stay until three. You've an hour yet.'

'I know that. But I've decided to leave now.'

She kissed me on the forehead, as if I was her brother, then she turned for the door. I didn't yet know her well enough to decide if she was genuinely hurt by my lack of appreciation for her drawing skills, if she really had been setting me a test and I'd somehow contrived to fail it by passing up on the opportunity to turn us into a family, or she was just teasing.

Confused?

I sure as hell was. And she was still leaving.

She was halfway out of the door when I said, 'Claire.'

She turned and smiled, ready to accept an apology, perhaps for anything.

However, if there is a space between the door and the jamb, I will put my foot in it. It is partly back to the honesty thing, but mostly down to stupidity and low-grade jealousy.

'Did Tommy like *his* picture?'

I meant it to be teasing.

Wrong.

'What?'

Like being on a water-park slide. Once you're off, you're *off*.

'Tommy – did Tommy like *his* picture?'

She didn't look angry or furious. She looked . . . *disappointed*.

'Did anyone ever tell you, Michael Ryan, that you have a mean streak?'

She went out then, slamming the door. I heard her go halfway down the wooden steps outside, then stop. There were a few seconds of quiet. She was either deciding whether to come back, or listening to see if I was coming after her. I didn't move.

Stupid *and* stubborn.

Claire hurried down the rest of the steps and away.

17

Welcome home, you son of a bitch.

What it meant was that Joe knew I would come home eventually, but that he wasn't about to go chasing me. He understood why I'd gone on the run, he just wished I hadn't. The *son of a bitch* wasn't serious. Joe said it a lot. He was just punching me gently on the arm, man to man, and saying *'You son of a bitch, it's good to see you.'* At least, I preferred to look at it that way. This confidence lasted all the way out to the car. I had the book with me. I showed it to Lena. She raised her eyebrows, then suggested going to McDaid's for a drink. I didn't object.

On the way there I sat studying Joe's copy of *Space Coast*. It was well-thumbed and the spine was cracked. On the inside of the front cover there was a sketch of me, rather than a photograph, and then some biographical information. In the corner of the sketch you could just make out a tiny *Claire*. Joe had circled this in red ink. As I flicked through the pages it became clear that he had made a detailed study of the text – underlining, boxing off, and the plentiful use of sarcastic exclamation marks. He paid particular attention to passages that he took to be about his daughter, and those which described the history and lay-out of Brevard. The book itself was a first-edition paperback which would have come out about a year after Claire died, by which time I was long gone from the Blue House. It begged the question – did he write the inscription then, and just hold on to it, or more recently, in the knowledge that his own death was probably approaching?

It was only a ten-minute run to McDaid's, and we were actually parking in the lot opposite it when I realised I hadn't spoken the whole way. Now Lena smiled kindly at me and said, 'We don't have to go in if you don't want to.'

'No, I'm fine. Honestly.'

At least, I *was* fine until we strolled towards the bar and I saw that Ambrose was *still* sitting there. Jo-Ann wasn't exactly sitting with him – she was perched on the windowsill to one side, with her apron on and a tray in her hands, but as the other tables outside were empty, and it looked fairly quiet inside, it appeared that she'd been there for quite a while. I stopped, ready to turn back, but just at that very moment Ambrose looked up and waved, and then I'd no choice really but to walk on up and introduce Lena. There was some small talk, then Lena excused herself to use the rest room, and Jo-Anne went inside with her.

Ambrose beamed at me. 'Haven't lost it yet.'

'Haven't lost *what*, exactly, Ambrose?'

'You and me both, Mikey, we're not in town five minutes, and we're both hooked up.'

'I am not *hooked up*.'

'Yes, you are. You should see the way she looks at you.'

'Ambrose. I've only just met her, and she's wearing sunglasses.'

'I know these things.'

'Yes, Ambrose. You are Dr Love.'

I'm not sure if it was entirely wise to show the book to Ambrose, but I did it, more to get off the subject than anything else. I explained to him about going to see Joe, and found myself apolo-gising for not taking him along.

'No worries,' he said. Then he looked at the inscription. 'Oooh. Spooky.'

'Spooky?'

'It's like he's talking to you from beyond the grave. Except, of course, he's not dead.'

I immediately turned to Lena, who was just returning to her seat. 'He has a Pulitzer, you know.'

'Two,' said Ambrose.

She smiled at that and said, 'So you're writing a book about Michael's return to Brevard.'

'Nope,' said Ambrose. 'I'm just along for the ride.'

I raised an eyebrow.

'That's very good of you,' said Lena. 'You two must be very close.'

I looked at Ambrose. He looked at me.

'We're working on it,' said Ambrose.

'Ways to go,' I said.

Jo-Anne had her apron off and her handbag over her shoulder. She stood somewhat awkwardly by our table. 'I'm finished now,' she said. She took keys out of her bag. 'Are you driving past the Comfort Inn?' Ambrose asked. Jo-Anne nodded, mumbled: 'Do you want a ride?' 'Love one,' said Ambrose. He stood up. 'You don't mind if I leave you two lovebirds, do you?'

I took a deep breath; even managed a smile.

Off they went, leaving only an awkward silence behind them.

'Sorry about that,' I said.

I wasn't surprised *at all* that Ambrose wasn't waiting in our room at the Comfort Inn.

Yes, *our* room. I was rich beyond my wildest dreams, yet I had been sharing a room with Ambrose for nearly three weeks. And when he wasn't home, I worried about him. He was a liability and a menace, he was a drunk, and an unpredictable one at that. He had won two Pulitzers and nobody cared, and he was insanely jealous of my book sales. Yet despite all of the above, I was better with him than without him. Alone, there had been too much darkness; with Ambrose there was at least the opportunity to hate someone else.

I dozed for a while, then was awoken from an interesting dream featuring Dr Lena Olson by the bedside phone. It was the front desk. The police were downstairs, wanting to talk to me. I asked about what. They asked me just to come on down. I huffed and puffed a bit, but there was nothing else for it. It would be like this for the next few days. A celebrity in town would be the victim of a hundred requests. A donation to the Police Benevolent Fund, most likely.

Downstairs there was a young-looking cop in a tan uniform. As I approached, he clearly recognised me and put his hand out.

'Mr Ryan – it's an honour, sir. Deputy Sheriff Newton.'

'Well, thank you. It's an honour to be here.'

He nodded and released my hand. He stood looking at me without saying anything. I raised an encouraging eyebrow and he seemed to shake himself.

'Sir, I read *Space Coast* when I was thirteen. Ten years ago.'

'Well, that's kind of young, son.'

'Dirtiest damn book ever allowed in our house. My daddy kept it under lock and key, but I knew where the key was.'

'And here you are in law enforcement.'

'Yes, sir. And about the tenth time I sneaked a peek at that book my daddy caught me and he whipped me good. That sure as hell taught me.'

'Well. It really wasn't *that* dirty.'

'Sir, you don't know my daddy. No – actually, you do. Sheriff Newton.'

I nodded. 'Yes, I remember the Sheriff.'

'He told me to come on down here, quick. It's kind of embarrassing, you being our special guest. He thought I better have a quiet word, sort it out.'

'Sort *what* out?'

'Sir, about an hour ago we were called to the Elm Lodge Seniors Village south of Interstate 95 – report of an intruder. We attended the scene, and it seems an eighty-six-year-old woman discovered the intruder sleeping in her room when she returned from her evening meal. Sir, we had some trouble rousing him, and at first he gave his name as Peter Pulitzer, but we soon established that he was—'

'Ambrose.'

'Yes, sir, Ambrose Jeffers of Brooklyn, New York. Mr Ryan, sir, he's down at the station now feeling pretty sorry for himself. He said he was your companion and that you would bail him

112

out. Sorry, sir, that's just a figure of speech, we're not charging him with anything, but Daddy . . . Sheriff Newton . . . would like to release him into your custody, if that's not too much trouble. Ordinarily we *would* charge him, but that would be kind of embarrassing, with all the celebrations this week. I don't mean celebrations. You know what I mean, sir.'

I knew exactly what he meant.

Junior Newton produced Ambrose. My 'companion' had a stupid grin on his face and an ugly bruise on his neck.

'You're a very lucky man, Mr Jeffers,' said Junior.

Ambrose jabbed a fat finger at him. '*You're* the lucky man. You're lucky I don't sue you for police brutality!'

'Ambrose,' I hissed, 'for fuck's sake, zip it. They're letting you go.'

'No!' Ambrose snapped back. 'I'm letting *them* go. Remember *Atticus*!'

I grabbed him by the back of his jacket and propelled him forward. He didn't resist. It was just for show: I knew it. I shouted my thanks back to Junior Newton.

'No problem, sir, you just get him home and keep him quiet. And, sir, my daddy says, "Welcome to Brevard".'

I stopped Ambrose for a moment and looked back at the kid. There wasn't much of a family resemblance.

'I'll bet he does,' I said.

I pushed Ambrose forward through the swing doors and finally let go of his jacket. He stood for a moment, breathing in the cooler night air.

'What sort of an idiot are you?' I asked.

'Any sort you like.' He was suddenly sober, and standing straight and in control of his faculties.

'Remember *Atticus*?'

'Yeah, I was thinking Attica, but *Mockingbird* kind of got in the way. But it's all about human rights, right?'

I stared at his neck. 'That's not police brutality at all. That's a lovebite, a hickey.'

'Yes, it is. I scored bigtime.'

113

He was smiling magnificently, and I couldn't but feel a little happy for him, at least until righteous anger kicked back in. 'Ambrose, what the fuck were you doing up there?'

'Wanted to see this Joe Roth for myself.'

'And did you?'

'Hell, no.'

18

Bob, I was young. In love, yes, but also sulky and stroppy and lazy and self-confident, and there was about an hour of *she'll be back* and *the grass is always greener* before panic began. What set it off was going into the kitchen and seeing my sketch stuck to the fridge. Except it wasn't the same sketch. It was *me* on the torn notebook page all right, but it was a recognisable me, filtered through Claire's eyes. It was all shades and opinions. It was delicate and intense. It was everything I had said the original wasn't. She had bluffed me again. Eighty-five minutes on this, then she'd tossed off a crappy version to see if I'd lie to her. I had this sudden awful and huge empty feeling inside, a hollow distress. At that moment Tommy's words came back to me: how she would grow tired of me and dump me, just as she had all of the others. I didn't want to believe that Tommy could be right, but suddenly it made sense. Why else would she have stormed off over *nothing*? She wanted to finish things and the flimsiest excuse would do. I could not let that happen. I *would* not let it happen.

I raced to the Blue House.

As I dashed up, sweaty and breathless, Joe was sitting on the porch reading a book. I don't know for sure if he was expecting me, but it did not escape my notice that his shotgun was resting against the wall behind him.

'Mr Roth, sir,' I panted. 'Is she here?'

He idly turned a page. 'Might be,' he said, without looking up.

'We had a fight. Over nothing. I was stupid. Is she here?'

His eyes flitted up. 'She's here.'

'Can I go in and talk to her?'

'If you can get through that door before I shoot you – yes, you can.' There was no humour to it.

'Joe, I came to apologise.'

Joe closed his book and indicated that I should sit opposite him. I lowered myself cautiously into a wicker chair. He was sitting a little to the right of the open front door; I could see the stairs behind him and, as I sat, the tips of Claire's feet about halfway up.

'I thought you might like to take a look at this.' He held up the book. It was a well preserved copy of *A History of Brevard* by Thomas Sitwell. 'It covers the early days of the town. You know, our family's been here right from the start. My father built half those buildings downtown, this one too. Owned the newspaper before me. Disturbs me Claire has no interest in taking over. Always thought the man she married might take an interest.'

I nodded.

'Son, this isn't the fifties, and it's got damn-all to do with me, but I have to tell you, she could have the pick of any damn man in this town and she seems to have picked you. But if I don't like you, you'll have a fight on your hands.'

'I understand that.'

'Now tell me about this novel. Has she read any of it?'

'No, sir.'

'Why's that? Is it no good?'

'I'm not in a position to say, sir. But she can't read it until it's finished.'

'And when might that be?'

'I don't know.'

'How far into it are you?'

'About halfway.'

'And how long did that take you?'

'Twenty-six years.'

'Is that supposed to be funny, or deep?'

'Bit of both, sir.'

Joe nodded. 'She must think you can make a living off of it.'

'I can't promise that. It's not up to me, but I'm giving it every-thing I've got.'

'So what happens, twelve months down the line, when you can't finish it or you can't sell it?'

'I keep trying.'

'And you still won't consider working on the paper?'

'No, sir.'

'You think I worked on it all these years just so I could sell up one day, and it's like I never existed?'

'I don't believe you will sell up.'

'Damn right I won't. Do you think I'm giving you a hard time?'

'Yes, sir. But I understand.'

'You could just tell me where to go.'

'Yes, I could. But then I fear you might shoot me.'

Joe reached back and took hold of his shotgun. 'Do you really think it's loaded?'

'I'd prefer not to find out.'

He cradled it in his lap. 'Do you love her?' he asked.

'Yes, I do.'

Claire's toes moved back out of sight.

'So what are you going to do about it?'

'Sir?'

'What are you going to do about it? It's a simple question.'

'I'm going to marry her.'

'Have you asked her?'

'No, sir.'

'I thought I told you to call me Joe.'

'I didn't think it was appropriate right now.'

Joe nodded slowly. Then he sighed and reached into his shirt pocket. He removed something which he cradled in his fist. It might have been a shotgun cartridge or a headache pill. 'You're not some preppy rich kid from New York, are you?'

'No, sir. Bog Irish and poor.'

'Then when it comes to it, maybe you could use this.' Joe opened his fist. There was a ring. An engagement ring. 'It was her mother's. When the time is right, you give it to her.'

He held it out to me, and I took it. He nodded. I nodded.

'Now go in and see her. She'll twist you round her little finger, if you let her. She's been doing it to me since she was in diapers.'

I smiled and went to move past him. He lifted the gun barrel out of the way. I stopped in the doorway.

'Joe? What if the time is never right and I just keep the ring?'

He nodded gravely. 'Then I will hunt you down and kill you, you son of a bitch.'

19

Ambrose had the address of Tommy's old house, and insisted on driving out there the next morning after another IHOP breakfast. I'd not been there before, obviously, so I was a little surprised to find that it was one of Brevard's grander dwellings. I suppose I had imagined something in a trailer park. Ambrose gave me his usual talk about how cathartic it would be for me to visit the house, perhaps speak to Tommy's family, while actually using me to facilitate his own research. We sat outside looking at it for a while, then Ambrose said, 'Let's go see.' I refused. We argued for a few minutes then he got out and slammed the door. He walked up the driveway and rang the bell. An elderly man answered, spoke to him for a few moments, then Ambrose returned to the car.

'Nope,' he said as he got in, 'only been there five years, claims to know nothing about his illustrious predecessor.'

'Claims?'

'All the publicity, you think no one's let slip this was the house where Tommy Ford planned the raid on the First National? He knows. He's just trying to protect the property value.'

I wasn't convinced that much planning at all had gone into the robbery. If there was, it was more likely sketched out on the back of a beer mat.

'Okay,' said Ambrose, examining his notebook, 'next stop is . . .'

Next stop was a rundown ground-floor duplex apartment in a complex overlooking Indian River. An elderly black woman answered the door. Ambrose talked to her for five minutes, then turned and waved me over. I had again told him I wasn't going to co-operate, but with the woman looking over I could hardly ignore her, so I walked across and was introduced to Lawrence Shaw's mother, Grace.

I told her I remembered Lawrence playing raucous guitar on a mean version of 'Gloria'.

She said, 'That Lawrence loved his music,' and invited us in.

The air conditioning was on full blast and the chairs were thick with cat hair. While she made coffee, Ambrose and I examined the many photos of the late Lawrence Shaw that hung on the walls. Lawrence with dreadlocks. Lawrence at graduation. Lawrence on the basketball court. Lawrence in a tux on one of the cruise ships with the rest of the band.

As Mrs Shaw came back in with the tray of coffee she said, 'How much are we talking about?'

Ambrose, without bothering to look at me, said, 'That'll be up to the network. Depends if Connie or Diane are involved – money goes up in that case.'

'That Diane seems like a nice lady,' said Mrs Shaw.

'You bet. But it's essential to do all the research in advance, you understand that?'

'Yes, sir.'

'Ambrose?'

He gave me a rather pained *don't complicate things* look.

'Ambrose?'

'Mr Ryan?'

I looked at the old lady. Her face was pinched with age and heartbreak. 'I'm very sorry about what happened to your wife,' she said. 'Lawrence was such a good boy, never in trouble as a kid. He loved his music, he had this dream about moving to LA and making it big there. He just loved to play. That band, some of them were his friends from when they were this high, and then they went off on those damn cruise ships and they changed. They changed. Got so he didn't care about his music no more.'

'Changed in what way?' I asked.

Mrs Shaw set her cup down. 'How you think? Black man shouldn't be exposed to those kind of temptations.'

I glanced at Ambrose. He reached across and took Mrs Shaw's hand.

She stood in the doorway, watching as we walked back to the car. I just stared straight ahead. Ambrose waved back. As we drove away I snapped: 'What the hell are you playing at?'

'Ah, these poor folks, you mention TV to them and they just can't stop talking.'

'Jesus, Ambrose.'

'No harm done.'

I groaned. A little further on I asked: 'Ambrose, *are* you talking to the networks?'

Ambrose snorted. 'Yeah, right, Shakespeare.'

We spent another hour on our little terror tour. The house where Tommy and DeMarcus were shot dead had been knocked down not long after the killings and was now a smallish apartment block. We had an address downtown for DeMarcus, but there was no answer to the door and the neighbours were out. Ty Whitelaw, Lawrence's fellow musician, had been of no fixed abode and apparently had family out west, but nobody local. At the car shop where Tommy had worked nobody wanted to talk. As we drove away someone shouted, 'And *Space Coast* sucked!' Ambrose gave them the finger, while at the same time muttering, 'Got that right.'

Since we'd arrived in Brevard, I'd been avoiding two locations. The site of the memorial garden, and the First National Bank. Although they were on Main Street, and opposite each other, there were enough intersections to allow me to negotiate downtown without coming upon either of them. I'd like to think that Ambrose knew better than to ask me to go to either, although quite possibly he was just biding his time. But I knew if I did visit either, it wouldn't be with him. Most situations I can predict how I might react; when I can't, I don't want anyone there who might be taking notes.

121

We parked opposite McDaid's grill. Ambrose was wearing a striped shirt, undone at the neck, and displaying his lovebite. The thought that Jo-Anne might also be showcasing a similar love wound was too much for me. I told him I was going for a walk, and before I knew it, or perhaps I did, I was heading directly for those two locations I'd been trying to avoid. But I didn't stop. I would have to do it sooner or later, and better to get whatever reaction there might be out of the way and in privacy.

I was spared the garden, at least. The space opposite the bank was fenced off and hung with tarpaulin to frustrate the curious. The bank itself looked exactly as before – oddly elongated to facilitate the drive-in at the end of the block. As I stopped by the entrance a security guard, standing outside smoking, nodded. He was a black guy, perhaps thirty. Ten years before, DeMarcus Hall had stood there and I'd gotten to know him reasonably well, calling by to take Claire to lunch in those carefree days before the return of Tommy Ford. Did he know then, while we swapped small talk about sports, what was coming? As we laughed and joked, was he practising nights with his gun, learning how to shoot innocent people and not give a damn about it? You never can tell. As I entered, the security guard said what a fine day it was, and I couldn't do anything except nod back and grunt.

It seemed smaller inside than I remembered, and brighter. The layout was pretty much the same. I went to one of the freestanding counters and stood pretending to fill in a form, but my eyes darted about, trying to imagine what it had been like. The blood, the horror, the screams, the panic, the *fucking* realisation that this was not going to end well. Claire would have been over *there*, her favoured spot. I wondered at what point she understood that it was Tommy Ford giving the orders. He was wearing a mask, but that gravelled, macho voice was so distinctive. All I knew was that she was the first to die. Three shots. All to the face.

I staggered. Held onto the counter.

As I steadied myself, I glanced up to see a clerk looking across at me; I forced a smile and focused on the paperwork. Less than a minute later, a voice beside me said, 'Michael?'

I turned to find a portly man with barely any hair, smiling kindly at me. 'Michael. It's Sheldon.'

I blinked at him for several moments, trying to place him. Sheldon. Sheldon. *Sheldon*. Sheldon *Adelson*. The bank manager. Claire's employer. But the Sheldon Adelson I'd known had been slim, with a full head of luxurious blond hair. Off-duty, he had often been mistaken for a beach dude. But I looked closer, and saw the remnants of his chiselled features, the hint of his yellow mane in the moustache that surfed above his thick upper lip. I guess time hadn't stood still for me either. I put my hand out.

'Sheldon,' I said, 'how are you?'

Sheldon had come to the Blue House to break the news.

'I'm just fine, Michael, just fine. Really good to see you. One of my staff recognised you right off. I . . . didn't expect to see you in here.'

I managed a smile. 'No, neither did I.'

'Come . . . come into my office. Please.'

He led the way. 'I can't stay,' I said almost immediately. He said he understood completely and phoned for coffee. We sat wordlessly for a while, then the coffee arrived and he began to talk. He said he'd taken a year off after the robbery. When he came back the first day, nobody recognised him. He patted his bald pate. 'Fell out, almost overnight. Doctor said it was stress.' Then he rubbed his belly. 'Donuts account for the rest.'

'It's not easy,' I said.

He nodded slowly, his eyes far away. Then he seemed to give himself a shake. 'Had a television producer on the phone with me yesterday, said he was working with you on something for *Oprah*.'

'Uhuh?'

'He had a lot of questions, but to be frank, I'm not really up for talking about it.'

'That's fine, Sheldon.'

'He didn't want to take no for an answer.'

'I apologise for that. He's just enthusiastic.'

'I didn't think she would be interested in smalltown stuff like this.'

'Actually,' I said, 'it's precisely the sort of thing she might be interested in, but it's not going to happen.'

'Okay,' he said. 'Good to know. I prefer not to . . . dwell. It's been hard for all of us. These last few weeks, with the garden, it's really brought it all back. I was invited onto the organising committee, but I really couldn't bring myself. Needless to say, the bank has made a healthy donation. Really, we can't do too much for those poor people.' This thought seemed to spark something off. He turned to the computer on his left and typed something into the keyboard, then waited a moment and nodded. 'I'm actually glad you called in,' he said. 'I wanted to have a word with you about your account.'

I just looked at him.

'I hope you don't mind,' he said, 'but it is significantly over-drawn, by several hundred dollars. And with ten years' interest . . .'

I stirred my coffee. Claire always said he was an ass.

20

Things seemed to move so quickly after Claire and I got back together (although we were only apart for about sixty-five minutes!). Without belittling the sweat and turmoil and hair-tearing that went with it, *Space Coast* moved relentlessly forward until I reached the point where, six months after my arrival in Brevard, I was relieved to finally type *The End*. It was a huge weight off my shoulders, but there was also an enormous sense of dread. What if it had all been a colossal waste of time? What if it really was Joe's telephone directory – too many characters, not enough plot? Part of me actually didn't care what editors or publishers thought. If one person liked it, then I would be happy: as long as that one person was Claire. I would still love her if she confirmed that it was garbage, but every cell in my body ached for her to love it. Meanwhile, every time I saw Joe he raised an eyebrow, but the time wasn't quite right to pop the question. It *really* wasn't right, because I had a plan in mind, and it depended on the weather, and the full moon and the boffins at NASA.

The day I finished *Space Coast* I printed it up, and called Claire. She seemed as excited as I was. I went round that night for dinner with her and Joe, and set the manuscript on the table. I'd put a bow around it.

'Christ,' said Joe, 'it's bigger than *War and Peace*.'

It wasn't, of course. Claire picked it up and clasped it to her bosom. 'I can feel my heart beating through it,' she said.

It was, in retrospect, exactly what I was trying to achieve. 'I am reading this tonight. I'm not coming out of my room until I'm done.'

'Christ,' said Joe, 'we'll need the paramedics.'

'Then Daddy's going to read it,' said Claire.

Joe laughed. I took from it that he had no intention of doing any such thing. He said then that he had his own news. For the past few weeks I'd been hunting around for a new apartment as the lease was up and the owners weren't for renewing. Now Joe announced that he was planning to move into the small apartment above his newspaper office. 'This damn place is getting too big for me,' he said, 'and you two need somewhere to put your heads down without me there to distract you.'

'Absolutely not,' said Claire, despite the fact that this was a licence to cohabit. Or because of it. 'This is your house.'

'Exactly,' said Joe with finality.

'That's very kind of you,' I said. In response, he raised one of his eyebrows, a dramatic prompt if ever there was one. 'Joe,' I said, 'I wanted to have a word in private with you anyway.'

Claire's eyes flitted towards me for just a second, then she focused all of her concentration on the cover of the manuscript. Her cheeks suddenly looked a little flushed. She stood up and took the manuscript to her room. Joe and I got a couple of beers and went out onto the veranda where I quietly explained my plan.

Joe nodded to himself for several moments. Then he gave a little shrug. 'You know, in my day, you didn't need bells and whistles.'

Nevertheless he agreed to help. When we went back inside, Claire reappeared and hovered expectantly. When nothing was said after twenty minutes she finally took me aside and asked what we'd been talking about. I told her it was about the wisdom of me moving in, and the maintenance of the air conditioning. Claire immediately said she was tired and was going to bed. She might start the book next week if she'd some free time.

I said goodnight. When I kissed her she turned her cheek

slightly. I was no longer concerned about our minor fall-outs or Tommy's warnings, because when we made up, and we always did, it was *spectacular*.

She phoned at 4.19 a.m. 'I hate you, you son of a bitch,' she said.

She was becoming more like her father every day. I managed a groggy, 'Why?'

'Because this book is fantastic.'

'Oh. So why do you hate me?'

'Because this book is so good I can't keep hating you, and I hate that, so I hate you even more. But I love the book.'

'Okay then.'

'I'm only halfway through. It may all be downhill from here.'

'It probably is.'

'If it is, you'll never hear from me again. Goodnight.'

She put the phone down. I returned to sleep, contented.

Three weeks later, on a Saturday a little after sunset, I drove Claire to a beach a mile out of town which hardly qualified as a beach at all, it was so small. But it was perfect for my requirements. It was completely deserted. She thought we were just going for a walk, but I produced a blanket and a picnic. We drank wine. We kissed. Time passed. After a while she asked, 'Why do you keep looking at your watch?'

'No reason.'

'Is there somewhere you have to be?'

'Right here.'

'All right then. Concentrate.'

We kissed. I drank some more wine. 'Are you cold?' I asked. She shook her head.

'I might get my jacket.'

Before she could respond, I hurried across to the car. It was only about thirty metres away. As I bent into the rear, pretending to look for my jacket, I snapped open my phone and called Joe.

'Well?' I said.

'It's delayed, Michael. Another hour.'

'Christ.' I cut the line and strolled back, wearing my jacket, sweat stuck to my back.

I poured her another glass of wine. I was more careful about checking the time. After an hour, and with nothing happening, I said I was going back to the car for another bottle of wine.

She said, 'I've had enough. And you're driving.'

'Just a little,' I said.

She gave me a look, then sighed with resignation. 'I suppose I'm off work tomorrow.'

I called Joe. 'Any minute,' he said.

When I got back Claire said, 'Who were you talking to?'

'No one. The wine . . . ?' I held the bottle up as evidence.

She held up her cell phone as *her* evidence. 'I phoned you. It is cooler. I wanted *my* jacket. Your cell was busy.'

'No, it wasn't. You dialled the wrong number.'

'No, I didn't. I called you. Your phone was busy. I left you a voice message. Who were you speaking to?'

'No one.'

'You were talking to someone.'

'Nope.'

'Michael. This is ridiculous. You've been looking at your watch all night. Who were you talking to, and who are you meeting?'

'I'm not meeting anyone.'

'Don't lie to me, Michael.'

'I'm not lying.'

I went to pour her wine. She put her hand over the top of the paper cup, but too late. It dribbled across her fingers. She snatched them away, cursed, and stood.

'Michael, what's going on?'

'Nothing's going on.'

'I want to go home.'

'We will, soon.'

'No, now.'

'We can't. Not right now.'

'Why not?'

'We're having a picnic.'

'Michael, I want to go home.'

'No.'

'No?'

'No.'

'Are you physically going to *stop* me going home?'

'If I have to.'

'Michael, please, tell me the truth.'

I swallowed. 'You can't handle the truth.'

It did not raise much of a smile. She folded her arms. 'Are you seeing someone else?'

'No.'

'Are you dumping me?'

I did not respond. Not because that was the idea, but because the sky behind Claire had begun to brighten, and with it came a roar, which grew, and grew. Claire turned. The light suddenly became intense, illuminating the entire sky, and the noise triumphantly intense. From Cape Canaveral to Mars, a finger of flame soared upwards at a delicious angle. Without thinking, Claire put her hand out for me to hold. When I didn't grasp it she looked back. I was down on one knee, holding out her mother's engagement ring.

'Will you marry me, Claire Roth?' I asked.

21

I stood in the shadows outside Dr Lena Olson's house for at least twenty minutes, debating whether or not to go in. She had said it would be an intimate dinner party, with just two other guests, and it might do me good to have a couple of drinks, it being the night before the commemorative events were due to begin. Since arriving in Brevard I had fended off a succession of similar invitations with varying degrees of good grace. Most were from people I did not know, but who wished to know me. Some were from relatives of the deceased. I turned these down despite Ambrose's protestations. He went along in my place, and asked the questions I could not, and would not, and had little interest in. He took Jo-Anne with him to at least two of these, and at one was caught in a bedroom with her and asked to leave. He now sported a hickey on the other side of his neck.

I was not in Brevard to socialise and small talk; I could not properly say why I was there at all, apart from some inclination to close the circle. Standing looking at Lena's house, with the warm glow of lights within, and the dark mass of the abandoned Blue House to my left, I felt awkward and scared. I could just as easily have gone to my former home: that is, not easily at all. I had wallowed in painful memories for a decade; if I slipped in there in the dark, I would surely drown in them. I had agreed to attend Lena's dinner party because she did not accept the bullshit excuses I had given everyone else. She told me it was happening, I should be there, and it would be a waste of a good steak if I wasn't. I did not know her well, but I felt I knew her well enough to predict that her other guests would not be intrusive or anything other than pleasant company. It was just the physical act of walking up those steps, of crossing from the darkness into the light. I had been in one too long, and was fighting shy of the other.

My cell rang and Lena asked where I was.

'Outside,' I said.

She appeared at the window, and I stepped out from under a tree. 'I'll come and get you,' she said, then cut the line before I could reply. I was not a halfwit or a drunk, so I crossed the road and was up her steps before the front door opened. When it did, she looked a little surprised, but smiled warmly.

'I'm sorry I'm late,' I said. She kissed me on the cheek and I offered her the bottle of wine I'd brought.

As she took it she said: 'This is a complete disaster. Neil and Terry have cancelled and the steaks look slightly green.'

'Green in a steak is not good,' I said.

Lena was nervous and I was awkward. As a result we both drank too much. It wasn't a bad thing. She kept apologising – for the steak, for the décor, for the fact that the house was still coming down with food and flowers which relatives, friends and patients had brought following her father's death and which were now largely on the turn.

'It's just been hectic at the surgery – but look at this place. What was I thinking, having a dinner party when I haven't even time to . . . Please – usually I'm much more organised.'

'It's fine,' I said. 'Please, relax.'

This, coming from me, with my leg drumming up and down and gulping down the wine like it was going out of fashion.

Eventually a calmer domesticity settled on us. We sacked the fridge and the cupboards, removing off-colour food, pouring rancid water from vases and rescuing the flowers which looked as if they might retain their petals for a few more days. As she rearranged some of these, Lena caught me looking oddly at them and asked me what the matter was, and I immediately became a little embarrassed and said nothing. But later, after a few more drinks, I confessed that the yellow flowers had reminded me of Claire; they were her favourite kind, and sometimes when I saw them, no matter where I was, I almost felt that she was right beside me. I immediately regretted saying it, because although Lena's immediate reaction was to nod sympathetically, she also looked away and the realisation dawned on me (because I was always slow on the uptake) that she had never quite gotten over her student crush on me but had suddenly understood that if anything was to happen between us, Claire would, in a sense, always be in the room. I don't mind admitting now that several times during the evening I looked at those flowers, almost willing a petal to fall off, as a weak indication that some manifestation of Claire might indeed be with us.

As the wine went down, our boldness went up. We sat side by side on a comfortable sofa. We ate – but mainly cheesecake. I said to her, 'So how come you're not married?'

'Nearly was, didn't work out.'

'How long were you together?'

'Five years. At medical school. He didn't want to move to Hicksville. Or, as it turned out, he didn't want to move with *me* to Hicksville. I heard he moved to somewhere even smaller than Hicksville.'

'I'm sorry.'

'I'm not.'

'So, no one here?'

'I think they're scared to ask. They put my daddy up on a pedestal, and now he's gone they've put me up there as well.'

I nodded, then spoke with cod gravity. 'It's lonely for us pedestal-dwellers.'

'I'm not a nun, Michael Ryan.'

'I should hope not.'

'Only the men I go for are not the men who go for me. How frustrating is that?'

'Tell me about it. The men I go for are exactly like that.'

She punched me playfully. 'What about you? Have you been celibate for the past ten years?'

I nodded mournfully for several moments. Then laughed. 'No, of *course* not.'

'Elaborate, please.'

'No.'

'A girl in every port?'

'No. Not *every* port.'

'But some ports?'

'One or two. And not just ports. Places of historic interest, and big industrial cities. I've travelled widely.'

'But nobody who you've wanted to settle down with?'

'Not settle down, no.'

'Why not?'

I shrugged. 'I get dumped a lot.'

'Really. Don't they know who you are?'

'Who am I?'

'You wrote *Space Coast*.'

'It was long ago and far away. I think only in Brevard am I invited to dinner parties.' Lena pouted. 'Sorry. Not you. The others. This is nice.'

'Nice cheesecake. Please don't tell.'

'Who could I tell?'

'The girls in every port. And even those in places of hishtorical interest.' She tried again. 'Historical. God, when you can hear yourself slur, you're really in trouble.'

'It's okay,' I said, 'where that girl was, that's how they pronounce historical. It was a city of hishtorical interest, it shurely was.'

Lena giggled delightfully. 'Don't make fun,' she said.

'I'm not, I'm chertainly not.'

'People in glass houses shouldn't throw stones.'

'*Glash* houses? Is that some new kind of—'

'Stop!' Her eyes were bright.

I pulled her gently towards me and kissed her softly on the lips. Then once more.

We parted.

134

Lena looked at me for a long time. Then she said, 'I'll make coffee.'

I changed the music. I looked at her framed certificates on the wall. She was gone for a long while. When I joined her in the kitchen I noted that the vase of yellow flowers she had placed in the middle of the table was gone. She was standing looking out of the window.

'Claire,' I said.

She turned. 'I'm not Claire.'

'Christ,' I said.

I walked out of the kitchen, through the lounge and out of the front door. Then I walked back through the front door, across the lounge and into the kitchen.

'I'm sorry,' I said. 'Schlip of the tongue.'

She did not smile.

'I'll go,' I said.

I went.

22

The preparations for the wedding of Mr Michael Ryan to Miss Claire Roth were planned with commendable efficiency by the latter, but mostly executed by the former. Claire had to work by day, whereas my novel was done, and besides photocopying and posting it to prospective publishers there wasn't much else for me to do. It was way too early to think about my next book, and despite continued hints from Joe about working on the paper, I had no intention of capitulating. I was mentally drained by *Space Coast*. I wanted to chill. Claire, obviously, had other ideas. We may not have had much money, but Joe knew a lot of people and was owed a lot of favours. Between the three of us, everything began to take shape.

I suggested that the ceremony take place on the beach, and Claire rolled her eyes. We would be married by Rev. Richard Schulze, in the picket white church at the top of Brevard Main Street on 4 April. Neither of us was particularly religious, and he knew it and did not seem to mind. Joe was a regular. Dick Schulze was a bear of a man. He had a kind word for just about everyone, usually delivered without the kind of clammy piety we expect from our priests. He took a look at our guest list and the traditional left-right division of the families and said, 'If this was the *Titanic*, she would roll over. Either you find yourself some friends, Michael, or we're going to need a rethink.' On my side, there was only me. 'And what about your best man?'

I had no best man. I looked at Claire. 'Would Joe do it?'

'He's giving me away,' said Claire.

'Ah.'

'You don't have to have a best man,' said Dick.

Claire looked at me.

'Yes, I do,' I said.

Later, Claire shouted, 'Why not?!'

'Because I hardly know him!'

'You hardly know anyone!'

'That's not my fault! I'm always with you!'

'You need a best man! He's the only man you know!'

'Claire, I can't just—'

'Yes, you can! This has to be perfect! I'm only doing it once!'

Which was all I needed to hear.

'Yesterday,' Paul de Luca was saying, 'this drunk came in, causing hassle – tough guy, you know? Kicked him with one of these babies,' he lifted one of his titanium feet, 'broke his kneecap. He cried like a baby. I felt like *The Terminator*.'

'You sound like exactly the kind of guy I need for a best man.'

He laughed.

'I'm serious,' I said.

'Me?'

'You.'

'Why me?'

'Why not?'

'I don't know anything about you.'

'That's okay. I'll write your speech. It'll sound like we've known each other since the cradle.'

'You really don't have anyone else?' I shook my head. 'That's a pretty sad state of affairs.'

We both nodded at that for a while.

'Claire would very much like you to be there.'

His eyes seemed a little brighter. Getting closer to me would necessarily bring him closer to Claire. When you're in love, every little helps.

'Your best man?'

'My best man.'

'With the titanium feet. Just like in *Forrest Gump*.'

I nodded. 'Just like in *Forrest Gump*.' Which, I suppose, made me Forrest.

'You're a good guy, Michael. And we're the only two writers in Brevard, aren't we?'

'Yes, we are.'

'And writers should stick together. Even though I have never read a word you have written, mainly because you won't let me, I know that you are a writer, and one day, if you keep at it, you will be right up there with me. It will be a very great honour to be your best man. I will have to buy new shoes.'

Paul was full of boundless confidence on his own territory – the video store – but outside of it he was still a little gunshy when it came to his feet. Which is why, a couple of weeks later, I was with him in a Payless Shoe Store. I was there to offer moral support, and to get my own wedding shoes. We were served by a seventeen-year-old-boy with bad skin who couldn't take his eyes off the titanium feet and was foolish enough to ask why Paul bothered with socks when his feet clearly couldn't sweat. My best man was just ripping into him about minding his own god-damn business when he suddenly lost track of what he was saying, and just waved the boy away. The change in attitude was enough for me to ask him if he was feeling all right, and he responded by asking me to fetch him another pair of shoes. He pointed towards a shelf at the back of the store.

I said, 'Get them yourself.'

'Please,' he said. 'My feet are sore.'

I looked at him. There was a bead of sweat on his brow, and he was avoiding eye-contact. Maybe he wasn't well. And, also, I didn't want to fall out with the only best man in town so close to the ceremony, particularly over something so trivial. So I walked across and picked up the pair I thought he had indi-cated, then held them up and called back, 'This them?' as I turned.

Paul wasn't looking. He was talking to Tommy Ford.

I understood immediately that Paul had sent me to the back of the store in an attempt to keep me out of the way, and in truth there was a small temptation to duck down amongst the racks of cheap shoes. But I just couldn't do it. Bob, you will know, I am a writer, not a fighter, but I was going to marry Claire come hell or high water, and I was going to be living in Brevard. I had no intention of spending the rest of my life hiding from Tommy Ford. So I took a deep breath and walked back over.

'Hello, Tommy,' I said.

He looked around, a smile already forming, then saw it was me. The smile didn't disappear. It grew wider.

'Chapters,' he said. He put out his hand. 'I understand congratulations are in order.'

I grasped it. He squeezed. I squeezed. 'Thank you, yes.'

'When's the big day?'

'April.' I was deliberately vague about the precise date. 'Are you back for long?'

'Just the weekend. Thinking about calling over to see my girl.'

My girl. You could interpret it several ways, but he knew what he meant, and I knew what he meant, and I wasn't rising to the bait.

'She'd like that,' I said.

It wasn't a lie, exactly. Claire hadn't had a falling-out with Tommy. In fact, I hadn't even told her that he'd warned me to get out of town. I just didn't want her worrying. She knew what he was like, but she still had a soft spot for him. At least part of her believed that if she found real true love, he would eventually give his blessing. Good girls find bad boys fascinating. It's a fact. And sometimes they delude themselves that they can change them.

Tommy was buff and bronzed and I knew he was itching for trouble, just knew. He just had too much class to let things kick off in a shoe shop. He would wait to do it under the cover of darkness.

I have to admit, my mind wasn't too much on the shoes after

that. Paul and Tommy were old buddies, but their small talk was awkward, and after a couple of minutes Tommy was off. We shook hands again. I watched him cross the road outside and climb into a jeep. As it drove past I saw the two guys from the band in the back and the bank security guard behind the wheel. It was the first time I'd seen them all together like that, but of course it meant nothing then. The robbery was still several months down the line.

Thinking about calling over to see my girl.

What if he meant right now?

No, Claire was at work. I was pretty certain he wouldn't venture into the bank. But she would be going home for lunch, just as she always did. Tommy would probably know that. I phoned her from the sidewalk and said I'd meet her outside work in half an hour. She said she couldn't wait to see the shoes. Then I drove Paul back to the video store. We didn't say much. When we arrived I kept the engine running. Paul didn't move.

'You should be careful,' he said.

'I'm always careful.'

'I'm serious.'

'So am I.'

'I've heard things, Michael.'

'I don't want to know, Paul. Sometimes, ignorance is bliss.'

'And sometimes it's lethal.'

I smiled at him. 'Paul, you're my best man. You'll protect me.'

He snorted.

I took Claire to lunch. I told her about Tommy. She said she knew. He'd called her cell phone. She recognised the number and allowed it to go to voicemail. She let me hear it. 'Hey, darlin',' Tommy purred, 'I hear you're getting hitched. Looking forward to it.'

23

Next morning, I had the mother-in-law of all hangovers. Ambrose lay in the bed opposite, smiling with satisfaction while I, unable to make it as far as the bathroom, dry retched into a half-empty KFC bucket. Apparently I had purchased it and the half-empty quart of whiskey that sat on the bedside table on the way home from Lena's abortive dinner party, but there was no memory.

When I lay back, caked in sweat, my shirt and jacket stuck fast and crumpled to hell, Ambrose said: 'Big day, Michael, you better get your act together.' He shook his head and laughed. 'What a state you were in. Would have undressed you myself, but didn't want you getting the wrong idea.' He caressed his wounded neck to emphasise where his predilections *definitely* lay. Soon he went out for breakfast, telling me he'd be back at twelve to pick me up in time for the service.

The service.

At the church where we were married, performed by the minister who married us. Imported, special, just for today.

Dick Schulze had moved to several parishes in different states in the ten years since the events at the First National, but he'd kept in touch with many of his former congregation. He had jumped at the chance to return to conduct the service and the dedication afterwards in the Memorial Garden. I had no particular desire to meet him, although it was probably inevitable. I was not on speaking terms with God, or His agents here on

143

earth. Last time I'd seen Dick, I'd thrown him against that wall in the morgue.

Lena.

It came back to me then that I had kissed her.

And the name I had called her.

Then run away.

I had her number. But what could I possibly say? 'You're very nice, but you're not *her*'? 'You're lovely, but you can *never* be her'? No. I would do what I had done before. There *was* a girl in many ports, but the dumping was almost always done by me. I know now that it was because I could not connect. I could not reveal. I could not communicate the incommunicable. I knew then that I would cut Lena off before anything could happen.

Cut and run, always. Cut and run.

The pain in my head was merely the physical evidence of the sheer folly of returning to Brevard, lacking even the shaky justification of a fool's errand. I'd allowed myself to be talked into it, and while I accepted that I had certain responsibilities to fulfil now that I was there, that would be the end of it. I would pull myself together, perform my civic duty and then get the hell out of town. I did not wish to re-establish relationships or build new ones. This was the final farewell. Life could start again, somewhere else. I was done with Brevard.

I showered. I shaved without inflicting too much damage. I had, at least, a suit hanging in the cupboard. I finally made it downstairs, aware both that I was running late and that Ambrose had failed to return. As I walked up Main Street I called him on his cell. He apologised. He was already at the church. Possibly it was deliberate. Perhaps he thought it would make a better story if I didn't show, or if I arrived late and as I began to walk down the aisle all heads turned and the good Reverend paused in silent condemnation.

That's him. Who does he think he is?

Fact is, they were running late. When I arrived at the church-yard, hundreds of people were still milling about outside. It seemed like the entire town had turned out, not just the relatives, but their friends, neighbours, every old resident who had been shocked by the events, every child weaned on the horror of it all and who had remained fascinated into adulthood, every charitable organisation and ladies' group, every civil servant, a representative of every city department, the press, the curious, the idle.

There was the Mayor, holding court; Adam from the newspaper; Sheriff Newton, Deputy Sheriff Newton; Ambrose and Jo-Anne; Dr Lena Olson. She saw me, I think, and looked away. I lost myself in the crowd. I didn't want to talk to anyone. I just wanted it over. Dick Schulze was in the doorway, shaking hands and pumping shoulders. A man I took to be the regular minister was beside him, looking a little peeved that he wasn't getting all the attention. I nodded and smiled where required, but continued to look purposeful in my circular momentum. At one end of the churchyard, standing by herself, I saw Grace Shaw, Lawrence's mother. I felt apart from it all. She *was* apart from it all. I went up and reintroduced myself.

'I know who you are,' she said. 'People are looking at me, but I got an invitation. I lost family as well.'

I didn't think people were actually looking at her; or, if they were, it was because in a small town everyone looks at everyone.

'Don't like this new pastor much,' Grace went on, nodding towards the church. 'Rev. Schulze used to listen. I said to him, "Rev. Schulze, sometimes I feel like my boy is right here at my shoulder", and Rev. Schulze used to say, "Maybe he is, Grace". I said this to this new guy and he looks at me like I've a screw loose. Rev. Schulze, he always had the time of day. Always trying to get me to call him Dick, but I ain't calling no reverend Dick, that's for sure.'

When I turned from her, Mayor Heise was immediately in my face, with an official photographer at his side, insisting on a picture, and when others saw me posing they crowded around: two news crews, an agency photographer, and a dozen others with disposable cameras and cell phones. I was *Space Coast*. As I stood, unsmiling, I wondered what Claire would have made of it. She had an admirable ability to remain poker-faced in embarrassing situations while flashing me a look that reduced me to hysterics. Then she would upbraid me for my behaviour. I often tried to work it the other way round, but she never fell for it, not once. What I would have given for that irreverence there and then: for her to puncture the po-faced gravity of that broiling afternoon and let me take the blame for it. But she wasn't there, and we were supposed to be remembering why.

'Michael,' Dick Schulze said as I finally entered the church. 'Michael.'

'Dick.'

'It's so good to see you. Nobody was sure if you would come.'

'Me included.'

'Can we talk later?'

'Yes, of course. I'll be at the dinner.'

It wasn't quite what he meant. He was a warm man, but he believed what he believed and I suspected he wanted to judge the condition of my soul.

Three rows had been reserved at the front for the direct relatives of the deceased. Two spaces had been provided for me, in the presumption that I would bring a partner and, true enough, he was sitting there, talking away. When I sat beside him, he continued right on. I stared straight ahead, but I couldn't help but be aware of what he was saying. Apparently we were cousins, and had always been close, and I was on a journey of self-discovery, and I was due on *Letterman* the following week. In return, these poor, fraught, never-to-recover people spilled their secrets. How they had found out; about the dreams their partners, sons or daughters would never fulfil. How they had clung to life. How they had been robbed of justice by the shooting to death of the bank robbers.

Ambrose turned to other relatives, behind. They had long ago forgiven the killers. They thought Sheriff Newton had been given no choice but to kill them. It was lucky he was there at all that day; he could just as easily have been on the other side of town. What if he hadn't been almost right outside when it happened? How many more innocent people might have been killed? Didn't the Sheriff get taken down to the State Capitol at Tallahassee and have a medal struck for him? He never talked about it but he was a god-damn hero.

Ambrose sucked it out of them. I kept my eyes to the front. Something didn't look quite right. Dick was there, almost ready to start. The organist was seated, turning the pages of her music book. There were very many flowers, including, naturally, yellow ones. As I watched, a petal fell from one. It floated lazily to the floor. I walked forward, crouched and picked it up. I held it in my fist and returned to my seat. People were looking at me.

Then I realised what was wrong. It was a funeral without coffins.

Something went wrong in the planning. The Memorial Garden wasn't large enough to take everyone who had been issued with invitations. And some who hadn't been issued with invitations felt they should have been and squeezed in anyway. The dedication was relayed through an ancient PA which crackled so much that Dick's words were rendered indistinct. I was prevailed upon to unveil the memorial plaque, together with Sheriff Newton. We shook hands before it and had our photos taken. There was applause. It seemed inappropriate and loud. Everybody seemed much too pleased with themselves. Maybe it was the hangover. As I stood there willing it to be over I opened and closed my palm, examining the petal as the colour sweated out of it, into my skin.

And then it *was* over.

As I pushed myself through the crowd and out onto the blocked-off road, I saw the ass of a bank manager standing in the doorway opposite, his uniformed staff grouped around him like a silent choir. I was looking for the doubtful comfort of Ambrose Jeffers when a familiar voice said: 'Didn't you write *Space Coast*?'

I turned. 'Doctor Lena Olson,' I said.

'I'm sorry about last night.'

'No. I'm sorry.'

'Everyone is going back to the Comfort Inn for coffee,' she said.

'Not me.'

She nodded. 'What're you going to do?'

'Buy you a drink.'

'Okay,' she said.

24

My wedding to Claire Roth was the best day of my life. Everything was perfect. *Claire* was perfect. Joe gave *me* a hug. Paul, as arranged, when asked to produce the ring, delved into his pocket and produced a Pluto fridge magnet. Claire roared. Everyone else looked at us as if we were bonkers. Then he revealed the ring. I slipped it onto her finger. We kissed.

In this day and age it is wrong to be too proprietorial, but I can't help it. Claire was *mine*. Relationships can be like books in a library; eventually there's a price to pay if you hold on to them too long. But Claire was like a gift-set presented at Sunday School, mine to treasure for ever. Bob, I can talk endless amounts of crap about how I felt about Claire that day, and after, and since, to this moment in the motel room, with the medication buzzing around my head, knowing what is coming. But none of it does her justice. Claire was Claire was Claire. Yes, I know the passage of time has caused me to place her on a pedestal. We fought often, and bickered, and we both said cruel things and thought them, but at the end of the day we were a perfect, perfect match. As we said our *I do*'s I could scarcely believe my luck. What's more, Claire genuinely didn't seem affected by the fact that I was on crutches, or that there was a police car outside.

If that day was perfect, those leading up to it were not. There are the usual traumas that precede a marriage, and we suffered those. But there were other things which were not of our own making. It started with the flowers. It was lucky that she'd ordered from a friend's store downtown. A week before the big day, someone phoned and cancelled the order, telling the assistant there that the wedding was off. Bryan was annoyed at the cancellation, but also sad for Claire. Fortunately he phoned to commiserate. Of course, it wasn't off. We could easily have dismissed it as a misunderstanding, as crossed wires (assistant was Polish, and his English not great), except for the fact that the caller had been specific about the names and date. He had identified himself as a family friend dealing with an embarrassing situation. With no little trepidation we began checking out our other arrangements, and discovered that the wedding cars had been changed to a different day and the reception at the Radisson had been brought forward by three hours.

We knew who it was, of course.

Or, I did.

Claire was for giving him the benefit of the doubt. She said there were lots of jealous people out there, and she had a point. She was lovely and amazing, and not everyone likes to see lovely and amazing people happy, particularly when they themselves have been rejected at some point. She wanted to phone him anyway, just to see how he'd react. I forbade her. Which, of course, was like a red rag to a bull. She phoned. Tommy's number was dead. She asked around and was told he was off on another cruise – but I had tasted his boots, I knew he was still here. There didn't seem much point in going to the police, since they were hardly going to drop everything to trace what amounted to a few nuisance calls. We just agreed that whoever it was wasn't going to ruin our day. We enlisted Joe to monitor the arrangements on a daily basis.

In the meantime I wrote a speech for Paul. I emerged quite well from it. But he was a writer himself, and wanted changes. In the absence of any organised stag night – I didn't have enough male friends to justify one – we agreed to meet up in McDaid's grill and do the work over a few beers two nights before my wedding. Bob, I'll tell you how mad it got – I took the car. That is, not at all. I wasn't interested in getting spectacularly drunk, there was no desire at all to throw up some last defiant salute to freedom. If I was walking into slavery, it was with eyes wide open. Bring it on.

The same semi-sobriety did not extend to Paul. He was still on a lot of medication, so he got drunk quickly, and then sick, and then drank some more and asked to go home. I drove him out to the video store which, although advertised as being open twenty-four hours, actually opened only *when I damn well feel like it*. There wasn't another similar establishment for thirty miles. I think, at certain times, there were a lot of frustrated men running around Brevard.

That night the neon was switched off, the store locked up and the car park empty. He had a basic studio at the rear and I managed to get him in there without him being sick again. He immediately lay on the unmade bed and fell asleep. I wasn't sure what the protocol was with titanium legs – whether to remove them or not. I decided to leave them in place in case he tried to get up in the middle of the night thinking they were on and fell over and killed himself.

Taking the keys, I went back through the store. I stood in the middle of the sales floor for a minute and laughed: my stag night, just me and two thousand porn videos. Then I locked the door from the outside and pushed the keys back through the mail slot. I stepped down to my car, but before I could get it open I was blinded by headlights. A door opened and shut. I shouted across, 'It's closed!' out of politeness, then another door opened. Two, then three figures were coming towards me, dark silhouettes, and I thought, This isn't good.

I would like to say that I fought them off. That I had secretly trained as a Ninja. Often since, I have thought of what I could have done. But the fact is, I did nothing beyond raise my hands against the first blow from what was probably a baseball bat, and for my trouble had two fingers broken. I was clubbed to the ground and beaten.

They did not say anything, and I in turn remained silent. I

did not try to reason or beg for help or cry or scream as they flitted in and out of the harsh beams of light. I curled up in a ball and they did what they did. I did not see their faces or their shoes. The punishment was coming in but I hardly seemed to feel it. I remember thinking, Be patient, it'll be over soon. Then I would get up and dust myself down. Except when it came to it, and as they roared away, and I tried to get up, I could not. There was something up with my leg. It was pitch dark out there, and I couldn't see; all I knew was the pain that had seemed trivial was now massive. Later I would learn that there was a bone sticking out.

I lay for a long time. My cell phone rang. And then what must have been the store phone somewhere behind me. My cell rang again. And again. I just couldn't get to it. Then I must have blacked out. Sometime later my eyes opened, with light starting to show in the sky and that phone ringing inside again, but then I heard vague, muffled curses and a minute later the jangle of keys as the door was unlocked. Then, from Paul: 'Jesus fucking Christ. I'll phone you back.'

At that point Claire thought I was dead. She told me later she had screamed at him not to cut the line, but too late. She raced there. She beat the ambulance, even though the hospital at Merritt Island was less than a mile away.

She held my hand, and it brought some brief measure of clarity. She said, 'Baby, I love you.'

'Jesus fucking Christ,' said Paul.

I woke in the hospital, surgery over, my leg held fast in a metal contraption, yellow flowers by the bed and a Deputy Sheriff outside the door. When a nurse came to check my vitals and saw that I was awake, she ushered the police officer in. He asked me if I knew who had done it.

I told him it was a very complicated suicide attempt.

They'd given me a lot of morphine.

25

They do say that the only real certainties are death and taxes, but I'm not so sure. Just as tax isn't the same for everyone, why not also death? Perhaps there are a hundred different categories of death and it's just a question of which one you fall into. Or maybe, with the right accountant, you can avoid it altogether.

And you know something? I wouldn't change a thing.

The path that led inexorably to my own demise was really laid that afternoon, after the service in the Memorial Garden. In the six hours we had to kill before the official dinner, Lena and I repaired to McDaid's Char Bar and Grill and Jo-Anne plied us with drinks. I don't recall paying for any of them, although I do have a vague memory of offering to buy the bar. Bob, I've so much money in the bank, I could have bought the *town*. I don't expect anyone to have any sympathy for someone with as much money as I have/had, so I try and forget about it. Besides, I've been gone so long, you've probably worked out a way to siphon it all off. Only joking. What *is* certain is that large amounts of alcohol, taken in the company of an attractive, funny woman, are not good for you if you've had your heart broken and have spent a miserable decade on the road. If I had been Lena, I would have given me a good slap. But, instead, she did something else. An hour before we were due at the Radisson – yes, scene also of my wedding reception – Lena took me home to her house and put me to bed. Us, to bed.

We were drunk.

We made love.

It was lovely.

That's all you need to know.

It flew in the face, of course, of everything I'd decided about Lena – but those thoughts had come in the abstract; being in her presence again was something entirely different. And also, there was the booze. Then some more. We did not stop drinking. It is crass and boorish to say that going to bed drunk with Lena was a way of killing the pain, but it is true. There was more to it, of course. And for her part there was certainly more to it than what is euphemistically known as a sympathy screw. This was not a doctor's bedside manner taken to the nth degree. There was definitely a connection, and in another life it might have been *the* connection, but it was not, it *could* not be. It was just absolutely right at the time. Look at that day: it was death, then death, then love, then right back to death. I treasure that time with Lena. I'm just sorry for what followed, and I take that sorrow with me.

The problems started almost immediately upon our arrival at the Radisson. There had been a certain decorum at the church service and again at the Garden, but later, people's inhibitions began to recede in direct proportion to the amount of alcohol consumed. That meant they started asking questions of each other and of themselves which might normally have remained unspoken, or which they had unknowingly internalised since the time of the robbery until released by the drink. Many of these questions and comments festered and grew on the main dining floor – they involved who did what on that blood-soaked day, why someone didn't do more, or made that decision, or made this comment. I know that Grace Shaw was driven from the room in tears. In retrospect I know that at least some of it was sparked off by Ambrose asking inappropriate questions. The top table, where I was obliged to sit with the organising committee, the Mayor, Sheriff Newton and the newspaper editor Adam Harrington, was not immune, and most of it came from me. Lena, being part of the committee, was there, but at the far end. She kept looking at me and smiling, and I tried my best to reciprocate, but the truth is I was growing angrier and angrier as the night wore on. It was mostly to do with Sheriff Newton, and partly to do with my consumption of red wine. It wasn't what he said. It was what he *didn't* say. The Mayor lavished praise upon him, paid tribute to his role in the events of that bloody day and even raised the efficiency of his marksmanship. The Sheriff responded with modest gestures and shrugs, but to me, in my state, they appeared both calculating and haughty. I thought that he was basking in it, and probably had been for ten years, when, with a little more application, the events of that day might have been avoided completely.

'If you'd arrested him the night he beat me up, none of it would have happened,' I heard myself say. 'They would all be alive. My *wife* would be alive.'

It rather quieted the table.

'Mr Ryan . . .' the Mayor anxiously began.

'Every single one of them would be with us. But then again, you might have missed out on your medal.'

'Michael . . .' It was Lena from the other end of the table.

'No, let him talk.'

Sheriff Newton had the kind of a face that erred towards pomposity. His look was not helped by a military buzz cut. In others it can emphasise the strong cut of a jaw or the bold intelligence of a brow, but in Newton it focused attention on his double chin and unkempt eyebrows. Others may not judge his features so harshly, or may question their relevance to his character, but I think everything forms you. He was a smalltown cop who had once been presented with a chance of glory, and he'd grabbed it with both hands. But, like the moonwalkers so long ago, the Sheriff discovered that afterwards there was nowhere else to go. He'd missed the limelight these past ten years and now, thrust back into it, he didn't want anything spoiling his second coming.

Everyone was looking at me, willing me to stop. But of course I couldn't.

'If you'd gone after Tommy Ford, arrested him then, he'd have been in prison. There would have been no robbery. Nobody would have died.'

'Michael, by the time we tracked him down he was out of state. He was in international waters.'

'So?'

'So, we couldn't arrest him, not without physical evidence or witnesses. Sure we wanted to talk to him, but you can't go out of state on a hunch. He looked sympathetically across the table at me. 'My hands were tied.'

I snapped out, almost without thinking. 'They weren't tied on the day of the robbery, were they?'

The Mayor tried to intervene again. 'Mr Ryan – Michael – please, we're here to pay tribute . . .'

'Pay tribute to what – the carnage? To a bunch of trigger-happy cops?'

I was aware, somewhere, that this wasn't strictly fair, that the police on the day could not have prevented the deaths of the innocents – Claire and the others had been shot down before law enforcement arrived – but I have also always believed that they could have saved the guilty and allowed us a longer revenge. So I said it. They'd shot first and asked questions only the dead could answer. We would never understand why, if they had an inside man, they had chosen to carry out the robbery on the one day in the month when there was the least amount of money there to be stolen; why the robbers had visited such violence upon the staff and customers when everyone was co-operating. It all came out. Only, as Lena told me later, it came out slurred and broken, with me standing, pointing, slobbering and staggering. I knocked over my glass, and in trying to save it, knocked over a bottle which crashed onto the floor and brought a cheer from the diners behind.

I walked out of the dining room. Or, I *fell* out, and into the rest room. I turned on the cold water too hard and it sprayed out, soaking my suit jacket and shirt, but I wasn't inclined to turn it off. In fact, I turned others on as well. Then I shut myself in a stall. I punched its walls. I was done with Brevard and its ghosts. As soon as the world steadied, I was going home. Except, of course, I had no home. I had a room and a bed and a pillow where I placed my head occasionally, and it could be in any one of fifty states or a hundred and fifty countries. I didn't know then, of course, that actually, I was home, because home is where the heart is. All I knew was anger and bile.

The hiss of the cold water gradually stopped as the taps were turned off one by one.

'Michael?'

The water was seeping in under the stall door, and I followed its meandering stream back to the puddle in which Lena's shoes stood.

'What?'

'What's *wrong* with you?'

'Take a wild guess.'

'You just exploded. We had such a nice afternoon. Will you come out? There's going to be speeches.'

'I don't want to hear any *fucking* speeches.'

'Michael, you're the guest of honour. Don't let these people down. You mean a lot to them.'

'Yeah. *Right.*'

'Please, Michael.'

'They're all so *fucking* full of themselves. There's going to be fucking *dancing* later on. Dancing! They're dancing on our fucking graves!'

'They're just trying to move on, Michael.'

'Right!'

'Michael, you've all had a difficult day. Everyone is trying to wind down. We've had a nice meal, a few drinks, and if people want to dance – well, that's their choice, isn't it? I'd rather dance than sit feeling sorry for myself on a toilet bowl.'

That sat in the air for a while.

Then: 'I'm going now, Michael. I'm going home. Thanks a lot.'

I watched her feet splash towards the door. It opened, and they disappeared.

I sat for about three seconds.

Christ!

'Lena!'

I charged, suddenly panicked, out of the stall, but as I turned for the door, my left foot slipped in the spillage and I fell sideways. The side of my head cracked off the sink. It was a sudden and intense pain and I must have blacked out, perhaps only for a second, but when I next became aware of myself I was on the floor, mesmerised by the sight of my own blood floating past.

26

There was blood caked on my pillow and a small bump under the matted hair on the left side of my skull, but I attributed most of the pain I was suffering to my second hangover in two days. The only difference between my drunken performances was that with this latest, sad effort I had considerably upped the embarrassment factor. I had let myself down in front of an audience. All I could thank providence for was that I would never have to see any of those people again. The social elite of Brevard could talk and gossip about me all they wished, I was gone. It was shortly after dawn. I could pack up the car and be on my way before anybody else surfaced. I would have no qualms at all about leaving Ambrose behind and just disappearing to Nova Scotia or Azerbaijan. I had the money, I had the time, and I definitely had the inclination. He could write what he wanted. I doubted if I would get to read it in Morocco or Phuket or wherever else I washed up. This decision to flee was made simpler by the fact that once again Ambrose had failed to return. His affair with Jo-Anne was really quite intense, and, I thought at that point, was the only positive thing to come out of the entire misadventure.

I took some painkillers then staggered under a hot shower and had several of those *oh no* flashbacks you get after drinking excessively. *Me* – screaming across a car park after Lena as she drove off. *Me* – catching a blood-spattered glimpse of myself in a liquor-store mirror and understanding with sudden and extreme clarity why I was being refused service. *Me* – being sick, folded down in a shop doorway and an old man patting my shoulder and telling me I'd be okay.

The pills did their work, and by the time I'd shaved and packed up – including rolling my bloodstained Armani suit in a ball and stuffing it in my case – I was feeling more positive. It was my life and I was beholden to nobody. I couldn't claim to be a wiser man for my experiences, insofar that I had known all along that any attempt to confront the past or *close the circle* was all very well in theory, but ultimately doomed to failure; but perhaps that was in fact the lesson of it – *listen to yourself*.

I was certainly not doomed to spend any further time with Ambrose Jeffers. When I went down to the lobby to settle the bill to date, I didn't tell them I was checking out. I would leave my card open for Ambrose to enjoy himself with Jo-Anne for another few days. After that he was on his lonesome. I was taking the car and I was heading north, or south, or west. Any direction, in fact, that took me away from Brevard.

I nodded through the usual mundane questions about enjoying my stay while they ran out the paperwork. The morning shift had now started, so hopefully they wouldn't have been aware of the state I had been in when I returned to the hotel the night before. I signed without at first looking at the breakdown, and only then did I realise that the printout ran to several perforated pages. I had used the mini-bar liberally, and made a few phone calls, but this seemed extraordinarily long. I studied the itemised items, then turned it for the clerk to examine.

'I don't think this is mine,' I said.

She was petite, with light freckles upon a face that blushed easily. She checked her computer and confirmed that it was. The print-out was dominated by a list of items identified only as Video C. 'I haven't watched any movies,' I stated, but even as I said it, jabbing my finger at the paper between us, the truth was dawning.

'Mr Ryan, I'm sorry, but our system . . .'

Somehow, in our brief few days in Brevard, Ambrose had

found time to watch eight different pornographic movies, and as far as I knew was planning to let me pick up the tab.

'It's okay,' I said quickly. 'My mistake.'

She nodded, then without looking up said, 'As you see, the titles of the movies don't appear on the print-out. It saves embarrassment.'

Now my face was as red as hers. I had never seen her before and might never see her again, but suddenly I desperately wanted to explain. She might once have been a devoted fan of *Space Coast* but in future would only picture me as some kind of obsessive masturbator. So in an effort to release us both from purgatory I said, 'I don't watch them, honestly. It's the guy I share with, Ambrose. He's at it all night long.' I cleared my throat. 'I'm not gay.'

She just looked at me.

I drove through Brevard, not at all sorry to see the back of it. Claire had been its only attraction. It was just another tourist town on Florida's Atlantic coast, too hot for comfort in summer, and mostly too hot for comfort at any other time of the year as well. The only real respite from the heat was the occasional hurricane. All you could say about Brevard was that it was *close* to somewhere that had once been famous but whose grandeur was long faded: Cape Canaveral and man's quest for Space.

Except there were loose ends. I drove to Alzheimer's Alley and the Elm Lodge Seniors Village and went in to say goodbye to Joe.

I stood at the end of the bed, just looking at him as he lay bloated and unresponsive while the machines surrounding him continued to control his every function. I touched his cool hand and bent to his ear. 'It's me, Joe,' I whispered. 'I'm sorry, Joe, I should have done better.'

I turned and left without looking back.

Then to Paul de Luca's adult video store.

I'd made no attempt to contact Paul during my ten years

away from Brevard, nor since my return. I had intended to, but kept putting it off. He was a good guy, my best man, but a more accurate description might have been my *only* man. Although we were both writers, after a fashion, I knew all along that he was more interested in Claire than me. I also knew that in the few days before I flew the coop after Claire's murder, I did not hear from him. I was too caught up in my own misery to regard it as some kind of betrayal, his not being there to offer support, but later I came to realise that he was devastated by her death and quite possibly blamed me for it i.e. if I'd never come to Brevard it wouldn't have happened. I suppose the one thing worse than unrequited love is unrequited love where the subject of that love is murdered. Unrequited love is all about hope, and with Claire's death, hope was gone. But he was still my best man, and now that I was leaving town I felt suddenly guilty about not getting in touch. I had thought he would pop up at one or other of the events of the previous day, but there'd been no sign of him. Maybe he didn't feel the need. Perhaps he'd gotten over her and was now happily married, and a successful porn baron and didn't want to rake up bad memories.

Maybe we would punch each other on the shoulder and hug. His store was set back from the highway, but advertised by a large red neon sign. The sign was still there, but it was switched off. When I drove into the lot it was weed-strewn and the store was shuttered. I parked and approached the door. Letters and catalogues spilled out of the letter box. I knocked anyway, without response, before walking around the back. There was a beat-up truck parked there, and beyond it a dilapidated mobile home. I ignored it at first, because Paul had always lived in the back of the store, so I tried peering through the windows there; but they were thick with grime and it was impossible to see anything. I was just turning towards the mobile home when there was a sudden and ferocious barking and snapping and this *thing*, this blur, came hurtling towards me, and I was so shocked I could only stand there and wait for the impact; it seemed as if its yellow, jagged teeth were mere centimetres from my throat when it gave a strangled yelp and fell to the ground at my feet and I realised it was at the end of a chain that was tethered to a pole cemented into the ground just outside the mobile's front door. My hammering heart gradually calmed, although the creature kept up its barking and snarling. It was some kind of a cross-breed, like between a Rottweiler and a black bear, with teeth a Great White would have been proud of.

'Easy, boy,' I said.

The creature fell suddenly quiet, and sat. I was just congratulating myself on my until then unheralded Dr Doolittle qualities when a voice behind me suddenly rasped: 'Private property.'

I turned to find an old man in a smart morning suit and white shirt. He was tall, patrician-looking, and not happy. The shirt collar had probably once fitted, but was now too wide for his neck.

'I was looking for Paul, he's an old—'

'Private property,' he repeated.

'I understand that, but—'

'The clue, sir, is in the word *private*.'

'I'm sure if Paul . . .' I nodded back at the mobile home and was rewarded with a brief glimpse of long, straggled hair and a beard. I expected the door to open then, but it remained resolutely closed.

'Paul!' I shouted.

No response. The dog whined.

The old man said: 'Sir, I choose not to entertain visitors. That's my right.'

I looked at him. I sighed. I held my hands up. 'All right,' I said, 'I'm going. Tell him Michael Ryan called, and I hope he's okay, and maybe next time.'

There would of course be no next time. I returned to the car. You go away, and you come back, expecting things to be the same, but they rarely are.

My final stop was the cemetery. I had sworn not to return, and I was actually half a mile past it when the thought occurred, and a further mile before I decided to act on it. Not so much for me, for him. I didn't believe she was up there, but I knew he would. You can call it sentimental bullshit if you wish, Bob. I just felt like doing it. I parked, then walked that narrow path again until I found Claire's grave. I had Joe's annotated copy of *Space Coast* with me. I knelt by her headstone and set the book down before it. 'There you go, sweetie,' I said. 'From him, to me, to you. Love you always.'

Then I walked away from her for the last of the last times.

There's a bridge across the Indian River you have to cross to get onto the I-95. Coming up to it, I got a fit of the shakes, and then the dry heaves. My head rocked and I sweated through my shirt and I had to slow right down and then pull over, with horns blasting in my ear and someone in a big rig screaming, 'Asshole!' at me. Across the road there was a group of people standing, maybe waiting for a bus. I ducked down out of view and retched again. It got so bad I couldn't raise my head above the steering wheel. I closed my eyes and willed it to pass. I tried to think of something nice and pleasant but the only thing that would come was that old man patting me on the shoulder as I threw up the previous night and telling me everything would be okay. I remembered then that he'd laughed in quiet support of my predicament. 'Youth is wasted on the young . . .' I tried to picture his face, but then I realised that I hadn't seen it at all, that I'd been too busy throwing up, my head down close to the ground, that my impression of his age was only to do with the rasp of his voice.

There was a knock on the window. I forced myself up and saw a tan uniform, too close, and then a familiar face.

'You okay, Mr Ryan?' asked Deputy Sheriff Newton, his earnest young face full of concern.

I hit the button and the glass eased down.

'Fine,' I said. He didn't flinch, exactly, but there was a little flare of the nostrils as he encountered the breath of last night's alcohol. 'A migraine.'

'You don't look so hot, Mr Ryan.'

'I'm fine, really. It'll pass. Thanks.'

'You've been sitting here an hour.'

I glanced at the clock. I had. I must have slept. It had been a false dawn, getting up too early when clearly I had still been drunk. I looked beyond Junior Newton. The people across the way were still waiting for their bus. I looked ahead to the inter-state, stretching away across the bridge, and then I retched again. Junior diplomatically looked away. When I resurfaced he suggested I went back to town and found somewhere to lie up for a few hours. It was an order as well, and he probably had a point. If all that time had passed and I still wasn't feeling any better, there was no point in even attempting to drive any further.

'Do you want I should give you a ride back?' he asked. 'You can pick up the vehicle later.'

'No, really, it's not too bad.'

I started the engine again, waited for a break in the traffic, then turned the car and headed back towards Brevard as Junior shadowed me in. I took deep, deep breaths and held them, trying desperately not to be ill again. When I pulled into the Comfort Inn car park, Junior continued on.

I reclaimed a key and returned to my room. Ambrose was lying on top of his bed, fully clothed but bleary and dishevelled.

'Just getting home?' he asked.

'No,' I said.

'House calls with the Doc?'

'No.'

'That was some performance last night.'

I lay down on the bed, facing away from him. 'Ambrose, I need to sleep.'

He was quiet for at least a minute. 'You know, I was thinking, they should hold a service and dinner like this every year. It would be fun.'

'Ambrose, I just need to sleep for a while.'

Half a minute passed.

'You put a bar on the porn.'

'Yes I did.'

27

I couldn't shift the headache, though the pain seemed to reposition itself from the all-over throb of a hangover to a frequent jabbing to the side of my head. The bump had hardened into something like a Frankenstein bolt under my skin. I asked Ambrose to go out and get me some water and fruit; he came back with a tortilla and a Diet Pepsi. I'm still not sure if he was trying to be cruel, hoping to prompt a reaction so he could write about it, or whether he was just plain dumb. Possibly it was a combination of all three. Perhaps it was frustration over not having access to the porn. When I showed him the bump he scoffed and said he had bigger zits. And it was true.

He left, I slept. I was woken by the phone. It was after eight in the evening. I'd instructed the front desk to screen my calls, but when I picked it up, this had been circumnavigated by using the house phone and, as it emerged, Dick Schulze calling every room until he got lucky. He was waiting for me in the lobby and wouldn't take no for an answer.

Eventually, I appeared. We shook hands and I told him how well he looked. He blamed it on a God-fearing lifestyle and a Bushmills before bed.

'I'll buy you dinner,' he said.

His first choice was McDaid's Char Bar and Grill. I asked for his second. He took me to Flaggs, a bar at the foot of Brevard pier. It had been a rough and ready place when I'd first come to town, and it hadn't changed. It boasted the biggest steaks in the country: they were also the toughest. There was a country and western band playing at the back, with a crowd of Hawaiian-shirted drunks singing and hollering along. They turned out to be accountants letting their collective hair down following a convention at the nearby Radisson. We took a table outside on the pier itself, with the crashing surf dulling the songs of Garth Brooks and Dwight Yoakam and the breeze fresh and calming. We drank beer.

I let him do most of the talking. He told me where he had served, and how congregations were mostly the same wherever he went i.e. ageing. We were onto dessert before I raised the subject of my behaviour at the dinner. He waved my half-formed apologies away.

'It was an emotional night,' he said, 'and not just for you. Many things were said by many people. There was at least one fist-fight. It was a good idea on paper, but I'm not sure if it turned out quite the way everyone expected. The whole day was like that.

'On the plus side, old friends met up, stories were shared, tears were shed and there was some remarkably bad dancing later on, not least by me.' He shrugged. 'Well, it's done now.'

We both watched the waves tumbling onto the sand. Not more than a few yards from where we sat, I had helped to save Paul de Luca's life. As if he was reading my thoughts Dick asked if I kept in touch with my best man.

I shook my head. 'He was conspicuous by his absence yesterday.'

'He hasn't been well.'

'What's wrong? Have his feet finally joined in with the rest of society and rejected him?'

'Maybe you should give him a call,' Dick said.

'Dick, to tell you the truth, the only reason he was my best man was because he was in love with Claire and I didn't know anyone else.'

'You were both writers.'

'After a fashion.'

'You know, after it happened, he came to see me. He was in quite a state. I'm not in the business of taking confessions, but he wanted to talk. It's amazing the connections you can make when you think about things too much: he had convinced himself that somehow, if he hadn't been saved on the beach that day, none of it would have happened. The bank robbery, the murders. He blames himself.'

'*Why?*'

'You met Claire because of him. Claire fell out with Tommy because of you. Tommy turned to the dark side because of that. Then everyone died.'

'Well, I hope you put him right.'

'I did my best. Although it's an interesting point. How different your life, for example, might have been if he'd been entirely consumed by that shark, instead of just his feet. Cause and effect. Isn't that what they say: a butterfly beats its wings in Sumatra and a building collapses in New York?'

'Ban the butterfly, that's what I say.'

'Alternatively,' Dick replied, 'perhaps it's just the Lord moving in a mysterious way.'

I gave him a long, cool look. 'You mean it might all have been for the good, the greater good?'

Dick quickly held up his hands. 'That's not a debate we need to get into right now.'

'Because there would only be one winner.'

He smiled, then shivered abruptly. 'Perhaps we should adjourn inside?'

The good Rev. Dick Schulze, as with many people who do not have a great capacity for alcohol, nevertheless insisted on drinking an awful lot of it. After we went indoors, he moved onto his preferred tipple, Bushmills. I stuck with the beer. I was already half-drunk again, but determined not to let it go further. I was leaving town the next morning, and this time a hangover wasn't going to stop me.

Around eleven, Dick began to nod off. I prodded him a couple of times, and he jerked straight before very quickly sinking back down. The third time I poked him there was no response at all. I sat quietly debating the moral dilemma of whether deserting a man in an alcoholic stupor was any more or less reprehensible for him also being a man of the cloth. I came to the somewhat superficial conclusion that if he'd been wearing his dog collar I would have stayed with him, but as he wasn't, and he was merely fast asleep, and a danger to no one, then it was quite all right for me to leave. Possibly my own alcohol intake, or top-up, had something to do with it.

Easing myself out from behind our table, I then tried to ask one of the bar ladies if she would keep an eye on him, but the music was too loud and the demand for service too great for me to make myself understood. I turned, gave Dick a final look, then started to push my way through the crowds towards the exit. As I began to descend the wooden steps outside, I stood to one side and held the door open to allow a black guy to enter. I half-recognised him from somewhere; he looked momentarily surprised, then nodded thanks.

Politeness costs nothing.

I began a leisurely stroll towards the Comfort Inn. Bob, I remember I was thinking about Ambrose, and hoping that he would be spending the night with Jo-Anne again as I intended to make another quick getaway in the morning, when I suddenly thought about the black guy again. Where *did* I know him from? He'd been wearing a baseball cap pulled down quite low, and the combined light from Flaggs's neon sign and the inside of the bar hadn't been brilliant, but there was definitely some recognition factor on both sides. Of course, I was the celebrated author of *Space Coast*, so that could have been his part of it, but where did I remember *him* from?

As I walked on, I went through as many of the events of the past few days as I could recall i.e. when I hadn't been extremely drunk – but still couldn't place him. Then I thought perhaps he was from *before* – yet he appeared quite young, perhaps mid-twenties, so he would have been a young teenager back then. The black couple in the apartment downstairs before I moved to the Blue House – did they have kids? Yes, a daughter. What about at the newspaper? Or the bakery? No. I just couldn't place him at all.

It didn't *matter*, of course, it was more just a way of killing time while I walked home, but sometimes when you have to remember something, dwelling on it only makes it harder. So I started to think about movies, and then sports, and then, being slightly inebriated, Lena and how awful it was to leave things like this. I actually took my cell out and found her number and looked at the screen, but in looking at it, it wasn't her number that I saw, it was *his* face – and suddenly I had his name and it just absolutely and literally staggered me. I actually stepped onto the road and a car blasted me and someone yelled at me for being an asshole again.

DeMarcus Hall.

Of course, it *wasn't* DeMarcus Hall. The inside man had been shot to death within the First National Bank, apparently surplus to requirements. Anyone can look like anyone, Bob, and it had been the briefest of encounters, but I'd gotten to know DeMarcus reasonably well, and even after ten years familiarity can return when prompted – and the similarity *was* uncanny. I tried to recall those newspaper articles I'd glanced at and the information about the gang Ambrose had thoughtlessly aired at the grill. Had he mentioned DeMarcus's family? Was there a younger brother? It didn't have to be a brother – could be a cousin, first, second or third. He was just such a spitting image of DeMarcus that I convinced myself there had to be some connection, especially for it to occur in a town as small as Brevard.

To all of this you might say: *'So what?' So you had a chance encounter with someone who looks like someone who had something to do with the death of your wife.*

It wasn't this guy's fault. Everywhere I looked there were reminders of the past, but none had given me this kind of a chill. There was just something about him, something that stopped me in my tracks and actually made me turn back towards Flaggs. I wanted to know who he was, what his connection to DeMarcus was, and above all, why this fleeting glimpse of a once-familiar face was affecting me so much. My head was suddenly pounding again and I felt vaguely nauseous, but along with it there was something of an adrenaline rush which I hadn't felt quite as intensely since the writing of *Space Coast*. Maybe it was what Ambrose had been waiting for and had promised would come – some invisible lever that might give me my inspiration back.

I picked up my pace. In fact, I broke into a jog. I was just approaching Flaggs, crossing the largely deserted car park out front, when a voice suddenly came out of the darkness.

'What you doing here, man?'

It was him. He was just a few yards away, pushing himself out of the entrance to a disused amusement arcade to my left.

'I just . . . you look . . .'

'What you doing here?' he repeated.

'Nothing, really, I—' I misjudged the speed at which he was coming towards me, and before I could react he had thrown a looping punch which caught me flush on the cheek and sent me down. He stood over me and waved his fist again.

'What you *doing* here?' he spat. 'Go back. Go fucking back, man.'

He shook his head, then stepped away, back into the night.

28

'What he was saying,' Ambrose opined, 'was *get outta my face mothafucka or I bust a cap in yo ass.*'

I cleared my throat. He sounded ludicrous. Ambrose was more *cul de sac* than street. New York may have been his beat, but I knew for a fact that he rarely ventured out of Central Park West. He had relied upon phone charm and loquacious e-mails to obtain the information which had won him his Pulitzer. His *two* Pulitzers. I don't know why he chose to drink with me in Brooklyn, well outside his safety zone, but he always arrived in a cab and always made sure there was one available for him to be poured back into at the end of the night.

'Yes, Ambrose,' I said patiently, 'I understand *what* he was saying. I don't understand *why.*'

It was gone two in the morning. Ambrose lay on his bed, I on mine, both of us fully clothed and drinking coffee. Ambrose now had five hickeys of varying hue. My cheek was red where I'd been struck, but it had been more the shock of it than the force that had put me down.

'Because he recognised you, your face has been all over the papers, and he saw that you picked up a family resemblance in him, and then when you went running after him, he panicked. He thought you were going to jump him, and attack is the best form of defence. I don't blame him at all. I would have whacked you too. He probably thinks you blame him for whatever his brother did. Or maybe what his *father* did – you follow me?'

I didn't think the math worked, but you never know, people start early, look older, or younger. 'But why did he say "*Go back. Go fucking back, man."* Exact words.'

'Go back to your hotel, go back home. Makes sense to me.'

But it still didn't feel *right*.

'Just forget about it,' Ambrose advised. 'Besides, you're lucky he didn't steal your wallet.'

'No,' I laughed, '*you're* lucky.'

Ambrose looked confused for just a moment, then said defensively, 'I pay my way.'

I raised an eyebrow.

'Fuck you,' he snapped.

We concentrated on the TV for a while.

Halfway through a *Kojak* re-run he glanced across. 'Okay, so we track him down, confront him, find out why he attacked you, what the legacy of the robbery has been. If he's walking around town, a double of DeMarcus, how's that going to affect people who remember DeMarcus and what he did? What happens if he walks into the bank? Do they hit the panic button? Maybe there's an inevitability about it all; maybe the family was doomed from like three generations ago.'

'Okay,' I said. 'I'll think of some more questions, you phone *Oprah*. Ambrose, he punched me. If I talk to anyone, it'll be the cops.'

The adrenaline had long gone by this stage, and the wisdom of running after some hood who happened to look like someone I had once known was no longer quite so apparent. I'd actually gotten off quite lightly with a punch. I was inclined to forget the entire incident.

Ambrose wasn't.

'No! Christ, Michael, you're looking a gift horse in the mouth. We find him, we talk to him. This could be the key to it all.'

'The key to *what*?'

'Well we'll know that when we find him.' He rolled up and off the bed. 'Now, I'm taking a crap.'

When he emerged, thirty-eight minutes later, I said, 'Ambrose, I'm going home tomorrow.'

'Christ,' he said, taking hold of the bathroom door and fanning it back and forth, 'was it that bad?'

'Ambrose. Listen to me. I've had enough. I'm going home.'

He crossed the room, his trousers undone, his shirt open and his belly spilling out. 'Yeah, well, let's sleep on it.'

'I don't need to sleep on it. I'm finished here.'

'Okay, whatever you say.'

We lay in the dark with the TV off and the lights off. I was just starting to fall asleep when he said, 'Kid shouldn't be that hard to find.'

Ambrose was not so much persuasive as relentless, so compromise was inevitable. We agreed to spend a morning searching for my DeMarcus lookalike. If we found him and he was willing to talk, I might extend my stay in Brevard into the afternoon. If we didn't, I would drive out and Ambrose would stay for another few days in order to break up with Jo-Anne in such a way that ensured that he, in his own words, didn't look like a complete bastard. I observed that he looked like one from whatever angle or timeframe you cared to judge him, and he swore at me.

The first stop was the downtown address we had previously visited. This time we were more successful in that there was someone in, but they had never heard of DeMarcus Hall. One of the neighbours did remember him though and confirmed that there'd been a wife and son, but that they'd moved out shortly after the robbery, didn't know where.

Ambrose was enthusiastic.

'There *is* a son, he's maybe still around, but his mother, the widow, probably changed her name back after the robbery. Doubtless she's married again.' He whipped out his cell. 'You can run but you can't hide from Ambrose Jeffers.' He said this

175

straight-faced, while I smirked. But he was good. His calls were slick. He lied through his teeth. City Hall. The library. Sheriff's Department. Everyone was remarkably co-operative. Dropping my name, and Clint Eastwood's (he was considering a movie version), certainly did the trick. DeMarcus's wife Ariel *had* reverted to her maiden name, married a chiropractor and moved to the West Coast. Her by then twelve-year-old son Oliver went with them. Ambrose tracked down the chiropractor to San Diego and called him. He explained his interest, and said how keen Denzel was to talk to everyone connected with the robbery. The chiropractor phoned his wife, his wife phoned Ambrose. She didn't want anything to do with any movie. He asked about Oliver. Oliver was in college in New York.

'Right now?'

'Yes, right now. He has exams.'

'Did you speak to him last night?'

'Yes, I . . . is he in some kind of trouble?'

'No, ma'am. Just sometimes kids say they're in one place and they're really somewhere else.'

'He's in New York. Why would Denzel Washington need to know where my son was?'

Ambrose cut the line. He turned to me. 'My gut feeling is, this isn't our boy.'

'It's patently *bloody* obvious this isn't our boy.'

He lifted his cell again. 'I'm not finished yet.'

But he was. From there on in, there were only dead ends. If DeMarcus Hall had any other family in the area, we couldn't find them. There *was* a chance that Oliver was misleading his mother about New York and instead headed south to attend the memorial events. He might have reached an age where he wanted to know more about his father and how he'd died.

If it really was the former Oliver Hall I'd encountered outside Flaggs, then I felt quite sorry for him. Losing a father is hard enough, but when they are also responsible for terrible deeds, how must that affect you? Nobody wants to share *that* grief. You inherit the guilt. As I sat in that car with Ambrose as he worked his cell phone until the battery died, Oliver was probably curled up in some cheap motel, now not only painfully aware of the full horror of his father's past, but also anguishing over the sudden realisation that his creator's propensity for violence was absolutely in the genes.

Sorry for him – but not enough to change my plans. I had problems of my own to deal with, but not in Brevard, and I had fulfilled my obligation to Ambrose. It was time to go.

We drove back to the motel and I packed up while Ambrose paced the floor. Then he started to gather his belongings as well. I asked him what he was doing.

'I'm coming with you.'

'What about your book?'

'You're the story, man. I go where you go.'

'And what about Jo-Anne?'

'She'll be fine.'

'Fine in what way?'

'I'll call her. Or I'll send an e-mail once I'm home.'

'Ambrose.'

'Has it anything to do with you?'

'It's just not very nice, is it?'

'Did I ever claim to be very nice? It's just a vacation romance. She'll get over it.'

'Does *she* think it's just a vacation romance?'

Ambrose shrugged. Then he sighed. 'I suppose the ring was a bad idea.'

'You gave her *a ring*?!'

'No, of course I didn't, you fuckwit! But she's after one, I can tell. Better to get out now, while I can – clean break. I'm with you all the way.'

'I'm only driving to Orlando, Ambrose. It's forty minutes away. You can wave goodbye to me downstairs, you can still work on your story and you'll also be able to put things right with Jo-Anne. Take a couple of days. It's on me. I'll even take the bar off the porn, if it makes you happy.'

'I already managed that,' said Ambrose.

'Well then.'

He thought about it.

All of twenty seconds.

'Nah. I'll come with you.'

Ten minutes later we were driving down Main Street and just coming up on McDaid's Char Bar and Grill. I was behind the wheel, with Ambrose ducked down low in case Jo-Anne was working outside.

'Going,' I said, as we drew opposite.

'Going,' I said as we reached the halfway point.

'Gone,' I said, as I glanced at it in my mirror.

A hundred yards further on Ambrose slapped the dash. 'Fuck it,' he snapped. 'Pull over here.' I stopped the car. 'Give me ten minutes.'

He opened his door and climbed out.

'Ambrose?' He glanced back, then crouched down and peered through the open window. 'I'm proud of you,' I said.

He laughed. 'I'm only going for one last ride,' he said, before bouncing away.

Half an hour later I was still sitting there. I'd gone through 193 radio stations without finding a song I liked. The moment I switched it off, my headache came back.

Great.

The waves of nausea had been coming and going all morning. Not quite as bad as on the bridge the day before, but hardly pleasant. My balance felt a bit off and the driving wasn't helping. I thought maybe my slip and fall in the Radisson had not only given me a bump, but had also somehow damaged my inner ear. Or maybe with lying on the soaking floor, water had gotten into my ear and now I had some kind of infection. My inclination was to leave Ambrose behind, but having him with me at least meant that he'd be able to take over the driving if I got sick again. But I wasn't going to hang around for ever. I decided to give him another ten minutes.

I got out and bought a Pepsi and downed four Tylenol in a drugstore opposite. The *Brevard Herald* was for sale. The cover advertised six pages of exclusive photographs inside recording the memorial services. I flicked through them with very little interest – there were at least six of me – but it was only in seeing one of the top table at the dinner and Lena looking so fine that I realised that I hadn't spoken to her since I'd made such a fool of myself. Even Ambrose had (eventually) shown the decency not to just run out on his woman. Lena, of course, was not *my* woman. But still.

I returned to the car and called her. Her cell went to voice-mail. I said nothing. I called the surgery. Her receptionist said she was busy, would I leave a message. I prevaricated. She said she had another call and put me on hold. I cut the line. As I slipped the phone back into my pocket I happened to look up – and there was the man whom fine detective work had led us to conclude was (possibly) Oliver Hall. He was just crossing onto the opposite side of the street, barely thirty yards away and moving in my direction. I had a sudden inclination to thank Dick Schulze, another acquaintance I had recently abandoned, and his Lord, for moving in such a mysterious way.

I moved my hand up to shield my face in case Oliver happened to look over. He had a wary kind of a gait and was tall and thin like his father. Once he passed by, I got out of the car. Last night had taught me that he didn't like surprises, so I thought I'd just tag along behind him for a while to see where he was headed, perhaps wait for him to settle somewhere so I could approach in a way that wouldn't cause him to hit me again. I had no idea what I was going to say to him. Maybe I could buy him a beer and we could discuss how much life sucked.

He was certainly a curious type. There was hardly a shop window he didn't look into or a car he didn't kneel beside so he could examine the interior. Even when the vehicles were occupied, he didn't let that stop him. Most people ignored him. One or two gave him a look, but he stared right back and they soon looked away. Then Oliver would smile to himself and saunter on. Cool, cocky, quick to anger. He was his father's son, all right.

I followed his snail's pace at a safe distance for several blocks.

Then he turned off Main and walked down the incline towards the harbour and the strip of rickety wooden houses that overlooked it. Developers had been trying to buy them up during my original time in Brevard and clearly hadn't succeeded. They were in a much worse condition than I recalled, every one of them a splintered, dilapidated mess. Oliver walked right up and peered through the first front window, then along to the next, and the next, almost as if he couldn't quite remember where he lived, or perhaps he was brazenly checking out which one would be best to break into. At the sixth house there was a girl, maybe six or seven, sitting on the stoop, her face smudged and tear-stained. Oliver moved up beside her and tried to pat her on the head, but she squirmed away. Then he slipped around the back of the house and entered it through an open side door.

I stood at the bottom of the steps and looked up at the house. The little girl regarded me curiously. There was music playing loud inside.

I said to the girl, 'I'm a friend of Oliver's. Are you a friend of Oliver's?'

She shook her head.

'Could you tell him I'd like to talk to him?'

She shook her head again.

I smiled. I mounted the steps and she ducked away in case I tried to pat her as well. I pressed the bell. It rang, but it sounded inadequate against the music. I opened the swing door and knocked on the glass. But the music was still too loud. I tried the door, and it was unlocked, so I pushed it open and stepped into a rather chaotic hall.

'Oliver?' I called.

There was no response.

I felt foolish and awkward, standing in this strange house. I should have just walked away. Really, it was none of my business what Oliver's story was. He had punched me, I just wanted him to know he'd got it wrong, and that I understood at least part of the confusion he must be feeling. I could give him the benefit of my experience, tell him that he should forget all this

180

shit in Brevard, that if he allowed himself to get caught up in it he'd end up living in the wilderness like me.

I jumped as a shout came from upstairs. It was loud enough to be heard above the music but not distinct enough for me to understand what it meant. I wasn't even sure it was directed at me.

'Hello?' I called.

The shout came again.

'Oliver? It's Michael Ryan. I wrote . . .' God, it sounded so weak, so embarrassing. 'I just wanted to have a chat. I don't want to get you into any trouble.'

I moved to the foot of the stairs. A third shout came, but this time, being a little closer, and it being a little louder, it sounded more distinct. It was a woman's cry, full of pain, and my thought was, Jesus, there's something happening here. He's come here for a reason, he's . . . *Jesus* . . . what if he's *murdering* someone?

Like father, like son.

My first inclination was to charge back down those stairs and out. This had *nothing* to do with me.

But I didn't, of course. I couldn't. I was no hero, but I had to do something, enough to put him off, enough to give whoever he was killing a chance. I looked around for something to use as a weapon. The kitchen would have knives, but there wasn't time. If I was to do anything, I had to do it *now* because the cries were growing increasingly desperate. But there was only a table with a small lamp upon it. That would have to do. I grabbed the lamp, ripping the plug out as I charged along the hall towards the source of that animal pain. The door ahead of me was open just a couple of inches. I kicked it hard and it flew back. I raised the lamp as I jumped through the gap, screaming, 'Let her go, you son of a bitch!'

Bob, there are moments in time that remain frozen in one's mind for ever. Picture if you will this scene – an angel of mercy wielding a small but not unattractive lamp suddenly appears in a somewhat messy bedroom expecting to find a young black man engaged in bloody murder, but instead discovers a rather overweight white couple engaged in vigorous sexual congress.

Imagine the look on their faces.

Or mine.

Imagine the sheer mind-blowing catastrophe of it.

Imagine me saying, 'I'm sorry. I was looking for Oliver.'

Imagine me hurling myself back down those stairs and out of the house and racing along the street.

Imagine me with that lamp still in my hand.

It wasn't funny, Bob.

29

'Mr Ryan, this is embarrassing for everyone, you being who you are and all, but a complaint has been made and we have to take it seriously. You understand?'

'I understand.'

'Good thing we stopped you before you crossed the bridge. You got much further and this went out of state, would have been federal – no turning back then. This way, we get it sorted out local, no one needs to know.'

If I was convinced that DeMarcus and Oliver represented a prima facie case of *like father like son*, the jury was still out on Junior Newton and his father. Where the Sheriff was bloated with self-importance, Junior appeared to be genuinely concerned about getting to the truth of the matter and then settling it quietly. He knew that no major crime had been committed and that the Andersons – that was their name – were kicking up seven shades of shit because they'd recognised me straight off and knew that I was rich beyond their wildest dreams. Junior had a duty to protect them, but also understood that it left me open to a legalised form of blackmail. How he dealt with the case would have a bearing on what happened further down the line if the Andersons decided to sue. Of course, I had been wrong about people before. For all I knew, Sheriff Newton himself was outside the door, pulling the strings.

Junior looked down at my statement. 'Gee,' he said, 'this must be worth something.' It was an honest comment, and accurate. I'd dicated it two hours previously while he typed it into a laptop, then he'd left me to stew for an hour. 'See, as it stands, you could be charged with trespass, theft—'

'*Theft?*'

'The lamp, sir.'

'The lamp.'

'You threatened assault with a deadly weapon.'

'A deadly . . . ?'

'The lamp, sir.'

'The lamp. Am I right in thinking that almost anything can be described as a deadly weapon?'

'Yes, sir, if you kill someone with it.' He scanned several more lines before looking across the table at me. It was just the two of us. No lawyers. Yet. I could quite easily have flown in a twenty-seven-strong team and scared the shit out of him. But I didn't want the fuss that would go with that, I just wanted to slip out of town as if nothing had happened. I was quite prepared to write the Andersons a cheque. I was mortified at having gotten things so wrong. 'This guy, this Oliver Hall – you say you were following him.'

'Yes, because he had assaulted me the previous evening.'

'An assault you didn't report.'

'There didn't seem much point. He didn't steal anything, he just knocked me down.'

'Yet you followed him. Why?'

'Because we'd had a misunderstanding and I wanted to sort it out, and at the same time I didn't want to scare him off, so I followed him.'

'If you don't mind me saying, it's an unusual way of doing things.'

'Yes, I realise that now.'

'Because you don't even know that's his name. You were following him because he looked like somebody you used to know.'

'Yes, I can see that it doesn't make a lot of sense now. At the time it seemed like a good idea.'

'So you followed him as far as the Anderson house.'

'Yes.'

'What did he do there?'

'He spoke to the daughter out front.'

'The daughter. You heard what he said?'

'No, I . . . well, I don't know that he spoke, but he tried to pat her hair. I just presumed something was said, because he immediately moved around to the side door.'

'He went to the side door and you . . . ?'

'Well, I didn't want to just walk in like I owned the place. I stopped at the front. I asked their daughter to go and get him, but she refused. Then I . . .'

'How'd you know it was their daughter?'

'Well, there were photos of her on the stairs. Is it relevant? She wasn't very helpful.'

Junior nodded thoughtfully. 'So you rang the bell, you knocked, but there was no response. Maybe someone else would have given up at that point?'

'But I'd just seen him go in, I knew he was in there, it was just that the music was so loud. If it had been quiet he would have heard the bell, and then it would have been his choice whether he came to the door or not, but as it was so loud, I just wanted to be sure he knew I was there.'

'So you entered the house.'

'I entered the house.'

'And did you see this gentleman?'

'No.'

'But you heard other noises, besides the music, and you decided to investigate because . . .'

'Because it sounded like someone was being murdered.'

'That's quite a big leap to make, if you don't mind me saying. I've just committed trespass on someone's property, I hear a noise and automatically there's a murderer upstairs.'

'It seemed like the right thing to do. If I *had* saved someone's life, you'd be pinning a medal on me right now.'

'But in actuality you discovered Mr and Mrs Anderson.'

'Yes. It's a sight I won't easily forget.'

'You threatened them with their own lamp.'

'No. I threatened – well, yes, but I didn't know it was them. Maybe I could have stayed and explained, but I panicked and ran off.'

'Did you see Oliver Hall on your way out?'

'No.'

'And the child outside?'

'She was gone.'

'Then you drove out of town with your friend, who I have to say has been making a nuisance of himself on your behalf.'

'That's Ambrose. His heart is in the right place, but his brain rarely is.'

It was supposed to be light and fluffy, but Junior merely nodded. He clasped his hands.

'Mr Ryan, I'm going to be straight with you. You are a famous man, and you've done a lot for this town. These past few days must have been very stressful for you, and nobody wants to see you get into trouble. But this . . .' he held up the printed statement '. . . this doesn't help.'

'What do you mean?'

'I mean this bullshit.' Junior tore the statement in two. And then again. 'Mr Ryan, this is a small town, a quiet town. We were in the limelight once, we really don't want to go there again. My daddy runs a tight ship here, and he really won't tolerate some drugged-up celebrity terrorising our citizens.'

'I—'

'Just be quiet and listen. We are not stupid hick cops, Mr Ryan.' He held up the scraps of paper, then let them flutter down. 'We destroyed *this* in five minutes. Maybe you did get jumped outside Flaggs, but it wasn't by Oliver Hall – Oliver *Alexander*, as he now is. For one thing, Oliver is white, like his mother. He wasn't DeMarcus Hall's natural child. I spoke to him in New York an hour ago, seems like a nice guy and not obviously possessed of the superpowers that would allow him to flit back and forth across the continent to wander our streets attacking people whenever he felt like it. Then there's the Andersons – bad enough you break into their house and see

186

what you see, but I swear to God, Mr Ryan, this stuff about their daughter outside, that's too much, sir.'

'All I said was—'

'Mr Ryan, their daughter died in a fire three years ago.'

I didn't quite know what to say to that. I held my hands up. 'Okay, so it wasn't their daughter, it was some other kid.'

Junior shook his head. 'They had a real tough time. You should know what that's like – you should know how cruel hearing something like that would be.'

'Yes – yes, of course. I really—'

'Mr Ryan, we will sort this out with the Andersons – you won't hear anything more about it. But as far as I can tell you've been drunk or drugged ever since you came here, and that's your decision, but I don't like it, and my daddy doesn't like it. What we're going to do is escort you out of town, and we don't want you back. Do you understand?'

'Yes, I do.'

'And you will take that fat fuck with you.'

'Yes, I will.'

'Okay then. That's the end of it.'

And it was. Except, as Churchill more or less said, it was merely the end of the beginning.

30

As I have made clear before, my realm is fiction. While I managed to scrape by as a journalist I never really embraced that world or showed any aptitude for it. I was not interested enough to chase stories. If someone else did the legwork and the facts were brought to me for conversion into a colourful story, then I could manage that, but actually seeking them out was anathema to me. In retrospect, therefore, I should have known better than to even briefly countenance writing a book based on my return to Brevard. I was not interested in other people's experiences of the massacre, their loss, their hopes or regrets, or in investigating any kind of wider communal guilt. I had lived with my own guilt for so long I was no longer even interested in *it*. I had, admittedly, summoned a brief flurry of interest following my encounter with (the man who wasn't) Oliver Hall, but that had been my fictional head at work, and it had only served to get me into trouble. I had made a fool of myself, and my only relief from that was the knowledge that it would survive only as local gossip. Junior would see to that. In return I was more than happy to comply with his advice to get out of town, fast.

Except . . .

'Assholes!' Ambrose shouted as I drove us out of the Sheriff's Department car park. Then louder: 'You're all ASSHOLES!'

189

There was no one about, and we had the windows up and the radio and cold air on. Nobody heard him.

'Chased out of town!' he spat. 'Never been chased out of anywhere in my life! I was six months in Chechnya, never got chased out of there! I was in Somalia, I walked tall and proud! Chased out of fucking *Brevard*, man.'

A little further on I said, 'We were leaving anyway.'

'Of our own choice!' Ambrose turned and looked back along the highway. 'No escort.'

'Were you expecting one?'

'Yeah. Kind of.'

A little further on and we were within sight of the big blue IHOP sign.

'Hungry?' he asked.

'No.'

'Sure?'

'No, Ambrose.'

'A few pancakes, what difference?'

'We promised.'

'Dripping in maple syrup.'

'Ambrose.'

'What harm?'

'Ambrose.'

'Ten minutes.'

'No, Ambrose.'

'Five.'

'Ambrose.'

'If they had a drive-through we could use it, but they don't, so – two minutes, that's all. Pancakes. Syrup. Eggs. Bacon. Ten minutes. It's not like we're in some sort of fucking exclusion zone. We're allowed to eat.'

'*No*, Ambrose.'

We got a booth. The waitress smiled and said, 'Ambrose.' She nodded at me. We ordered. Ambrose sat back. He had a smug look about him.

'Did you tell her?' I asked.

'Who?'

'Jo-Anne.'

'Yeah,' he replied. 'Kind of. I've been called back to the office, this latest blow-up in the Middle East.'

'I wasn't aware of a blow-up in the Middle East.'

'It's pretty hush-hush.'

The waitress brought juice and coffee.

'Jo-Anne's not stupid,' I said.

'No, she's not. But I can be very convincing. So, you think you're going to write this book?'

'I don't think so. No.'

'Shame.'

'Uhuh. You?'

'I've made some notes.'

I nodded. He nodded. I stirred my coffee.

'Just seems a pity,' said Ambrose.

'What does?'

'To finish it this way – you know, run out of town.'

'I fucked up, Ambrose.'

'Yes, you did. Absolutely. But I was thinking, you know, you're just about the most famous person ever to come out of Brevard. You'd think that if you said you'd been mugged, they'd be falling over backwards to find out who it was so that their precious reputation wasn't damaged any further. You'd think they'd want to parade the guy and say, "This is what happens when you mess with us".'

'I broke into someone's house, I threatened them.'

'With a *lamp*. You were trying to make a citizen's arrest.'

'Ambrose, I'm past caring. I just want to go home.'

He looked at me. He knew I had no home. *Property*, yes. *Home*, no.

Our pancakes arrived. Ambrose immediately tucked in. The waitress smiled indulgently. 'Someone's hungry,' she said.

'Yes, ma'am,' Ambrose grinned back, syrup already dribbling down his chin.

'You're a big hit with waitresses,' I observed as she left.

'I know,' said Ambrose. 'I'm very impressive to serving women.'

I wasn't hungry. In fact, when I looked at my pancakes, I felt ill and then somewhat dizzy again. Almost sea-sick. I should have picked up something for my ear infection at Walgrens.

'Did I mention that I won two Pulitzers?' It was a rhetorical question. 'Well, you don't win two Pulitzers without following your instincts. And something about this set-up I don't like.'

'Which set-up is this?' I asked.

'Well, you know, the longer I do this, the more I realise there's a lot more shit goes on than you can ever imagine. Those geeks who see a conspiracy theory around every corner, sometimes you shouldn't just write them off.'

'So there are aliens amongst us. Kennedy, Princess Diana and Mother Teresa were all assassinated by Opus Dei or the Boy Scouts, right?'

Ambrose stopped chewing and adopted a thoughtful look. 'No, not Opus Dei.' Then he smiled. 'No, I mean you'd be surprised how often there's a little grain of truth in these things.'

'If you say so, Ambrose. And what has this got to do with me?'

'Well, let's say there are two ways of looking at what's happened. The normal, rational one which says that yes, you've been partying hard—'

'I haven't.'

'Let me finish. You've been partying hard, you thought you saw someone who looked like someone, you made an honest mistake, time to go home. Okay?'

'Okay. And the irrational one?'

'That you didn't see someone who looked like DeMarcus Hall. You *saw* DeMarcus Hall.'

'The same DeMarcus Hall who was shot to death in the bank?'

'Well, what if he wasn't? What if he escaped? Butch and Sundance managed it.'

'No, they didn't, they died in a hail of—'

'If you choose to believe that version.'

'Ambrose, that's just plain stupid. For DeMarcus Hall to still be alive you'd need a miracle *and* a conspiracy.'

'The Red Sox won the World Series – there's a miracle *and* a conspiracy.'

192

'Ambrose.'

'I'm only trying to help.'

'Well, you're not.'

'I'm just saying, as a Pulitzer Prize-winner – twice – what if somehow DeMarcus Hall survived the robbery, and he lay low for ten years, but he heard about the memorial services and was drawn back in . . . maybe he has some unfinished business.'

'That's impossible.'

'Unlikely, I would agree – but not impossible. You spot him, he tries to frighten you off.'

'Ambrose, he walked down Main Street in broad daylight!'

'So maybe he was saying to someone, "Look at me, here I am, you don't scare me".'

'That's ridiculous.'

'So some Japanese soldier walks out of the jungle fifty years after World War Two is over – is that any more ridiculous?'

'It's not the same thing.'

'He's cocky, maybe he's all hopped up.'

'Hopped?'

'He's saying, "You try anything, I'll tell all".'

'Tell all *what*?'

'Who else was involved in the robbery.'

'Ambrose, I don't need this shit.'

'Nor I. But it's out there. Michael, the way I see it, is all we have to do is track this guy down, satisfy ourselves that he's *not* DeMarcus Hall, then we can drive out of Brevard with our heads held high and our journalistic integrity intact, and we won't spend the next twenty years wondering what if it was him.'

I sat back. I gave him a long, hard look. 'Ambrose,' I asked, 'are you sure this isn't just another way for you to stay for another shag?'

Ambrose shook his head sadly. 'You really don't know me at all, do you?'

'Ambrose . . .'

'So if you're not going to eat those fucking things, pass them across.'

31

For some reason I was dreaming about Dumbo and the stork delivering him to his mother as the circus train wound its way across country, except it was me she had in her mouth, not the little fella with the big ears. I asked her what time it was, and in answering she opened her mouth and let go of me and I fell and fell and fell, and just as I was about to slap into the ground I heard her answer:

'Just after midnight.'

I opened my eyes, not having remembered closing them, and Lena was standing before me. I blinked at her. There were certificates on the wall and a computer on a desk and a plastic sheet beneath me. I sat up and immediately winced, the side of my head alive with little jagging pains.

'Easy there,' said Lena, helping me back down.

'I don't understand. Where am I . . . ?'

'You just can't bear to leave us, can you?'

'Lena . . .'

'Do you remember what happened?'

'No, no, I . . .'

'Do you even know your own name?'

'Yes, I do.'

'It is?'

'Michael Ryan.'

'Not the shit-heel Michael Ryan? Your friend Ambrose brought you here. You fainted outside an IHOP.'

'Fainted?'

'Collapsed. Blacked out. Keeled over. He should have taken you to the hospital. I think he thought you might save some money, coming here. You won't. I charge double after hours.'

Her coolness was to be expected. However, I had no memory of fainting *at all*.

'Where is he?' I asked.

'He left. He said he had to meet someone.'

Well, *that* figured. I tried sitting up again. This time I took it a little easier. 'I'm sorry,' I said, 'it must have been the heat. I think I'm a little dehydrated.'

I went to swing my legs down, but Lena held her hand up. 'Not so quick, mister. Tell me about this.' She reached up towards the side of my head and I instinctively pulled away. She raised an eyebrow.

'Sorry,' I said. 'Sore.'

'I should think so. When did you do this, and how?'

'Night of the dinner,' I said. 'Drunk.'

'Really?'

'I'm sorry, Lena, I never meant—'

'Forget it. You didn't think about getting this checked out?'

'It's just a bump.'

She rolled her eyes, then leaned a little closer and took hold of the top of my head and my jaw and gently angled my skull for a better look.

'You've been feeling nauseous, dizzy?'

I sighed.

'Christ, Michael, you should have gotten this seen to.'

'It's not that bad, really.'

She looked at me doubtfully. 'Do you have any other symptoms?'

'No. I'll be fine. Really.'

'I'd like you to go to the hospital for a scan.'

'No.'

'No?'

'I'm not even supposed to be here.'

'*Here?*'

'In town. We've been invited to leave. Ambrose didn't mention this?'

'He all but dumped you at my door.' Lena folded her arms. 'Okay, Bashful. Tell me what you've done.'

I cleared my throat. 'Well . . .'

'You may be a bestselling author,' Lena concluded, 'but you are also an idiot.'

'I know that. All I want to do is have a quick look around for this guy, really just to get Ambrose off my back, then leave town. I promise I'll go and have a scan as soon as I get home. And, well, I really am sorry about what happened, that night.'

Lena held her hands up. 'It's done. Now, about this leaving town nonsense. You know, Sheriff Newton isn't such an ogre. If I explain to him that you need medical treatment, it really won't be a problem. As for the man who attacked you, I'm afraid Ambrose has been putting ideas in your broken old head. DeMarcus Hall is one hundred per cent dead. You forget, the day of the robbery my dad was right there, about to go into the bank when it all happened. He attended the victims, the good guys and the bad. He pronounced DeMarcus dead at the scene. In fact, he attended the cremation. I remember because he said how awful it was because there were only a few people there, and they kind of raced through it. The whole town was mad at what he'd done. Anyway, the point is, Ambrose is full of shit. But then I imagine you're aware of that. And perhaps you're full of shit too.'

'I really am sorry, Lena,' I said.

'Yeah, well. Just go and get checked out, all right?'

'All right.' I sat quietly and kept my eyes on the floor.

Silence descended.

Eventually: 'Where are you staying tonight?'

I shrugged. Then I checked for my wallet. It was gone. I looked at her helplessly.

'I've either lost it, or Ambrose has it. And, uhm, my cell phone.'

'So you not only can't afford a hotel room, but you can't pay for my services either.'

'That's, uhm, pretty much how it looks,' I said. 'I can write an IOU.'

'Jesus Christ,' said Lena.

She showed me her couch.

'Nice couch,' I said.

She brought me a quilt.

'Nice quilt,' I said.

She went to bed.

I lay in the dark. She was right, of course. I'd been feeling unwell and muddled ever since I'd slipped in the rest room at the Radisson. Now that the obvious had been pointed out, it made sense to go and get checked out. Perhaps if I'd gone sooner I wouldn't have jumped to so many daft conclusions about my assailant, nor given Ambrose's loopy theories the time of day. DeMarcus Hall was dead, his stepson was white and happy in New York, the bank robbery had been carried out by a gang of drugged-up rockers working alone, and we were being ordered out of town because of my behaviour, not because of some larger conspiracy.

Through the side window I could see the dark mass of the Blue House.

I turned away from it. I drifted. I dreamed that Claire was behind me, snuggled up. She stroked the back of my head and whispered, 'Everything will be all right.'

It was warm and comforting and I could have lain there for ever, except – a door opened upstairs and a light came on and I heard a soft pad along the landing and halfway down the stairs. I looked up to see Lena standing there, her dressing-gown tied at the waist, yet revealing.

'Do I have to hang a sign out, Michael Ryan?' she asked.

Then she turned back up the stairs.

She didn't.

But for a long ecstatic moment I wallowed in the memory of my wife's embrace, before mounting the stairs to betray her again.

32

I allowed myself to believe that everything might somehow be okay, that as you slept gently beside me, Lena, and the sun rose and beamed through the front window, that this was how it could be. I felt refreshed, my headache was gone. I showered and dressed and planned to make you breakfast, but your fridge was mostly empty. I borrowed your car and drove to Publix. It had just turned eight, but it was already busy – Floridians are early risers. I chose fresh orange juice, eggs, smoked bacon, crois-sants, strawberries and honey. There was a special needs kid in a green overall and a big name badge identifying him as Simon helping to stack shelves. He asked if he could help me and I thanked him, no. I commented that it was a beautiful morning and Simon said every morning was beautiful.

Then it started.

The sensation was odd. Like you're in a plane and you think your hearing is fine until you get to a certain height and you swallow and suddenly everything becomes twice as clear. Except as I experienced this sudden clarity there was also a very strange and contradictory diminishing – as if a vacuum had been created and the sounds around me that weren't required had been sucked out and others that were more pertinent became exaggerated. The trolley being wheeled towards me was silent, as if its wheels were slightly elevated; the heels of the woman pushing it should have been click-clicking on the tiled floor, but they were barely audible. I stopped, confused, and glanced back at Simon to see if he was experiencing the same bizarre phenomenon, just in time to see him drop a can of pears, which struck the floor and rolled with little more than a whisper. Simon chased after it, muttering something, but I could only tell that because his lips were moving. Yet there *was* sound – exaggerated sound – footsteps, fast, running, from a different aisle. It was as if everyone else was above the water, and I was beneath. Their sounds were drowned out, and all I could hear were these footsteps conducted *through* the water because whoever was making them had been cast into these depths alongside me.

As strange and unsettling as it was, I could not help but hurry forward, because at that moment they were my only reality. I pushed the cart before me, shadowing the footsteps from the other side of the aisle – except, when I came to the turn, I seemed to emerge from the sensation as suddenly as I had entered it. The checkouts ahead of me suddenly were alive with conversation. An ancient, sun-blasted septuagenarian apologised for not moving her cart out of my way and I mumbled, '*Thanks.*' I pushed to the next aisle and looked for the source of those rapid steps, but there was no one there.

I stood, staring up the aisle, trying to settle myself. I *had* heard them. There *had* been some kind of a vacuum. But here was normal life, all around me. My head was throbbing again and the nausea was back. I gripped the bar of the cart for support. There was movement behind me and I spun. It was Simon, looking genuinely concerned.

'Excuse me, sir, are you . . .' he began. But before he could finish, the sound had whooshed out again. His lips were moving but there was nothing coming out.

The footsteps were back, but from the aisle where I'd just emerged. And more: laughter. A child laughing.

I spun the cart around and moved quickly back to the first aisle.

There, at the very top of it, the briefest glimpse of a little girl.

Shoppers moved their carts to one side as I raced after her. I apologised, I thanked them. My own voice sounded impossibly loud. I paused at the top and looked left and right: there she was, perhaps twenty yards away. A row of freezers ran across virtually the entire width of the store, and it was into one of these that the girl was peering.

As I drew closer I realised it was the little girl from the steps outside the Andersons' house. She was dressed in a mucky pair of red dungarees, cut off at the knee.

'Hi,' I said.

She spun towards me, her face white with shock, before springing away and into the entrance to the opposite aisle.

'No – please! Wait!'

With her escape route clear, she stopped and looked cautiously back.

'Please – it's okay. I know you – it's all right. I saw you at the house, the Andersons' house – remember?'

She examined me for several moments before giving the shortest nod.

'Who are you with?' I asked. 'Are your parents here?'

She shook her head. 'I'm playing.'

'What's your name?'

'Meg.'

'I'm Michael. Why did you run away, Meg?'

'Mommy told me not to talk to strange men.'

'That's good advice. Is she here, your mom?'

Her brow furrowed, and she looked suddenly very serious. 'When they come, where will you hide?'

'When who come – your parents?'

She glanced behind her as a clattering sound, followed by laughter, drifted across from a further aisle. 'I have to go,' she said abruptly. 'I'm not allowed here.' She immediately darted away along the aisle.

'Meg!' I called, moving after her. 'Meg!'

By the time I made it down to the end of the aisle, there was no sign of her. The other sounds were continuing to drift across, so I turned towards them. Shoppers glided silently by, seemingly unaware of the jarring metallic crashing and the laughter that went with it. I pushed my cart past one aisle, then another, but as I approached the third my head jagged viciously and I shut my eyes against the pain. When I opened them again my ears had popped and I was back, my world no longer muted but alive and vibrant – yet there were still remnants of that noise, a cascading, collapsing sound. As I turned the corner I saw Simon crawling about on all fours, trying to gather up dozens of cans of food that had fallen from a shelf which had come unstuck at one end.

I let go of my cart and went to help.

As I knelt beside him he looked helplessly at me. 'It wasn't my fault,' he said, and I could see he was on the verge of tears. 'It wasn't my fault.'

Before I could respond, there was a shout from the other end of the aisle. 'Simon!' A red-faced man in a red short-sleeved shirt and blue tie, flanked by two shelf stackers in Publix uniforms, came hurrying up. 'Simon! Just leave them!'

'Wasn't my fault,' Simon moaned, reaching for another can. I picked two up.

'Sir!' the manager-type said, reaching out to take them from me. 'Sir, thank you, but everything's fine. We'll clear this up. Simon – the storeroom, *now*.'

The boy slowly got to his feet and tramped sadly away.

'I think the shelf collapsed,' I said.

The manager-type looked doubtfully at it, then at the retreating Simon. 'I appreciate your assistance, sir.' Then he sighed. 'We don't always get the employees we deserve.' He nodded at me before moving to a position where he could better direct the other shelf stackers as they set about clearing up.

'Hi.' Lena was coming down the stairs, but I didn't turn. 'I thought I heard the car.'

There was hesitancy in her voice, despite the intimacies. It had been our first night together without alcohol.

My hands were cupped around a cold Publix coffee. The breakfast items I'd purchased remained in a plastic bag on the table before me.

'I brought breakfast.'

She peered into the plastic bag and jauntily commented, 'And you're expecting me to . . . ?' But then as she moved in front of me she stopped. 'Michael – God, you look rough.'

She immediately put her hand to my brow. I'd been sick on the way home. Stopping, opening the door, driving on. I had barely made it from garage to kitchen. My legs were weak, my hands shook, my throat was tight.

'Sorry,' I began.

'Shhh.'

'I wanted to surprise you.'

'You did. Last night. For such an old man, you're pretty slick in the sack.' She hunkered down beside me and squeezed my knee. 'You, sir, need to go to hospital. What were you thinking of, sneaking out like that?'

'I felt fantastic.'

'But not now.'

My head was too sore to shake.

'Just give me a minute,' Lena said. She disappeared. Then she was back, wearing black jeans and a white T-shirt. 'Okay, can you make it to the car? If you can't, I can phone for an ambulance.'

'No – I'm fine.'

She helped me up, and out. I did feel like an old man. She settled me into the front of her Lexus and secured the seat belt. She drove fast but smooth. I rested my head against the open window and allowed the rush of morning air to cool me. Lena called ahead as she drove. 'They're waiting for us,' she said.

'It's just a hangover.'

'Right.'

'I went to Publix. It's their air conditioning.'

'Okay.'

'My balance is all over the fucking place. But this is nice. We should go for a picnic.'

'Okay.'

'It was lovely last night.'

'Yes, it was.'

'I must be forgiven.'

'The jury's still out.'

Lena checked my pulse with one hand as she drove. Then she stepped a little harder on the gas, at least until we ran into traffic downtown. She cursed. She drummed her fingers on the dash. She checked my pulse again. We inched forward. We got stuck at a light. People crossed from both sides. I stared at them, and they stared back, although probably at Lena. She was a lot prettier than I was. There was one woman, on my side, who stood where she was. I admired her legs. Then I realised she was looking at me looking at her. She smiled. I smiled. Her smile vanished, her mouth dropped open, she began to back away.

I whispered it, and it must have come from my brain, but it was an involuntary spasm, because no sane, cogent individual would ever have said: *'Claire.'*

Because it was impossible.

Lena turned. 'Sorry?'

With the people crossing for the other side, she was moment-arily obscured. But it was 100 per cent definitely her. Power surged through me. The imbalance vanished, the nausea was gone, my legs were suddenly mine to command again. I yanked at the door handle.

'It's Claire!'

I leapt out. There were people crowding the sidewalk, moving towards me, but I surged through them. I caught glimpses of her, moving away.

'Claire!'

I was dimly aware of Lena shouting from behind, and car horns sounding, but nothing was going to stop me. It made no sense, I must have known that, but there, then, the impossible was real, because I had seen it; our eyes had met and I had felt it. Somehow, somehow she had survived and returned. I was thinking, Amnesia, kidnap, a complicated switch and scam – anything, *anything* – because she was alive.

She was *alive*!

Yet I couldn't get to her. As soon as I pushed someone out of the way, someone else appeared to replace them, blocking my way, forcing me off the sidewalk.

Someone screamed, 'Get off the road, asshole!'

Then there was space, but no sign of her.

'Claire!'

She was scared, of course she was scared, caught off guard, ill-prepared with an explanation, an excuse, not understanding that there and then I required neither. I required only to hold her in my arms, to crush her to me, to kiss her and love her and thank Christ for salvation.

I just . . . couldn't find her.

'Claire!'

The lights were at a crossroads with several smaller roads leading off; there were alleys between stores, there were the stores themselves, there were a dozen possibilities. She could have gone in any direction, but every time I started one way I panicked that I was allowing her to escape another way.

'Claire!' I bawled. 'It's me! Claire!'

'Michael!' I spun around, but it was Lena. 'Michael, *please.*'

'It's Claire. Good Christ, it's Claire! Claire!'

I was screaming hoarsely. The surge of adrenaline that had propelled me out of the car was already fading, but I kept on. The horns multiplied, incessant.

'Michael, it's not her, it wasn't her.'

'I saw her! Claire!'

'Get in the car, asshole!' a driver yelled.

'Lena, please – you saw her, you must have.' Panic gripped me. I staggered in one direction, then another, pulled by possibility and hope and confusion.

A flash of neon, and short burst of siren, then Junior Newton was there, his squad car pulled up on to the sidewalk. Now he stood with his hands raised, trying to calm me.

'Mr Ryan, sir.'

But there was *no way.*

Claire.

Alive.

'Claire! Claire! Please God, Claire! Don't leave me! Don't hide – not now! I know you can hear me! Claire!'

'Mr Ryan, if you don't quiet down, I'm going to have to restrain you.'

I ignored him.

I knew I would have to make a bold decision, choose one direction to go in and pray it was the right one. She had only had a few moments in which to hide, and with the panic of discovery she must surely have chosen the closest – *there*, the alley running between a pawn store and a lawyer's office flanked on either side by lock-up garages.

Make your decision.

Go!

Now!

I was just moving towards it when I was struck behind the knees and immediately collapsed. A moment later, Junior had me pinned and was cuffing me. I tried bucking against him, but he pressed my face down into the sidewalk. I used every iota of strength to try and get to my feet, but iotas were in short supply. He kept me down with one hand.

'Just take it easy,' he said.

'Michael.' Lena, to my left, a syringe at the ready. 'It'll be okay, Michael, it'll be okay.'

'No – please, don't. Lena, in the name of God, don't!'

But it was too late.

33

Whispers. Ambrose. Lena. A stranger's voice – deep, authoritative, saying, 'Internal bleeding could make him delusional, yet
you say he's largely coherent?'

'Largely,' Ambrose said.

Lena tutted.

The quiet hum of fluorescent lights. The antiseptic smell.
Merritt Island Hospital.

I drifted.

Intravenous Valium. Lovely.

Ambrose was reading a *USA Today*, perched on a windowsill, the
window open, smoking, about six inches from an oxygen tank.
He folded the paper.

'You're awake,' he said.

I closed my eyes.

When I opened them he was still sitting there; same shirt, same
paper, different headline.

Lena, bending over me, whispering, 'What's your name?'

'Pope Benedict.' My voice sandpaper dry.

'I'm serious. What's your name?'

'Pope Leo the Third.'

'Please.'
'Michael Ryan.'
'Do you know where you are?'
'Yes, I do. The Vatican.'
'Do you remember how you got here?'
'Yes, I do. Stabbed in the back.'
'Who is the President of the United States?'
'If I say Reagan do I get to sleep some more?'
'Yes, you do.'
I slept.

This much I know, or overheard, or imagined. I had something called a keloid scar, which is a wound that has healed but it leaves a thick, ugly reminder. Asking who the President of the United States is, is one of the standard questions used to deduce whether you're a nut job or not. I'm not sure what they ask the President if *he* cracks his head. They carried out a CAT scan whilst I slept. This highlights the structure of the brain and the bone surrounding it. If they see a dark shadow forming over the surface of the brain this indicates internal bleeding, and it also shows where they need to drill to drain it. But they seemed confused. There was no evidence of brain *bleed*, but seemingly plenty of evidence of the effect. They kept me under observation. I kept *them* under observation, although with my eyes closed.

'How do you feel, Michael?'
'Fine.'
They reduced and then removed the sedation. I got up. I walked around. They shone lights in my eyes and checked my bloods.
'The tests are clear,' said Lena.
'That's good.'
'Concussion is like an insult to the brain. It doesn't cause permanent damage, but you have to have bedrest and refrain from physical activity.'
'I *was* in bed, but I didn't refrain from physical activity. You are clearly to blame.'

Lena blushed. 'I mean, you were charging about all over the place, so your brain didn't have a chance to recover; you were drinking, you were dehydrated, you were overheated.'

'So what now?'

'More rest.'

'Okay.'

'You can stay here. Or you can come back to my place.'

'And what about physical activity?'

The blush intensified. Then: 'Only under medical supervision.'

'Okay. Does this mean I'm not being run out of town?'

'I had a word.'

'What about Ambrose?'

'Him too. Under sufferance. He sat with you night and day.'

'He wanted to be there when I died, or to record what I said in my sleep.'

'He cares about you.'

'He cares about himself.'

'I care about you.'

'I know that.'

After three nights in hospital, I came home to Lena's. She made me lie on the sofa and brought me decaf. I watched a lot of cable and read newspapers.

'Don't you have patients?' I asked.

'You're my patient.'

'Don't you have other patients?'

'Yes, I do. They will have to be patient.'

Later, she did have to go to her surgery. Fortuitously, Ambrose arrived just as she was leaving. It was like the changing of the guard. He brought beer with him, but did not offer me any. I didn't miss it. I asked him about Jo-Anne. He grew defensive. I asked him about his wife. He ignored my question.

'I like Brevard,' he stated instead. 'Kind of place you could come if you jacked your job in and wanted to write a book.'

'You're writing a book?'

'In a way, it would have been better if you'd died on the operating table.'

211

'Thanks, Ambrose.'

'I mean, purely from an aesthetic point of view; it would make for a cleaner ending. It's a bit like Truman's *In Cold Blood* – he couldn't finish it until the killers were executed. They kept appealing against the death sentence. Truman thought they were doing it to spite him.'

'I'm not sure which is more depressing – you being disappointed at my failure to croak, or you equating yourself with Truman Capote.'

'Truman Capote never won a Pulitzer.'

'Does that make you a better writer, Ambrose?'

'I always trust the jury. If Junior Newton had shot you dead in the middle of the sidewalk, it would have been perfect.'

'Sometimes I wonder exactly who has the brain injury.'

'Did *Space Coast* win *anything*?'

I closed my eyes.

As Ambrose's watch came to an end, Rev. Richard Schulze arrived. He stayed for an hour and a half. He did not mention my having left him comatose in Flaggs. He did mention God, and salvation and the afterlife. I asked him where he got his information. He had a lot of arguments, but at the end it all boiled down to faith. He told me he thought I was mellowing. I told him I thought he was senile. We agreed to differ. He was going home the next day. He said he was sorry to be leaving. He hadn't realised how much he'd missed Brevard until he'd come back. He'd served all over the States, but Brevard felt like home. I didn't feel the same way.

We ran out of conversation. Dick did not leave until Lena returned. As she came through the door I sneezed. I was developing a bit of a headcold. All I needed.

We made love. Carefully. At the end she checked my pulse. Then I checked hers. They were broadly similar.

I made her breakfast in the morning.

When we were finished, she said: 'I think you're okay.'

'I think you're okay too.'

'No, I mean better.'

'Better than who? Or *whom*?'

'I was going to say I think you've recovered from your concussion, but now I'm having doubts.'

'Another physical workout should prove things one way or another.'

'You mean like a jog?'

'Like a jog, but horizontal.'

'Not a marathon?'

'In my condition? Certainly not. But not a sprint either.'

'Okay then.'

I took her back upstairs.

Afterwards she pretended to stamp my head. 'The all clear,' she said. 'It's official.' I sneezed again. 'Colds don't count,' she said. 'You're still better.'

'I'm safe to be left alone?'

'You're safe to be left alone.'

'You trust me not to set fire to the house, or dance naked in the streets.'

'I trust you.'

'I'll make you dinner for coming home.'

'I still want you to rest.'

'I will.'

'I still want you to take it easy.'

'I promise.'

She kissed me.

'I could get used to you,' she said, then put a finger to my lips to stop me replying. She smiled and moved to the shower.

I lay back on the bed, and waited.

When I heard her car accelerate away, I dressed quickly and walked to the front door. I scanned the neighbourhood. Nobody seemed to be watching. I pulled the door shut behind me and started walking.

I was going to find my wife.

34

Bob, I should explain my thinking, even if barely enough time has elapsed to allow me to describe it with the benefit of hindsight. First of all, I am not normally a devious person. But at that point I had to be. As soon as they reduced the sedation, I began zooming in and out again. Was I going to tell them that? They would have kept me there, they would have *operated*. They would have drilled a burr-hole in my skull and sucked out the very convergence of blood and bone and who knows what else, that was providing me with the kind of profound clarity that allowed me to see and hear things which others could not.

Bob, I know you well enough. You will be sitting there, shaking your head, thinking, I was quite enjoying this little story of his, but now he's lost it, he's really lost it – and you're entitled to think that. All you have to allow is that I believed it, and at least part of that came through applying logic to the illogical. That is what I set out to do that morning.

I knew everyone else thought I was delusional, but my wife *was not* a delusion. We had locked eyes, she had reacted with shock and fled. If she had been a delusion, would we not have embraced and made love and floated off somewhere? DeMarcus Hall was not a delusion. He had *punched* me, for heaven's sake. I *still* have the faint remnants of the bruise. Could they *both* have survived the robbery only to clumsily give themselves away – to me, of all people – ten years down the line? I think you will agree, absolutely not. But I was also certain that I was not seeing actor lookalikes or mysterious twins. If someone had hatched a wild conspiracy (and believe me, I had thought of it) to fleece me out of my millions, they would surely not have left so much to chance, and they would at least have gone to the trouble of making my wife look a decade older. She looked *exactly* as she did on the day of the robbery. It was a Casual Friday, no bank uniform. She always spent a couple of days planning what she was going to wear. *That* casual. Yet she was as real as my fist in front of me, and yet not there, like a limb that has been amputated, but you can still feel pain through it.

While I was recuperating in hospital I received a visit from Adam Harrington of the *Herald*. He said he was up seeing someone else and had heard I was a patient, but I was pretty certain he was just trying to avoid being rejected by phone. I wouldn't have, actually. I had my own questions. We bandied small talk for a while before he got to the point.

'I was parachuted into Brevard a few years ago when Joe Roth sold up, and I wanted to impress the troops – show them their new editor could also write a story – so first week I did our main story: the fire at the Andersons' house. It was a real heartbreaker. I've been kind of close to them ever since. So, they came to me yesterday – said Junior Newton was trying to talk them out of taking suit against you.'

'Uhuh?'

'So, I was wondering if you wanted to, you know, give your point of view.'

'Not really, no.'

He nodded. I nodded.

'Had to ask,' he said.

'Are you running a story?'

'Haven't decided. Junior Newton asked us to sit on it, and as he's the source of half our news stories, I'm not keen to get on the wrong side of him. But still. Celebrity mayhem, and all that.'

'It was hardly mayhem.'

'Well – they were very upset.'

'That's understandable. They were making love.'

'It wasn't so much that. It was more because you claimed to have spoken to their daughter.'

'It was an honest mistake. I just presumed she . . . well, I'm sorry.'

'Okay. I can tell them that. They've just – never gotten over it. You couldn't, really. I know if anything ever happened to my . . . well. You know what I mean.'

I nodded.

'Mrs Anderson, Beth, she goes up to Meg's grave every day, without fail.'

I was pale anyway, but what colour was left drained away.

'Meg.' I just said it, statement not question.

I had seen pictures of her dotted about the Anderson house during my brief visit without really taking them in; yes, there had been some similarity between the child on the wall and the one I'd spoken to outside, but to a childless man all children are the same. If Adam noticed my shock, he did not react. I nodded numbly as he chatted on, but when I failed to engage further he took it as a hint and made his excuses.

DeMarcus Hall. Claire Roth. Meg Anderson. I was seeing living, breathing people. The problem, of course, was that nobody else could see them.

Okay, Bob, sitting there in your plush office, and remembering that pre-*Space Coast* you were something of a scholar, you must know that history is almost always a question of interpretation, usually by the victor, and that every indisputable fact comes with a caravan of denial and contradiction. My reality was nobody else's, and I respect the fact that from the outside it must have looked as if I had taken leave of my senses. I had surely suffered a brain injury which the hospital had failed to detect and as a result I was slipping in and out of an ultra-realistic but nevertheless completely imaginary world.

Fair enough. But *my* indisputable fact is that it was real to me, and it offered something that *your* real world could not: the chance to be with my wife again. You know that I would have swapped my life for hers in that bank that day in an instant. Bob, God forbid, but if something dreadful happened to your wife and you were given the opportunity to be reunited with her, would you not seize it with both hands? If, say fifty years ago, some professor offered to save your wife's life with a heart transplant, or a face transplant, or to grow a new kidney from stem cells, would you have told him he was mad and try to have him locked up because those things simply weren't possible then? Or would you have taken the chance, knowing it was your only hope?

Bob, this was *my* only hope. I had to embrace what I was experiencing, I had to follow it through. Of *course* I was aware that it wasn't normal, that I might be doing myself irreparable damage by not confessing that my 'delusions' were continuing and getting the right treatment, but I simply could not. My only purpose in hurrying downtown on that sweltering morning was not to embark on some bizarre adventure, nor was I setting out to solve a mystery (both of which occurred, as you will see); it was simply my overwhelming desire to find my wife.

Wouldn't *you*?

'Absolutely fucking barking, my friend.'

That was Ambrose's interpretation of my behaviour. The problem was that I could not predict when my zooming in and out would occur, and all that morning it failed to oblige. I was still certain of my chosen path, but I was frustrated by my inability to find it. Ambrose had discovered me wandering helplessly back and forth in the area of the traffic signal where I had seen Claire, and insisted on taking me to the grill.

'At least Uri Geller could bend spoons,' he observed. 'A small market, but a lucrative one.' He sipped his beer, then set it down and clasped his hands before him, and gave me what amounted in Ambrose to a serious word of advice. 'Kiddo,' he said, 'bite the bullet, tell them what's happening, get yourself sorted out.'

'I shouldn't have told you. I shouldn't have fucking told you.'

'Too late, my friend.'

'Ambrose, she's out there, I *know* she is. Okay, explain this to me – how could I have known that the Anderson kid was called Meg? It happened six or seven years after I left Brevard.'

'Michael, how do I know you didn't ask the neighbours or phone the *Herald*, then you backtrack it into your little dream story?'

'But I didn't, I swear to God.'

'God – you mean the guy over there with the long white beard? Don't tell me you can't see *Him*.'

'Please, Ambrose.'

'Michael, you deliver it well, you sound normal, but it's utter bullshit. Ross Perot used to try the same trick.'

I rubbed at my brow in frustration. I wanted to be rubbing at it because of the pain, because that would be an indication that I was about to zone out again, but I felt 100 per cent normal.

'Okay,' Ambrose said, 'let's say for the sake of argument that these aren't delusions from a damaged brain, and there really are ghosties walking amongst us. Aren't there going to be thousands of them? Isn't that sidewalk going to be busting with them?'

'I don't know, Ambrose.'

'Aren't they going to be crowded around this table, listening in?'

'I don't know, Ambrose.'

'Maybe if you are there, folks, you can give this drink of mine a little nudge, show us what you're made of.' He sat back and indicated his beer. 'Go on, shake it, baby.'

We sat and looked at his beer.

Jo-Anne came out and saw us staring at it. 'Something wrong?' she asked, running her fingers along the back of Ambrose's neck. He glowed.

'Not with you in the world.' He winked, then lifted his beer and sipped. When she went back inside he said: 'She's a lovely big woman, but clingy.'

'Ambrose,' I said, cutting to the chase, 'what's required here is a leap of faith.'

'What's required, my friend, is a mallet, and a drill.'

Ambrose volunteered to drive me back to Lena's. We passed

the traffic signals where I'd seen Claire. He made me point out exactly where, then waved across. 'See anything?' he asked, then laughed and drove on.

He didn't take me home. Instead he parked opposite the First National. He turned the engine off, folded his arms and stared across. 'You will have to agree,' he said rather solemnly, 'that our efforts to research this book, *either* book, have been pretty half-assed. You've been morose and uncooperative . . .'

'. . . and you've been too busy fornicating with a comely barmaid.'

'Granted.'

'Your point is?'

Ambrose shrugged. Then: 'Maybe the point is, there's still a book to be written, and maybe it's different to the one we imagined. Maybe it's not all about you. Maybe it's about a bank robbery that went wrong. Maybe a cover-up. Or a conspiracy.'

I sighed. 'Ambrose, please, we're not back to conspiracy theories.'

The bank manager, Sheldon Adelson, surfer dude gone to seed, appeared briefly in the doorway, shaking hands with a client before disappearing back inside.

'There is something about that man I don't like,' Ambrose observed.

'He's a pompous ass. It tends to go with the job.'

'More than that. I find him shifty.'

'*Shifty*? Isn't that a bit *Scooby Doo*?'

'Don't knock it, your *life* is a bit *Scooby Doo* right now.'

'How is he shifty?'

'He's evasive, and defensive.'

'Because he gave you the brush-off? You can't blame him for that.'

'No, no, you can't. But when I called in to ask if he was aware of Oliver Hall having any family still in town, the thought of Oliver being around seemed to spook him. It wasn't particularly relevant at the time, so I filed it.' He tapped the side of his head.

'And it's relevant now?'

'Now that I think about it, maybe. You see, everyone's been busy making a song and dance about the anniversary of the massacre, but it's all surface, do you know what I mean? Nobody has actually sat down and asked what really happened, and why it panned out the way it did. I mean, these guys go into their home-town bank, where the chances are they'll be recognised, where there really can't be that much money, and they just start shooting for no reason. The violence is way out of proportion. It's actually counterproductive. You rob a bank, you get in there, you shut the doors, try not to draw attention to yourself, get the money and get out quick as you can. If you start shooting, then the chances are the cops are going to be waiting for you when you come out. Does that make sense to you?'

During my ten-year exile from Brevard I had not thought much about the actual mechanics of the robbery or why it had exploded into such awful violence; it was difficult enough living with its consequences.

'I don't know, Ambrose. Maybe they were just amateurs, and they panicked, and once one started shooting, they all joined in.'

'Yeah. Maybe. Well, what about the two who made it out? They hole up outside town, but next thing is, they're shot dead too. No negotiating, no demands, nothing except a medal for Sheriff Newton.'

'He was dealing with a massacre, he was out of his depth. And you forget, most people *liked* the result. At the dinner, they would have carried him on their shoulders if they'd had the strength.'

'Well, it's something else to think about. I also don't like the fact that as soon as I started asking questions, the cops tried to run me out of town.'

'I was under the impression that you got run out of town for being obnoxious. And, incidentally, you're still here.'

'Only because you had a timely brain seizure.'

I smiled. 'Happy to oblige.'

We looked at the bank some more. Customers came, customers went.

'Are you going to turn yourself in?' Ambrose asked suddenly.

'No, I can't. Are you going to rat me out?'

Ambrose briefly drummed his fingers on the steering wheel before giving a little shrug. 'As far as I'm concerned it's your life, you can do what you please with it. I reckon you can get away with it right up to the point where you drop down dead from a brain swell.'

'Thank you, Ambrose. I appreciate it.'

He nodded in response. Then, hesitantly, 'In return . . .'

I sighed. 'So it's not friendship, it's a deal.'

'It's friendship *and* a deal.'

'All right, Ambrose. Whatever you say. What can I do for you?'

'Well, I think a million dollars ought to do it.'

'What?'

Ambrose laughed abruptly and slapped at the wheel. 'If you could see your face. Second thoughts, you probably can, my astral buddy. But yeah – a million bucks ought to do it. Michael, did I ever tell you about my Pulitzers? I did? Well, to tell you the truth, I'm too old and I'm too out of shape to go pounding these mean streets any more, but there's definitely something about this whole set-up that doesn't smell right. So how do you feel about cutting some corners and letting some of that money you never seem to spend do the talking?'

'You've lost me.'

'Simple. We let it be known that there are dollars available to anyone who comes forward with new information about the massacre. I'd be interested to see what it flushes out. Maybe have a word with our friend at the *Herald*, get him to splash it across the front. Something like *'Space Coast' Author Offers $1m Reward* ought to do it.'

'One *million* dollars?'

'I'm not expecting you to *pay* a million. But it's a nice round number, and the rubes will surely fall for it.'

I thought about it.

Then some more.

My head jagged suddenly and I winced. Ambrose didn't seem to notice. He and I were on two different but parallel courses.

I wanted my wife back, and he wanted to know why she had died in the first place. We were both pursuing the same ghosts His approach was practical but expensive. Mine was impossible but cheap.

'Well?' he asked.

I just looked at him.

'If a million's too much . . .'

I would ask his questions of the dead.

35

I told Ambrose I was going to buy flowers for Lena. I didn't ask him to accompany me or give him the opportunity to invite himself. I just came up with the best excuse I could think of, got out and started walking. There was no telling how long I would remain in 'the zone' and I had to strike while the iron was hot. Publix seemed the best place to start, given that it was only a block away and I'd already had one encounter there. I glanced back once, and the car was already gone.

Good.

I hurried through the doors into the welcoming cool of the store, already aware that the dynamics of this 'condition' were changing again. My initial encounters with DeMarcus Hall and Meg had seemed so normal that I had not thought there was anything odd about them until much later. Then my hearing had begun to be affected by it, so that anything abnormal became exaggerated while everyday sounds diminished. I had also felt nauseous. Now, though I was very much back in the zone, there seemed to be a more even balance between the real sounds and the other, exaggerated ones. Thankfully, the old sea-sick feeling was much diminished.

As I picked up a cart and began to reconnoitre the aisles I tried to look as much like a normal shopper as possible. I plucked items at random from the shelves. I kept my speed down. But I was straining to hear something. My heart hammered expectantly. I was *convinced* something would happen, because thus far, whenever I entered the zone, it always had. Even in the hospital I had heard things, but I had stopped myself from investigating, for fear of giving myself away. This time I was determined to face whatever was there. It wasn't a case of me having nothing to lose – I had *everything* to lose. I had been given a glimpse of Claire, and it wasn't enough. I had to see her again.

I circled for nearly half an hour, my cart full – and I was still in the zone, the longest yet – before anything happened.

A bottle smashed.

It happens a dozen times a day in a large supermarket, I'm sure, but there was something about this one, something more precise, cleaner.

I hurried towards it, judging it to be perhaps three aisles away. As I drew nearer there was a PA announcement overhead, directing a cleaner to aisle seven – but as soon as it ended I realised that it had masked the sound of exaggerated footsteps, more than one set of them, moving in my direction, but as yet still hidden. For the first time in my life I felt the hackles rise on the back of my neck.

'Mister!'

It was Meg's voice – behind me. But I couldn't see her.

'Mister! Here!'

Then I spotted her elfin face poking out of a v-shaped space beneath a display cabinet half a dozen yards up the previous aisle.

'Quickly!' Meg was waving me frantically towards her.

The footsteps would become something physical in moments. What could she know that I didn't?

Everything.

This was not my world, it was Meg's.

I abandoned the cart and dove beneath the display. Meg backed up, giving me just enough space to crush in beside her. She put a finger to her lips and took my hand in her own and squeezed it. I don't know what I was expecting, but it felt warm. I was hiding, but I wasn't paralysed: I began to twist around to give myself a better view, and it was only Meg's nails suddenly digging into me that stopped me in the nick of time.

Three pairs of feet, two in track shoes, one in battered army boots, appeared inches from our hiding-place. I felt ludicrous, and pathetic – but I was also filled with an abject horror. Bob, I might argue now, sitting here typing this, that it was only out of consideration for the child that I remained hidden, but I cannot lie. This dread was real. It was . . . and how can I say this without you throwing this manuscript across the room in frustration at the absurdity of it? It was *evil*. I *felt* it then, but I *knew* it later.

After what seemed like an eternity, but which could only have been a matter of seconds, the feet moved out of my line of sight, and their sound rapidly receded. Meg held tightly on to me for another few minutes, and only relaxed her grip when she was quite sure they were gone. She squeezed past me out of the hiding-place and, as a child will, by the time I emerged behind her she had already wiped her tears away and was smiling.

As I brushed the dust from my knees, I realised we were not alone. Simon, with a cart full of Diet Pepsi ready for stacking, stood staring at me.

'Oh, hi,' I said. I nodded down at our refuge. 'I dropped a quarter.'

Simon didn't look convinced. I glanced at Meg. She was staring at me with a look of astonishment on her tiny face.

I smiled at Simon and turned away. Meg walked with me.

'Sir?'

I stopped, took a deep breath, then turned.

'Is this your cart?' Simon asked.

I shook my head. I turned again.

'Sir?'

I stopped. Meg slipped her hand into mine.

'Sir, thank you for helping me with the spilled food. I keep knocking it over. Mr Williams says I am a klutz and should be locked up.' Simon lifted three twelve-packs.

Meg pulled at my hand. 'Mr Williams farts when nobody is looking. He stinks.'

'Simon?'

He heaved the cases onto a shelf and turned. 'Sir?'

'Mr Williams farts when nobody is looking. He stinks.'

Simon looked stunned for several moments, then a grin spread across his heavy features and he began to giggle softly. 'Mr Williams farts,' he said. 'Mr Williams stinks.' He lifted another weight of Pepsi. 'Mr Williams farts, Mr Williams stinks.' He laughed out loud and returned to his stacking. We could still hear him halfway up the aisle.

When we turned the corner I looked down at Meg. She was staring up at me, wide-eyed. 'What?' I asked.

'He sees you.'

I glanced around. 'Who?'

'Simon. Simon sees you.'

'Yes, of course.'

'How does he see you? He doesn't see me.'

The penny dropped, at last. 'I know. I don't know why.'

'But he sees you.'

'Yes, he does.'

An elderly woman, pushing a cart, said, 'Are you talking to me?'

'No, sorry. Talking to myself.'

I hurried on. Meg looked even more astonished. '*She* sees you. He sees you, she sees you. Does *everyone* see you?'

The beach was only a block away and with the late-afternoon coolness, largely deserted. We sat in the sand. Meg drew matchstick men with her fingers. 'I have to go home soon,' she said.

'Where *is* home?'

Her face creased up into a *you're mad* look. 'Home is home. Mom and Dad.'

'Okay. Can *they* see you?'

'No, of course not.'

'But you still live there?'

'I look after them. They're very sad. I make them sad.'

The breeze off the sea was pleasant. A woman in a white bikini jogged past; she kept her eyes straight ahead.

'Meg,' I asked gently, 'do you remember what happened, with the fire?'

She dug her fingers further into the sand and shook her head. 'I'm just here, and they're there. Why can they see you? Why can't they see me?'

'I don't know.'

'It's not fair.'

'I know it's not. Meg – the men in the Publix. Who are they?'

'Bad men. They hurt you and kill you. I don't want to talk about them. They're *mean*.'

'Okay, and are there others – good people, like you?'

Meg shrugged. 'Sometimes you don't know who is who and then they speak to you and they scare you.'

I changed position, moving round so that I could look directly at her. 'Meg? I'm looking for my wife and I think she might be here. I love her very much and I haven't seen her for a long time. If I tell you what she looks like, will you tell me if you've seen her?'

She nodded slowly, but kept her eyes on the sand.

'She's a little smaller than me, she has blonde hair down to her shoulders, and she's beautiful. Her eyes are brown, her nose is kind of—'

'Are you Michael?'

I stared at her, stunned. 'Yes, I'm Michael. You know her? You know Claire?'

'Claire is nice. Claire is my friend.'

My heart was preparing to *burst*. 'Meg, do you know where she is? Can you take me to her?'

Her brow furrowed suddenly, and she jabbed at the sand again. 'If you help me first.'

'Meg, I have to see my wife. Is she close? Can we go now?'

The girl studied her drawing. It was of a house. Although she had attempted to give it detail, it was an impossible task because of the fineness of the sand. She shook her head and gave me a look that was somewhere between mischievous and duplicitous. 'First you have to help me.'

If our positions had been reversed I would probably have tried to bargain as well. But they weren't, and I was so close to finding Claire – and, for all I knew, just as close to zoning out again and possibly losing her for ever. After all, how was I to know how long this all would last?

'Meg, this is really important to me.'

'Really important to *me*. They can see you.'

'Who can?'

'Mom and Dad.'

I suppose there was a rather depressing inevitability to it. She wanted me to tell them she was all right and missed them and loved them and to ask them when she could come home. I tried explaining what might happen if I turned up and started claiming to be in touch with their . . . and I just stopped myself from saying '*dead* daughter' . . . their *invisible* daughter – that I'd already gotten in trouble with the police after speaking to them the last time, but she *literally* dug her heels in.

'It's what I want,' she said firmly.

I had not studied the house closely before, but it was now easy to see a contrast between the older, brittle lower half and the upper level which was made from timber of a more recent hue. It would probably have been better to just knock down the entire structure after the fire, but perhaps it wasn't an option.

Meg took my hand when I hesitated before mounting the steps, pulling me forward. I rang the bell and after a short delay Mrs Anderson, her hair tied back, her face devoid of make-up, answered the door, and looked understandably surprised and not a little embarrassed. Last time we'd met she was naked and her husband, not exactly a bronzed Adonis, had been ramming into her from behind. I wondered briefly if Meg got to see *that* from time to time.

'Mrs Anderson,' I said, 'I'm sorry to trouble you, but I was wondering if I could have a word with you?'

She glanced behind. 'My husband said I wasn't—'

'Pop's not home,' said Meg. 'Pop's at work.'

I kept my eyes fixed on her mom. 'I understand completely.

I understand that you're upset. I just wanted to come by and apologise in person.'

'Tell her,' Meg said.

'I'm sorry,' said Mrs Anderson. 'I can't—'

I held up my hands. 'That's fine. No worries.'

I began to turn away. Meg tugged at my sleeve.

'It wasn't . . .' Mrs Anderson began. I stopped. 'It wasn't what you did – or saw – that upset him so much. It was Meg.'

I nodded. I turned again.

'Perhaps,' Mrs Anderson said, 'you'd like some lemondade, on the veranda?'

It was pink lemonade, sweet with just a little fizz. We sat on either side of a white plastic table. Meg perched on the fence.

'It was a Friday evening,' Mrs Anderson said, her hands clasped in her lap, not looking at me, but in Meg's direction, which made it rather unsettling. 'Bob had finished work, and we had a few beers to celebrate the weekend starting. We weren't big drinkers. But this time, maybe we had a few too many. Meg, she wanted Bob to play with her, but he was tired – you know, he was such a good father, but that time, he was just tired. He told her no, later, but she was just at that age, had to get what she wanted, and she created such a fuss that Bob sent her to her room. Of course, she was a headstrong little thing, and she wouldn't stay put. Half a dozen times he put her up there – never did whip her, not once, we don't believe in that – but he lost his temper, sure, and that last time he just locked her in. Well, we were both smokers then, there was always lighters about the house and I suppose she'd found one and hidden it in her room. Kids do that. That's what they figured, anyways. Thing is, we heard her screaming, but we thought she was just misbehaving again, and we let her scream, reckoned she'd get tired, fall asleep soon enough. Just let her scream. First thing we knew about a fire was a neighbour came running up, saying there was smoke coming out of the back window. Lord knows we tried to get up there, Bob burned all his hands, wasn't nothing we could do. Nothing we could do. I just loved that little girl.'

There were tears in her eyes and tears rolling down Meg's cheeks. She moved off the fence and kissed her mother's cheek. Mrs Anderson blinked, and a moment later touched her cheek, but that was all.

Meg returned to the fence, pulled herself up and nodded for me to start. It was awkward, embarrassing and despicable, but it had to be done. I made several consoling comments, then: 'Mrs Anderson, do you ever feel Meg's presence, you know, around the house?'

'How do you mean?'

'Do you ever, you know, get the feeling she's right there with you, watching over you?'

'Well – what a strange question!'

I was trying to be as delicate as possible, and to not come across like the lunatic I had previously shown myself to be.

'The reason I ask is that at home, in New York, I have a certain, ahm, reputation, or, should I say, I am known to have a certain *ability* – a kind of sensitivity – when it comes to the . . .' I couldn't help but glance up at Meg, who was staring intently at her mom. 'The, shall we say the *missing* – the *invisible*, as it were.'

Mrs Anderson nodded uncertainly. She had taken something of a chance, inviting me to sit with her, and now doubts were surfacing. She reached out to flick a fly off the table, but in so doing turned her wrist slightly to sneak a look at her watch.

It was not going well, but I had to keep at it.

'Mrs Anderson, I'm going to tell you something that you might find rather shocking. You've no reason in the world to trust me, and several reasons not to, but I have to tell you, I have to be honest with you because, well, I think I might be able to help you. You see, that day I entered your house, that day I caused all that fuss, I spoke to your daughter, right here, right on that step.'

Mrs Anderson was just in the act of raising her glass. She set it down again without drinking. She looked at the step. 'Well, I . . .'

Her eyes flitted across to me, and then beyond. I followed them, and saw Mr Anderson pulling up outside the house. He climbed out, waved cheerfully up.

Mrs Anderson stood abruptly, pushing her chair back, 'Mr Ryan, I'm going to have to ask you to leave.'

'Tell her!' Meg hissed.

'Mrs Anderson,' I said quickly, 'you have to believe me. I can talk to your daughter.'

'*Please*,' said Mrs Anderson.

As Mr Anderson approached, he saw who it was and his grin faded. 'What the hell are you doing here?'

I stood and held my hands up. 'I just came to apologise and—'

'He says he can speak to Meg, he says he can speak to Meg! Tell him to go, Bob – tell him to go!'

As I'd seen to my cost, Bob wasn't exactly a sculpted Adonis, but he was a big man. As he came thumping across the porch towards me, I backed away. I had to keep Meg on my side, and getting into a fight with her father was hardly going to help that cause.

'Mr Anderson – please just take it easy. I know we got off on the wrong foot, but if someone could speak to your daughter, if you could speak to her . . . wouldn't you take that chance?'

'You son of a bitch!'

'Haven't we been through enough?!' his wife cried.

I was now up against the rail at the back of the veranda. I made one last attempt to get through to them. 'Please – ask me anything – ask me anything about Meg, something I can't possibly know, and I'll be able to answer it. If I can't, I swear to God I'll write you a cheque for whatever you want – you name it. Please!'

Bob swung for me. I ducked under the punch and threw myself over the fence. It was a smart enough move, but I ended up in an undignified heap in the neighbour's flowerbed. Bob towered over me from the veranda.

'You bastards think you can buy anyone, don't you?' he snarled.

His wife appeared beside him, placing a restraining arm around his waist. She looked sadly down at me. 'You of all people should know what it's like to lose someone.'

I got to my knees. 'I do know. Mrs Anderson, I'm trying to find my wife again, and Meg's helping me.'

'You bastard!' Bob spat.

'I'm calling the police!' Mrs Anderson spun on her heel.

Bob tried to vault over the rail, but he wasn't quite athletic enough.

Meg appeared beside me. 'What are you doing?' she demanded. 'You have to tell them!'

I didn't respond, I didn't even look. I stood and brushed down my trousers as Bob gripped the rail and glared down at me. 'You get the hell out of my neighbourhood,' he spat, 'or I swear to God . . . !'

I took a step back, but I couldn't leave it. 'Mr Anderson, please, just one question. Ask me anything about your daughter. The police have already arrested me once – why would I risk it again if I don't believe one hundred million per cent that I can talk to Meg? Why?'

There was, somewhere in the far distance, a siren. With the knowledge that the police were close, and having shown me who was boss by chasing me off the veranda, Bob evidently decided that he didn't have anything to lose. His mouth curled up in contempt as he spoke. 'All right, bigshot, tell me this. Meg had a toy, a panda, her favourite toy in all the world. You tell me its name.'

Meg knelt beside me. 'Pierre,' she whispered.

I looked up at Bob, relief flooding through me. Everything was going to be okay.

'Pierre,' I said.

The big man shook his head disdainfully. 'You need to be locked up, ass-hole.'

I turned to Meg, but she was gone. The sound had shifted again, that airplane popping, and I was out of the zone, back in the real world. There was just dirty-kneed me in a strange garden, Bob glowering at me from his chipped veranda, and the police siren, closer, ever closer. I got to my feet and started running.

36

I was going to say that it was like being a teenager again, hiding out in the back bedroom while my parents defended me against a scurrilous allegation which I was, in fact, guilty of. But the truth is I was always a good, straight A's kid, even then a writer, not a fighter. And it was not my parents out front, standing up for me, it was Lena Olson, my doctor, my lover. I couldn't quite hear her argument, but it sounded robust and it must have been convincing, because the squad car eventually roared away. However, I did not for one moment believe that just because Lena had defended me, she was going to let me get away with it.

When she came in she was furious. She had every right to be.

'You promised me!' she raged. 'I *trusted* you!'

'I'm sorry. I just wanted to apologise.'

'They're good people. They don't deserve this shit. And neither do I!'

'I know. I'm sorry.'

She glared. I stared at the floor. I was still out of breath. I had run through a lot of gardens. I had torn my skin on shrubbery. There was a slight sense of elation that I had managed to avoid the police and make it back to base, but it was more than adequately countered by my embarrassment at getting myself and Lena into this situation.

Pandas.

Never fucking there for you when you need them.

Bob, all joking aside, I was almost overwhelmed by confusion and despair. As if a travel agent had shown me the Promised Land in a brochure, then yanked it away from me and stolen my deposit. I had been convinced that Meg was real, but when it had come to proving it, she had let me down badly; or I, in imagining her, had let myself down. Whatever I was seeing, whatever delusions I was embracing, they had failed me. The only reasonable conclusion I could come to was that Meg did not exist and that Claire was nothing more than a fantasy. I had been in denial: just because the doctors had not found a brain injury, it didn't mean it wasn't there. It was a tiny, minuscule leak that defied technology but manifested itself by plunging me in and out of a strange fantasy world. If I did not seek treatment immediately, next time it might dunk me down so hard that I could not resurface. I would be lost in an eternal pursuit of my dead wife.

I could not continue like this. I was a fool, an embarrassing fool. It was time to come clean to Lena, to confess that I was still in the grip of my delusions. I think she was aware of my turmoil, for when she next spoke, her tone was softer.

'Michael, are you okay?'

It was the perfect opportunity.

'Yes, Doctor.'

She even managed a smile. 'Truth?'

'Yes, Doctor.'

The *truth*, which I fully realised only in that instant, was that I was more scared of losing Claire than I was of losing my life. *All* of the facts were pointing in one direction. Yet hope lay in the other, and I just couldn't let it go – at least, not yet. I had already gotten myself into hot water by making rapid-fire decisions, and now I was on the verge of making another while still sweaty and disorientated by the catastrophe at the Andersons' and the subsequent pursuit across town. I was 90 per cent set on giving myself up for treatment, but wouldn't it be better to calm down first, get my thoughts in order? Perhaps sleep on it?

Bob, I can see now how much like a gambler or alcoholic I was. Every addict is a living contradiction: self-aware *and* delusional. The victory was always in the next hand, heaven in the next drink. That was me in a nutshell, and I was incapable of doing anything about it except lie some more.

She came to me and put her arms around me. 'I worry about you,' she said.

'I worry about me,' I said. I kissed her brow. 'Look, my head was sore, I poked around looking for some painkillers, but you have just about everything locked up. I found a bottle in a cupboard, no label, I just took a chance. They *did* work. But then I had a drink with Ambrose and everything got a little fuzzy. I should have called you. I think Ambrose put it in my head that I should go and see them; he thought it would do me good, and help our book. So I went, but it was a bad idea. I'm sorry.' I felt no guilt at using Ambrose as a convenient scape-goat. The guy owed me.

'Are you sure you're all right?'

'Yes, I'm fine. I didn't mean to embarrass you. I didn't mean to upset the Andersons. Maybe I should call round and apologise.'

'Michael! This isn't funny. Sheriff Newton was all for dragging your ass down to the station.'

'You talked him out of it.'

'Only because I like your ass here.' Pause. 'Where it can do some practical good.' She kissed me again. 'And also, Sheriff Newton is an arrogant prick.'

I liked Lena a lot. Perhaps I was even starting to love her. The problem was, that even as I kissed her, at least part of me was thinking, Are we alone? Is Meg here in the room with us? Is *Claire* here? I was already slipping right back into believing in that world. I could not relax, I could not concentrate, and it was only a few moments before Lena sensed it. She stiffened against me, then turned away and muttered something about making us dinner. I felt terrible, but what could I do or say? I just needed a little time. It wasn't much to ask. Or *not* ask.

* * *

We lay in bed, together but apart. We did not make love. She wanted to know what *this* was – our relationship. She had wanted to keep it light and fluffy, like a holiday romance, but the entire experience was so tied up with tragedy that she thought it might more easily be described as a funeral romance. I had almost forgotten she too had lost a loved one, and a lot more recently than I had.

'People will say we're two lost souls finding each other,' she whispered, 'except, my soul isn't lost.'

I stroked her shoulders and back. She was lit only by moonlight coming through the open window. 'Your father died. It's a *little* bit lost.'

Lena nodded gently. 'I deliver bad news every day, people die, and then I help their loved ones grieve. I ought to be immune to it. But the more I practise, the more I realise that you can have the most loving, rewarding relationship in the world, and at the end you'll still ask yourself why you didn't do this better or that better, why you didn't say this, or why you said that. It's the nature of things. Then, time passes, people recover, they create new relationships, they love again. Do you know what I mean?'

I nodded against her, even though I was living, breathing evidence of someone who could not move on. I was older, but not wiser.

'Michael – if holiday romances always end in tears, what about romances that *begin* with tears . . . Do they end with smiles and love?'

'I hope so,' I said, and kissed the back of her neck. She snuggled up. After a few minutes, and a little to my surprise, her breathing eased into sleep.

As the moon rose higher and its reflected light brightened the bedroom further, I pushed myself up on one elbow and watched Lena as she slept. She was so beautiful, and bright, and funny. Just like Claire. Yet nobody who knew them both could ever have argued that I was attracted to Lena because she reminded me of my wife. They were *completely* different people. I have said previously that there was no hope for my relationship with Lena because no one was ever going to replace Claire, but I realise now that this was not only harsh, but also quite irrelevant. Lena was never going to be a replacement *anything*; she wasn't a spare part to be slotted in when something goes wrong with the original. She was absolutely her own wonderful person. When I was with her I felt happy and relaxed in a way that I hadn't been in years – and this *despite* everything that was going on. In the past, when I got myself into situations, my instinct had always been to run away, but in Brevard, my instinct was to run to Lena.

I was falling for her.

I was up really early. I'd spent half the night trying to decide which course of action was right – continuing this mad pursuit of Claire, or submitting to further medical investigation and probable surgery. By eight a.m., and no closer to a decision, I could hear Lena moving around upstairs. I called up to see if she wanted coffee.

'Yes,' she shouted back, 'and sex.'

The doorbell rang.

Lena shouted down, 'Tell them to go to the surgery!'

When I opened the front door, Mrs Anderson was standing there. I was surprised, and a little worried. I looked around her for Bob.

'I'm sorry,' she said. She was red-eyed and pale.

'Sorry?'

'For getting the police, for chasing you off, for Bob throwing you over the fence.'

'Well, he didn't actually—'

'He told me what you said.'

'I . . .'

'Meg had the panda since she was a toddler. She wanted a Winnie the Pooh, but the store was sold out, so we bought the panda instead. She insisted on calling it Winnie. He went everywhere with her. But on the day of the fire she said out of nowhere that Winnie was a stupid name for a panda. She said from now on she was going to call him Pierre.'

Lena shouted, 'Who is it?'

We ignored her.

'Pierre the Panda. Before I could tell Bob, she was dead. I never did tell anyone. Mr Ryan, nobody else *knows*, nobody in the whole wide world. You've been talking to my daughter. You've been talking to my Meg.'

Without really knowing why, I stepped forward and I hugged her. She cried against me. Hope was reborn, and honesty be damned.

37

As I embraced Beth for the third time – that was her name, and she insisted I call her by it; *Mrs Anderson* was much too stuffy now that we had made up – Bob gave me a sheepish thumbs-up from the car. It took a while to get through to her that I could not just turn *it* on like a tap, that there was no point in her waiting around for something to happen. She peppered me with questions and I answered as many as I could; as far as I could judge, everything I told her conformed to her memories of her daughter. I didn't tell her about our experience in Publix or the 'bad men'. Eventually she agreed to go, but only because Bob was late for work and she needed him to take her home first. I walked her to the car, aware that Lena was watching from inside. I made a show of shaking hands with both of them, while quietly promising to drop everything and race to their house as soon as anything started to happen. Beth asked what time did I think I'd be visiting, and I had to explain again that there was no predicting it. She gave me another hug. She glowed.

As they drove off, I pounded my fist into my hand and said, 'Yes!' Everything was different now. These were not delusions. It wasn't a case of me seeing things, it was a case of everyone else *not* being able to see them. The doors to perception were split asunder.

'What're you looking so happy about?' Lena was at the front door, already dressed for work.

'I've been forgiven,' I said, 'by an act of Christian charity. It restores your faith in human nature.'

'Well, good for them.' She came up and kissed me. 'I'm late for work.' Then she smiled and purred: 'But I can be later.' She kissed me again. 'Five minutes. Maybe ten. What do you say?'

Last night's inquest into our relationship was clearly forgotten. Of *course* I wanted to make love to Lena, but with my hopes of meeting Claire revived, I was suddenly concerned that my going to bed with Lena might now constitute a real betrayal. I hesitated, and she detected it *again*. She cooled immediately.

'Second thoughts,' she said, and left it like that. She hurried down the path to her car. As she unlocked it, she looked back up at me on the porch.

'Promise me something,' she said.

I nodded.

'Today, don't do anything silly.'

'Okay,' I said. I sneezed.

Lena looked at me. There was no 'Bless you'.

Patience is a virtue. I did not have patience. I paced. I *willed*. Nothing happened beyond the slow development of a headcold. I sniffed and snorted while I rehearsed what I would say to Claire. Nothing sounded right. I had waited ten years to see her again, and I was going to wing it. What, after all, do you say to someone under such circumstances?

Long time no see?

Luckily, I was able to channel my impatience into anger. Ambrose appeared at Lena's shortly after nine with a freshly printed copy of the *Brevard Herald*. He laid it out on the kitchen table, and beamed.

'Jesus Christ,' I said. The headline read: $1M REWARD FOR FIRST NATIONAL MASSACRE INFO.

There was a second, smaller headline beneath: MICHAEL RYAN TO BREAK 'CONSPIRACY OF SILENCE' accompanied by a photo of me, clearly taken at the memorial dinner. I appeared red-faced. I looked drunk.

'Jesus Christ,' I said.

'You're the man,' said Ambrose.

'Jesus Christ,' I said again.

'The man not happy?' Ambrose asked innocently.

'What the fuck do you think?'

'You gave me permission.'

'I did *not*.'

'Well, you were about to, then you charged out of the car to buy flowers. You were distracted. I thought this might help you to focus.'

'Jesus Christ, Ambrose, this is crazy.'

'Well,' he said, 'you're the expert on crazy.'

Despite the size of the headlines, the article itself was relatively restrained. It recounted the facts of the robbery as they were reported at the time, and featured several quotes from Ambrose, who was described as a multi-Pulitzer Prize-winning reporter who was working with me on a book about the massacre. He explained that I had experienced severe psychological problems as a result of the robbery and the loss of my wife, and that it was only now, ten years down the line, that I had felt well enough to investigate the circumstances surrounding it. I felt there were a number of questions which remained unanswered and I was offering the reward in the hope that members of the public would come forward to tell their story. Ambrose's cell phone number was printed in a little black box in the middle of the text. There was no mention of *Oprah*, no *Letterman*; no hint that Springsteen was about to immortalise the robbery in song. When I expressed my surprise, he shrugged. 'You can give that crap to the rubes,' he said, 'but you sure as hell don't want to see it in print.'

'And has your phone been ringing nonstop?' I asked.

'No, but the ink's hardly dry. I have every confidence. It'll just be a question of sorting the wheat from the chaff.' He nodded to himself for a moment, looking thoughtful. 'Chaff,' he repeated. 'Not a word you hear a lot of these days. But apt.'

I shook my head. '*You're* fucking *apt*.'

His cell rang. A smug, superior smile appeared. 'Here we go,' he said, and answered in a deep, authoritative voice. He listened for quite a while. 'Love you too,' he said at the end of it.

'Jo-Anne?'

'Wife.'

It did start, slowly, but by lunchtime it had snowballed. Ambrose made himself at home in the lounge, plumped up on the sofa with his feet on the coffee-table. I brought him drinks and snacks while he fielded the calls and made notes. He was very good at cutting through the waffle and weeding out the cranks and his questions were sharp but delivered with a surprising politeness. He suited his demeanour to that of his callers, and he could suss them out in an instant. He became a Southern gentleman, a god-fearing Christian or a cussin' redneck as required. Lena, returning at lunchtime, got to hear Ambrose extolling the virtues of aromatherapy massage and talking to trees to one caller, while rolling his eyes at us.

I made us coffee and we adjourned to the small gazebo in her back garden. Lena seemed withdrawn, slightly austere.

'Tough morning?' I asked.

She ignored the question. 'Michael, what's going on here?'

'Oh, don't worry about Ambrose. I can ask him to leave. With a cell phone you can go anywhere, it's amazing.'

'I mean, what's going on here, with us?'

I laughed, trying to keep it light. 'Is that not more like a three-month question, rather than a three-day?'

She remained grim-faced. 'Michael, we've crushed three days into three months. Sometimes I feel like I've got you one hundred per cent, other times it's like you're not here at all.'

She was right, of course. And she deserved a straight answer, but I could not give it. The only proof I had of my breakthrough was Meg, and she was really no proof at all.

Lena set her coffee down. I set mine down. She took my hand. 'Michael,' she said.

'Is this how you deliver bad news, at work?'

'It's not bad news. It's commonsense. I was in love with you when I was a student, and you didn't know it. Then you came back and I got to be with you, and it was great. And before your head gets too big, you're not perfect, and sometimes I want to throttle you, but I am falling for you. But I don't sense it coming back from you. I think this is just a fling to you. If it is, then tell me that now, and move on, because I don't want you to break my heart.'

My head jagged.

You see, in comedy, timing is everything. And the line between comedy and tragedy is a thin one indeed.

I was holding hands with a wonderful woman who should be loved, while dying to get to a fantastic woman who had been loved, and might be loved again.

'Michael?' Her voice echoed distantly. 'Is that all it is to you?'

I raised her hand and I kissed it.

Then I stood up and walked away.

38

Bob and Beth Anderson sat on the sofa in their front room, backs erect, eyes front. There was coffee on a tray, together with an unopened packet of double chocolate chip cookies. They said, 'Is she here?' about twenty times.

She wasn't.

It was embarrassing. I was a carpet salesman who'd forgotten his samples.

Bob had roared home from work moments after Beth spotted me hurrying along the sidewalk. He fiddled with his tie, loosening it, then tightening it, then loosening it. I could tell he couldn't quite believe he was doing this. It was, after all, based on the name of a panda. Pierre had not survived the fire. Eventually, after perhaps half an hour during which the small talk had evaporated into awkward silence I suggested going out to look for Meg. 'She's probably out playing somewhere,' I said, not very convincingly.

'She's out *playing*,' Beth dreamily repeated, squeezing Bob's hand. He patted it. They clearly loved each other. Their burden was not an easy one, and in many ways worse than my own. My only fault was coming into Claire's life in the first place; theirs was indirectly causing their daughter's death.

Then, without any fuss, she was there, walking through the open door. Meg sat on the arm of my chair and began to suck her thumb.

'They understand now,' I said gently.

'I know.' She appeared sullen.

Bob and Beth stared at me. 'You're talking to her?' Beth asked. I nodded.

'Tell her we love her very much,' said Bob.

'She can hear you,' I said.

They looked awkwardly at each other. Then Beth inched forward. 'Meg,' she said, taking care to shape her words distinctly, as if she was speaking to an elderly relative, 'we love you *very much*. Are you *okay*?'

Meg clasped her hands around her knees and began to rock back and forth. She bit down on her lower lip.

'Meg?'

'Tell them I hate them.'

'Meg!'

'Tell them I hate them!'

My only real interest was in gaining Meg's co-operation in finding Claire, but I couldn't bring myself to be so harsh.

'She says she loves you very much and misses you.'

Tears rolled down Beth's cheeks. Bob put an arm around her shoulders and squeezed her.

'No!' Meg yelled. 'I don't love them! I hate them! They locked me in my room! I can't ever come home! I hate them!'

'She says she wishes she could come home . . .'

'I was screaming, I couldn't get out and they were drinking beer . . . !'

'She doesn't blame you for what happened, it was an accident.'

'I hate them! Tell them!'

'Ask her if she remembers what happened when we brought the puppy home.'

'Bob,' I gently reminded him, 'she can hear you.'

'Meg – do you remember what happened when we brought the *puppy* home?'

'They said I was allergic to it and got rid of it. I hate them! They spoil everything! They're always fighting! When Mom's asleep he looks at DVDs with women with no clothes on, except she's not asleep, she's drinking vodka.'

'Meg says she was allergic to it.'

'Yes, she was,' said Beth, nudging her husband. 'Yes, she was!'

'You're not telling them what I say – you have to tell them what I say!'

'Meg, are you an angel?' Beth sat forward, eager for confirmation. 'You were our little angel.'

'You locked me in my room! You locked me in! You locked me in and something happened and I can't come home! You . . . assholes!'

'She's *like* an angel,' I began tactfully, 'but more mischievous.' Meg screamed and suddenly struck out at me, catching me on the side of the face. I tried to cover it by changing position. 'She stays the same age – and plays . . .' I waved my hands in what must have appeared to be a rather vague manner while actually giving Meg a shove off the arm of my chair; she landed on her bottom and let out a shocked cry . . . 'and she can still be quite a handful. Was she prone to temper tantrums?'

'Yes, she was,' said Bob.

'But she had a heart of gold. They only ever . . .' Beth trailed off. She was staring at me. 'Your face – you're bleeding.'

My hand went to my cheek. Sure enough, blood. Meg had caught me. 'Sorry, cut myself shaving this morning,' I said. 'Thought it had healed.'

Meg stood defiantly by the arm of the chair. 'Wasn't my fault,' she said. 'You pushed me.'

'You deserved it,' I said. 'Now behave.'

'Will not.'

Her parents looked concerned, and confused.

'I'm sorry,' I said. 'Sometimes the signal fades in and out. If you could just give me one minute.'

I crossed the lounge and beckoned for Meg to follow. She stayed where she was. I went back and took her by the hand. She resisted. I dragged her across the room. She wailed: 'Let me *go*!'

It must have looked bizarre, but I was past caring. I needed Meg, but I didn't need *this*.

I led her out onto the porch, then positioned her before me

and crouched down to her eye-level. I became aware of Bob and Beth watching through the glass. I moved us along.

'Now *listen* to me. You whined and whined about getting to talk to your parents, and now you have the chance, you're fucking it up.'

She looked genuinely stunned by the f-word. 'Momma says you shouldn't say—'

'Be quiet! Meg, this is serious. This might be your only chance to speak to your parents, *ever*. I hardly understand this myself, but for some reason I am caught between two worlds, yours and theirs. I don't know how long it will last. So *please*. I understand you're annoyed with them, and if you want to sulk and be mad at them, that's up to you, but I'm telling you, you might regret it for the rest of your . . .' I stopped. I sighed. I took her by the shoulders. 'Please. Talk to them. They love you so much.'

She stared at me, and her eyes got that squished-up look kids get when they try to stop themselves from crying because they think they're too old for it.

'Okay?' I asked.

Meg nodded.

I think, if they could have, the Andersons would have kept me there all day, or for ever. Meg sat on the floor and chatted happily. She was a delight. They laughed. They cried. I laughed. I cried. I edited and occasionally fabricated. There were things about Meg's world I didn't understand, and which she either couldn't grasp herself or didn't yet have the vocabulary to explain. That would hopefully come as and when I got to speak to Claire. Or perhaps this world was as strange and unknowable to its denizens as it was to me.

Eventually I said, 'I have to go.'

I'd been in the zone for nearly two hours, I was drained emotionally and physically, but the purpose of all this was to get to Claire.

'No,' said Meg.

'Please stay,' said Beth. 'Talk some more.'

'No, I can't, but I will come back.'

'You *have* to stay,' said Meg.

'No, you promised to take me to Claire.'

'Later.'

'No, Meg. I did this for you, now you have to keep your end of the bargain. Remember, caring is sharing.'

She screwed her face up. 'I'm not a *baby*!'

Bob looked to where he supposed Meg was standing. 'Mr Ryan has been very kind,' he said gently, 'coming to help us like this, but he has to go now, and you have to let him.'

'But I don't want him to go!' I didn't relay this to them. '*Tell* them I don't want you to go!'

'No.'

'What does she say?' Bob asked.

'She says that's fine,' I said, and gave her a look.

She pouted.

It took a further fifteen minutes. More tears. Beth hugged me and went upstairs. Bob shook my hand and walked me out.

'This means a lot to Beth,' he said as we stepped onto the veranda. He closed the door behind us. He had taken a full and lively part in the proceedings. He had shed tears. It didn't stop him saying, 'I don't know how you do it, but it's very convincing.' He took out his wallet, removed a $100 note and held it out to me.

I shook my head. He raised an eyebrow and crushed the note into my top pocket. 'Thanks for coming,' he said. He turned back to the house.

'Aren't you going to say goodbye to Meg?'

He stopped. He snorted. Then he went back inside.

Meg slipped her hand into mine. 'He locked me in my room. I prefer my mom. I *like* my mom.' She smiled up at me. 'Let's go and find Claire. I like her too. She lives in a big blue house.'

39

It worried me and frightened me that Claire had chosen the Blue House as her, if you will, place of residence. Had she been there when I'd first returned with Lena and cried over the fridge magnets? Was she just next door when I was having my first drunken relations with Lena? Mostly, though, it excited me. Now she was just a few hundred metres away, in our house – in our *home*. As I hurried along the sidewalk Meg kept telling me to slow down, but I wouldn't. *Couldn't.*

Then the house was before me, standing dark and austere in the early-evening gloom. I rushed up the steps – and then rushed right down them again. In my excitement I'd forgotten that I needed the keys to get in – Claire was hardly going to answer the doorbell. I charged across to Lena's, ran up her steps, opened the front door (which she always kept unlocked) and then darted down to the utility room where she kept her keys hung on a series of hooks. I picked out the Blue House keys and was just heading back to the front door when Lena stepped out of the kitchen, a coffee in one hand and a bread-knife in the other.

'Oh – it's you! I thought—' she said.

'Lena – can't stop.'

'Michael, what's going on?'

'I can't stop!' Down the steps, back to the Blue House, shirt sticking to my skin, no sign of Meg. Good!

'Michael?' Lena was behind me. 'What are you doing?'

'Not now, Lena!' I had the door open. I jabbed in the alarm code. It hadn't changed in a decade. Nothing in the house had changed in a decade.

'Claire!' I switched the lights on. 'Claire!'

I turned into the front room. 'Claire! It's me! I'm home!'

Out again, along the hall into the kitchen. 'Claire!'

Room to room to room.

'Claire!'

Of course – she'd be upstairs, in our bedroom. There, to be reunited!

Halfway up.

'Michael.' Lena, pale in low wattage. 'What are you doing?'

'Get *out*!' I charged up the stairs. Our bedroom. Lights on. 'Claire!'

Empty.

Bedroom to bedroom to bedroom. Bathroom. 'Claire!'

'Michael.'

I spun. Lena again. 'Fuck! Will you just get out!'

'Michael, she's not here.'

'Shut up! You don't know what you're talking about!' I surged past her, back down the landing and into our bedroom. 'Claire!'

'Michael . . .'

I stood in the middle of the floor, barely able to breathe. Was I doing something wrong? Was I scaring Claire? Could she just blink out of view? Could she walk through fucking walls? Anything was possible – anything!

I ran to the window and yanked it open. 'Meg!' I shouted. 'Meg – she's not here! Meg! What's happening?'

But of course there was no Meg, and I credit you with realising before I did that I had zoned out again. Of *course*! It was both a relief and a huge frustration. I had been under for several hours, the longest yet by far – and it didn't mean they weren't there. I just couldn't see them. I put my hands out in front of me. I turned in a circle. Was I touching my wife? Was she standing there, tears rolling down her cheeks the way they were rolling down mine?

'Claire,' I said. 'I'm back, I'm home.'

There was only the sea breeze through the open window.

I sat on the edge of the bed, and my head slumped down.

Lena came across and went to put her arms around me. 'Don't!' I snapped, raising my own hands to stop her. 'Just *don't*. Just leave me alone. Please.'

'I can't—'

'Just do it! This is my fucking house! Get out!'

She stood her ground. 'Michael – you're not well. You must know that. I want you to come with me, we need to go back to the hospital. Okay?'

'No.'

'Michael, *please*.'

'No! Just leave me alone!'

'I can help you, but only if you come with me now.'

'Get out!'

'Michael, if you don't come with me, I'm going to have to call for help.'

'I *can't*! Just leave me alone. Just *go*.'

Lena shook her head slowly. 'Okay,' she said. 'Have it your way.' She backed out of the room, the way you would if you were scared of being attacked.

Had it come to that? That she was scared of me?

I didn't wish it, but maybe it was good that she was scared. She had been kind to me, but I didn't need her interfering now that I was *this* close to seeing Claire. It was just a matter of being patient. I would stay in the house until my head jagged and I was back in the zone again. Lena cared, of course she did, she was worried for me, but I couldn't explain because she wouldn't understand. It was *my* house, and what I did in it was my business. If anyone tried to stop me, Christ, I would make them pay. I was the richest man in Brevard *by far*. I could have bought and sold the entire town.

Jagging out was inevitable.

All I had to do was wait.

Easier said than done.

'Claire – if you're there, give me a sign. Do something.' I looked from the curtain to the mirror to the bedside lamp. Was it too much to ask that one should billow, the other mist up, the lamp switch itself on?

Yes, of course it was.

Before, the memories associated with this Blue House had been too overpowering for me, but now they seemed to welcome me in. It was my home, it would always be my home. I should embrace it. I would move back in. A home with my wife in it half the time was better than no home at all. There had to be life here again. I opened the remaining bedroom windows. Then I systematically went from room to room, switching the lights on, opening those windows, allowing the salty air in and the musty air out. I hurried downstairs. I opened the windows there, and then returned to the front room and knelt down before my CD-player. My CDs were the only thing about the house that weren't ten years out of date – because I'd never really had my finger on the pulse. The Stones were timeless, The Beatles, The Who, The Byrds. I selected The Kinks.

'Lola'.

I blasted it.

I was gripped by a euphoric belief that all would be well as long as I was here in this house, that all of my problems thus far in Brevard had been caused by interaction with other people; that if I was just left alone I could cope perfectly well with whatever life or death threw at me.

'Let It Be'.

A song for every occasion.

There was wine in Joe's old cellar – vintage in terms of my lifespan. I opened a bottle, poured a large glass and returned with it and the bottle to the front room in time to catch the neon glow of a police car as it came to a halt outside. A moment later, an ambulance pulled in behind it.

Ah.

I turned the music down. Closed a window. As I looked out I could see neighbours on the other side of the street standing in their front gardens looking across. Okay, so music blasted out of an apparently deserted house in a quiet neighbourhood must have caused a little head-scratching. Perhaps I was disturbing the peace. But they weren't going to bust me for that. The ambulance told me that Lena had been as good as her word and had brought the paramedics to help subdue me and take me away. The cops were coming up to the front door; the paramedics right behind. Lena was with them. The question was, was I within my rights to stand at the door and argue with them, or could they just grab me and take me and worry about the legalities later?

There was a heavy and sustained knocking on the front door.

America – land of the free and the litigious. I turned the music up again, then took the front-door keys and walked through to the kitchen. I slipped out and across the garden and hopped over the fence, with Smokey Robinson and the 'Tears of a Clown' masking my escape.

40

The tourist season was over, so most of the stores on Main Street were already closed, although it was only early evening. I chose one with a well-shadowed entrance and hid there while I decided on my next move. Once the fuss had died down I intended to sneak back to the Blue House and wait for Claire. Now that I had time to breathe, I realised I might have handled Lena better, and blasting the music had been foolish, but I hadn't hurt anyone. I just wanted to see my wife again: what was so unreasonable about that?

For the moment, returning there was out of the question, and so was seeking refuge in any of my usual haunts – the Publix, the grill or the Comfort Inn. I was fairly certain the police and paramedics had only attended because Lena had persuaded them that it was a life or death situation, so they weren't just going to leave it with a cursory search of the house; they were performing an essential public service, saving a sick man's life. Besides, I was the celebrated author of *Space Coast*, not just some ordinary Joe; there would be press and promotion.

I checked my messages. Ambrose had left three, wanting to know where I was and why I wasn't picking up. He said there'd been lots of calls following the newspaper article 'and not all of them crappy'.

I called him.

He said, 'Where the hell are you?'

'I'm here.'

'Lena's looking for you. She says you need urgent medical attention. She has a habit of stating the blindingly obvious.'

'Do I sound like I need urgent medical attention?'

'Well, no more than you normally do.'

'Good. Then come and pick me up.'

He said he'd be there in ten minutes. He wasn't exactly a friend, and he wasn't exactly trustworthy. So when I told him where I was, I wasn't exactly truthful; but I could see our proposed meeting-point from my hidden position and would know if he arrived with back-up and butterfly nets.

As I waited in the darkness I became aware of an elderly couple hurrying along the street opposite. There was nothing special or distinctive about them, but they seemed nervous and glanced behind them several times before turning sharply off into an alleyway and out of sight. A few moments later, a teenager came past on a bike, riding hard in the opposite direction; he skidded to a halt almost directly opposite to me, looked both ways then he too turned into the alley. I was just passing the time, waiting for Ambrose, and curiously wondering what the attraction up that alley might be when another figure appeared, this time running along the opposite side of the street – and not just running, but from his anxious glances back, very clearly running *from* something. I was just having a little wager with myself over whether he too would turn into the alley, when he stepped into the full glare of a streetlight and I saw who it was.

Oliver Hall. No – not Oliver Hall. DeMarcus. Not a copy. The original.

No jag, no warning, just straight into the zone.

I thought later that whatever *it* was, it was accelerating; wherever the dividing line had been, it was disintegrating, but there and then the sight of DeMarcus running past was beyond analysis and just thrust me straight into action. Ever since this weirdness had come upon me, my only source of information had been a confused child, but DeMarcus, even though he'd thumped me on our last encounter, was at least an adult and would surely

260

know more. Even if I had to punch it out of him. You see, he'd taken me by surprise last time: now it was my turn.

'DeMarcus!'

I stayed hidden in the store doorway, as DeMarcus spun towards me, shocked, and peered into my darkness.

'Who the fuh . . . ?'

I thundered across the road, adrenaline surging through me. I wasn't particularly in shape, but I knew I had the beating of him. He was tall and wiry, but not like a boxer with hidden muscle; he was just skin and bone. He took several steps back while raising his hands in a vain attempt to protect himself. I thumped into him, forcing him back across the sidewalk and into a wall.

I stuck my face right into his. 'DeMarcus, fucking DeMarcus Hall.'

His eyes widened. 'Oh man, not now – not now!' He was shocked by my attack, but he was more scared of something else. He tried to push past. I thrust him back.

'You're not going anywhere, you murdering son of a bitch!'

'I didn't, it wasn't . . .' His eyes flitted left, then he threw himself against me again, but there was no strength to him. 'Not now, not now,' he pleaded. 'They're coming, they're coming!'

He tried it again, and this time I let him have it: a clean punch to the jaw. He dropped, but I think it was more the shock of it; it probably hurt me more than it hurt him. I cradled my hand and he scrambled away, jumped back to his feet and started running. He turned into the alley. I would have gone after him, but I was distracted by new sounds – exaggerated footsteps, ribald echoing voices, laughter, just as I'd heard in the Publix that day with Meg. As I turned towards them I realised that even a moment's delay had been too long, for they were upon me.

Ty Whitelaw.

Lawrence Shaw.

And bringing up the rear, but effortlessly dominating, Tommy Ford.

Bob, you're probably 500 steps ahead of me, but I swear that even though I'd previously been assaulted by DeMarcus Hall, had followed him across town, and only moments before had thrown him against a wall, I had never once considered the possibility that Tommy Ford and the rest of the gang would be part of this new world. I had been so focused on finding Claire that everything had been channelled towards that. But now here he was, 'alive', and closing in. And worse – they were armed with pistols and assault rifles, just as they had been on the day of the robbery.

This was what Meg had hidden from, this was what the seniors and the cyclist had fled from, what even DeMarcus Hall was so frightened of – Tommy Ford, calling the shots in Ghost Town.

I froze.

I didn't know whether to run and hide, or plead, or try to brazen it out. This was so entirely new and unexpected I just couldn't conjure up any kind of coherent response. The last time I'd met Tommy Ford, he and his gang had beaten me to within six inches of my life. Now here he was, right in front of me, broad shoulders intact, muscles poking through his T-shirt, his sarcastic grin spread across his chiselled jaw, every inch of him as alive as you or me.

I held my breath, I stared ahead, I avoided eye-contact.

Ty and Lawrence joined Tommy. I was surrounded.

Tommy leered right into my face. 'Just can't drag yourself away, can you, boy?'

Say nothing. Stay calm. Don't provoke them.

'Look at you, you smug fuck,' he sneered. 'We ever find that wife of yours, boy, we'll fuck her over good.'

'Shoulda finished him off the first time,' said Ty.

Lawrence nodded beside him. 'If I could just smash his fucking Ivy League face.'

'He's not fucking Ivy League,' snapped Tommy. 'He's fucking Irish.'

They weren't aware that I could see them! It was an astonishing, possibly life-saving development. They were menacing and threatening me, but didn't think they could do a thing about it. I had presumed there would be a way for the people of this world to recognise each other, but it seemed not. All I had to do was play to their beliefs and act like I couldn't see them either.

I looked at my watch.

'Fucking Rolex,' said Ty. He pushed his face right up into mine. His breath was rancid. 'Big writer, aren't you, so fucking superior.' Then he shook his head. 'Come on, they're around here somewhere.' He turned away.

Lawrence went with him. Tommy stood where he was.

I took out my cell phone and began to study it.

Tommy drew his fist back and swung at me. I refused to blink or react, even though it came within an inch of my face. He held it there for a long moment, then dropped it and cursed.

'Come on, Tommy,' Lawrence shouted back.

Tommy gave me one last hard, frustrated look before going after his companions.

At that moment, of all moments, I sneezed.

'Bless you,' said Tommy, his back already to me.

'Thank you,' I automatically responded, a lifetime of politeness coming back to haunt me.

It almost, *almost* passed Tommy by. He walked on several yards, then spun around, just in time to catch my eyes flitting away from him.

'Good God Almighty,' he whispered. 'You're *here*.' I couldn't stop myself from looking at him. 'You're *fucking* here . . .'

No excuses – I ran.

But he caught me before I was halfway up the block. I was on the ground then and he was laughing uproariously as the others joined in with the beating.

41

Funny: I'd been so impatient to enter this world, now I was begging to get out of it. But just as I couldn't choose when to visit, I couldn't choose when visiting time was over. I lay on the ground and took it. I choked up with blood and heard Tommy's voice at my ear. 'Welcome to *my* world, Chapters.'

Then Ty, urgent: 'Tommy! There she is! Fuck!'

The beating paused, then I heard shouts and whoops and racing footsteps. I forced my eyes open and saw the three of them charging away towards a vision, tiny because of the distance, but unmistakable: at the very far end of Main Street, in the middle of the road, was Claire, standing defiantly. As they drew closer she sped off to one side and disappeared into the darkness; a few moments later it swallowed up Tommy and Ty and Lawrence as well.

Bob, it was an odd mix of emotions: relief that she was there at all, and fear that they might catch her. The *possibility* of her seemed to act as something of an anaesthetic and I managed to drag myself up. Claire had put herself in the line of fire for me – she had drawn the enemy away to give me a chance. I supposed that if they failed to catch her they would come back for me, but my inclination was to go in her direction. That, after all, was my only purpose in being here. Yet as I got to my feet I lost my balance and sat again. I had taken quite a pounding and my faculties were not yet my own again. I jumped suddenly as hands were placed on my shoulders.

'It's okay.' A face appeared, silhouetted by the streetlight above. 'Just take it easy for a moment.'

His voice was vaguely familiar. As his hands ran quietly and expertly down my back and around to my chest, it came to me who he was – the old man who had sympathised with me when I'd thrown up in the street.

I winced.

'Ribs,' he said. 'Can you walk, do you think?'

'I don't know.'

With Claire gone, with Tommy and his gang disappearing after her, my immediate thought was that I'd zoned out again, this time seamlessly. But it was immediately dismissed by his next suggestion.

'Get you off the street before they come back, eh?' The old man eased me up. I staggered and he held onto me. In so doing, he also staggered. He was nothing but skin and bone; his face emaciated. 'This way,' he said.

He led me a little way down the sidewalk, then into the alley I'd seen the seniors and the cyclist turn into. We moved along, weaving from side to side.

'Where are we going?' I asked breathlessly.

'Just along here.'

'You . . . helped me before.'

'I did. And here we are again, proving my point. Youth *is* wasted on the young.' He gave a rattle of a laugh as he directed me to the left and a strip of garages that adjoined the rear of the Main Street stores. He knocked gently on the fourth one along, and after a short delay a bolt was pulled back and a side door opened. The old man led me into darkness.

I heard the door being closed behind us and the bolt being eased back into place. Then a light was switched on: a weak bulb, but enough to dazzle me. Then, as my eyes became accustomed to the light I saw that I was surrounded – the seniors were there, the cyclist, at least a dozen others I'd never seen before, all just standing, staring at me. The curious thing was, I didn't feel threatened at all. In fact, they seemed scared of *me*.

I nodded around them, I gave them a reassuring smile, but

before I could say anything there was a noise from outside and the main garage door was suddenly yanked open. I spun towards it, expecting to see Tommy, but there was only a man standing there clutching a cardboard box, looking as surprised as I was.

'What the fuck!' he shouted.

I was back out of the zone, standing half-broken, alone in the garage.

'Sorry,' I mumbled, 'taking a piss.' I lurched towards him, then past. He turned with me, and seemed in two minds what to do. He wanted to give chase, but the box in his hands was either too heavy or too fragile to set down quickly.

He settled for yelling, 'I'm calling the cops!'

I made it back out onto Main Street. I'd blood in my mouth and one eye was half-closed; my ribs ached and one leg was dead. I didn't know where to go or what to do; I was elated and confused and frustrated.

Claire. Far away, so close.

Although I'd come out of the zone I was still moving blind – I could jag right back in at any second and find myself back with Tommy and his boys, ready and waiting to finish the job they'd started. I was limping along and for all I knew, they were right beside me, screaming abuse. Lights flashed ahead of me and I stopped, but then a moment later, a familiar car pulled up and Ambrose grinned out at me. 'Sorry I'm late,' he said. 'Following a lead.'

I leaned on the roof for a moment while I tried to catch my breath, then pushed myself off and moved around to the passenger door. When I collapsed into the seat, Ambrose got his first proper look at me.

'Jesus Christ, Michael, what happened *this* time?'

'Fight,' I gasped. 'Over nothing. Drive on.'

'I'm taking you to the hospital.'

'No, you're not.'

As we pulled away from the kerb, a police car turned onto Main Street and moved slowly past us.

'Do you want to report something?' Ambrose asked.

I shook my head.

We drove in silence for a couple of minutes. Then Ambrose nodded across. 'We're like twins, aren't we?'

My head was resting against the window. 'How do you figure that?'

'We're both regular shit magnets,' said Ambrose.

We adjourned to his favourite watering-hole, the IHOP. According to the clock on the wall it was just after ten p.m. As a place to recover it wasn't a bad substitute for the hospital: it was also a twenty-four-hour operation, and the food was better. All you had to do was make sure you ordered coffee once in a while and the waitresses didn't disturb you, except for coming by to check for ants on the racks of maple syrup which sat on every table.

'Michael – do you want to tell me what's going on?' Ambrose asked, although only after he'd scoffed down a healthy serving of pigs in blankets – sausages rolled in pancakes to you and me.

'No, Ambrose. I don't.' I rested one elbow on the table, and put my head on my hand. I was tired and sore. 'Tell you what,' I wearily suggested, 'why don't you talk, and I'll listen.'

He shrugged. 'What do you want to know?'

'Nothing. Anything. Who to make the cheques payable to.'

He smiled. 'Relax. The way I'm playing it, you'll owe zilch. I got some useful information, though. I heard from our old friend, Mrs Grace Shaw, mother of dear Lawrence.'

I was currently sporting his footprints on my back. 'Uhuh?'

'Eager to blame everyone but her own flesh and blood, but she told me a little more about the dynamic of the outfit. So far, at least from my perspective, we've seen Tommy as something of a caricature – you know, ex-Marine, living on past glories, the muscle, humping around gear for a two-bit cabaret band, all the hard work, none of the girls. Grace said it wasn't like that at all: he was their manager, he set up the cruise-ship gigs, he handled the money. She said after the first cruise Lawrence didn't want to go back, said it wasn't the sort of music he wanted to be playing, but Tommy had made him sign this contract, he forced him back. She said that after the first few cruises she saw a big change in him; he was jumpy, withdrawn, he wasn't eating. I do believe he was either allergic to Neil Diamond, or he had acquired a drugs habit. Grace confronted him – told him he wasn't going back, he could bust that contract; hadn't he walked out of a dozen jobs before – what was the difference? Well, the difference was Tommy. He came to see Lawrence, and next thing, he was back on the ships again.'

'So Tommy called the shots,' I said tiredly. 'How does that expand our knowledge of the universe?'

'Well, seems one time Lawrence was home she talked him into coming off the dope, took him away up-country somewhere, the whole cold turkey thing. And during the worst of that he let slip he was making all this money and soon they'd be rich enough to take off somewhere. She said to him, "Where is all this money, 'cause you haven't got a red cent?" and he said it was coming, that Tommy was looking after that end of things, and how great Tommy was because of it.'

'Tommy kept his wages so he wouldn't spend it on dope. Good for Tommy.'

'She didn't mean it like that. She said that Lawrence wasn't earning much on the ships, that the tips were shit. He was talking real money.'

The waitress came by and refilled our coffee. She had a smile for Ambrose. He could charm everyone, it seemed, except me.

'So what are you thinking? That Tommy was using the band for cover to pull a few deals on these exotic Caribbean islands?'

'Something like that, yeah. But something went wrong. Maybe he tried to go one deal too far – he lost their stash and had to make it up by raiding the First National. Or he ended up owing more than he had, so he had to raise some cash, urgent, to pay off the . . .' Ambrose raised his hands rather sheepishly '. . . the cartel.'

I stirred my coffee. I was in no position to criticise anyone for being too fantastical. But I did, nevertheless. 'Aren't we getting a little *Miami Vice* here, Ambrose?'

He shrugged. 'Who gives a shit? It happens, doesn't it?'

It did. Of course.

'Even if it's true, what difference does it make? How does it alter what happened to Claire?'

'Ah, but then we move on to caller number seventy-three.'

'Seventy-three? You got seventy-three calls?'

'I got around a hundred and forty, but this was seventy-three. Wouldn't leave his name, so he plainly wasn't interested in your money, which I suppose gives it a little more weight. He worked in the First National; he was only there for three months, transferred in from another branch to cover a staff shortage. This was before the robbery, and he'd left before it happened. Anyway, this guy's the last of a dying breed, a smoker, forty a day, and there was a place behind the bank they went to if they wanted to light up. Your pal DeMarcus was one of the few other smokers, so he got to know him pretty well. Said he was a nice enough kid, not exactly a rocket scientist. But what got him was that one day DeMarcus showed up for work high as a kite, all over the place. Bad enough in an ordinary job, but he was a secur-ity guard in a bank, he had a *gun*. Thing is, that witless fuck Sheldon Asshole didn't fire him on the spot, didn't have him arrested – he just sent him home. DeMarcus was back in work the next morning, like nothing had happened.'

'Well, maybe Sheldon's just a swell guy.'

'Michael, we've both met him, we know what he's like. And Phone Guy pretty much said the same, which is why he called, because at the time he thought it was just plain wrong. But, like most of us, he decided that it was none of his business, and within a few weeks he was back to his regular branch. He thought about it some more after the robbery, and actually called it in to Brevard Police, but he never heard anything back, so he forgot about it until he saw the paper.'

'Did he have a theory as to why Sheldon was so charitable?'

'No. It just struck him as odd.'

'But no doubt *you* have a theory.'

'Well, what if Sheldon can't fire him? What if DeMarcus is cocky enough to turn up spaced-out because he has something on his boss? What if Sheldon enjoys the odd toke himself, and

DeMarcus is his dealer? What if there's a line through from Tommy to DeMarcus to Sheldon?'

'Lot of *ifs*,' I said.

'We're in the *if* business,' said Ambrose, and ordered some Key Lime Pie.

Interesting as these little snippets were, I wasn't sure if they amounted to anything. Even if they did, they seemed largely irrelevant to my own perilous position. I couldn't get that image of Claire out of my head. That day at the traffic signals, she'd been so surprised to see me – but this time she had deliberately drawn off my assailants. She must have known that I was part of her world now and that we would meet again. Yet my beating had stopped so abruptly when they'd spotted her, and they'd taken off in pursuit of her so quickly – there was a desperation about it. What had Tommy said? *We ever find that wife of yours, boy, we'll fuck her over good.* Did that not suggest that they had never yet managed to locate her? How could that be? In ten *years*? Perhaps in a city you could manage that, but surely not somewhere as small as Brevard.

Ambrose glanced up at the clock and said, 'God damn, what time is it?'

The clock still said it was just after ten. I checked my own watch. It was half past midnight. The IHOP clock had stopped, probably had been for years. I showed Ambrose the time and he swore again. He delved into his back pocket and produced his hotel-room key. 'Here,' he said, pushing it across the table towards me. 'Put your head down – you need it.'

'Ambrose, I can afford my own room.'

'Hey, the old team back together again. Use it, man, you're paying for it anyway. And besides, I'm going back to Jo-Anne's for a while, then I'm hitting the road first thing.'

I nodded before this information fully filtered through. When it did, I asked why.

'Why don't you just *listen*?'

'I *am* listening.'

'Tallahassee – ring any bells?'

'State capital, right?'

'Yes, boss, but fuck that. Peter Czech?'

I shook my head.

'I just spent ten minutes telling you about him.'

'Sorry,' I said.

'Christ, sometimes I think you're on a different planet.'

I had been thinking about time, and our concept of it, how Claire and DeMarcus and Meg and Tommy looked exactly as they had on the last day of their lives, even though it was ten years down the line. Their lives were continuing in one respect, but stuck in another. It was the difference between my watch and the stopped clock on the wall. What if time existed for them, in that they experienced it, but it did not adhere to our concept of it?

'Peter *who*?'

Ambrose rolled his eyes. 'Czech. He was the entertainment director at Carnival Cruises, responsible for hiring the band, and for firing them.'

'They were fired?'

'Oh yeah.'

'Why?'

'Well, he said that was the sixty-four thousand dollar question. And I think he meant literally. He wants paying for any information.'

'So – shall I give you a cheque for sixty-four thousand dollars?' I asked.

Ambrose laughed. 'Son, you have *way* too much money. Of course I don't want a fucking cheque. I'll have it out of him for nothing, but it means me going to him. He retired, broke his back in an accident on board ship. I suspect Tommy may have had something to do with it. Anyway, I'll find out tomorrow. And if you're very good, I'll tell you too.'

Ambrose drained the last of his many topped-up coffees, then stood. 'Come on, I'll drop you back to the hotel. The key will get you through the fire door. No one needs to know.'

'Thanks, Ambrose,' I said. And I meant it.

I walked slowly to the car. He held the door open for me. It was difficult to bend, with my ribs the way they were. I grunted and groaned. When we pulled into the Comfort Inn car park he said: 'Are you sure you don't want to tell me what you've been up to? Or are you saving it for your book?'

'Saving it,' I wheezed.

'Michael Ryan,' he said, just as I opened the door, 'you wouldn't know a good story if it came up and bit you on the ass.'

I heaved myself up and out, closed the door and leaned back in through the open window. 'Fuck you,' I said. 'And thanks for letting me use my own room, you horny son of a bitch.'

Now I wish I'd said something different, because that was the last time I saw him alive.

42

Three worlds, Bob – your world, Claire's world, and dreamworld. When I fell asleep I still dreamed. Claire was there, of course, but so were my parents, and you, Bob, playing a guitar, though I'm sure you never have, then a tsunami was coming ashore at Brevard and we were all charging away from it, although I noticed Paul de Luca surfing on top, pursued by a shark. There was fear and adrenaline involved, as in most dreams, but none of the pain that had made it so difficult for me to get to sleep in the first place. Just as the wave was crashing down on us I leapt out of the way and back into *now* – and I was suddenly aware of movement in my room.

My eyes opened instantly. I couldn't see anything, but I could smell something sweet – perfume. I had been sleeping with just the top sheet over me – and now I felt it being pulled gently back.

My Claire.

This was the moment, the realisation of an impossible dream. When you live in a turgid situation, you never dare hope that change will come, yet when it does you are so shocked you hardly know what to do or say. You cannot respond: you have to be led.

Her lips on my chest. Warm. A hand moved down my side. It reached my shorts and slipped inside.

I began to respond; it was nice . . . *but* . . . it had been ten years and some mad notion inside me told me that this was too direct, that there were words that must be spoken, explanations that must be delivered, making up that must be done even though there was no falling out. She was just going straight for it. I wanted *this* desperately, but I also wanted the preliminaries – the holding and hugging and kissing, the *words*.

'Claire . . .' I whispered.

Her hand slowed, like clockwork winding down. It stopped. I remained in her grip. She whispered: 'Ambrose?'

'Michael.'

'Holy Christ!'

She tumbled out of the bed, while I scrambled for the lamp. Just as it came on she cried, 'No – don't!' but too late. Despite it taking a moment for my eyes to adjust to the light, I still got to see Jo-Anne bent over, naked, reaching for her underwear. It is not a sight I will forget. Do you remember that scene in *It's A Wonderful Life*, Bob, where James Stewart pretends to lasso the moon and drag it down for Donna Reid? Well, this was just like that, except when he dragged it down it wasn't the moon at all, but a huge white ass.

'Turn it off! Turn it off!'

'Okay! Sorry! Sorry!'

There were more curses as she frantically tried to retrieve her clothes in the darkness. She was a big girl, and Ambrose was eight-tenths pancake. When they made love it must have been like *When Two Soft Worlds Collide*.

'Mr Ryan, I'm *so* sorry!'

'It's okay.'

'I thought—'

'I know. May I put the light—'

'No!' More heavy breathing as she struggled on. 'I am *so* embarrassed.'

'It's okay, it's all right.'

'Can't find . . . there you are. Okay. All right. Just let me . . .' She took a deep breath, let it out, then took another. 'Okay – the lamp.'

I switched it on. She looked at the carpet. 'Don't tell Ambrose.'

'I won't.'

'Please.'

'I swear to God.'

She managed a grateful smile. 'He was supposed to come last night, but he didn't and his cell was switched off. He's been working so hard – he's exhausted. I thought, He's given me a key, why not use it? It'll be a nice surprise.'

'It was certainly a surprise.'

She put her hands to her face. 'I'm mortified.'

'Don't worry about it.' Given the level of our recent intimacy, it was surprising how awkward it felt getting out of bed in my shorts. Jo-Anne averted her eyes. I fumbled into my trousers and crossed to the little kitchenette to make microwave coffee. As I waited for the *ding* I coughed raggedly, and the pain of it caused me to crease down and grip the sides of the counter.

'Mr Ryan – are you okay?'

'I'm fine.'

'You look like you been beat up.'

'Yes, well.'

'You let me get that.'

It was actually a relief. I had crossed so rapidly from the dream state into the state of arousal that my body hadn't had time to remember that it was supposed to be in agony; now as the memories came flooding back, I found I could hardly move. My head pounded. As Jo-Anne removed the cups from the microwave I turned suddenly to the sink and retched. I lay with my arms over the taps and my head down to allow the cold water to run over it. My T-shirt had ridden up enough for Jo-Anne to see the bruises.

She said, 'You should be in a hospital.'

I shook my head.

'Then see Lena.'

'No.'

'Ambrose said you and her had a falling out, but he also says she loves you and she'll help you if you ask her.'

'I can't.'

'Why not?'

It was a straight, honest question and I'd no answer. I turned off the tap and limped back to the bed. I got on it and sat with my back against the wall. Jo-Anne followed with the coffees and handed me one. She sat at the foot of the bed, took a sip, then smiled kindly. 'She, Lena, she came to the bar looking for you, said you weren't well. She had tears in her eyes, said if I saw you, to tell you to call and she would do exactly what you wanted her to do, that there was nothing to be frightened of. I asked her what she meant but she wouldn't say, but I tell you, Michael, it's a free country – you can believe whatever weird shit you want. Hell, I was a Scientologist for about a week. But she does care, so I think you should phone her and get yourself looked at, and if you're worried about her pulling a fast one, you tell her from me, if she tries anything I'll track her down and I'll sit on her, and if she tries anything else, I'll bounce.'

'Well, I . . . thank you, Jo-Anne. Appreciate your . . .'

'Just phone her.'

'Okay. I will.'

'I love that man,' she said abruptly.

I nodded.

She sipped her coffee. 'He's so funny, and warm, and smart. Beats me how a man like that never got married.'

I nodded some more.

Jo-Anne smiled. 'I know he's married. We play a kind of a game where he pretends not to be, and I go along with it because it's easier that way. But I check his cell sometimes and know he's been talking to her.'

'He's talked about moving down here,' I said.

Her eyes lit up. '*Has* he? What did he say?'

'Just . . . that.'

She nodded. 'I understand. You being his best friend, 'n' all.'

It didn't surprise me that Ambrose might have described me as his best friend. *Nothing* about Ambrose surprised me. In fact, it wouldn't have surprised me if at that very moment he was on the interstate, heading north, going home to his wife and child and keeping his cell switched off so that gullible fools like me or Jo-Anne couldn't make him feel guilty.

'Jo-Anne. Ambrose is—'

'I know what he is. I also know I can come on a bit strong – I don't want to frighten him off, you know what I mean? But if he's gone, he's gone. I'll get over it.'

It was difficult to tell from the room itself whether Ambrose intended to return. If he had packed up and left, he had done so carelessly. There were still items of clothing and books and magazines littered about, but nothing you could describe as essential. His travelling bag was gone, and so was his washing gear.

When I looked back to Jo-Anne, there were tears in her eyes. She was a lovely woman, but scary. Nevertheless, I moved down the bed, ignoring the pain, put my arm around her and gave her a cuddle. 'He will be back, Jo-Anne. He's gone to Tallahassee to interview someone. Once he gets a sniff of a good story he forgets about everything, but he will be back. I'll keep trying his phone, all right?'

'Thank you.' She squeezed my leg and kissed my cheek. She stood. 'You call Lena.'

'I will.'

She crossed the room, but hesitated before opening the door. 'Mr Ryan? As I'm here, you don't fancy . . .' She raised her eyebrows suggestively. 'Nobody would have to know.'

'Jo-Anne! *No.*'

She studied me for a long moment, then shrugged and stepped out of the room. It came to me suddenly that Claire had always told me it was good to water down rejection with a compliment, even if you had to lie.

'Jo-Anne!'

She appeared back *instantly*. 'Mr Ryan?'

'Thank you for the thought,' I said. 'And nice ass.'

She looked rather surprised. 'Oh. Thank you. Nice cock.'

I was going to call Lena, but I kept putting it off. I called Ambrose instead, but his cell went straight through to voicemail. Five times. I left laconic messages. The final one said, 'I saw your girlfriend's big white bum.' I thought he might be intrigued enough, or jealous enough, to call back. He didn't.

*   *   *

Eventually, I called Lena.

'Michael? Are you okay? Where are you?'

'Yes, yes, and wouldn't you like to know?'

'Michael . . .'

'I don't doubt that you have the technology to track down my cell phone. I expect there'll be SWAT teams outside my hidey-hole in a few moments.'

'Michael, this isn't funny.'

'No, it's not. It's the exact opposite.'

'If you won't tell me where, will you at least tell me how you really are?'

I was lying back on the bed, loaded up with painkillers from a machine in reception. It wasn't so much the beating I took, it was the pains in my head.

'I've felt better,' I said, 'but that's not why I'm calling. I just wanted to apologise for everything. I haven't been nice to you, and it's not your fault. I don't expect anyone to understand what's going on, Lena, but I would like you to.'

'I'm trying to, Michael. I just want you to—'

'I've seen Claire, and I'm going to see her again.'

There was a sharp intake of breath. *'Okay,'* she said.

I cut the line.

An hour later I got fed up with waiting for Ambrose to respond to my messages. I called information and asked for Peter Czech's number in Tallahassee. He wasn't listed. That in itself wasn't unusual. I called Carnival Cruises. It was the middle of the night, but they had a skeleton staff on duty to deal with complaints from rich people. I stopped short of saying, 'Could you put me through to someone who'll be impressed enough by my famous name to divulge personal information,' although that was the intent. I was connected to several different departments until finally the name clicked with someone. I told her I was an insomniac writer preparing a book set on a cruise ship in the 1990s; I said it would be like *Titanic*, but with a happy ending. I said I wanted to track down a former entertainment director called Peter Czech for research purposes. She couldn't divulge that information, but if I liked she could call him and give him the option of calling me back. I told her that would be perfect. She checked her computer. No Peter Czech. She checked her paper records. No Peter Czech. She tried different variations of Czech, but drew a blank. I apologised and said I must have been misinformed. She volunteered to find someone knowledgeable of that era. She made it sound like it was about a hundred years ago.

Maybe it was.

I no longer trusted time.

I thanked her and rang off. I lay back. I was still not unduly worried. I hadn't been paying much attention to Ambrose when he'd said the name, I could quite easily have gotten it totally wrong, or it might just have been another crank caller leading him on a wild-goose chase. Ambrose could also have just made the whole thing up as an excuse to get out of town. He was devious. I knew that. I'm sure Jo-Anne did too.

I called Lena again. Without preamble I said, 'My head is killing me.'

'Tell me where you are.'

'No, Lena, not yet.'

'Tell me. Please.'

'I know how this looks from the outside. The problem is, I'm not on the outside. I have a chance to put things right and I have to do it while I can.'

'I don't understand that, Michael. Will you please explain it to me?'

'How can I? I can't show you. Maybe it's like Dick Schulze says, sometimes you just gotta have faith.'

'I think that was George Michael.'

We chuckled. It was a good sign.

Lena told me she was in bed. She wanted to know everything I was thinking or seeing. I hesitated. She said, 'Look, I think you're nuts anyway, what harm can it do?'

'What good can it do?'

'Well, it might help to talk it through and get a sane person's reaction to it.'

'Your bedside manner is flip and dismissive.'

'I'm off duty, this is the real me.'

'I think I preferred the nice lady doctor – can I have her back?'

'Michael, talk to me. Tell me how it started.'

I closed my eyes. 'You know how it started. I got drunk, I fell over, I banged my head, I started seeing things.'

'There were no indications before? No sickness, no nausea?'

'Apart from those associated with intoxicating liquor? No.'

'Okay then, from the moment you banged your head: tell me.'

I decided to tell her how it was. I didn't see the harm in it. I gave her as much detail as I could. She was a patient listener and didn't get frustrated when I went back and forth exploring tangents and dead ends. She asked about Meg. Then she wanted to be sure that the man who'd helped me outside the Radisson was the same man who'd led me to the garage if I hadn't seen his face the first time.

'Some voice, same cliché – youth is wasted on the young.'

I waited for the next question. And waited. Then:

'Sorry. This guy, had you ever seen him before?'

'No, why?'

'Because I think nearly everyone you're encountering when you . . . zone out . . . they're people you've met before, even if you don't recognise them straight off. They've lodged in your subconscious and now they're coming out, as it were. Claire, of course, Tommy and the rest of his gang – but also people who were less important to you but nevertheless might have some bearing on your story.'

'My *story*?'

'Your *experience*. Don't get fractious. Is it possible that the people you saw in the garage, the seniors, the young man on the bike, you've met them before? When you lived here ten years ago?'

'I don't know. I don't think so. I suppose it's possible. But not Meg – she wasn't even born. How would I know stuff that nobody but her own mother knew?'

'Yet her husband wasn't convinced.'

'He wouldn't be convinced if Jesus Christ Himself turned up on his doormat.'

'Is it not possible, Michael, that somewhere along the line you might have read about Meg, or you've overheard something that you haven't even been aware of overhearing, but it has lodged itself somewhere in your memory, and this is it coming out?'

'Only Meg and her mother knew the name of that panda. How could I possibly know that?'

'Because the Andersons are traumatised by their loss, because they deal with it by drinking heavily, and when they drink they talk about their daughter, at *length*. Do you honestly not think that in the three years since Meg died, she hasn't told the story of the panda before? The fact that she doesn't *remember* telling it is neither here nor there.'

'But how would *I* know it?'

'Isn't it possible that you picked it up somewhere and you were able to regurgitate it because of your accident?'

'Okay, it's possible. But is it likely? What are the chances of it? And after you work that out, what are the chances of me then being able to fit it so neatly into my . . . *experience*?'

'Is it any less likely than you being able to communicate with a different world? With ghosts?'

'I didn't say they were ghosts.'

'Didn't you?'

'I don't know.'

'Are they not all dead – Claire, Tommy, Meg? If you can see them, and you know they're dead, are they not ghosts?'

'*Lena*. I can only tell you how it is, and when I'm there it's real, it's not a dream. They're not ghosts who can walk through walls, they are real people, made of flesh and blood. What if it's like . . . a different dimension? Perhaps when we die it's not the end; we continue to exist in some form, we just move to a . . .' I laughed. 'This sounds like shit, doesn't it?'

'Yes, it does. But shit happens.'

'So what do you suggest?'

'You're not going to tell me where you are?'

'I can't. I have to see this through.'

'In that case I'm going back up to the hospital, and I'm getting a second opinion on that CAT scan.'

'Because sometimes brain surgeons ain't no brain surgeons.'

'Excuse me?'

'Nothing. Go check the scan if you want, but it's not going to make any difference.' She sighed. 'Lena – if I could get one piece of evidence that would absolutely prove to you that what I'm experiencing is real, what would it be?'

'Prove to me, or to the scientific community?'

'*You.*'

There was a rapid knock on the door. I shouted: 'Hold on!' Then back to Lena. 'Well?'

'Give me a moment, I'm thinking.'

Another rapid knock: not unduly heavy, but longer.

'I'll be there in a minute!'

It started again, and did not stop.

'Sorry, Lena, just give me a—'

'If you go back there, Michael, and you meet these people, I want you to ask a question. I want you to ask them if they know someone called Walter.'

'Walter? Who's Walter?'

'He was a patient – maybe he's there too, okay?'

'Walter . . .' But I'd had enough of the thumping. 'Just hold on,' I said. I set the phone down on the bed, stomped across to the door and yanked it open. 'Will you stop the f—'

Surprise.

'Meg!'

'I've been knocking for ever! Why didn't you answer?'

'Meg, I'm sorry, I didn't—'

But she wasn't listening. She was pointing along the corridor. 'They're coming!' she cried in terror. 'They're coming!'

43

We charged down the walkway, hand-in-hand. The elevator was halfway along. The light above showed it rising. I didn't understand the physics of this world, or how they could ride an elevator, and perhaps they couldn't, but I wasn't about to take the chance. We turned left, pushed through a set of storm doors and raced down another corridor towards the fire escape – then stopped stone dead as Lawrence Shaw emerged from it.

I spun Meg around and we backtracked a dozen yards to where the corridor branched off to the right. We plunged right along it – realising too late that it was a dead end. I cursed and turned back in time to see that Lawrence had been joined by Tommy and Ty, the three of them moving swiftly towards us.

Meg had her head screwed on tighter than mine. She yanked me towards a garbage chute, then let go of my hand and hurled herself through it. She actually giggled as she disappeared through the swing doors.

I think she presumed it would be like a helter-skelter, a fast curvy slide to a soft landing. In reality, after a short plastic directional ramp it was a straight fall down into jagged plastic sacks. I know because I followed straight after her. Luckily we were only two floors up. Meg was covered in crap and screaming at the sight of the blood seeping out of a long slit along her arm. I climbed out of the dumpster without any new physical injuries, but with my old ones raging. There wasn't time to console or calm her, I just grabbed her and limped away.

The garbage-disposal-room door gave out onto a small fenced-off area at the rear of the car park. There was a gate with a lock, but it had been busted open and lay hanging off its hinges. We darted through the gap and straight on until we came to a wire fence which protected a public access route to the beach between the Comfort Inn and the Sea Breezes Motel next door. To discourage its use, the hotels had allowed the undergrowth on both sides to build up and hide the route from casual view, which was good for us. I lifted Meg up onto the top of the fence, and she climbed down the other side. I scrambled over a moment later and then we ran along the path, out of sight until we emerged onto the deserted beach. The wind was up and although the sky was lightening now, stormclouds were already gathered and preparing an assault. We ran along the edge of the powdery sand, ready at any moment to disappear into any one of the other hotels along the strip if we saw Tommy and his crew coming.

After perhaps half a mile, and with no sign of our pursuers, we collapsed down in the sand and tried to catch our breath. My T-shirt and trousers were stained and ripped; had there been even a casual observer, I would have looked like a crazy derelict, sitting there, talking to myself.

Luckily, Meg had gotten over her initial horrified reaction to her injury. The cut was long, but not deep. I ripped one arm off my T-shirt, and then the other, and fashioned a very rough bandage. It looked kind of ludicrous, and was soon dyed red and flapping in the wind. Meg wasn't very impressed with my nursing skills. She stood up abruptly and said she wanted her mom.

'Meg . . .'

'Mom will kiss it better.' She started walking.

'Meg!' She stopped, looked back, and sniffed up. I felt terribly sad for her. The realities of *this* hadn't completely sunk in. 'Thank you for coming to warn me.'

She screwed her face up into a *don't be stupid* look. 'I didn't. They *followed* me. Claire sent me to get you.'

Lump in the throat. 'Claire?'

'Who else?'

'Meg, where is she? Where's Claire?'

She smiled. She pointed. 'Over there.'

'Over there' was not actually just 'over there'; more like '*way* over there'. Meg was actually pointing at Brevard Pier, back the way we'd come, at least a mile along the now swirling sand, its outline hazy against the pounding surf.

My approach was necessarily slow and frustratingly circumspect, rather than a mad dash across the sand, because I knew that if Tommy had followed us to the beach, I would have to get past him again to get to the pier. So I worked my way along using stacks of chained-down sunbeds and serial *No Beach Access* signs for cover. It took perhaps twenty minutes, and felt like twenty years. I got a few odd looks from early-morning joggers and beachcombers as I darted from one hiding-place to the next.

But fuck 'em.

My Claire, on the pier, so close, so far away.

There was no sign of Tommy or his crew, but even as my excitement grew I forced myself to slow down, to stay hidden, observant. If Claire was on the pier, and they followed me onto it, we would be trapped. Thunder rolled ominously above and waves churned. The first shards of lightning licked out of turbulent skies. Rain pelted down, cracking hard against the wooden slats and the tarpaulin roofs of the bar and souvenir stores which stretched half of the pier's length. Two elderly men carrying fishing rods and wearing sodden T-shirts hurried past me as I stepped up onto the pier and made a dash for their cars. Imagining this, Bob, you're probably thinking that all this scene needed was for some lush music to swell up as I approached my date with destiny, but it was so intense, with the wind and the rain, the thunder and lightning and the roar of the surf, it didn't need music, or it felt as if there *was* music, all in glorious surround sound.

And yet, little things are sent to try us.

Between the end of the stores and the bare second half of the

Bateman

pier, there was a gate which fishermen had to pay to pass through. A guy in a slick yellow raincoat was just about to lock it down and didn't see me coming until I'd already squeezed through.

'Hey!' he shouted. 'Pier's closed till the storm's done!'

From the gate to the end of the pier, it was about twenty-five yards.

There she was.

Bob, I'm *from* fiction, I'm *of* it – this was my *French Lieutenant's Woman*, this was my *Wuthering Heights*.

I wasn't distracted by the gatekeeper yelling, 'Asshole!' and then, 'It's your funeral!'

Claire faced the ocean. I stopped half a dozen yards short. I said nothing, but she knew. She turned slowly, or maybe she turned normally and I saw it in slow motion. She had been my life, and then she was gone, and now she was back – and much as I was filled with hope and relief, there was also a palpable dread and a sudden panicked urge to delay. Everything that had happened in the past few days had felt real, but this was the test of it. I was terrified that if I went to hug her she would, literally, slip through my fingers, that I might find myself alone on a treacherous pier, screaming and cursing at the wind, or worse, lying on a hospital bed, after surgery, with the crushing realisation that it had all been nothing more than a demented fantasy.

She looked *perfect*. She smiled hesitantly. 'Michael – is it really you?'

'If you're really you, then I'm really me, and we're really us.'

The smile widened. 'A *yes* would have sufficed. I didn't know if you would come.'

'Of course I would. Did. Christ.'

'Michael – I'm scared.'

'I'm scared too.'

Four or five rapid breaths, then I stepped forward, my mind screaming *Don't zone out, don't zone out, don't . . .*

Claire rushed into my arms.

We were in the middle of a god-damn tropical storm, and

288

even though we were soaked and buffeted and the pier was literally swaying beneath us, we were our own oasis of calm. Bob, for Christ's sake, can you *imagine* it?

She kept saying, 'Don't go, don't leave me.'

I told her I wasn't going anywhere, though I'd no control over it.

Then, abruptly, she pushed herself away. With the rain I couldn't tell if she was crying. She stared at me. She looked totally lost. Then she came at me, hands flailing, punching and slapping and screaming: 'This isn't real! Go away! Stop it! Stop it! Please God, go away!'

I enveloped her so that she couldn't move her arms. I held her tight. I urgently whispered, 'It's real, it's real, it's *real*,' over and over. She banged her forehead against my chest and I crushed her against me until she stilled. I could feel her heart racing. I pushed the damp hair out of her face and said, 'I'm here, I love you, I missed you, I'm home.'

44

In Florida, storms that would have scared Noah into a life-preserver come and go in an hour and leave barely any evidence beyond a few scattered palm fronds and gurgling storm drains. Before very long the sun had poked its head out again and we were able to dry out as we walked along the beach. My arm was around her shoulders, her arm around my waist. It was romantic, but also a conscious effort to stop each other from disappearing. Waiters from the Radisson were ferrying out stacks of white plastic chairs and setting them out in lines for the start of the day's beach weddings. The first party was already on the sand, waiting patiently, while up above the bride emerged from the hotel with her bridesmaids battling to keep her train under control in the swirling breeze.

My hand traced the outline of Claire's arm, and moved down to her bottom and the top of her leg. It ran across her back and touched her hair. Her hand moved across me in the same way. Our hands touched and Claire grabbed hold of mine and squeezed hard. After a few moments she stopped me and looked up, her face stern.

'Michael, you have to tell me what's going on. Where are we? Why are we here? When can we leave?' I went to touch her face, but she moved out of the way. 'Tell me, please, I can't stand this any longer.'

'Claire . . .'

'Tell me! I can't keep on running. I'm tired, Michael.'

'Claire, I don't *know*.'

'It just keeps going on and *on*.'

'I know.'

'Michael, it's been weeks and weeks.'

I got her to sit down in the sand. 'Claire, darling – I need you to tell me whatever you can about what happened to you, right from the start. Can you do that?'

She put her hand on my leg and moved it slowly up and down. She nodded and her brow furrowed in a visible act of concentration.

'I was just here, and . . . I couldn't get away.' She began to dig her other hand into the sand, just as Meg had done.

'Claire, do you remember the last morning we were together? You went to work . . .'

The hole was getting deeper.

'I went to work, and then I came home, and you weren't there, and I didn't understand. I ran around looking for you everywhere and I met other people who couldn't find their loved ones, or who were just lost, and we were all confused and frightened. It's been like that ever since. Then you appeared from nowhere and it scared me at first, and I hid from you – but then Tommy attacked you and I did what I could.'

'You saved me.'

'I love you. But I don't understand.'

'What do you *think* is happening?'

'I think . . . I'm in a coma in hospital and this is all going on in my head. But it's so *real*. If I fall, it *hurts*. I just want to go back, Michael. I want to wake in the morning with you beside me. I want to make breakfast, and make love, and do what we do, not this – not *this*.'

Bob, I was struggling. I had been convinced that once I got to talk to Claire I would have all the answers I needed, but she had turned the tables; she was looking to *me* for explanations. I had cursed the fact that I was drifting uncontrollably between these two worlds, but how much worse was it for her? We had in the past, so far as I knew, always been scrupulously honest with each other, but now I wasn't completely convinced by what she was telling me. She had brushed over the events at the bank too quickly. Perhaps it was too painful to go back. God knows I found it hard, and I hadn't even been there. But I could hardly press her on it. Her distress was palpable.

With the resurgent sun warming us we recommenced our walk along the beach and I gradually coaxed more out of her. It came in little pieces, but it was hard. She veered between exasperation and frustration; there was anger, and tears, but also smiles and hugs.

She described endless days of wandering about Brevard watching 'real' people go about their business. When I asked if she followed them into their homes, if she watched them fight or make love, it was with some relief to me that she said no. That wouldn't be right, she said.

When she was tired she went home to the Blue House. You see, Bob, when you exist in Claire's world, you open doors and you sleep in a bed and you use the bathroom – little things like that are the same, it's the bigger picture that is confused, out of focus.

'Tell me about Tommy,' I said. 'Was he here right from the start?'

'I suppose. Yes.'

'How many of you are there?'

'I'm not sure. Twenty, maybe.'

'Some who worked in the bank with you? Some who were customers there on the last day you remember?'

'How do you know?'

'I don't, I'm just guessing. But there are others as well?'

She nodded. 'Yes, of course. Just ordinary people.'

'Do they know how *they* got here?'

'No – I don't know. Look, we were just all *here*, but it took a while to get us together, to come out of hiding. We were so frightened of everything – we couldn't understand why the other people couldn't see or hear us – but gradually we recognised each other and now it's like a support group.' She smiled. 'Do you know what I mean? We help each other through this. But not everyone . . .' She took a deep breath. 'Tommy tried to take charge. He started ordering people about, and then he killed—' She looked suddenly horrified. 'He killed Billy James. He shot him dead. Billy owned the gas station on Merchant, remember? He was shot dead the month before we were married, in a robbery.'

'So *he* knew how he came to be here?'

'I suppose.'

I looked at her. She looked to the ocean.

'It's okay,' I said. I squeezed her shoulder. 'Tell me what happened.'

'Billy didn't like being ordered around. He stood up to Tommy, so Tommy shot him, just like that. Shot him right in the chest. It was horrible.'

'And what happened to Billy James then?'

'He *died*.'

'But his body, what happened to his body?'

'We buried it, what do you think?'

'Okay. I'm sorry. Of course you did. Then . . . ?'

'Well, Tommy realised he could do whatever he wanted, that there were no police to stop him or his gang. He wanted to control everything. And that's when he decided I would . . .' her eyes flitted to mine '. . . that I would be his. He said I *owed* him.'

'What did you owe him?'

'I don't know.'

'Claire . . .'

'I don't know!' She turned angrily towards me, her face flushed with anger. 'What do you want me to say – sex? I don't know how his mind works!'

'I'm sorry, I didn't mean to—'

'He just does what he wants! All we can do is run and hide.' She took a deep breath. 'Michael, it's not just Billy James. He's killed six of us altogether, and he says he's going to keep killing until they give me up. These people, they're protecting me, they're hiding me and distracting Tommy and they're risking their own lives to do it. But you're here now – you'll look after me. You always look after me, don't you, Michael?'

'Of course I do. Of course I will. I swear to God.'

She hugged me and peppered me with desperate kisses – then broke off abruptly.

'We have to go now. It's not safe outside.' She put her hand out to me. 'Please.'

I took it. I had no control over how long I would be in her world, but I knew that while I was in it, I was never going to let go.

Bob, I'm sure you're thinking to yourself, how must this have looked to an outsider? I was apparently talking to myself on the beach. Then I was hurrying down Main Street, hand-in-hand with no one. If it had looked as I have described it, I would surely have been a suitable case for treatment. But it didn't. I saw myself in a store window – there was no sign of Claire, of course, and my hand wasn't even sticking out as if I was holding hers. I just looked harried, as if I was late for an appointment, but otherwise quite normal. I can't explain it. There is so much I can't explain. It is just a fact that I could function in both worlds without looking – well, as Ambrose might have said – mental.

Elated as I was to be reunited with Claire, I was also aware of a real, concrete fear growing within me, as if the terror that enveloped her had also thrown its dank cloak around me. The doorways seemed darker, the footfalls louder, the light breeze wheezed uneasily. As we passed the grill, Jo-Anne was just clearing abandoned drinks from one of the outside tables. She saw me, gave me a wave, then looked confused as I merely returned it and hurried on.

'Michael!' she called after me, 'Did you hear anything from—?'

'I'll call you later!'

I had not devoted a single thought to Ambrose's absence; he was not my concern. My concern was Claire, her warm hand squeezing mine so hard, hurrying me along, not noticing her old friend Jo-Anne, her only aim to get us to a safe haven.

And a familiar one at that.

We turned down that same alley. The Old Man who had brought me there the first time opened the garage door and ushered us in, then quickly locked it behind us. They were all there, as before, almost swaying, as if caught between wanting to embrace me and a desire to hide. They had the haunted look of people who had been hiding in darkness for too long.

Claire looked around them, her head nodding almost imperceptibly, before breaking into a wide smile. 'This is Michael,' she said. 'This is my husband.'

Still they looked at me, their eyes filled with the same fear I'd seen in Claire's.

Then little Meg squeezed through the circle and came forward to take my other hand. 'He's on our side,' she said, looking reassuringly around the circle, before raising her finger to the side of her head and twirling it around. 'Even if he is nuts.'

The Cyclist laughed, and then the others joined in, hesitantly at first, and then as their confidence grew, more heartily; they surged forward, real, live human beings, patting my back, shaking my hand and peppering me with questions about how I came to be here. When, for a brief moment, there was enough of a gap in the crowd for me to see into the corners of the garage, I was surprised to see DeMarcus Hall sitting there. Our eyes met. He looked sheepishly at me for a moment, then at the floor.

'What's DeMarcus doing here?' I whispered to Claire even as the questioning continued and the gap closed.

'He's with us.'

'But he was—'

The Old Man put a hand on my arm. 'He's with *us*,' he said simply.

Another hand, on my other arm. The Cyclist. 'You can speak to them?'

'I'm sorry?'

'You can speak to our families. Meg told us. You spoke to her parents. You can give them messages from us?'

'I . . .'

'You have to speak to my girlfriend. She's getting married. She's marrying my best fucking friend. She can't do that. She used to hate him. He really used to piss her off and now she's fucking marrying him. You have to tell her . . .'

The Senior couple pushed right up close in front of me. 'We shouldn't have done it,' the man said. 'We're sorry now – we just thought it would be easier on everyone.'

'We weren't well,' said the woman, her teeth crooked, her white hair nicotine-tinged, her eyes red. 'Our daughter, she hasn't gotten over it. We want her to get on with her life. If you could just tell her we—'

The Cyclist pulled my arm again. 'Do you understand? I can't do anything, but *you* can. You can tell her—'

They buzzed around me, vying for attention. I did my best to placate and promise and sympathise, but it was impossible; their demands were too many, too confusing. Eventually the Old Man stepped in and urged them to give me space and promised I would take time to talk to them all individually. He was possessed of a calm, natural authority, but even with this they only reluctantly allowed him to extricate me. They were like passengers on a sinking vessel being denied assess to a packed rescue boat, frankly doubting the reassurances that another one would be along shortly.

It was only when we at last had a little space that I realised that Claire was no longer holding my hand, or was even by my side, and for a moment I panicked, but then the Old Man guided me towards the back of the garage where the light was weakest, and I saw her kneeling beside DeMarcus, talking quietly to him while he continued to stare at the ground.

'Poor kid,' the Old Man said quietly, 'forced out by Tommy and not trusted by the others. Claire's the only one who talks to him.'

Hearing her name, Claire smiled up, then returned her attention to DeMarcus, who was indeed looking rather miserable.

Good. 'Doesn't she know he . . . ?' I asked. The Old Man nodded. 'Well then, why does she bother with him?'

'She's forgiven him, Michael.'

Now, looking back, I realise I shouldn't have been surprised. It was exactly what Claire would have done. But then, something about seeing them together made me snap. It wasn't just that, it was the culmination of all of the emotional turmoil and the physical battering I had endured over the past few days – and, who knows, years. It just all bubbled out.

'This is so fucked up,' I spat. 'It doesn't make any sense, none of it!' I jabbed a finger at the Old Man and then moved it around the others. 'Do you even know how you came to be here? Any of you?'

Silence fell. Claire looked at me, disappointed. Her saviour in his moment of crisis.

The Old Man spoke with that same calm authority.

'We are just here, Michael. We don't know how long for – all we can do is make the best of it.'

I suddenly felt rather ashamed. After all, I still had an escape route. The anger drained out of me.

'Sorry,' I said.

The Old Man smiled benevolently. His face was sallow, pinched, his eyes were kindly and now, I realised, vaguely familiar.

'I know you,' I said. He nodded gently. Where had I seen him before? I stammered an embarrassed, 'I'm sorry, . . . but I do know. . . '

'Michael. It's me – Dr Olson. You've been sleeping with my daughter.'

45

From amongst the piles of cardboard boxes and rusting file cabinets in the garage I managed to salvage a crumpled notebook and a thick black marker pen with which to make notes of the names and addresses and the messages to be passed to their relatives. My theory was that if I wrote on something from *my* world, it wouldn't disappear the moment I zoned back out. *If* I zoned back out.

After the rush upon my arrival, they now queued patiently. Dr Olson stood at my elbow while I made notes. He did not seem to hold it against me that I had slept with his daughter, and appeared to understand my recent treatment of her. He looked vastly different to the neighbour I remembered: I will explain the reason for this later.

As I made notes, Claire relieved one of the young men who'd been keeping watch on the alley outside so that he could join the queue. She perched on a stepladder and peered through a small triangular window set into the brickwork above the main door. But she kept looking back at me and smiling. Even as I listened to those poor souls, crazy thoughts were sweeping through me. I was going to make love to my wife. I knew that, we both knew that, but I was thinking, What if she gets pregnant? What if there's a baby born with the ability to flit between these worlds, but not the understanding?

I shook myself. *Don't even think it.*

Dr Olson calmly introduced each member of the company before asking them to provide the address of their closest relatives and some item of information that only the latter would understand or recognise. These varied immensely. For some it was a childhood adventure, a treasured toy; for others it was a first kiss or a bedroom nickname. All of this was at first conveyed to me in a sensible, matter-of-fact manner. But when it came to asking what messages they wanted passed on, several of them cracked. They were angry because their loved ones had betrayed them or been unfaithful or just plain forgotten them. They jabbed accusing fingers as they told me; they shook their heads and shed tears, and I couldn't do much but nod in response. It was Dr Olson who quieted them time and again with a soft, 'We may not have much time – what do you really want to say?' You could almost call it a graveside manner. It changed them again. Rage, bitterness and regret banished, to be replaced with simple timeworn phrases. *Tell them I love them, Tell them I'm okay, Tell them I'm watching over them*. It was a powerful testament to love and family, and also dreadfully heartbreaking. They were entrusting me with a weight of responsibility that I had avoided for years. Talking to Meg's parents had not been about Meg, it had merely served to further my own attempts to track down my wife. This was different. I was their only hope.

Me.

It took over an hour to get through them all, and when the last had turned away, a curious kind of quiet settled upon the group. It was only in reading down my notes that it dawned on me what they all had in common – none of them were there because they had died of natural causes. They had been killed in the bank massacre or had died by fire, or by drowning, or by accident, or by their own hand. Dick Schulze had once talked to me about purgatory and how many believed that the souls of suicide victims would be condemned to an eternity there. Well, perhaps he was nearly right. Purgatory wasn't confined to suicides. It was a place for people who died before their time.

Claire, still perched on the stepladder, caught my eye. She nodded at DeMarcus and raised an eyebrow. I raised an eyebrow.

She gave me a look. A Claire look. I sighed. She gave me the look again.

She was always the boss.

I lifted my notebook and moved to the back of the garage. I stood in front of DeMarcus.

'You want your name on this list?'

He shrugged.

'You tell me who I should contact, and tell me something only they'll recognise, and whatever message you want to pass on.'

He stared sullenly at his shoes.

'Up to you,' I said, and started to turn away.

'Okay,' he said.

I stopped. I glanced up at Claire. No quarter there. I turned, my pen raised.

'Anyone?' he asked.

'Sure.'

'I'll spell it for you. A.'

'A.'

'S.'

'S.'

'S.'

'S.'

'Hole.' DeMarcus grabbed his balls, shook them in my direction. 'Asshole,' he laughed.

Claire had been relieved of her lookout duties by Dr Olson when I returned to the front of the garage. 'Thank you for trying,' she said, which, I suppose, made it worthwhile. She glanced back up at DeMarcus. 'Tommy really messed him up.'

'Tommy?'

'DeMarcus had a bad habit; Tommy fed it, then controlled it, so he controlled DeMarcus. Tommy could get him to do whatever he wanted.'

'Am I supposed to feel sorry for him?'

'We all do stupid things, Michael.'

'What DeMarcus did wasn't stupid. It was lethal.'

Our eyes met, and locked.

'It's gone, Michael,' she said.

'No, it's not. It will never be gone.'

She gave a slight shake of her head. Then she crossed to DeMarcus.

'Claire.'

She ignored me.

After the initial flurry of excitement, they had settled down into a kind of wary observation of me. I was with them, but not of them. I had a means of escape, a tunnel into which they could not squeeze. I even felt it from Claire.

While I waited for her to finish with DeMarcus, I studied the notes I'd made. It wasn't going to be easy trying to deliver these messages. Proving myself to Meg's parents had been an ordeal: now I was facing it twenty times over. It wasn't like I was a cop coming to break bad news, it was *good* news – but I knew it would be resisted rather than welcomed. I would have done exactly the same if the positions were reversed.

'Dr Olson?' I had moved to the foot of the stepladder and was looking up at my old neighbour as he sat with his face pressed close to the dirty glass. 'Is there anyone who isn't here, who I should add to this list? I was told there was someone called Walter, but there's no one here of that—'

'Walter?' He looked across the room, at the little groups sitting chatting quietly, then lowered his voice. 'Sure, there's a Walter. How do you know about him?'

'Lena said to ask about him.'

Dr Olson smiled to himself. 'Good old Walter,' he said.

'Do you want me to add him to the list, in case I go back sooner than—?'

'No . . . no.' Dr Olson nodded down at me. 'Walter won't be sending any message, at least not the type you write down.'

'Sir?'

'Let me tell you about Walter, son, but not too loud, eh?' He indicated the lower steps of the ladder. I glanced back at Claire, then sat down. Dr Olson took another look out of the window, then, satisfied, bent towards me. 'Walter killed me,' he said.

* * *

We sat on the floor, me with my back against the wall, Claire between my legs, leaning into my chest. The others slept or chatted quietly in small groups.

I whispered, 'I want to take you to the Blue House.'

She pressed against me. 'Soon,' she said.

My eyes opened to complete darkness and the sudden panicked awareness that Claire was no longer sleeping against me. I had barely slept in the past few days, and just when I wanted to spend as much time as possible with Claire, exhaustion had claimed me. I was sure I'd zoned out, but I still called her name.

'Shhh.'

I scrambled forwards and collided with her, crouched down on the concrete floor just in front of me. Her own hand found me and pulled me closer. She pressed her warm lips to my ear. 'They're outside,' she whispered. I could feel her shaking against me.

A moment later the door was rattled.

An old woman let out the tiniest cry from somewhere behind me.

But a lock was a lock.

The breathing from within sounded tremendously loud.

We waited.

And waited.

Perhaps another ten minutes passed before the Cyclist appeared silhouetted in the triangular window. 'They're gone,' he said.

There was no sudden explosion of relief, no urgent chatter. It was the norm. Five minutes later, when they were absolutely certain, the light was switched back on.

'Christ,' I whispered to Claire, 'how can you live like this?'

'We have no choice.'

Coming from Claire, the born optimist, it was hard to take, and in the quiet of the garage my response came out sharper and louder than I intended. 'Is there no way to fight back? There are three of them, and more than twenty of you.'

'They have guns,' the tall Bank Teller snapped right back.

'They've killed many already,' said the Senior man.

'Michael,' said Dr Olson. 'Nobody wants to die.'

Claire took my hand. 'It will be bright soon – it'll be better then. With all the people, the traffic, it's easier to avoid them.'

'Okay,' I said.

As it brightened outside, the light was switched off and we began to vacate the garage. The dust motes swirled with each opening of the door. It reminded me of movies I'd seen as a kid about the French Resistance, clandestinely listening to a secret radio, and then slipping away in ones and twos so as not to arouse suspicion. In this scenario, I suppose *I* was the radio, their only conduit to the outside world; the difference was that for them there was no hope of relief, no invasion, no massive airborne landing. There was just Michael Ryan, celebrity recluse and fuck-up.

DeMarcus went out by himself, head down, avoiding eye-contact. Claire and I left together, of course, but as Dr Olson was going to Lena's he tagged along. Meg, not wishing to be parted from Claire, came too. I wasn't entirely happy about that. As the doctor stood waiting to lock the door behind us, I realised that I'd forgotten the notebook and darted back inside. It was exactly where I'd left it before falling asleep, with the cover turned back – but my eyes were immediately drawn to the bottom of the list. I'd left the space beside DeMarcus's name blank for obvious reasons, but now, written there in the thick, disjointed strokes of a child, was:

My stepdaddy Eric Stratton lives on Pine Road, no. 475. You say, the Big D is OK, and how those Blue Jays doing?

We turned onto a Main Street already busy with morning traffic. Meg ran ahead, skipping happily, with Claire and I following, hand-in-hand, and Dr Olson behind. He could only walk quite slowly, but Claire and I were so busy with each other that we didn't realise how far he'd fallen behind. We stopped to allow him to catch up, but Meg, unaware, ran on ahead to the junction. By the time we reached it, she was already 100 yards further on to the right. We were just following along behind when Claire suddenly clutched at me and pulled me back out of sight, colliding with Dr Olson in the process.

'It's them!' she hissed.

I cautiously peered around the corner. Meg was standing staring across the road, transfixed by the sight of Tommy and Ty emerging from the public car park opposite her. They crossed the road at an angle, away from her but clearly moving towards us. With the pedestrians on both sidewalks, and the traffic bumper to bumper, they had not spotted Meg. Even if they did, she was small and fast and a mistress of tiny spaces, I think she could quite easily have escaped them. But in that moment I also understood that Meg was not frozen in terror for herself, but for us.

Claire pulled at me. 'Michael, please come,' she begged.

I began to move with her. Dr Olson had already set off, but he was painfully slow. There simply wasn't time for all of us to make it. I had to do something – lure them away. I had been beaten and battered, but I surely had enough strength left in my legs to give them a run for their money. Claire must have guessed what I was thinking, because she suddenly took a firmer grip on me, but before I could loosen it there was something else to distract us.

'Tommy can't catch me! Tommy can't catch me!'

Meg's tiny little sing-song voice.

I pulled away from Claire and back to the corner. I saw Meg standing shaking her fist at Tommy, taunting him.

Tommy laughed back at her, but continued on towards us.

'Tommy can't catch me! Tommy can't catch me!'

He pivoted suddenly and charged back up the sidewalk towards her, with Ty falling in behind. Meg took off, confidently twisting in and out of pedestrians, certain of her escape route – but she could not have guessed that Lawrence, until now undetected on her side of the road, would step out from behind a parked car and sweep her up into his arms. She screamed and kicked and fought, but he had her.

Christ, no, Christ no. She had sacrificed herself.

I turned to Claire. *'Run!'*

'No, Michael, no!'

'Please, Claire!'

'Michael, you can't – not now! *Please!*'

But I had to. I couldn't leave Meg like that. With no clear idea of what I was going to do, how I was going to get the child back, I stepped out from the corner.

They were already gone.

No – *vanished*. There was just the hum of traffic and the inane conversations of innocent passers-by.

I pivoted back to Claire. She was gone too. Dr Olson – into thin air.

I was back in my world. Yet they were there, I knew they were there, all of them. I just couldn't see them or touch them.

I could do nothing but yell threats at Tommy and his gang.

Nothing but promise Meg that I would get her back.

Swear to Claire that I would return and that everything would be fine.

46

So, Bob, I was ranting on a street corner. In deadly peril one moment, the next standing like a fool while passing Brevardians avoided eye-contact. Trying to get my act together while fully aware that Tommy might be standing right in front of me hurling his own abuse and throwing punches that could not land.

I was helpless. My head was pounding again. I did the only thing I could think of: I called Lena. When she answered, it all came out in a despairing, disconnected rush. She patiently coached me to slow down, and then stop. She wanted to take me to the hospital.

We settled on IHOP.

She picked me up and we drove wordlessly. We took a booth and ordered coffee and pancakes.

'Michael, I have good news, and I have bad news.'

'*I* have good news,' I countered, 'and *I* have bad news.'

It wasn't exactly a Mexican stand-off. What had happened to me was so recent, so distressing, that I genuinely did not care what her news was. How could it be of any relevance, when Meg was seized and for all I knew Claire as well, and I was utterly helpless to do anything about it?

'Lena, I met her, I met Claire.'

'Michael . . .'

'She's alive. She's as real as you are.'

307

'Michael, *stop.*'

'I was with her all night and not just her, there's—'

'Michael. Ambrose is dead.'

A blow to the chest. I stared at her incredulously. 'What're you talking about?'

'His car went off the highway outside town; it was only found late last night. He had multiple injuries. I believe he died instantly.'

'Ambrose is dead?'

'Yes, Michael.'

'He's not fucking dead. He went to Tallahassee. He's interviewing someone.'

'No, Michael.'

'This isn't *fucking* happening.'

'Michael, this is real. *This* is *real*, do you understand me?'

'He drove off the road? It's a straight road. How do you drive off a straight road?'

'There may have been a collision with another car before he left the road, since there was some damage to his vehicle. Sheriff Newton is—'

'He hit another car, on a straight road?'

'It happens.'

'Christ.' I stared at the table. Our pancakes arrived. The waitress was chirpy and as she put the plates down tried to draw Lena into some gossip about a schoolteacher who was suddenly back on the market, but stopped when she realised it was one-way traffic.

Ambrose *dead*? He was a lying, cheating, violent drunk, my occasional friend and part-time rival. How could he be dead? I wondered if Jo-Anne knew. I was pretty sure she did. It was a small town and news travelled fast.

Christ.

'Michael. I got a second opinion on those scans.'

'Oh fuck that, Lena!'

She recoiled slightly. 'The good news is we found something. Something that might explain these hallucina—'

I exploded. 'Ambrose is dead!'

'Michael, *please.*' Other customers were looking at us. 'Yes,

Ambrose is dead. It's terrible and if there was anything I could do about it, believe me I would. But there is something I can do about *you*, so will you please just listen?'

I glared.

'You have an aneurysm. It's tiny and that's why we didn't see it, but it's the position of it, right up against an artery. It's affecting the blood supply to your brain. Michael, these things don't get smaller of their own accord; if it's getting bigger, that means longer periods when you're in the grip of these . . .' She stopped herself from saying it. '*Are* they getting longer?'

I glared some more.

'You need to trust me. I know what I'm talking about. I know it's real for you, but it *isn't*. And if it's getting bigger, it will kill you and I don't want that to happen. Do you? Is that what you want?' She reached out to me, but I avoided her touch by sitting back. 'Michael, it's not real. *She's* not real.'

I produced the folded notebook from my back pocket, opened it to the first page and pushed it across the table. 'This is a list of names of the people I've met there.'

'This is ridiculous.'

'They are all people who should be dead but who are not. People who are stuck there. Beside each name there's a fact which only they or their loved ones could possibly know. Then I've written the messages they want me to pass on.'

'What are you now, Michael, some kind of medium?'

'It doesn't matter what you call it. Just read it. Please.'

She held my gaze for a moment, then sighed. She scanned the list, her lips moving just a fraction as she repeated each name. She glanced up. 'I know some of these people,' she said. 'They were my patients. But this isn't proof.'

'I could not know these things.'

Lena nodded patiently. 'Michael, you've been through the newspaper archives, you spoke to relatives, mixed with people at the service, the dinner. All that information goes in, and now it's all coming out, but because of what's happening to you it's been twisted into this . . . I don't know, into some fantastic, frightening fantasy.' She took my hand, and held it tight. 'I need to get you to the hospital. I need you to trust me. You're a bright, lovely, intelligent man – deep down, you must know that none of it is really possible. You *must*.'

It was heartfelt and might have been persuasive if I did not know what I knew.

'I met Walter,' I said, and watched the colour drain from her cheeks.

'You listen to *me* now, Lena. *You* listen. Everyone I've met is there because they came to an untimely end. Many of their deaths were violent.'

'But what relevance—'

'Your father was dying of cancer. One of the doubtful benefits of being a doctor is that you know exactly how ghastly different forms of the disease can be. Your father was a proud man, Lena, and he wanted to die with what he considered to be dignity.'

Her eyes were moist. And cold. 'It is a matter of public record that my father shot himself.'

'Is it a matter of public record that in the end he wasn't physically strong enough to pull the trigger himself? That you helped him? That it would have been easier to kill him by administering an overdose of morphine, but that that would have pointed the finger at you, so you followed his wishes and helped him to shoot himself?'

'That's outrageous. It's . . . it's . . .'

'*Walter* is not a person, Lena. *Walter* is a joke, a nickname you and your father gave to the gun he kept in the house ever since he left the Army. A Walther PPK, isn't that it? It was your little secret, and you kept it right to the end when you muffled it in against his chest and pressed his fingers against the trigger even though you could hardly see for crying.'

'Stop this, Michael.'

'And he loves you for doing it.'

'Stop it!'

'And he forgives you.'

'Michael! Please!'

'And it's not your fault he's stuck there with the rest of them.'

Tears rolled down her cheeks and she shuddered. 'You could not know this,' she whispered. 'You could not know. Who told you? *Who told you?*'

47

There is probably nothing as intense as a holiday romance. Doesn't matter if you're a spindly ten years old or an overweight thirty-five. Parting to go different ways is traumatic enough; imagine how much more cataclysmic that parting becomes if one half of the fledgling partnership *dies*. I found Jo-Anne sitting in the tiny reception area at Brevard morgue, her make-up run and her eyes inflamed. As soon as she saw me, she jumped up and threw her arms around me.

'I knew you'd come!' she cried. 'They won't let me see him.'

I talked to a whey-faced clerk, and he tried to give me the same crap he'd given her about not being the next-of-kin. I asked for someone older and wiser, and eventually his manager arrived, and he recognised me and said it wouldn't be a problem, and asked when I was going to write another book.

We were led down a corridor. I asked Jo-Anne if she was sure she wanted to see Ambrose broken and battered. Would it not be better to wait until the undertakers could do their job and perhaps achieve what he had never quite managed in life: make him look presentable? I suppose I was trying to channel my own last-minute jitters through her. But Jo-Anne was adamant. She was stronger than I was. Nevertheless, her nails dug into my flesh as we were shown into the chilled room and Ambrose was pulled out of a wall on a sliding shelf.

He did not look as dreadful as I had imagined. The thing about internal injuries is that they are, well, internal. Discolouration and bruising yes, but not the mangled mess I had feared. But still, Jo-Anne did what I could not. She took his cold hand.

We said nothing for several minutes. She wept quietly.

Eventually I said: 'He won a Pulitzer, you know?'

'Two,' said Jo-Anne.

Ambrose was dead; I was a dead man walking. I knew it. Lena knew it. She was numb for a while following my revelations in IHOP, but then she began to pepper me with questions and demanded forensic detail, not just about her father, but about my whole new world: she had heard much of it before, but that had been filtered through the prism of disbelief. Now she made me go over it again and again. I would not say that she was completely convinced, but there was a huge shift in attitude. She was virtually certain that Walter was a secret shared only with her father, but a tiny part of her could not discount the possibility that perhaps she had talked of it in her sleep or that her father had mentioned it in conversation with me many years before and I had unknowingly filed it away. She was a doctor, but she was also a bereaved daughter, and hope does not confine itself to breeding or profession. She desperately wanted to hear from her father again. When she looked at the list of names in my notebook again her eyes seemed to glow.

'You're going to go and see them, aren't you? All their loved ones.' I nodded. 'Michael, that could take days; you may not have that much time.'

'I have to try. I have a . . . responsibility.' It was not a concept I'd been familiar with in many years.

Lena shook her head gently. 'You have a responsibility to yourself. If you were to ask Claire what she would prefer – you living in this world, or joining her in her world, what do you think she would say?'

'It doesn't matter. Claire is in danger. I have to save her.'

'And if you do, your intention is what?'

I shrugged. 'I don't know. To stay with her.'

'So you actually *want* this aneurysm to grow to the point that it kills you?'

'I suppose.' I had not actually thought that far ahead, but it was the obvious conclusion to my adventure.

'Michael, this world of yours has its own rules. You've told me that everyone there has died before their allotted time. By murder or accident or . . .' Her eyes flitted away for just a moment. 'Or suicide.'

'Yes.'

'Then if this aneurysm kills you *here*, it will be from natural causes. You will not end up *there*. You will have sacrificed yourself for no reason.'

It was a rather pertinent point and I cursed myself for not thinking of it.

Okay, so if I managed to save Claire, I could not expect to remain with her – but it still had to be done. I couldn't just abandon her. And some time with her was better than no time. Besides, time *there* was very different to time *here*. It was warped. Didn't Claire think she'd only been gone for a matter of weeks? As long as I returned there and rescued her, our time together could last for years before my time ran out here. Besides, what alternative did I have? Was I supposed to just walk away and leave my wife under threat?

I still had the unenviable task of passing on the bad news to Ambrose's wife. I supposed he had her number somewhere, and hoped to find it amongst his personal effects. It would mean calling into the Sheriff's office and persuading someone else that I was the nearest there was to a next-of-kin.

As it was, I got a free ride, because when I emerged from the mortuary, with Jo-Anne remaining inside for a few private moments with her lover, Junior Newton was hunched down beside Lena's car, chatting.

He smiled up at me. 'Mr Ryan,' he said, 'I happened to be talking to the morgue and they mentioned you were here. Daddy – Sheriff Newton – was hoping you could come down to the station. He'd like to talk to you.'

'Sure,' I said. 'Do you want me to follow you down?'

'Why don't you ride with me?'

It was delivered without menace, and anyone else might easily have taken it as a kindness rather than an order, but my experiences of the past few days had left me rather paranoid, and I chose to take from it that I actually had no choice in the matter. I looked at Lena.

'I'll call you later,' I said.

My eyes flitted to the passenger seat and my notebook. Lena gave an almost imperceptible nod in response. There was nothing incriminating in my notes, but a list of people who'd died under unusual circumstances and messages from them wasn't exactly evidence of a balanced mind, and I had the feeling that I would need to appear sane and normal if I was going to go one on one with Sheriff Newton.

I was kept waiting in the reception area for thirty minutes. I sat by a large window, with the back of my head against the air-conditioner-cooled glass. Junior got me a coffee, then water, and apologised several times; then his shift was over and he apologised again on his way home. Eventually another cop led me down a corridor to the Sheriff's office. He knocked on the door and a gruff response indicated that we should enter. Sheriff Newton was behind a desk busy with opened files. He didn't rise or offer his hand; he nodded at a chair opposite, but set some way back. I moved it forward. The other cop left. Sheriff Newton finished typing. He pushed the keyboard to one side and clasped his hands. There was no preamble.

'Indications are that the deceased's car was forced off the road. No witnesses. We have microscopic paint from the other vehicle – might be able to trace it, but it's a long shot.'

'Is it a murder investigation?'

'Early to say.'

'And . . . what do you think?'

'What do I think?' He shrugged. 'I think maybe he argued with someone in a bar, maybe that someone followed him, tried to scare him, it went too far. You think that's a likely scenario,

316

Mr Ryan, given your knowledge of the deceased and his lifestyle?'

'It's possible,' I said.

Sheriff Newton nodded slowly. 'Or perhaps someone read that newspaper article of yours, didn't like it, thought they'd teach Mr Jeffers a lesson and maybe give you a warning.'

It sat in the air for a while. He was a superior type, and particularly enjoyed it when he felt he had something to be superior about.

'Sheriff, we were just looking for information for a book.'

'You don't think there was a full and proper investigation at the time? You think I didn't look under every stone there was?'

I wasn't looking for a fight, I was just putting in time until I could return to Claire.

'Sheriff,' I said, 'we were simply trying to throw some more light on it. Time changes things. And a reward helps. Whatever we found, we were going to turn over to you.'

It was a lie, but I hoped it might pacify him.

Wrong.

Newton turned slightly away in his swivel chair, so that he was looking out of his office window and across Main Street. 'Let me suggest a different scenario to you, Mr Ryan, then maybe you'll give me your opinion on that. The Mayor, in his wisdom, comes up with the bright idea of commemorating the most miserable day in this fine town's history, and in so doing dredges up a lot of bad feeling, a lot of bad memories. You with me?'

'Yes, I am.'

'Wasn't a great day for Brevard. A lot of mistakes were made – some of them right here in this office. You still with me?'

'Yes, Sheriff.'

'Okay. So that's a pretty volatile mix to start with. Now into this mix comes two guys – one of them very well-known, a real celebrity, more money than he knows what to do with, the other a reporter who tells everyone he meets he's won a god-damn Puh-litzer.'

'Two, actually.'

The Sheriff's eyes flitted back to me, just for a moment. Lights of a turning car swept across the office.

'Now never mind the volatile locals, these guys are two of the biggest drunks you're ever likely to meet. They have a stand-up, kick-down fight in a motel just a few miles down the road from here, nearly get themselves arrested, only for a passing patrol to get a more important call.'

I wasn't aware of *that*.

'One of them, the famous writer, his behaviour is pretty erratic. He talks to himself, he charges about yelling things, he breaks into a house and threatens the occupants, he says he can speak to the dead, his own doctor says he needs to be locked up. Every time you see him he's more battered and bruised than the last, and still he's talking to god-damn invisible people. He's probably not even aware that after the robbery, we brought in security cameras, put them all over town – you can hardly move without someone watching. And I'll tell you, Mr Michael Ryan, we've been watching you a lot.'

I wasn't aware of that, either.

'Mr Ryan, I know our people pretty well. We've had our bad times in Brevard, but that was ten years ago. These days we're really rather peaceful. Fact is, only trouble we've really had this last while, we can trace right back to you and Mr Ambrose Jeffers. So I'm going to say this to you, Mr Ryan, no lawyers present, no charges brought: first thought I had when I heard this might be a murder was, where were you when this happened? Where were you when his car was forced off the road?'

I half-laughed, but his gaze remained steady and hard.

'Are you suggesting . . . ?'

'I'm asking you a straightforward question. I know how rich you are, Mr Ryan, I know you could have half the lawyers in the state batting for you in thirty minutes, but right now, just the two of us, where were you?'

Where was I when Ambrose died?

I was standing in a garage with a bunch of spooks.

48

Smalltown justice can be a bizarre and elusive thing. Of course it was ridiculous of Sheriff Newton to connect me to Ambrose's death. I think his point was that he intended to investigate it without any interference or contribution from me, and if he couldn't find who was responsible, it was entirely within his powers and abilities to make it look as if I was involved. He had also stolen a march on me by calling Ambrose's wife in New York to break the bad news. He thought I'd caused enough problems already by my behaviour and with the newspaper stunt. Without explicitly saying it, he had issued a second order for me to get out of town.

The truth was, I was about to get further out of town than he could possibly imagine.

Still, it made sense to call Lena to make sure that she would corroborate my lie that I was with her all of the previous night, and I was intent on doing just that as I hurried out of the station. However, I was distracted by a sudden outburst from the front desk. A man with long scraggy hair and a body odour that could fell trees was ranting to an embarrassed deputy about his dog getting shot and demanding to know what was going to be done about it. Other police officers, sitting at desks to the rear, were struggling to keep their faces straight. I was halfway through the doors when I heard the deputy say somewhat more sternly: 'Mr de Luca – just fill in the form.'

I stopped and turned to stare at the dishevelled mess standing with his back to me. 'Paul?'

The aggrieved man turned towards me. A mess of thick grey hair covered the upper half of his face, so that I couldn't actually tell if he was looking directly at me. He was wearing a ripped brown knee-length leather trench coat and black motorcycle boots. But it was still, very plainly, the man with titanium legs.

'It's Michael,' I said. 'Michael Ryan.'

Paul's lips opened just enough for me to see cracked teeth, set like burned tree roots in the undergrowth of his unkempt beard. He nodded once, then immediately twisted back and jabbed a stained finger at the cop. 'You find out who did it, or I swear to God!' Then he strode past me and out of the station. He was halfway down the sloping wheelchair access ramp before he stopped and looked back at me still standing in the doorway.

'What're you waiting for?' he shouted. 'Come on!'

I was expecting to have a quiet chat with him in the privacy of his vehicle, but I had barely closed the door before he stamped on the accelerator and his pick-up roared us away without even a cursory check for oncoming traffic. He drove hunched forward like a nervous learner. Every few moments he glanced in the mirror for signs of pursuit.

After a mile or two I decided to break the silence by asking who 'they' were.

He shot me a look. 'What?'

'You said *they* shot your dog. I was wondering who *they* were.'

'Who do you think?' he snapped.

'I don't know, Paul.'

'Well, you fucking should, because you'll probably be next.'

Before I could respond to that, he thumped the horn and yelled abuse at a slow driver ahead, before pulling the truck violently off the highway and up the short incline onto his property. He drove around the yard several times, allowing the lights to sweep back and forth across the open ground surrounding the video store and into the undergrowth beyond the garbage-strewn wire fence until he was satisfied we were alone, before bringing the vehicle to a screeching halt in front of his home.

When he pulled down the back of the truck, I saw that it was packed with groceries in beige Publix carrier bags. I helped him carry them up the steps to the front door. He fumbled with the lock, then pushed me in ahead of him and slammed the door shut behind us. He stared back out through the glass for fully two minutes, as we stood in complete darkness, before flicking a couple of switches, one for the interior lights and the other which instantly floodlit the yard.

His accommodation was a mess. It smelled of dog and beer. Paul carried his Publix bags across to the kitchen table and set them down. I followed suit. For the next few minutes we unpacked the groceries, side by side, in complete silence. The fluorescent light didn't do his complexion any favours. He'd been a bronzed beach god when I'd first met him; now he was wan and ill-defined. After a while, and somewhat hesitantly, he muttered gruffly, 'Heard you were back.' He lifted two cans of peaches and placed them on a shelf.

'Yeah,' I said. 'Not one of my better ideas.'

'So how come?'

'I . . . don't really know. I was persuaded.'

'You shouldn't have. Wakes things up.'

'I called to see you, Paul, a few days ago. You weren't here.'

'I'm always here.' He lifted some more cans.

I took a couple, and began feeding them to him. 'Well, maybe you didn't hear me. Met your dog though, then some old guy chased me off. He seemed very protective of you. They both did.'

'Ivan's an attack dog, that's why I got him. Don't know about an old guy. There's nobody lives near me. Anyone comes near the house, Ivan would takes lumps out of them. Damn dog didn't stop barking from dawn to dusk. But I loved him.' He sighed.

'Paul, what happened?'

'To Ivan?'

'To Ivan. To you. Paul, I've been gone a long time.'

His eyes flitted, red and sad. 'Not long enough,' he said quietly.

* * *

There were tins of fruit, vegetables, soups, but mostly there was beer, too much for any domestic fridge. What wouldn't fit he piled up on counters and crammed into cupboards. At some point he'd tried storing beer in the freezer and it had expanded and exploded. The twisted remains of a tin lay on the flushed brown ice like the wreck of a crashed aircraft. He'd also bought enough cigarettes to keep a Chinese bookie and his extended family happy well into eternity. When the groceries were away we sat at the table with a couple of warm beers. Paul rolled a joint with single-handed expertise.

'Do you think I would ever have had a chance with her?' he suddenly asked after his third toke.

'Claire?' He nodded. 'I don't know.'

'She was just getting to know me, the real me, when you showed up.'

'I'm sorry, Paul. I know you loved her. She really liked you, I know that.'

'Did she talk about me at all? Do you think if the shark hadn't—'

'I just don't know. It was a long time ago.'

'Was it? I can remember every single thing she ever said to me. Every word.'

It didn't surprise me. He'd been obsessive then – and it had clearly festered for a decade.

'So can I,' I said.

'Those bastards. Those fucking bastards.' He ground the remains of the joint into an ashtray, then immediately began rolling another. He opened a second beer.

I took a sip of my own. 'What did you mean when you said I'd be next?'

His eyes remained fixed on the joint. 'Stands to reason. Shoot my dog to keep me quiet, come after you to stop you poking your nose in. Ten years I've kept my mouth shut, and I wasn't about to open it, but they shot my dog. No call for that. Now I don't care who knows.'

There was a prickle of sweat on my back. I leaned forward. 'Who knows what, Paul?'

His eyes flitted up for just a second before focusing back on the joint. 'All that shit,' he half-mumbled.

'All *what* shit? The robbery?'

'Yes, the fucking robbery.'

'About Claire?'

He shook his head. 'I don't know about Claire. I just know . . .' He trailed off. He lit the joint and inhaled deeply. 'I just got sucked in, Michael. You know what Tommy was like, he was very persuasive. All those fucking Marines are. What did I ever do? I wrote a couple of books and ran a video store. He went off and killed people. He was tough.'

He offered the joint. I shook my head. He inhaled. When he exhaled he coughed a little.

'Before he went out on those cruises, he was okay, I could handle him. But he came back different. The other guys in the band, they came back all cracked up, but Tommy, he came back smart, straight, big ideas. He'd set up a lot of deals and the money was coming in – big money. That's why he came to see me. He couldn't just walk into the bank with a suitcase of money and put it in his account. He wanted me to do that for him – you know, put it through the business.'

'Launder it.'

'Yep. And I did. Smart, right?' He didn't wait for a response. 'Smart because I never made a dime out of it, smart because Tommy made sure I got hooked on that shit first, then he kept me supplied as long as I looked after his money, and any time I had second thoughts, he'd just withhold for a while until I came running back. Michael, these legs, these fucking legs – I was in constant pain, I needed something. Fucking Tylenol didn't cut it.'

'That's okay, Paul. I understand.'

'No, you don't. Nobody does. It just grinds you down.' He looked to the window for a moment. 'Anyway, I got off the junk – nearly killed me, but I got off it. That was later, though. Back then, I just went along with Tommy. He kept me sweet, but man, there was just too much money coming in, and I was getting more and more fucked up so I wasn't as careful as I should have been. I started forgetting and putting money in the bank that hadn't been cleaned, and one day Sheldon called me in.'

'Sheldon Adelson? The First National?'

'Smooth-as-shit Sheldon. Tells me he's been keeping a personal eye on my account and he's done the math, and that for me to be making that much money, every man woman and child in Brevard must be buying porn on a weekly basis. I tried to joke with him, told him he'd be surprised how many pillars of the community came through the store, but he wasn't buying. He said some of the notes had been traced: some were forgeries, some stolen. Well, I was panicking then, because at the end of the day it was my account, and I was paranoid anyway – I was thinking the cops are in the next room, taping this, and any minute they'd bust in. Then Sheldon asks if I'm interested in cutting a deal, and I thought he meant with the cops – you know, give up my connections in return for soft time, and maybe I would have gone with that but he was actually talking about cutting *him* in, in return for not calling the cops. What was I supposed to do? I mean, he had the money anyway, didn't he? If I tried to withdraw it, he'd just call the cops. So I agreed to split it with him.'

'Split Tommy's money, that is.'

'Exactly. I was just buying time, Michael. I wanted out of there.'

'And?'

'I walked.'

'And you told Tommy.'

'Tommy was off on another cruise. He showed up a couple of weeks later, with more cash. I didn't tell him. I needed – what do you call it? An exit strategy. I was going to take off with my half, except, fuck, I was a junkie, and junkies are always making grand plans but they never seem to happen, do they? Couple of months pass, then Tommy turns up one day, wants his money. So I have to tell him. He goes ballistic Only reason he doesn't kill me is, if something happens to me, the account gets frozen – fucking Sheldon keeps the lot.'

'So what's to stop Tommy having one of his quiet words with Sheldon?'

'He tried, but turns out Sheldon isn't just Sheldon, Sheldon has influence all over town. Tommy was chased out.'

'And then he came back, all guns blazing.'

Paul nodded slowly. 'So you see? It was my fault. If I hadn't gotten on the shit, I wouldn't have let Tommy use me like that, and Claire never would have died. Someone said you kill the things you love. That's what I did. I loved her, man, I really loved her.' Tears began to drip down his cheeks. 'I'm sorry, I'm really sorry . . .' He paused to take another smoke. 'He didn't need to do that, man, he didn't need to.'

He was my best man, and worst man.

Given his appearance and demeanour, and his prodigious appetite for dope, I had been surprised by the lucidity of Paul's recollections, but eventually the joints began to take their toll. His words became vague and he rambled off on tangents that only occasionally veered back towards reality. I deduced from one single thirty-five-minute stream of consciousness that he blamed himself for what happened in the bank and shut down his video business. He retreated into a fug of dope, rarely going out and growing increasingly paranoid and chaotic as the years ticked by. He'd heard I was coming back for the anniversary events and shortly afterward received a visit from some heavies who'd warned him to stay away and to keep his mouth shut. I presume they were not unconnected to Sheldon Adelson.

When Paul nodded off, I removed the joint from his lips and set it in the ashtray so it could burn itself out. That left me with a decision about my own exit strategy. It was a long walk back into town. I could easily borrow his pick-up, or I could phone Lena, which I'd neglected to do earlier.

Alternatively, I could sit and wait to zone out.

Talking to Paul, going to see the Sheriff – these things were important in their own way, but they were a sideshow to the main event. The bank robbery, the massacre, they had ruined both our lives, but they were history, beyond our control. My wife wasn't the past, she was the future, and she was in danger.

If the aneurysm was growing as rapidly as Lena seemed to think, then my zoning out should have been happening with increasing frequency, but it had been hours since I'd deserted Claire and Meg. I desperately wanted to be able to will myself back there, but it was beyond my control.

Still undecided, I got up and briefly inspected the other rooms. They confirmed my first impression that ten years of insular, drug-fuelled madness had turned Paul's home into a complete shithole. It didn't need a springclean, it needed to be burned to the ground and rebuilt from scratch. His bedroom was particularly rank; there were cartons of rotting Chinese food all over the floor, many of them spilled over piles of paperback books which had tumbled from sloping shelves. On the top of a cheap dressing-table I noticed a framed photo lying face down – it was the only item in the room that wasn't covered in a thick layer of dust. In fact, it had been recently polished. When I turned it over, I saw Claire looking back at me.

My stomach did a little somersault.

The photo was slightly fuzzy. Claire was wearing the blood-stained zebra-striped bikini I'd first seen her in on the beach, and I guessed that Paul had taken it from the news footage of the shark attack. Given that he'd been in a coma at the time the clip had been broadcast, he must have tracked it down later.

I heard movement from the kitchen, and not wishing to be caught snooping, I turned briefly into the bathroom and pulled the toilet chain; it made a grinding sound and didn't flush. When I walked back up the hall I saw that the kitchen light was switched off. Paul had recovered sufficiently to move from the table to the door and was now standing in the semi-darkness staring out across the yard. He was clutching what appeared to be a shotgun.

'The sleeper awakes . . .' I began, but Paul cut me off by holding a finger to his lips. The lights of a car swept over the derelict video store in front of us, and then moved along the far side, out of sight.

'Paul, what's with the gun?'

The car swung back around, and as it came to a halt in front of the house there was a flash of red and blue neon and a short *whoop* from its sound effects department. Brevard Police.

Paul visibly relaxed. 'About fucking time,' he muttered. He put a hand on the door, but staggered as he tried to open it.

'You've had enough blow to stun an elephant,' I said, moving across to steady him. 'Maybe I should have a word with them.'

'My dog, my problem,' he replied, and this time successfully pulled the door open. 'He's in the outhouse. If they can extract the bullet, maybe they can find whoever shot him.'

'I'm not sure they'll want to go to that much effort.'

He nodded back at me before stepping onto the porch, shotgun under his arm. He moved down the steps as the car doors opened and two cops got out. For the briefest moment I thought about joining him and then asking the cops for a lift back into the town, but I quickly reconsidered. I still hadn't firmed up my alibi with Lena and I wasn't yet sure how serious Sheriff Newton's threats were, so staying out of the way of the forces of law and order was definitely the preferred option. Instead I moved further back into the darkened kitchen and tried to keep an eye on them through a small window above the sink, but they'd already come closer to the steps and were out of sight. However, I could hear Paul arguing with them. He didn't seem to appreciate how unusual it was for cops to bother with investigating something as mundane as the death of a dog, particularly in the middle of the night, and that if he continued to be obstreperous they could easily bust him for dope.

There was a sudden crack and flash.

You don't have to be familiar with a gunshot to recognise it.

My appalled first thought was that it was Paul in his anger who had let loose, and I was halfway to the door to try and stop him causing further harm when I saw his pallid face pressed against the glass. Then there was another crack and he slipped down out of sight.

I stood virtually paralysed in the darkness.

'Get him inside.'

Three words – and paralysis fled. I took a step back, then another. I padded down the hall, my mind choked and confused and numb. The front door opened as I turned into Paul's bedroom.

I moved across to the back window and tried to open it, but it was locked. No key.

Steps in the hall.

I crouched down and crawled under the bed while desperately trying not to disturb any of the cartons of food or adult DVDs that littered the floor. I just managed to crush myself against the back wall before the light was switched on.

Seconds passed like hours.

Then it was off again and the footsteps retreated. A drag-thump-drag sound before something heavy was dropped on the kitchen floor.

'This place fucking stinks.'

'Not for long.'

The front door opened, closed, opened again. A sloshing sound and the ominous smell of gasoline.

A sudden roar and then flames licked out along the hall.

Kill the man, torch the crime scene.

I scrambled out from under the bed to the door. Thick black smoke choked the hall. I ducked down low and hurried along to the bathroom. The window here was also locked. I pressed my face against it. The view was over the yard at the back of the house; so far as I could see, there was nobody out there. With the intense heat already causing glass to shatter in other parts of the house, one more wouldn't sound out of place. I heaved a set of scales through it, then pulled myself awkwardly up until I was perched on the base of the windowframe. Yet instead of jumping down, I had what I can only describe as a Road to Damascus moment. The thought struck me that if I stayed in the house and allowed myself to be overcome by the smoke, it would give me exactly what I wanted: my own personal untimely death, a swift passage back to Claire's world, on my terms, to my own schedule, not according to the vagaries of blood circulation. I could so easily turn back into the smoke and suck it greedily in, embrace it, safe in the wonderful knowledge that soon I would be reunited with—

God, no!

There was a huge difference between committing suicide and just handing victory on a plate to whoever was ultimately responsible for my wife's death. What was the point in giving myself up to fire and smoke when I was still capable of fighting my enemies on two fronts – in this world and in Claire's – and at the very moment when the extent of the conspiracy had just been revealed, from Paul to Tommy to Sheldon – to the Sheriff's department?

I pulled myself through the shattered window and dropped down onto the rough asphalt yard. I crouched there for a moment, trying to decide which part of the surrounding fence to aim for; it was topped with barbed wire, so it wouldn't just be a straightforward race up and clamber over. I picked what looked like the least well-protected spot and was just about to charge across when the police car swept around the corner and its lights flashed across me. For a blessed moment I thought they hadn't seen me, but a dozen yards further on, the car braked suddenly. Now I had no choice at all. I raced across to the fence and hurled myself at it. I grabbed on and hauled myself up. The barbed wire at the top was tangled and sharp, but not impenetrable. I tore through it without regard to flesh or fashion. I hurled myself from the top, landed hard and rolled blindly forwards into a thick bank of shrubs and bushes.

'Ryan!'

I kept my head down and pulled myself forward through root and branch.

Gunshot!

Another! I pressed my head into the ground. Another!

'Ryan!'

With my head in the dirt I couldn't tell if they were silently climbing the fence or had found a way around it or through it or beneath it. I willed them away.

Then in the far distance I heard the wail of a fire tender, closely followed by a panicked shout: 'Junior! Come on!'

Junior! So the nice guy act was just that. Like father like son.

The siren grew louder.

If I could just stay hidden for a few more minutes, then there would surely be too many people around for Junior and his pal to do anything.

At that moment, my cell phone rang.

Timing is everything.

I felt frantically in my jacket pocket, but it wasn't there. I twisted around . . .

There! It had slipped out less than five yards back and was now glowing invitingly and in time to every elongated note it issued. Almost immediately the bullets began to yip around me.

49

Lena drove up. As I yanked the door open and jumped in, she was full of apologies for the delay. 'There's a fire down there,' she said. 'The traffic's backed up. Police are searching cars looking for someone.' It was only at this point that I turned to face her and she got a proper look at my smoke-blackened face, torn clothes and scratched and bleeding hands.

She remained admirably calm. 'So, you weren't out for a late-night walk – you weren't trying to clear your head.'

'No.'

The glow from Paul de Luca's home was clearly visible against the night sky, though it was at least three miles away. I'd scrambled that far across fields and along ditches.

'And if we could drive, that would be appreciated.'

Lena pulled the car back out onto the highway. As she drove she checked my pulse with her right hand, then tutted. My head had been aching for the past hour, and now I was seeing little stars. I thought it might be an early sign of zoning out, but I couldn't be sure. It happened, and each time it was different. If it was to be the big one, the one I wouldn't come back from, it made sense to tell Lena not only everything that had happened at Paul's but also to try and explain the small measure of the understanding that had come to me on the Road to Damascus and again afterwards, during my long stumble through the dark. She had to know so she could pass it on, make them pay in case I couldn't. So it all came out, rapidfire. She kept telling me to slow down. She asked for clarification on this, and this, and this. The days of her dismissing my stories as hallucination were gone. She looked horrified as I told her about Junior Newton.

'They're all in it, Lena. It's drug money. It's why Sheriff Newton made sure Tommy and his gang were wiped out. I think they only let Paul live because he's so fucked up. They thought they got away with it, but then the Mayor, new to town, comes up with this crazy anniversary proposal, and it all bubbles right back up to the surface.'

'But if Paul's dead, then there's no one to testify.'

'It's a bank, Lena. There's always paperwork, records, computers. You can delete things a hundred times from computers, but it never really disappears; there's always an expert who can get to it.'

'So what do we do?'

'You keep driving, get out of state, go to the FBI.'

'*Me?*'

'Lena, I can't go. You know that.'

'And neither can I. Not yet.' She glanced across. 'There's something we have to do first.'

'What?'

'I can't tell you, you just need to come with me.'

'Why can't you tell me?'

'Because then you might back out. Please. It's important.'

I rested my head back and closed my eyes. The lights of oncoming cars weren't helping my head. I felt *wavy*. I sighed. 'Lena, please, just tell—'

'We'll be there in a minute. Just go with me on this, Michael, then I promise I'll do whatever you want.'

In recent days I had misled her, betrayed her, confused and lied to her. I could do this one thing for her, whatever it was, before I plunged into the unknown again.

'Give me a clue,' I said.

'You've heard of killing two birds with one stone?'

'I have.'

'Well, this will be killing a whole flock.'

We arrived at the Radisson, scene of previous humiliations. Lena switched the engine off and looked at me. 'I thought we could go straight in, but if they see you like this they'll walk.'

'They?'

'Just stay with me on this.'

We walked into the hotel, her arm around my waist, either to give me support or stop me running off. I was shaky, unfocused, aching to cross over, but I just couldn't make the jump. Lena directed me into the men's room, and followed right in behind. I leaned against the row of sinks while she soaked paper towels and began to rub at my face like I was a helpless kid. She peeled my jacket off, examined it, then decided it was beyond redemption and threw it into a waste-bin. My T-shirt wasn't too badly marked and my trousers, despite having been dragged through dirt for hundreds of yards, were dark enough to hide most of the stains once the top layer of dust had been brushed off. Lena cleaned the jagged barbed-wire scratches on my hands and arms as best she could, but there was really no hiding them. She left me alone for a couple of minutes before returning with a black sports coat under her arm.

'Lost property,' she explained, slipping it over my shoulders before looking me up and down. 'It ain't pretty,' she said, 'but it'll have to do.'

Then she kissed me.

'What was that for?'

'For free. And because I love you. Now let's go.'

'Lena . . .'

'Come on. They're waiting.' She led me out of the men's room and across reception towards the function room where the memorial dinner had been held. She paused at the double swing doors and put a hand to my face.

'This is the only way to do it, Michael. Just go for it. And I'm sure there are other towns I can work in.'

She smiled, then pushed forwards and I followed in behind her.

What had been a hubbub of conversation faded to nothing as we entered a room packed to the gills with the mothers and fathers and brothers and sisters of the tragic dead of Brevard.

'Christ,' I whispered.

Lena took my notebook from her bag and placed it on the angled lectern, then tapped the microphone. I settled onto a plastic chair behind her.

'Ladies and gentlemen,' she began confidently, 'I am Dr Lena Olson. Most of you know me already, many of you since I was a kid. Some of you I inherited as patients from my late father.' There were nods of appreciation around the room. 'First of all, I want to thank you for coming. I would prefer to have visited you all individually, but that simply wasn't possible, for reasons which will become clear. I do have new information about the deaths of your loved ones, but it is not quite as straightforward as that.'

An overweight man in a McDaid's apron stood up at the back of the room. 'Doctor Olson, how can you have information for all of us? You know what happened to my boy, but Dorothy over there, lost her man in a fire. There was the robbery . . . but there's no connection between us all.'

'Mr Webber, please. If you'll just be patient and hear us out, then there'll be plenty of time for questions.' Lena glanced back at me, raised her eyebrows, then faced front again. 'Now, I'm sure you know all about Michael Ryan, his book and his loss; you may also have witnessed some of his rather, um, eccentric behaviour over the past few days – I know it's been the hot topic of all the local gossip.' There were scattered nods and whispers. 'To tell you the truth, if I'd had my way, after witnessing some of it, I'd have quite happily signed him into a secure institution.' I smiled, and there was some nervous laughter from the floor. 'However, there is a rational explanation. Mr Ryan, we have discovered, is suffering from an aneurysm of the brain.'

She paused dramatically. She had their complete attention. 'I could give you a long and complicated explanation of his condition, but the simple fact is that this aneurysm is dangerously constricting the bloodflow to his brain, and it could kill him at any time, quite possibly within the next few hours. We could operate, we could save his life, but with each minute that passes, that becomes more dangerous and the chances of his survival diminish. However, he has chosen not to have this operation yet so that he can be with us tonight, so that he can tell you what he has discovered. What he will tell you will sound incredible, perhaps unbelievable – crazy, even. I can't tell you what to believe, that's up to you, but I can say that there are things that are inexplicable to medical science. We don't know everything.' The audience were starting to shift in their seats; worried glances were exchanged.

'Somehow, what is happening to Michael Ryan has given him an insight into . . .' She looked at me, and for the first time her voice faltered. 'Michael, I can't explain this properly.'

All eyes were upon me as I stood up and walked to the lectern. 'It's okay,' I said quietly. 'I'll do the rest.'

Lena managed a half-smile. She touched my hand as she moved away.

I gripped each side of the lectern and looked around the audience. They were just ordinary people who'd been hurt, and I was about to inflict further pain. There was no point in giving them even a potted version of what had happened to me in recent days. I would lose them right from the start. Instead I reminded them about *Space Coast* and the millions I had made, and said that I would give up every cent I had in order to have my wife back – and that I was sure they would do the same to be reunited with their lost loved ones. They were with me on that.

I looked down at the file and picked a name at random. 'David Caldwell's parents – are they here?'

An elderly couple cautiously rose from their seat towards the back of the room. 'Yes, I'm David's father,' said the old man.

'David was a keen cyclist: he was killed in a road accident in 1993?'

'June twenty-fourth,' said Mrs Caldwell.

'Mr Caldwell, David's bike was a birthday present. It was

expensive, you warned him to look after it, but did you know he lost it the following day, and your wife went out and bought another one without telling you, so there wouldn't be a row about it?'

Mr Caldwell's mouth dropped open a fraction, then he turned to his wife, but she was busy staring at me. 'How could you know this? I drove one hundred miles to a bike store, so no one local would know. I never told. Our David was killed that night. How could you know this?'

Instead of replying, I picked another name. 'Tracy Yeoh – is her brother here?' A Chinese boy of about fourteen stood with his arm half-raised. His parents sat on either side of him. 'William – Billy – you were with your sister in the basement when you found your dad's gun. You wanted to put it back, but Tracy insisted on playing with it. You went to tell your dad, but before you could get up the steps, the gun went off and she died. Ever since, your parents have blamed you because they thought girls don't play with guns – but it wasn't you, was it?'

Billy stood wide-eyed.

'Son, Tracy wants you to stop blaming yourself, and she also wants you to know you spend far too much time on your PlayStation.'

Bob, this might read quite slowly, but the words were tumbling out of me because I knew I had to get to as many of them as possible before they lost patience and stormed out. While I could see that the people I'd already named were stunned, most of the others were becoming agitated, and I don't blame them – I was getting on like some carnival huckster. They'd come expecting revelations, not *Revelations*.

'Eric Stratton – DeMarcus Hall's stepfather?' A grizzled black man in the front row nodded. 'Mr Stratton, I don't know what this means, but DeMarcus just says the Big D is okay, and how are those Blue Jays doing?'

Mr Stratton broke into a wide grin. 'Son of a *bitch*!' he exclaimed.

A sallow-faced man in a plaid shirt jumped to his feet three rows back. 'Lena! What is this?'

Lena raised placatory hands. 'Mr Penske, if you just give him a chance . . .'

Mr Penske shuffled along the line of chairs and into the aisle before waving a fist in my direction. 'I won't be part of this . . . charade!' He stomped angrily towards the doors. A woman in the back row burst into tears before getting up to follow him. To my right, four young women – sisters, I think – stood up as one.

I was perilously close to losing them.

'Mr Penske!' I shouted.

'I won't listen to your crap!' he shouted without turning.

'Mr Penske! I've spoken to your father!'

He spun. 'You have no right!'

'Mr Penske.' My head jagged suddenly and viciously. I held onto the lectern and tried to focus on my notes. 'Mr Penske, please.'

'You are an affront to God! You are trying to make fools of all of us!'

Mr Yeoh jumped to his feet. 'We did not blame our son! It's outrageous!'

'Listen to him!' It was Mrs Caldwell. 'Nobody knew about the bike! Nobody!'

Another woman, away to the left, shouted: 'I knew about it! I saw you bring it home!'

Lena appeared beside me and leaned into the microphone. 'Please, everyone!'

More people were getting to their feet – not all of them to leave, some were actually offering support – but the meeting was quickly descending into a shouting match.

My head jagged again and I staggered against the lectern. Lena held me up. 'Michael . . .'

'It's okay – it's all right.' My voice was ragged, but I still had the advantage of the microphone. 'Mr Penske!' He was halfway through the doors. 'You switched off your father's life support, but he could still hear you.'

That stopped him. Those who had been following him out paused as well.

'All the things you'd never been able to say to him came pouring out! He was an alcoholic, he beat you nearly every day when you were a kid, but you never told anyone, not even your mother! He wants you to know he's sorry, that he couldn't help himself, that he's proud of you.'

Mr Penske shook his head. Tears sprang. But still: 'You should be ashamed of yourself.'

'No, Mr Penske. *He's* ashamed of *himself*.'

An old man who'd been leaving directly behind him put a supportive arm around his shoulders – but then suddenly bent down to kiss him on the forehead. It was an extremely familiar gesture, but Penske didn't react at all, he just continued to glare back at me. The old man looked up at me then, and nodded, and I realised that I knew him, that Lena's father had introduced us in the garage. It was Penske's dead father.

And he wasn't alone.

David Caldwell, the Cyclist, stood with his parents; Tracy Yeoh, hand-in-hand with her brother, but he wasn't aware of it. Here, there, everywhere.

'They're here,' I whispered.

Lena gripped my arm and gave me a concerned look. 'Who?'

It was surreal, but exactly what I needed. I bent back to the microphone. 'They're here! They're all here with you.'

Towards the back, someone shouted: 'You're fucking mental!'

'You should be locked up!'

'No! Listen to me. They're here – there, and there, and there.' They couldn't help but look about them and wonder, and even hope, but of course there was nothing tangible. But they *were* there. I had zoned out and now *they* were crowding into the hall and taking their places by the sides of their loved ones. They waved at me, they smiled, thumbs up, encouragement. I clicked my fingers, trying to remember a name. In the front row was Mark Nesbitt, the nineteen-year-old student who'd been in the bank about to negotiate a loan when he'd been shot dead by Tommy Ford. He was standing directly behind his parents, one hand on his father's shoulder, the other on his mother's. 'Mrs Nesbitt, your son is with you. You can't see

him, but I can. I can ask him anything you want. Just ask –
please!'

Mr Nesbitt looked incredulously about him. Mrs Nesbitt put
a hand to her shoulder. 'Ask him where I keep my jewellery.'

Everyone was watching, even Mr Penske.

'Matthew, where does your mum keep her jewellery?'

Matthew stroked his mum's hair and smiled up. 'She doesn't
have any jewellery.'

'You don't have any jewellery.'

Mrs Nesbitt immediately burst into tears. 'Oh my God . . . oh
my God.'

'Is my husband here?' A woman had come to the front of the
stage.

'No,' I said.

'I believe you,' she said. 'He was never here when he was
alive either.'

'Mr Ryan?' Michelle Del'Appa, the nurse who'd been shot in
the bank, had been one of the first in the garage queue, extremely
keen to tell her daughter Ronnie that she was marrying the
wrong guy. Ronnie sat hand-in-hand with her chosen man;
Michelle stood in front of them, glaring down. Ronnie's eyes
widened as I looked at her. 'Mr Ryan,' said Michelle, 'you tell
Ronnie he's a no-good son of a bitch.'

'I can't say that, Michelle, I'm in enough trouble.'

'Is that my mama?' a startled Ronnie asked.

Before I could respond, Michelle cut in. 'You tell her he's been
seeing another woman, works in a nail salon on Main.'

'Ronnie, your mother says your boyfriend's been messing
around with a woman who works in a nail salon on Main.'

The boyfriend's mouth dropped open.

'This true?' Ronnie demanded of him, and his reaction told
her it was. She immediately began to batter him around the
head. Laughter broke out. All around, people began to stand
with their hands out, pawing at the air, trying to touch their
loved ones while the objects of their affection hugged and stroked
them. Dozens of questions were shouted out and I answered as
many as I could, but it was like a conductor fighting for control

of an orchestra with every player reading from a different sheet; it was anarchy in the best sense – joyous, free, impossible.

My head jagged horribly, so bad that my legs almost gave out from under me. It jagged again and I gave an involuntary, 'Fuck!' But the questions didn't let up. People crowded around the stage vying for attention with charismatic fervour: and not just those of this real world, but from Claire's world as well. I was their only link, their only hope; it all had to be channelled through me.

A dog barked somewhere close by. The questions continued to rain down, but some of them began to fade away, as if Claire's world was gaining the upper hand. The dog, still hidden from view, barked again, but this time ferociously. On hearing it, the dead of Brevard began to back away.

My head jagged for the third and most painful time. Lena couldn't prevent me from collapsing to the floor. When I looked up, she had been joined by her father.

I was being helped by *two* Dr Olsons, the living and the dead.

Lena squeezed my hand. 'Michael, I have to get you to the hospital.'

'Claire,' I whispered. 'What about Claire?'

Old Dr Olson had my other hand. 'Tommy has her, son, Tommy has her. You have to come.'

There was a snarl from above and we both looked up into the dripping jaws of a huge black dog.

Ivan.

Paul de Luca's dog.

A ghost dog wearing a thick leather collar connected to a steel chain firmly held by the same black-suited old man who had chased me from Paul's yard. His stern, crumpled face looked gravely down at me.

'It's the Judge,' whispered Dr Olson. 'It's Judge Wheeler.'

My head jagged excruciatingly, forcing my whole body to arch upwards in agony. As it settled down again I tried to speak, but the words would no longer come; my peripheral vision was clouding, even the words of the departed now sounded distant and indistinct. There was a look of panic in Lena's eyes, a glaze of desperation in her father's. I was losing them, losing Lena as much as Claire, losing two worlds. I had sought battle on two fronts, and been defeated on each.

I was too late . . . too late . . .

'Stay with us, Michael,' Lena implored. 'Please, stay with us.'

50

There was a fantastic jolt, a feeling of intense cold. I was no longer in that crowded hotel room, but in a hospital theatre, standing amidst wires and tubes and digital screens and electronic pulses, with scalpels and drills laid out on metal trays, but untouched, with surgeons and nurses in smocks, their eyes fixed on screens, ignoring me, standing there, feeling great, perfectly healthy. There was an incessant, high-pitched and annoying whine which seemed to mesmerise them.

Abruptly, the nurse explained it: 'He's gone.'

They parted, and I saw another version of myself, lying on an operating table, my head shaved, my eyes vacant, my heart stilled.

I let out an elongated sigh.

Dead.

While my body had battled against an intruder, my mind had given me a glimpse of my dead wife and allowed me to briefly hope that we might one day be reunited. It had meant well: but now the physical battle was over. I was dead before the surgeons had had a chance to operate. I was gone from one world and barred from another by having the temerity to die from natural causes. Yet here I was, looking at myself, thinking, feeling, breathing; not some lost soul floating around. Where was I? What new world was this? And why were the surgeons continuing to stand over my corpse? Why were the nurses poised, ready for action? I was *dead*. They should at the very least have been harvesting organs so that some life might come from my tragedy. But they stood, they watched, they waited. The nurse who had pronounced me dead had a tear just below her left eye. With the mask and cap I hadn't realised: it was Lena.

I shivered. It was freezing.

'Michael.' I spun to find Lena's father behind me. He smiled 'I've been waiting for you.'

'I don't understand. I'm dead, Doctor Olson, I shouldn't be here.'

'You're dead, Michael, because they killed you.' He nodded around the surgical team. 'And now we've no time to lose. You must come with me.' He moved towards the swing doors with his familiar laboured gait.

'Killed?' I hurried after him. 'What do you mean?'

We moved through the door and I was surprised to see Sheriff Newton and Junior standing in the corridor outside.

'They're here to arrest you, Michael,' said Dr Olson. 'They believe you murdered Paul de Luca.'

'But they killed him!'

'I know that. They're panicking.'

Just a few yards further along there was a room reserved for relatives of those undergoing surgery – and it was packed full. It seemed that at least half of those who had attended the meeting in the hotel were there. In addition, Adam Harrington, the editor of the local paper, chatted and took notes. Jo-Anne sat in a corner staring at the ground.

'What are they all doing here? They're wasting their time. I'm dead.'

'No, you're not.'

It was all I could do to stop myself from grabbing him and throwing him against the wall. 'Jesus Christ,' I hissed, 'will you just tell me what's going on?'

'You've heard of cryonics, Michael?'

'Cryonics? I've heard of . . . I don't know, cryogenics. Is it the same thing? It's crazy guys with terminal illnesses who pay a fortune to have themselves frozen so that in a thousand years someone can defrost them and cure them. Is that what they're doing?'

'Not quite. I haven't heard of this myself, but Lena has been very good. Everything they've done she's explained out loud, I think entirely for my benefit. They have deliberately stopped your heart. There is now no brain activity. To all intents and purposes, you are dead, Michael. Every monitor in there shows that. But what it really is, is a state of suspended animation. They've developed this technique just in the past few years, Michael. They've removed your blood, cooled it right down and fed it back in so that it brings your body temperature right down to what it would be if you'd . . . say, fallen through the ice on a frozen lake. What they're doing in there now is cutting off the blood supply to your brain; you see, if there's no blood, there's nothing to feed the aneurysm, it collapses in on itself. That means they can go in and cut out what's left of it. It's bloodless surgery, Michael. When they're done they'll close you up, restart the bloodflow and use electric shock to get your heart going again.'

'And this works?'

'Sometimes.'

'Sometimes?'

'It's new, Michael, it's experimental – it's the last resort. The aneurysm was killing you, but the surgeons have jumped the gun and literally switched you off – which is why you're back here with us.'

We were now in the hospital's reception area. Dr Olson stopped as we approached the front doors. 'This is as far as I go, Michael. I'm going to stay with Lena, and I'm going to watch over you.' He reached inside his jacket, removed something wrapped in a dark cloth and handed it to me. 'I want you to have this.'

Heavy metal.

'Walter,' I said.

'Walter. Whatever we're touching when we go, we bring with us. My great good fortune was to bring Walter. Michael, I'm too old and decrepit to tackle Tommy, but you can. You have to save Claire. Tommy has her and he also has Meg. You have to save them.'

345

I unveiled Walter. 'Where are they?'

'I don't know – they keep on the move – but you could try the bank.'

'Why there?'

'It's where they ended, it's where they began.'

I stared at the gun. 'How long do I have?'

'Lena says sixty minutes is the absolute limit; they can't bring you back after that. But it all depends on the surgery. If they can remove the aneurysm quickly they will do it, and that means you'll have less time.'

'But how will I know if I'm running out of time?'

'The Judge, watch out for the Judge.'

'Why?'

'He always appears when death is imminent. If you see him coming, your time's up.'

It was all so fucked up.

But what choice did I have? I had to find Claire and Meg. I had Walter to help me, but Tommy and Lawrence and Ty were armed to the teeth, as they had been on the day of the robbery. I had never been in a fist-fight I had won, and I had never fired a gun in either anger or sport. I had a maximum of sixty minutes, and if the Judge turned up, quite possibly much less. The odds were stacked against me.

Why then this huge feeling of elation, this adrenaline rush?

Perhaps because for the first time what I had to do was defined. I wasn't stumbling into the unknown, I wasn't running scared or hiding. I had a purpose, a determination, a magnificent goal.

I pocketed the gun.

I shook Dr Olson's hand.

I started running.

51

Dawn, but instead of the familiar sunrise a sea mist had rolled in, poisoning everything with a dank greyness. I arrived at McDaid's Char Bar and Grill and from the shelter of its doorway peered up the street towards the First National. I was surprised to see that the bank's lights were on and the front door was lying open. I knew enough about the physics of Claire's world to know it wasn't Tommy's work, but it didn't mean he wasn't inside. It wasn't beyond the bounds of possibility that a second bank robbery was taking place; however, lights blazing and doors open was either remarkably careless or incredibly brazen.

I removed Walter from my pocket and began to cautiously move from doorway to doorway until I was close enough to the bank to be able to see inside. I couldn't detect any movement. I inched closer and was just venturing up to the open doors when Sheldon Adelson suddenly crossed in front of them. He was carrying a bottle of vodka by the neck in one hand and a scroll of fax paper in the other. As he walked towards his office he had to actually push himself off a wall to correct his trajectory enough to get through the open door.

I moved inside, pointing Walter this way and that. I checked the tellers' stations, the clerks' offices at the back and the staff canteen before arriving at Sheldon's office. I was still new to the experience of being invisible, so it felt strange watching as he took a hefty drink and studied the fax paper he'd spread across his desk. He shook his head once, then opened a drawer to his left, removed a gun and put the barrel in his mouth. He closed his eyes and pulled the trigger.

It just clicked.

Sheldon immediately threw the gun down and burst into tears. As he buried his head in his hands I moved behind him and looked down at the fax. It showed a reproduction of the front page of the next edition of the *Brevard Herald*. The head-line read: JOURNALIST'S MURDER LINKED TO BANK ROBBERY. The story below wasn't much more than specula-tion, but there was clearly enough in it for Sheldon to realise that the net was closing in. I had no particular feelings about Sheldon choosing to commit suicide; in fact, it would surely have meant his sudden arrival in this new world and I could have pummelled him for more information about his role in the robbery. But as it was, after a further few moments of tearful despair he started to pull himself together. He took another drink, then pushed his chair back and opened a locker behind his desk. He pulled out a canvas bag and hurried into the open strongroom, where he began filling the bag with bundles of used dollars. Having failed to commit suicide, Sheldon had decided to get out of town, fast, and there wasn't a damn thing I could do about it.

I cursed to myself – not because he was getting away, that didn't really matter, but because I'd allowed myself to get distracted. As soon as I'd established that Claire wasn't in the bank I should have moved on. I was running out of time.

I turned out of the office – then stopped abruptly as some-thing hard and rigid was jammed into my back.

'Hands up,' a voice growled.

My quest was over before it had properly begun. I had been stupid and naïve – careful going into the bank, but careless trying to leave it. I raised my hands.

'Now turn around.'

I turned slowly, then gave a huge sigh of relief. 'Paul!'

Paul de Luca stood before me, as unkempt as ever, his face stern, his eyes wild with confusion. He didn't lower his shotgun.

'Michael? What's going on? Where am I? I'm dead, I'm fucking dead – that bastard cop shot me – and now you're here. We're both dead, aren't we, Michael? We're both dead!'

'Take it easy, Paul – it's not as bad as you think.'

'Where are we then? Am I dreaming? Is it heaven or hell?'

'It's a bit of both, Paul.'

'What do you mean?! How can it be?'

'It's like purgatory, it's like a waiting room. Now could you lower the—'

Instead he shook the old shotgun at me. 'How can I have this, then? How can I have a gun in fucking purgatory? I'm on some god-damn trip but I can't seem to wake up! I've been wandering around for hours. I see people, but they don't see me. You're the first who can actually do so. Are we the only ones?'

'No, Paul. There are others.'

'You've met them?'

'Yes, I've met them.'

'Who are they? What do they know? Michael, you have to tell me.'

'Paul . . . Claire's here.'

The change in him was as sudden as it was remarkable. The craziness in his eyes faded and his cheeks flushed. *'Claire?'* he whispered. It was a calculated revelation on my part, and it worked. He lowered the shotgun. 'I don't understand.'

'She's here,' I said quietly, 'and she's been asking for you. That's the good news.'

I was aware of another difference in Paul, but it took me a while to realise what it was. It came to me as we jogged along Main Street.

'Paul,' I said, 'your feet. They're back.'

'Yes, they are. Or maybe they were here the whole time.'

We had a Walther pistol and an ancient shotgun between us, and time against us. Or, in fact – against me. I had not told Paul that my presence here was temporary, but instead emphasised the need for speed because of the imminent danger Claire was in. As soon as I told him about Tommy and Lawrence and Ty, he declared that he intended to shoot them on sight. He blamed them for everything that had gone wrong in his life. Even the shark.

With the sea mist cloaking everything in mystery it would have been easy for Tommy to spring a trap, and I suppose I would have welcomed that, since it would at least have brought him into the open. Brevard is not a large town, but it seemed pretty huge, running this way and that. The initial adrenaline rush had faded and I had this disturbing premonition of spending my entire hour looking for Tommy rather than saving my girl. We entered Publix via a goods entrance, we swept through my former motel, we scouted the garage and street where he'd beaten me up, but there was no sign of him, his gang or his prisoners. Then it came to me all of a sudden: even in this world he had to sleep. Claire had told me they were drawn to the places they had lived in before. She returned to the Blue House at night; next door, Dr Olson watched over his daughter. Wouldn't Tommy go home as well? And I knew exactly where it was, having been there with Ambrose.

'You sure?' Paul asked breathlessly. ''Cos I'll run anywhere, but these legs are out of practice.'

'No, Paul, I'm not sure.'

But we started running again.

It took us another, vital ten minutes, but it was the right decision: there, at an upstairs window, I saw Meg's face pressed against the glass. Almost as soon as I spotted her, she moved away. I don't even think she saw us, but it didn't matter. This was it, and the prospect of confrontation filled me with both elation and terror. What would I find in there? Meg was still alive, but at what cost? What if Claire had been forced to give herself to Tommy to save Meg? What if Tommy had forced himself upon her regardless? Might she even have voluntarily taken up with him because her one hope, me, had disappeared when she needed him most?

The house was set back amongst palm trees, several blocks from the beach, and fell just short of being a mansion. The sea mist was beginning to lift as we approached, although not yet sufficiently to allow the sun to peek through.

We hurried across the dewed grass and began to scout the outside for some means of silent entry. Despite the robbery, Brevard remains the kind of town where it's safe to leave your home unlocked at night, so it wasn't difficult. There was a window wide open at the back; it had wire mesh across it to keep the bugs out, but it was easily peeled back. We slipped through into an expansive kitchen before moving into a tiled hall which had half a dozen rooms leading off. We quickly checked these before coming to a sweeping staircase. We began to cautiously move up it, a step at a time. Paul had his shotgun raised to his shoulder, I had Walter in one sweaty hand, stretched out in front.

I had thought it would be easy to pick out Meg's room, but at the top of the stairs there was a long hall which looped around in a circle and which threw my sense of the interior geography off. There were eight doors on the seaward side of the house, all of them closed. There was nothing else for it but to try them all.

Bedroom. Empty.

Bathroom. Empty.

Bedroom – the old man Ambrose had chatted to was asleep, all by himself.

Bedroom. Empty.

Bathroom. Empty.

As I put my hand on the door handle of the fourth bedroom and began to turn it, a hole was blasted right through it at head height.

My head height.

If I'd been standing directly in front of it I'd have been dead. But I'd seen enough cop shows to know better. Yet my heart was hammering, my stomach churning. This was entirely new territory for both of us. We pressed ourselves against the wall on either side of the doorway, quite undecided what to do – but then the decision was made for us. After just a few seconds, what was left of the door opened slowly and DeMarcus Hall emerged, gun first.

Before he could take a second step I had my gun at the side of his head, and Paul matched it from the other side.

DeMarcus froze. His eyes went wide. 'Don't,' he breathed.

I put a finger to my lips and whispered: 'Where is she?'

His eyes rolled back. I stepped into the doorway, gun first – and immediately there was a cry from the far side of the room as little Meg charged towards me and jumped. I clutched her to my chest with one arm, at the same time ranging around the room with Walter. But it was empty.

I kissed her on the top of her head. 'Where is she, Meg? Where's Claire?'

Her pale tear-stained face looked up into mine. 'I don't know. They took her – *he* made me stand at the window. I'm sorry, Michael. I'm sorry!'

She started to cry again. I hugged her tight. 'It's okay, it's all right.' I turned back out of the room and snapped: 'Is Claire in the house?' at DeMarcus. He shook his head violently.

'They took her away. They made me do it, man, else they were going to kill me. I didn't touch her, man, ask her, ask her.'

Meg stretched across and slapped him hard. 'He's a *snitch*,' she cried. 'He told them you were coming. He saw you at the hospital – he wants back in their gang.'

Paul nudged him with the twin barrels of his shotgun. 'But first a small rite of passage, eh, DeMarcus? That's how Tommy works – you always have to prove yourself.'

'They *made* me,' he responded weakly.

I let Meg slide down my chest to the floor, before pushing Walter up and under DeMarcus's chin. 'Tell me where they've taken her.'

'I don't *know*.'

'I'm counting to three, DeMarcus. I haven't time for your bull-shit.'

'I don't—'

'Two . . .'

'What happened to one?!'

'Thr—'

'Okay! Okay! Just don't shoot, man . . . *please*!'

'Then where are they?'

'The beach, man, the beach.'

'Why there?'

'I don't know, I swear to God.'

I looked at Paul. 'What do you think?'

'You know what Tommy's like – a big Marine and an arrogant son of a bitch with it. He doesn't think you're worth wasting time over. He's happy to leave this bag of shit to do his dirty work.'

I lowered the gun. 'Or he knew there was a fair chance DeMarcus would fail miserably and then rat him out. Maybe he wants to be somewhere he can see me coming.' Paul nodded. 'Either way, Paul, I have to go now. You find some way to secure DeMarcus, then follow on with Meg – okay?'

'No, Michael. There are three of them – you can't—'

'I have to.'

Written down it sounds gung ho, but that's not how it was. All I knew was that time was racing by, and with both Paul's exhausted legs and Meg slowing us down it might easily run out completely.

I ruffled Meg's hair and promised to see her soon – she wasn't quite sure what to make of Paul – then sprinted back down the stairs and out of the house. My route to the beach was as the crow flies, cutting through gardens and hurling myself over fences. I had just landed from one such effort when I heard, from somewhere away behind, a single gunshot.

The sun had finally broken through and the last vestiges of the mist were dissipating as I erupted onto Brevard Beach, but the change in the weather was too recent to have yet attracted early-morning traffic. I looked to my left, away from the town. There was only one figure there, perhaps a quarter of a mile away – and my heart immediately sank. Even at such a distance I could see that it was a man walking a huge black dog.

Judge Wheeler.

I turned to my right and started running. If he was coming for me, he would have to match me for speed.

The sand stretching in front of me was completely clear all the way up to Brevard Pier. It suddenly made sense to me that if Tommy was seeking somewhere he could easily defend, with enough elevation to give him a clear view over the beach on either side, then the pier was ideal – and there was I, running straight at him. The instant I had this thought I switched to a zigzag pattern – and a second later there was a loud crack and the sand whisked up to my right. Then another shot, left; another, just ahead. There was nowhere to hide, nothing to do but keep running and dodging. Another shot, another, sand churned up here, and there, and there.

They were at the far end of the pier leaning against the guard rail. Maybe Lawrence and Ty weren't trained marksmen, but Tommy was. I'd seen his guns before and knew it was neither his equipment nor my laboured manoeuvres in the sand that were making him miss.

He was playing with me.

My only advantage, and it was a very, very small one, was that he didn't know that I was armed. He could mess around for as long as he wanted because he was sure I had no means of getting at him.

The closer I got, of course, the clearer a target I presented. One bullet zipped past my face, another dug in by my ankle *so* close that my reflex action was to dive to one side. I tried to pick myself up but the gunfire was chewing the beach up all around me. It was impossible to move. I could only watch helplessly as Lawrence and Ty dropped off the pier onto the beach and began to move nonchalantly towards me.

Tommy was out of sight on the pier for a moment – then reappeared, dragging Claire behind him. He lifted her up onto the rail, but she tried to fight back, flailing at him. In response he gave her a sudden hard shove. Claire pawed at the air for a moment before falling backwards. She hit the sand hard and lay still. My heart was in my mouth. I hardly even cared about the fact that Lawrence and Ty were now only twenty yards away and so confident that they were casually reloading as they walked. I only had eyes for my wife as she remained prostrate on the sand. Thank God – at last she rolled slowly over and began to drag herself onto her hands and knees. Her head came up and our eyes met for just the briefest moment before Tommy landed beside her and yanked her up by her hair.

There was barking from behind.

Judge Wheeler was closing in.

Lawrence and Ty began to raise their guns. I knew they were going to kill me.

It was now or never.

My hand shot into my jacket pocket for Walter, but as I tried to extract him the barrel got caught in the lining. I pulled and pulled, but I couldn't release him. I looked up, panic-stricken.

Two shots blasted out.

Ivan barked ferociously.

I expected my second death.

But it was Lawrence and Ty who were hurled backwards to land in gory heaps close to the waterline. For a moment I thought that for some reason Tommy had shot them himself, but no – he wheeled away to his right and was raising one of his guns to aim at the onrushing figure of Paul de Luca while using his other hand to keep a firm grip of Claire's hair.

'Let her go!' Paul screamed as he charged across the sand, his shotgun tight against his shoulder 'Let her go, you son of a—'

I think Tommy and I realised at the same time how little of a threat Paul was. He'd loosed both barrels and clearly hadn't had time to reload. He was only too aware of this himself, for as he bore down on Tommy he dropped the gun off his shoulder and twirled it around so he could better use it as a club. But his born-again legs just weren't fast enough.

Tommy calmly shot Paul between the eyes.

He fell, dead before he hit the ground.

Claire screamed.

Tommy smiled, then roughly pulled her around so that she could see what he was about to do to me.

Except that by then I had freed my own gun.

Reader, I shot him dead.

52

There was a huge sense of relief, of course, because Claire was free and in my arms, but there was no elation, no triumphant yell. It wasn't exactly a hollow victory because I'd achieved exactly what I'd set out to achieve – Claire was safe and Tommy and his gang were vanquished – but it had eaten up my allotted time and at any moment I would be whisked back to my world – or perhaps even to somewhere else entirely.

Claire took my hand and led me across to look down at Paul, white and still in the sand with Ivan, his massive black dog, whimpering beside him.

'Poor Paul,' said Claire. 'He . . .'

'He loved you.'

'How can you love someone so much, when it's not returned?'

I smiled. 'Claire, you don't understand men at all. As long as there's the tiniest hope it might be returned, then we'll battle through anything.' Tommy lay face down, just a few yards away. 'It was *his* problem as well, wasn't it? And he killed you because of it.'

'No, Michael. That wasn't unrequited love, it was jealousy. And it's not why he killed me. He killed me because I betrayed him.'

'With me?'

'No, darling. I betrayed him in the bank.'

'I don't understand.'

'Oh Michael, haven't you worked it out? I was supposed to be helping him. I had to tip him off when there was the most money in the vault. I had to disable the alarm.'

I stared at her, incredulous. 'But why would you do that?'

'Michael, to save you! Don't you see? He was going to kill you. He hated you. He was going to jump you and take you out to the Everglades and feed you to the alligators. He told me. The only way to stop him was to do as he asked.'

'Claire . . .'

'Do you think I could have lived with myself if something had happened to you? I had no choice, Michael.'

'You could have told me. We could have dealt with it together.'

'How? By running away? Or confronting him? Or telling the police? We would have been looking over our shoulders for the rest of our lives. I just wanted to be with you, to be happy, to let you write, to live in our Blue House and make babies.'

'But he *killed* you.'

'Only because I tried to be too clever. I told Sheldon and I thought he would tell the police and they'd set a trap for Tommy, and then he'd be out of our lives for good. But nothing happened. Tommy took me into the vault, and there was hardly any money there at all. I knew right away what Sheldon had done. He'd stolen it himself and was going to claim that Tommy had taken it all so that later on, the bank could claim insurance money, and he'd have millions stashed away. Tommy couldn't see that, of course, but he knew he'd been set up and that's when he did it.'

'It wasn't worth it, Claire, it just wasn't worth it.'

'It doesn't matter now. We're here, we're together.' She kissed me again – cheek, nose, forehead. But as she moved to my lips, my body gave an involuntary flex against her, strong enough for her to notice. 'What is it, Michael?'

I stared at her, quite unable to respond at first, because I knew exactly what it was. The surgery was over. They were feeding the warmed blood back in. I was on my way home. Claire could see the despair in my eyes.

'You're going, aren't you?' she asked, her voice tiny.

'Claire – I'm sorry.'

I stroked her hair and explained in a few stark words why our time had to end before it had properly started.

Ivan growled behind us and I expected to find Judge Wheeler at my shoulder, but as we swung round we saw instead figures swarming across the beach towards us. I spotted the Cyclist amongst them, pushing his bike, then the young gunshot victim from the meeting in the Radisson. Dr Olson was there as well, moving with renewed vigour. As they drew closer I realised that everyone I'd met in the garage was there, except for DeMarcus, but there were others too, others who had also been driven into hiding by Tommy and his reign of terror.

Claire clapped her hands together and pointed as little Meg burst through them. She raced past Dr Olson and across the remaining stretch of sand and straight into Claire's outstretched arms.

'I knew I'd find you!' she cried. 'I knew!'

Claire hugged her tight as the others crowded around, clapping and congratulating us, before moving on to look down at Tommy, making absolutely sure that he really was gone for good.

Meg twisted out of Claire's grasp and padded across to stand over Paul's body. As we joined her she said quietly, 'He saved my life.'

Claire put an arm around her shoulders and gave her a reassuring squeeze, then smiled up at me, but it quickly faltered. I glanced around to find that Judge Wheeler was now standing directly behind us.

'No,' Claire whispered, her hand slipping into mine.

Judge Wheeler was ancient and grey. His stone face looked as if a smile hadn't cracked across it in millennia.

'Is there nothing that can be done?' I asked.

'This is the law.'

'Please,' Claire begged, 'it can't end like this. There must be something.'

'I only enforce the law, I do not make it.'

'But it's not right!' Claire cried. 'If the law was the law, Michael wouldn't have come here in the first place! There has to be a way to allow him to stay!'

As Judge Wheeler shook his head, Dr Olson placed a hand on Claire's shoulder. 'Claire. Perhaps – perhaps you should allow him to go back.'

Claire looked at him incredulously. 'He's my husband. I *love* him.'

Dr Olson smiled kindly. 'I know you do, of course you do, but by trying to keep him here you're robbing him of a full life *there*. We don't know how long this will last. What if it all ends tomorrow and there's nothing else? Maybe you should give Michael a chance.'

Claire looked at me. 'Is that what you want, Michael? Would you go back without me?'

'Claire, I don't think I have a choice.'

She shook her head violently. 'No, we do have a choice, we must have a choice. Judge Wheeler, there must be something, *please*.'

The heat suddenly flushed through me again, but this time it was so intense that I staggered forward.

'Michael!' Claire cried, clutching at me.

I steadied myself against her. I held on. 'It's starting,' I whispered.

'No!' Claire's eyes were mad with anger and frustration. 'Judge!'

The Judge was already shaking his head again. 'I'm sorry. It's the law.'

A familiar, yet unexpected voice came from behind us.

'Well, I say the law is an ass.'

Even as I turned, his name was already on my lips. 'Ambrose . . .'

And it was him, making his way nonchalantly through the watching crowd, looking exactly as I remembered him: a bemused mess with attitude. He came right up to stand beside us; no handshakes, just the hint of a wink.

'Ambrose,' I said again, aware that my voice was weakening. 'I wondered when you'd turn up.'

'Oh, I was here ages ago. Just keeping my head down. Reporters, we're here to be objective, not to get involved.' He looked pointedly at Judge Wheeler. 'Unless, of course, there's an honest-to-God travesty of justice. Then it's our absolute duty.'

They locked eyes. When he spoke, Judge Wheeler's lips barely moved. 'What exactly do you mean, sir? What travesty?'

Ambrose was always a confident sort, and when he put his mind to it, could be quite intimidating and very convincing. 'I mean, sir, that if this was a proper court of law, there'd be a jury sitting over there, and they'd say that this young couple deserve a second chance. They've been through enough, they've sacrificed themselves for each other – in fact, they make Romeo and Juliet look like a holiday romance. That jury would throw out whatever case there was against them. It would set them free.'

'Sir, there is no jury. And the law is the law.'

Ambrose sighed. 'I thought you might say that. Well then, perhaps I should introduce my surprise witness.'

'Your . . .' the Judge began.

'Well, not so much witness as evidence. *Voilà*!' He held up a bottle of Budweiser.

I thought for a moment that he had taken leave of his senses. 'Ambrose, please,' I said. 'I don't have time for this.' There were things I had to say to Claire, *last* things. But then I was rocked again, a surge of heat and power so massive that it knocked me completely off my feet.

As I fell to my knees, Claire went down with me. 'Please!' she cried, looking in desperation from me to Ambrose to the Judge. 'Do something!'

Ambrose responded in characteristic fashion. 'Relax,' he said. 'I know what I'm doing.'

With Claire's help, I struggled back to my feet. I was determined not to go lying down. I wanted her to remember me fighting it, defiant.

Ambrose shook the bottle at the Judge again. 'I was holding this when my car was forced off the road, and such is my love affair with beer that even as I was about to die, I wouldn't let go of it. So I came here, and I find out from these nice people

361

crowding around us that that's how it goes, that whatever you're touching when you cross over, you bring with you. Doesn't matter if it's a bicycle or a shotgun or a bottle of beer. So, Judge Wheeler, do you not think there's a possibility that it might work both ways? I mean, just because it hasn't been tried before, doesn't mean it won't work.'

The Judge was looking quite thoughtful.

Claire stared at Ambrose. 'I don't understand.'

'What he is suggesting,' Judge Wheeler observed, 'is that if Michael Ryan goes back, perhaps whatever he is holding at that moment goes with him. That perhaps the law works in reverse as well.'

Claire's eyes widened and her face flooded with unexpected hope. 'Michael?' She took my face in both her hands and kissed me hard on the lips. 'Michael . . . it could work, it could work.'

Even if it was just a flicker of hope, it was hope where there had been none, a possible in the land of the impossible.

Claire clasped her hand in mine. 'We can do this,' she said.

I nodded, but in truth I could barely focus on her; the heat was swelling up, there were little stars exploding behind me. The others were crowding in around us, wishing us luck and telling us to pass on their love to their lost ones, but they were too close. It was too claustrophobic, I felt as if I was about to explode – I needed out. I needed space, I needed air. I forced myself forward, pulling Claire with me, and we stumbled down to the water's edge. We splashed into the calm blue, the heat now as intense as anything I have ever felt.

It was happening, it was happening, we were leaving.

Ambrose had to be right.

I looked at my Claire. 'No matter what . . .'

She put a finger to my lips. 'No matter what . . .'

Our eyes locked.

'I love you.'

'I love you.'

'Claire!'

It was Meg, storming down the slight incline towards us. 'Take me with you!' she yelled. 'Take me home!'

She threw herself at Claire, and it was Claire's lovely, beautiful, natural reaction to let go of my hand and catch the little girl in her arms.

And in that dreadful, eternal moment, I was gone.

53

Close to the end now, Bob, and the wheels are in motion. I've made the call to Newton and told him my accountants have traced the stolen money from Sheldon to him. This isn't quite true, but will be in a few days. My bean counters are the best in the business and they have the muscle to get into every bank transaction and offshore account known to man. Sheldon has gone on the run, but he will be found and he will talk. I've asked Newton if he wants to come and put his side of the story for the book I'm writing, and I feel I know him well enough to predict that he will come here – but for an entirely different purpose: to shoot me dead. In so doing, he will deliver to me the greatest gift imaginable while condemning himself.

You should see me, Bob, head shaved and neat stitching job. The operation was a little touch and go for a while. The aneurysm, as predicted, collapsed when the blood supply was halted, but it took them slightly longer than envisaged to remove it. Instead of the maximum sixty minutes, their work extended to seventy-five. My blood supply and heart were successfully restarted, but they were very worried about brain damage. However, everything appears to be functioning normally, although you may of course conclude otherwise when you get to this point and realise my intent.

Lena has spent a lot of time trying to talk me out of it. She thinks it is a waste, what with the surgeons having battled so hard to save my life, for me to throw it away now. But of course, the point is that I'm not throwing it away. I'm just moving out of state. She has told me she will not interfere. She is beautiful and lovely, and if things had been different we would certainly have been together, but I can't change the way things are. She is frustrated that I will not even let her stay in the motel with me – but how can I?

Claire is here.

I feel it.

I have not spent too much time wondering what might have happened if she had come back with me. I have already experienced one miracle; a second would be asking for too much. It's enough for me to know that I'll soon be reunited with her. Does it really matter where?

I have not been short of visitors either. I'm not sure what Lena has told them of my plans, but the parents and brothers and sisters and friends of the departed have been turning up with messages for me to pass on to their loved ones. It is an odd feeling – a happy sadness, if you will.

Last night I got a call from Dick Schulze. He made it sound like he just wanted to shoot the breeze, but I think it was probably Lena's last throw of the dice. He was out in Oklahoma or Nebraska or somewhere and was telling me how beautiful it was, and that I should come visit, recuperate out there. I thanked him, but told him I had other plans. We ran out of conversation after a while, and there was quite a silence before he said, 'Michael, how is your relationship with God these days?'

I had not actually considered this, but, put on the spot, I said: 'Somebody up there likes me.'

He laughed. When we were saying goodbye he said, 'God bless you, son.'

Bob, I don't know how this will turn out. All I know is that this place I'm going to will make me happy. If it doesn't exist at all, then it's no one's loss but my own, but I have to find out. So what if it's all in my mind? If that's what the afterlife is, then great! As a kid you think of heaven as this vast expanse of whiteness where all the good people go, then when you grow up you

either stop believing in it or adapt it to your more mature requirements, like it might have a Starbucks. Now I think that maybe
it's not such a big place, that maybe we all have our own personal
heavens where we get to be reunited with the people we love,
the people we have met, in the places where we were happiest.

Maybe it's like a Garden of Eden where you get a second
chance to confront the serpent.

For years I blamed myself for Claire's death – for being so self-
centred and egotistical that even after we were married I insisted
on writing my book while she slaved away in the bank every
day; for not facing up to Tommy earlier; for not recognising the
pressure Claire was under to co-operate with him. There must
have been signs, but I was so into myself I didn't notice. Those
ten years apart were my purgatory, then I was given a second
chance to put things right, and I did, I *won*. Would you expect
me to turn down the rewards that come with that victory?

Absolutely not! No false modesty here. I'm claiming my prize.

Bob, this has all come out in a rush and I'm sure there are
bits I've forgotten or maybe I've got some names wrong or not
explained things properly, but it's the best I can do. I know you
will have reservations about publishing this. You may think it
might damage my reputation or legacy or standing with the
critics, but really, who gives a shit? This is my story, and I stand
by every word. Publish and be damned! I know I was. But it all
turned out well in the end.

Adios, amigo!

Backward

I must confess that I stayed up so late reading Michael's story, his history, his confession, that I slept in the next morning, with the result that when I called Lena at her hotel she had already left me three increasingly irate messages before giving up and heading for the airport. Instead I e-mailed the manuscript to her and got out of commenting on it by using the rather miserable excuse that I hadn't yet had time to finish reading it because of my hectic work schedule.

It was a relief actually, because I wasn't quite sure what to say. The problem was that I found the book to be not only profoundly moving, but also very disturbing. Some of it was believable, while other parts had me convinced that these were nothing more nor less than the extensive ravings of a very sick man. I even had the wild thought that it could be a rather surreal literary hoax, that perhaps Michael's loathing of being in the public eye had led him to concoct this fantastical story and then stage his own death in the hope that he might finally be able to sink back into the obscurity he craved. Certainly he had the money to carry it off. But no. If you'd met the man you would know that was not the way of him.

I could of course have called Lena at home in Brevard to discuss my feelings, but I kept putting it off in the hope that these might crystallise into something definite. Unfortunately I couldn't settle myself to one coherent take on Michael's story,

369

and so the days turned to weeks, and then to months. While I prevaricated I wouldn't let the manuscript out of my grasp, so that essentially nothing happened with it. My loyalty to Michael was conflicted by my loyalty to my own reputation. Should I treat it as a work of fiction? Or risk the ridicule of my colleagues and the literary press for presenting it as fact?

The brouhaha surrounding Michael's death had died down sooner than I expected, and in fact there was no huge surge in the sales of *Space Coast*. As a result many of the projects and proposals that I had been immediately bombarded with soon faded away. My interest, of course, had been piqued by the new book, and so I kept a quiet eye on developments in Brevard, mostly through visiting the *Herald*'s rather proficient website. I learned that Sheldon Adelson had been arrested by the FBI in New Orleans and was to be charged with defrauding the First National out of tens of millions of dollars. A month or so later, Sheriff Newton and Junior went out deep-sea fishing. US Coastguards discovered their boat floating empty three days later and towed it back to Brevard. A forensics team found signs of a violent struggle on board and concluded that both men had perished. I had two thoughts about that – one, that Newton probably knew enough about crime scenes to make it look as if there had been a violent struggle; and two – and this shows how much Michael's book affected me – if they were dead, did that mean that their 'ghosts' were now stalking Brevard?

After a while, and satisfied that justice was being served, I stopped visiting the site. Although Michael's book remained very much in my mind, parochial events in Brevard did not.

Then, fate took a hand.

I received a call from the property management company I retained to temporarily look after the Blue House ten years previously. As with most publishers, I tend to pay scant attention to what happens outside of my own environment, that is, in Manhattan or here in the Hamptons, so it was with some surprise that I learned that in the past few days the east coast of Florida had been struck by a hurricane which had come ashore just north of Brevard. In the grand scheme of things it wasn't particularly devastating, but the Blue House, being old and wooden, had been one of the few homes in the town to suffer serious damage. The roof was gone, two walls were in imminent danger of collapse, and most of the furniture and contents had been smashed up. Building inspectors had already recommended that what was left of it be knocked down. Seeing no alternative, I gave the go-ahead for this, and as the condition of the house made it a matter of some urgency, we agreed that the demolition should take place three days later.

Shortly after this I received a rather short e-mail from Dr Olson, saying that she had recovered a number of items from the house, including some of Michael's original notes on *Space Coast* and a virtually complete early draft, which she thought might be of some value. I e-mailed back that I would be happy for her to send them on to me. She e-mailed back that she would be happy for me to come and pick them up as she was exceptionally busy right now and there was a lot of other material that would need sorting through.

I had no particular desire to return to Brevard, but I did have some responsibilities to the estate of Michael Ryan and also, in truth I was intrigued by the notion of getting hold of a first draft of *Space Coast*, and the contribution it might make, both to the understanding of his work and to my own retirement fund.

Due to work commitments and the time of year, I couldn't get a flight until the following evening – that is, the night before the demolition was due to take place. I left it to my secretary to arrange my hotel, and it wasn't until I was in mid-air that I realised she'd booked me into the Radisson, scene of so many of Michael's adventures. It was after ten by the time I arrived in Orlando, picked up a car and drove out to Brevard, just as I had a decade previously. As an act of courtesy I phoned Lena to let her know I'd arrived and that if she wanted, I could come over right away. She said the morning would be fine.

I was curiously unsettled to be back in Brevard again, although only one-hundredth as unsettled as Michael must have felt on his return. I had several drinks in the hotel bar before wandering into the function room where Michael had addressed those tragic relatives. A wedding reception was just winding up. I was trying to picture what it must have been like for Michael and Lena to put themselves on the line before so many doubting relatives when a matronly woman asked me to dance to the last song. It seemed easier just to agree to it, so I moved sluggishly back and forth, feeling rather foolish, while she grooved gracelessly; then her husband came over and tried to pick a fight with me. I quickly retired to the safety of my room where I endured a rather sleepless night.

After breakfast I walked along Brevard Beach which, despite the greyness of the water and the fact that various pieces of flotsam littered the sand, remained every bit as glorious as I remembered it. After my restless night, the sun on my face served to reinvigorate me, so I decided to continue walking rather than return to the hotel for my hire car. After about twenty minutes I cut away from the sand and took a public walkway through two imposing apartment blocks and found myself looking at the devastated Blue House. I had underestimated its distance from the hotel, and overestimated my own fitness. I was sweating profusely and had my jacket off and shirt open, and was just standing there thinking about happier times – Michael and I and Claire, sitting on that porch drinking beer and dreaming dreams – when a voice said: 'It's a terrible mess, isn't it?'

I turned to find Lena standing at the bottom of her garden, arms folded. I nodded.

'You look like you could do with a glass of lemonade.'

'Wouldn't say no,' I replied.

She led me into her house and kitchen, and while she took what I presumed to be homemade lemonade from the fridge and began to pour out two glasses, I stood rather awkwardly in the doorway.

'Lena,' I said, 'I'm sorry for not being in touch – you know, about the book. The truth is, I didn't know what to say.'

She handed me a glass, and took a sip of her own. 'It's quite a story,' she said.

'It is. I just don't know what to do with it. I have to think of his reputation. *Space Coast* was such an important work, I don't want that to be coloured by people thinking . . . well, you know what I mean.'

Lena took another sip. 'Let me show you what I managed to salvage.'

I followed her into a small dining room where she immediately presented me with the bulky early draft of *Space Coast* and the notebooks. These would certainly be going home with me. The contents of the cardboard box sitting on a pine table in the middle of the room were a different matter. It was full to the brim with paperwork, much of it water-damaged, which she had clearly scooped up indiscriminately. There were dozens of old bank statements and utility bills, Claire's pay slips and copies of rejection letters *Space Coast* had received prior to my dynamic arrival on the scene. There were also three more notebooks containing Michael's diary entries covering the time from his arrival in America up to his wedding to Claire; I put these to one side.

Towards the bottom there was another thick cache of documents. A quick examination of them revealed that they pertained to Claire's father's work on the *Brevard Herald* and were therefore of no interest, but as I was about to replace them in the box, I noticed one spiral bound notebook sticking out at an awkward angle. Being a man who can't resist neatening things, I pulled it out, intending to place it on top of the pile. However, it was with no little surprise and shock that I recognised the title, and indeed the handwriting on the sticker which adorned the cover.

'Good God!'

Lena peered over my shoulder. '*Redemption and the Myth of Orpheus*,' she read aloud, '*by Robert Naiffy*. You wrote this?'

I shook my head in disbelief. 'I *half*-wrote it.' I flicked through the dozen pages, the memory of it flooding back. It was all in my meticulous handwriting, and came to a stop mid-sentence three quarters of the way down the page, at which point I'd clearly given up my original dream of becoming a classical scholar. 'When I first met Michael I'd just run away from college and was trying to set myself up as an agent, but I always carried this with me. I was always promising myself that one day I'd go back and finish it, but then I just lost track of it. It must have been here all these years.'

'Well, it must be nice to have it back. Maybe you can finish it now.'

As I thumbed through it again, I could see that it wasn't exactly as I'd left it. Several passages were underlined, and there were notes in the margins in what I now recognised as Michael's handwriting. I pulled out a chair and sat. I kept looking at the essay. Lena could see that I was disturbed by it and asked what was wrong.

'Nothing *wrong*, exactly. Just . . . do you know the story of Orpheus?'

'Unless it's been a movie, probably not – but it's Greek mythology, right?'

I nodded. 'Well, Orpheus was the greatest poet of Greece, which was the civilised world, really. It was said that he could charm wild beasts and coax rocks and trees into movement. His wife, Eurydice, was killed by the bite of a serpent, but he wouldn't accept that she was gone and went down to the underworld to bring her back. The underworld was guarded by a three-headed hound, named Cerberus – his job was to keep the living and the dead apart. But he talked his way through. His poems were so beautiful that Hades finally agreed to allow Eurydice to return to the world of the living. However, Orpheus had to meet one condition – he must not look back as he was conducting her to the surface. But just before the pair reached the upperworld, Orpheus did look back, and Eurydice slipped back into the netherworld again and was lost.'

'Why did he look back?'

'Curiosity.'

We sat in silence for a little while before Lena quietly said, 'It's Michael's story, isn't it?'

'It's a corruption of it. You can see where he is Orpheus and Claire is Eurydice . . . and Tommy is the serpent and Paul de

Luca's dog might be Cerberus.' It was all falling into place. 'And Judge Wheeler is Hades – or he could also be the surgeon who operated, who has control over life and death. Lena, it's exactly the way you said it in the book. Whatever the aneurysm did to him, it released all this knowledge he'd stored up, and converted it into these incredibly realistic visions, hallucinations, whatever you want to call them. Except it's only half of the Orpheus story, because I only got to discuss that part of it in my paper before I gave up.'

'But what happened in the rest of the story?'

'It doesn't matter – he only read the first half, so that was all he had to draw upon. He had to create his own ending – a happy one. You see, Lena, there was a whole cult that grew up around the Orpheus myth. It revolved around the soul's fate after death. Orphism believed that man's salvation depended on his knowledge of the truth. Michael was denied access to the truth by his own guilt over what happened to Claire, and he refused to go looking for it. It's almost as if his subconscious or his soul, whatever you want to call it, forced him to search for it inside himself because everything he really needed to know was already in there.'

I had struck a chord, though clearly only with myself. Lena was nodding along to what I was saying, but also, I realised, looking out of the window rather distractedly. I looked where she looked and saw that a truck towing a crane and large wrecking ball was just drawing to a halt outside.

I glanced at my watch.

It was time to flatten the Blue House.

Except – when we emerged into the sun, the truck was stopped some yards short of the Blue House, its progress interrupted by a large group of people blocking the road. I thought at first that it was merely neighbours eager to witness the destruction getting in the way, but as I drew closer I saw that they were not actually facing the house, but the driver. He had emerged from his cab and was standing scratching his head rather helplessly as his bemused crew clambered down from the truck to stand with him.

As I followed Lena down the steps and across the garden I asked her what was going on, but she just kept walking. We were spotted as we approached and the crowd began to turn towards us.

'Lena?'

She stopped and turned. As she did so, everyone, with the exception of the wrecking crew, moved in behind her so that they were all facing me. Many of them were holding photographs or drawings or small toys in their hands. Lena nodded once and they immediately held them up, either in the air above their heads or at chest height.

I looked at these pictures of children, and fathers and brothers, mementoes of departed loved ones.

I nodded at Lena. 'I have the feeling I've been set up,' I said.

'I'm sorry, Mr Naiffy, there wasn't any other way,' Lena said. 'You have to understand how we feel about the Blue House.'

'And how do you feel?'

'It shouldn't be knocked down. It should be built up.'

They broke into applause.

When it had quietened again, I asked why.

'Because these people were hurt and lost, and Michael Ryan gave them hope.'

'Hope?'

'Hope that there is something else, that when we die it isn't the end. We want to rebuild the Blue House exactly as it was; we want to restore the damaged furniture, return the papers. If we can imagine that Michael and Claire are still living there, then we can imagine that all of our loved ones are still with us.'

'Lena, if you don't mind me saying – that is completely barking mad.'

She smiled. 'But that's where we stand, Mr Naiffy, and will continue to stand, until you call off the wreckers and agree to restore the house to its former glory. If you like, you can think of it as an investment. When Michael's book is published, people are going to want to see where they live.'

'You mean to turn it into some kind of tourist attraction?'

'Why not? As long as it's still there, it doesn't really matter. Please, Mr Naiffy.'

I looked at her, and this time at the people actually holding the photographs and toys and mementoes. There was conviction and determination in their faces, and I knew that I had no real choice in the matter.

'Okay,' I said.

'*Okay*?'

'Okay.'

'To calling off the wrecking crew? And to rebuilding the house?'

'Okay. Yes. To everything.'

'Yes? Just like that?'

'You said the magic word, Lena.'

Her brow furrowed. '*Please*?'

I shook my head. '*Investment*.'

Well, we'll know pretty soon. I suspect the Blue House will serve as a good enough marketing tool, and that tours will begin and loyal readers and converts will be guided around the restored house and imagine that Michael and Claire continue to keep home there. They will pass from the stolen fridge magnets in the kitchen to the study where Michael worked, and from there to the bedroom where love was made, repeatedly, and they will imagine that Michael and Claire are lying there still, in each other's arms. And perhaps I will imagine it as well.